MW01175021

David C. Walker

WILD WORLD

Copyright © 2012 david c. walker
All Rights Reserved

ISBN-10: 0987969609
EAN-13: 9780987969606

Published by Mulvey Books a division of W.C. Investments Ltd.

WASHINGTON, DC

Spring 2008

Myron Klass was one of those young men who knew what he wanted to do with his life by the age of sixteen: He would go to Washington to work on Capitol Hill. He would eschew family life by remaining a bachelor, thereby freeing up even more time to focus on politics, the first and only love of his life. Having started out as an aide to his local Democrat congressman, he was acutely intrigued by the everyday maneuvering of American politicians. From the beginning, he had learned the art of helping those more powerful and knowledgeable than he, and partly due to such skills, Myron's knowledge of what had happened in Washington since his arrival in 1970 was mind-boggling. He loved to flaunt his knowledge, often waxing eloquent in front of the newer recruits, especially because, as an older, single person, he was subject to far too many rumors about his sexuality. He didn't care because he knew that most of the powerful politicians he had come across had secrets of their own. His long nights in Washington bars naturally raised questions about his drinking but he was in cahoots with his regular bartenders who delivered his signature vodkas disguising his favorite tipple as Perrier on the rocks.

Along the way, Myron gravitated toward international security as the focus of his congressional committee work. The atmosphere was more professional and thoughtful and less partisan, as the players appreciated what was at stake. Republican presidents and congressmen had teased and forgiven him for his Democrat roots; they appreciated that he understood the issues about which he offered discussion and advice. Above all, as he thrived in the world of secrets and gossip, they knew he could be trusted with the most delicate of issues.

Now, he sighed as he headed out of his office into a rainy Washington evening. How did people keep getting into the same trouble?

The bar at the Fairmont wasn't a favorite, but Todd Aykroyd thought it was the most private. "Tonight," he explained over the phone, "I think that it's essential that we be alone." The weather discouraged Myron from any thought of walking, and he ducked into the first cab that drove by his building. He had to admit that Todd's call excited him, as four decades had taught him that a good spymaster paid attention when one of his men came in for a talk. Occasionally Myron explained interesting incidents in complicated files for the entertainment of friends, who knew from the outset that no amount of begging would get them the whole story. In addition, close associates were amazed how few of the culprits in his tales he had actually met. It was a bit of a shock to hear him pass judgment on these unknown souls, but he was unrepentant, perhaps a little nonchalant in his approach. Myron repeatedly commented at many Washington watering holes: "I'm the big-picture fellow on whom presidents and senators alike rely for analysis and advice. I never travel outside of Washington and never phone unknown contacts. Todd is my eyes and ears. He comes to me when new plots unfold against our great country. I'll decide which are dangerous and which are simple nuisances. That's my turf and my genius."

Todd was already at the bar finishing his first cocktail, a very dry Bombay Safire gin martini on the rocks with a twist; now he was scooping up handfuls of dry, roasted peanuts, a sure sign that he had encountered a plot that he alone could not place in either category.

He began his tale in a deliberate, slow manner, recounting a story passed to him by friendly agents in South Africa. He knew he would need his companion's help, sooner than later.

JOHANNESBURG, SOUTH AFRICA

Early 2008

Juan Moreno usually didn't leave himself open to the characters thrown together that evening at the Ndau Lounge at Johannesburg's Hyatt Regency hotel. It was one of those unavoidable times when his trucking interests took him far from his Madrid home. After several pleading calls from the South African cabinet minister responsible for the country's preparation as hosts for the continent's first World Cup, he felt he had no choice but to make the trip. Local politicians knew how much money his company was making by transporting European goods to the various sites; so far, because of high level interventions, no one had missed a payment. But his business went beyond the obvious freight shipments. If his luck held out, the checks would keep coming in from this African country well after the 2010 football matches. It was always his job to find out what was needed and how he could deliver the goods. He made excellent use of his time on this trip to confirm their orders for armaments difficult to find quickly on the open market. This Juan did with his eyes closed.

Sitting alone outside in the hotel's lush garden bar, Juan was gradually joined by other suppliers who had met him at the various receptions sponsored by the government to generate positive news about South Africa's first grandiose national project. A couple of engineers were particularly interested in his views on trucking in Africa. They were all there to build local transportation facilities for the World Cup crowds, facilities that would include a new rail link for a high-speed train being built by a company out of Montreal.

They were chatting about where the next big construction projects might be, offering opinions about the usual hotspots in China, India, Brazil and Russia, when an Australian engineer spoke up. "I'm part of an engineering group backed by one of our big Aussie banks," he said. "Last year we came across an interesting proposal to build a new highway in North Africa that would run from the Tunisian border east through Morocco and Algeria. I'm not quite clear on all of the route details, but if you wanted the job, you knew that you had to pay off officials in a big way, especially those Algerians. The governments were searching for an international company that had the resources to construct and maintain the new roads, bring in a huge amount of cement and steel, manage local professionals from at least three countries, train a young workforce, and, of course, have enough left over to engage a long list of advisors. Now here's the kicker: the winning bidder had to accept a confidential agreement that prohibited any role for Americans and Israelis. That cut out most of our competitors. We badly wanted this deal, as construction was to start right away. We lost the bid. Why? The Chinese and Japanese scooped up different sections; they were willing to play the game and pay off whomever. Anybody here heard anything about this?" Nobody responded.

It was interesting but not riveting gossip for most of those who were sitting, schmoozing, and drinking whatever local beer they preferred. Juan shrugged and pretended as though the conversation offered him trivial, unimportant intelligence. Nothing was further from the truth. He kept abreast of the region's politics and understood in great detail what had happened. He knew the names of every corrupt official that the Asians had paid in each country. However, this definitely didn't strike him as the crowd with whom to share any really valuable information. Instead, he simply sat back and took in the conversations floating around him. Because of his slight build and very dark complexion, Juan literally disappeared in small gatherings, a quirky attribute that he found useful whenever he simply wanted to listen and not be questioned regarding his take on the political events of the day. He worked in stealth, keeping his opinions out of conversations.

Juan's alert scrutiny of others attested to his carefully camouflaged world wherein he employed his transport company to supply terrorist organizations in North Africa and the Middle East. It was a complex world, to say the least, but he, and his father before him, had managed to keep a low profile, avoiding all but the most astute of watchers. An endless number of security agencies had reports after a major attack on western allies hinting something like "there is a chance that it was Moreno's support that made this possible," but they offered no thread of evidence connecting him in a convincing fashion with any specific act of terrorism. He lived handsomely in Madrid, where many political allies and business friendships protected him from international inquiries; he was never interviewed, and he never left careless clues about his activities lingering after any cocktail conversations.

A fidgety but otherwise nondescript character at the corner of the table caught Juan's eye. Hugh Parks was very interested in the conversation and looked as though he wanted to chime in, as did a few others. Juan was immediately interested in this fellow's efforts to dress properly since Juan never failed to present himself immaculately wherever he was. What was missing was any exposure to European style; here was someone trying hard but removed from a sophisticated lifestyle. Without losing sight of this new stranger, Juan's mind drifted back to the conversation. The work for outside contractors in South Africa was slowing down, which made them anxious to talk about the next opportunity, pass the information back to corporate headquarters, and hope for another assignment. Several were asking for leads but both Juan and Hugh contributed nothing up to this point. The difference with this gentleman, Juan speculated, was that he worried that others might think that he didn't belong at this table. That was to his way of thinking an unforgivable flaw that always led to major errors. The challenge of anticipating how this oddity would blunder at least made Juan's evening interesting.

Juan didn't wait long. A few minutes later, after Hugh hurriedly went through his mental list of contacts, he found one to flash at his new best friends. He started into his usual con job, much to the bemusement of Juan, who was grading the participants as though this were a class project.

"You know, this is probably of no consequence, because your friends, the big guys, always wrap up all of the major business opportunities before the rest of us even hear about them," Hugh began. "But I have friends in Calgary up in Canada who have a problem: Plenty of ambition and bags of money, but nowhere to go outside of oil and gas. I've been working with a scientist back home—don't panic; he's good—on how to improve access to all the resources found across Canada. We're looking at new materials for building all-weather roads. We have patents for new generators to produce electrical power for remote communities. We have plenty of ideas but no contacts here in Africa. These countries have the same problems as Canada. Lots of wealth in the ground but no one knows how to get the show on the road. So I was sent here to build up business for my buddies back home. They'd love to work and invest here but have no contacts. That's why they hired me."

Any close friend from back home in Western Canada would have picked up signs that Hugh was lying. For starters, he was avoiding eye contact especially when one of the engineers asked him a technical question. Having only read a few short newspaper articles on the flight from Canada, Hugh was in no position to detail these scientific discoveries. He is anxiously seeking a new crowd, concluded Juan. His one liner answers are not sustaining him back in Canada. The Aussie asked the obvious questions: "Are you looking for an international partner? Who is your Canadian friend with big money?" Without missing a beat, Hugh put forward a name he had read in the business section of a Canadian newspaper, *The Globe and Mail*. "This guy owns a great NHL hockey team—as important as your football teams—along with Canada's largest oil company; he's into everything. I sit with him during hockey practices. He's always looking for projects like this and will back me, 100 percent guaranteed." Juan laughed quietly to himself, speculating that some poor fellow back home had likely unknowingly signed an African road contract at least 5,200 miles from Calgary via his new agent 9,800 miles away. Hockey was Hugh's favorite hook to capture the interests of Canadian investors, but it didn't work with this crowd.

As the group began to disperse, someone suggested a final breakfast to exchange ideas about staying in touch and hopefully working on another project. Hugh quickly jumped in. "Let's do something different, since we're all leaving tomorrow. Why don't we meet late morning out at the casino, Emperor's Palace? It's on the way to the airport. Besides, I don't really like breakfast at this hotel." Everyone agreed and went off to their rooms. Juan sat a few minutes alone to finish his wine. Hugh passed by the patio outside—likely, his new watcher was willing to wager, on his way to a less expensive hotel.

The intervention was typical of Hugh, as Juan would later learn. Hugh's work did take him to South Africa regularly, although his Winnipeg friends joked that none of them had actually ever seen a plane ticket in his hand. Yet, given the general Canadian tendency to get into difficult, if not immoral, situations in the African mining business, it was natural to find a character like Hugh sitting in a hotel in Johannesburg scheming with the locals or other visiting developers. The trips were also a good way to launder cash. He was always hiding funds from different schemes, sometimes in his condo in Buffalo, in a bank in Barbados, or here in South Africa. Once, while pleading poverty with tax collectors back home, he told his wife Joanne that he had magically returned from South Africa with lots of extra money in his pocket from a particularly lucky streak in a local casino.

Tonight, he was returning to the Rand Club to sleep in a modest room. As his bill would be sent back home to the Manitoba Club, where he was a member, it would be months before he would have to pay the invoice.

The next morning, Hugh boldly stated that he had arrived early at the casino on a whim and had just won over $25,000. "Great bets, just now, at the tables." The yarn made Juan even more wary, although he loved stories about characters like this who laundered money without blinking. Where did the money come from, and why did he travel here to pick it up? As Juan knew a thing or two about stashing cash, he guessed that Hugh had a few hundred thousand tucked away with a local business partner.

"This road being built up north from here sounds interesting," Hugh began tentatively after having breakfast with two others who had decided not to join in the usual casino games. "Maybe I can sell them our new paving technology."

Juan replied, "You have to be really careful around North Africa; you don't know what everyone is up to, including governments. The religious upstarts are all copying the Taliban in three or four countries. They have their own photo IDs, compulsory military service, crop insurance, cops, and small business loans. The whole routine makes my team crazy—drivers often have to pay twice to get anything done. It makes the trucking business tricky and expensive."

The third bystander, an American investment dealer named Michael Sage, piped up. "This project is nuts, but we'll still make a ton of money. I'm not looking for another deal in South Africa or anywhere else on this continent. I prefer to be in North American markets. Hugh, what do you do in Canada? And your friend, the hockey mogul you talked about last night, how do you help him make money?"

"I enjoy my work here," Hugh said. "I represented Bombardier and set up the transit deal with the government. I represent many Canadian companies who have no clue how to obtain government support. That's my specialty."

As Hugh took a dramatic pause, Juan quickly looked around. This guy was taking a chance; there was no doubt in Juan's mind that Hugh was making up this story as he went along.

Hugh continued to embellish his story. "Harvey Shepherd has a lot of financial clout, and I'm his go-to guy. He thinks big, and he's put together significant companies in different fields to spread his risk. He turns to me when he needs for something to happen quickly and quietly." As Juan suspected, Hugh inwardly conceded that Shepherd would be surprised to hear that he was now his agent in Africa. Someday, Hugh promised himself, he would ask Shepherd for a meeting, just to see where it might lead._

That's what made Hugh seem like such an odd character to Juan. The Canadian's carelessness and huckster-like persona were a stark contrast to Juan's precise, minimalist approach to newcomers. Hugh was open to everyone, searching for new opportunities, perhaps finding a hapless soul who could be convinced to part with his money. Juan did not invite casual friends into his life, nor did he sit around in bars idly gossiping about his work.

But, Juan thought in his usual practical manner, business deals frequently require both the ability to convince others to follow and the management acumen to get the job done. Despite his reservations about Hugh, Juan had one idea that he wanted to test in front of these strangers as a way to help out his son Angel. He opened up carefully. "I work out of Spain, but I rarely visit countries where we have to operate in dangerous situations. This trip is an exception. You never know when something can go wrong and you might suddenly face a jail sentence because you didn't pay enough to local officials or to one of the competing gangs. Often you have to pay both. If I stay in Spain, nobody can touch me. Our specialty is trucking, and we have a long history of getting the logistics right. We organize everything that moves out of Europe, including equipment for big construction projects, and we supply both trucks and drivers to the front doors of North Africa and the Middle East. Newcomers don't know who to bribe, in what language and for what amount, especially as the records are not always as good as they might be for European security forces."

He paused before throwing a line to the Canadian. "Hugh, you have a guy with money and buddies who like to work for good pay but only from time to time, right? Are they smart?"

"Sure. Not all went to university, but some did. Bottom line is that no one has gone to prison." No one laughed at his feeble joke.

"We may be looking for a few specialists over there to help my son set up an American trucking business," Juan said.

Michael, who had not yet said anything, spoke up. "Not really my field, but if you need financing in North America, I can probably help out. We put together this deal in South Africa all on our own. We just got paid our first installment, so I'm off to the next scene. Our company—we're really just an investment house—has a little experience in transportation."

The three exchanged business cards, talking loosely about how they might help create Juan's proposed business. Hugh figured he could pull together a scheme back home, as the Spaniard obviously knew little about the Americas. It would not be the first good deal for Hugh to come together for the wrong reasons. By helping Juan and his son, Hugh was convinced he could help himself and his investment team.

After Juan settled into his seat for his flight to Dubai and then on to Madrid, he sat still, staring without emotion at the two business cards in front of him. He had not been surprised when they handed over their cards; no, he was horrified only as he watched himself respond as though he were a robot. Rarely did he give out his card. He now had another problem. While he was in South Africa, he had changed his cell phone cards several times, as was his habit. He had scribbled his original cell number on the back of one of his own cards as a reminder to reinstall it. Now either Michael or Hugh had that number.

Annoyed, he brushed away this concern; there was not much he could do while sitting in a Boeing 767. He turned his attention to meetings arranged by his bank during his brief stopover in Dubai. Since there were no direct flights from Johannesburg to Madrid, he had no choice but to take this long South African Airways' route back north. Dubai was the only transit point where he felt safe from the Americans, who were watching him at all times. If he flew through London, Frankfurt, or Zurich, as did most travelers, he wasn't sure what might happen to him. All he knew was that his old nemesis, Aykroyd at the U.S. Drug Enforcement Administration, would soon know that he was out of Spain and going someplace he shouldn't be—and available for capture by one of his agents. By flying this route, Juan could not only prevent this from happening but also meet some important clients who needed more than shipping containers. He would be on his way on an Emirate Airline flight to Madrid before anyone had figured out what he was doing.

This latest venture had proven that his style was unbeatable. His trucks had been used in South Africa's preparation for the World Cup. The manifests stated that the containers were filled with construction material, but in reality, the government had secretly acquired new weapons in case they had to turn against fellow countrymen in the months leading up to the crowded events. If anyone found out about these purchases, there would likely be large-scale thefts from warehouses. Juan knew the players and was happy to outmaneuver the Israelis in arranging these sales and stealthily delivering the armaments. He was, as usual, nowhere near the shipments when they arrived in South Africa. Instead, his loyal agent, Martin Belanger, was on the dock with a cell phone to let Juan know exactly what was happening.

Juan had already decided that getting involved with either Hugh or Michael would lead to catastrophe, no matter what continent they were on. They were without too much talent, a judgment he made when he had all too speedily emptied them of any useful ideas. He half-heartedly appreciated Hugh's brazenness, and he guessed that the Canadian's style oscillated daily from tender support to bullying. Juan's personality was not entirely different; he was driven by a mixture of barbarity and civility in his plots. His underlying determination was well-hidden. Those around him who saw it kept quiet; that side of Juan was silently recognized by only a few. He was once described in an American briefing note as the most thoughtful of arms dealers, one who could "write the book on intellectual rigor at the level of a destructive genius." A walk with Juan in a Madrid park, away from prying eyes and listening devices, was where he explained (to fellow conspirators, of course) his plans for supplying armaments mostly across North Africa and the Middle East. The polite transportation czar quickly showed his special guests what it took to win in the terrorist business. He left them with the same message during each walk in the forest: if you can't stand the stench of destruction, go home now.

After Juan was off to Johannesburg's O.R. Tambo International Airport, Hugh and Michael continued their discussion and left together in a taxi. "What do you think his next project might be?" Hugh spoke first; Juan's conversation lingered in their heads, and neither wanted to say much out loud. He continued: "I remember him saying that he needed a team to set up a small company for his son to move freight in and out of North America. He said there may not be much traffic at first but that he would like someone over there to run his business while he prepares Angel for his chance to succeed in America. Michael, should we get back to him? Is there something in this for us?"

Michael paused before replying. "There is probably something, but it won't be clean. Did you notice that neither of us was allowed to ask any questions? He didn't give us many hints, either. Some stuff I can live with, but I don't want to touch drugs—it would involve too many gangs. As long as it doesn't involve drugs, that's all I care about. My guess is that the opportunity is more suitable to you and your friends up in Canada. My business partners won't have the stomach for this. So if you're asking if I'm really interested, the answer is, I don't think so. International operators like Juan use local suckers and stay away from the mess themselves. He wouldn't care for a second if anything happened to us."

Hugh thought about that and then said, "If he wants to set up a small trucking company, I could do that quickly. I can find drivers and get their papers to haul merchandise across North America. We don't need many routes to make a few bucks. Maybe you know someone with trucks for sale?"

"Oddly enough, yes. Truckers are under incredible pressure these days to produce better profits. In this recession, nobody is moving anything; the trucks are sitting empty in the yard or are being driven with small loads. I have stayed in touch with a few truck owners from my college days. We could probably find a company for sale that would suit you and Juan."

Hugh tried another angle, hoping to hide his weakness. "I'm not so sure I'm the guy who can find the money. Can you point me anywhere?"

"Hmm, you have a couple of options. One that might be best for you is to find a small company that's a little bit of a corporate orphan. The owners might help you finance a deal just so they can get out of a losing venture. I actually know of one opportunity."

The taxi driver interrupted, inquiring about their airlines.

"The prospect for you, Hugh, is this." Michael stopped for a moment to pay the cabbie. Hugh made no move to offer his own cash. "The current investors are led by Aird Investments out of Philadelphia. I've worked with them over the years. They bought Aerospace International Systems in California, and it included a small trucking company. They're definitely not happy. They like the aerospace business but not trucking."

"What do you mean?"

Michael spoke quickly, as both had to catch their flights. "Their main business is to store older planes on a former air force base. Sounds straightforward, right? What's really going on is that the planes they have in storage aren't leaving that airport empty as they head to their new homes around the globe. No, they have cargo shipments never declared on the manifest. I know for a fact that our national security people are watching them. Remember that America is the world's largest supplier of armaments and nearby Mexico one of the largest drug traffickers. I don't think the people at Aird have any idea of the real role of their trucks.

"I've been told that the investment house has turned one of their young MBA researchers onto the file. He'll be their cover in front of the pension fund investors by providing the business case to get rid of the trucks. No one will read a single word about drugs and guns. When that happens, you can make your proposal to Juan. If I hear more, I'll let you know. Bye for now."

Once Michael settled into his seat for his direct flight back to Atlanta, he promised himself that he would never to speak to that Canadian again. It would be too dangerous to answer even one of his calls.

Conscious of his projected image, Hugh hung around the departure gate at the airport as long as he could, afraid that one of his new friends might see him heading back to the economy section of the plane. He was thankful that no one had asked him directly why he had attended all of the high-level receptions over the past week. The real story was that a local farmer from just outside Winnipeg was supplying all the sod for the new football pitches. When Hugh read the newspaper article, he had correctly guessed that this fellow wasn't interested in attending the high-powered events, so Hugh offered to represent him at no cost and grasped his chance to interact with many cabinet ministers. The opportunity made his work as a peddler of mediocre software more respectable, as these chance encounters were duly photographed and reported back to his investors as bona fide sales meetings.

Hugh passed the time on the long plane ride to Frankfurt thinking about the personalities he had just met by happenstance, especially the character from Spain. He was certainly different from Hugh's Winnipeg contacts. Not one to bring a book on even the longest of trips, Hugh spent the flight mapping out plans for taking advantage of his chance encounter with Juan. He could smell a profitable scam. He was reassured by the fact that it wasn't the first time that he initially felt lost because he didn't have a history with the major players. There was definitely an opportunity once he learned more about the game he was entering. For instance, if that Michael was right about planeloads of contraband flying out of a remote Californian air strip, was that all that was happening there? If they were smart enough to organize the stuffing of empty planes, how about the trucks? Hugh knew the answer to his rhetorical question. Maybe Juan would analyze this opportunity the same way. It was time, he decided, to prepare a new confidence game.

Hugh hoped that his efforts over the past several days would be appreciated by his investors on Winnipeg's Bison Board. He thought his latest jaunt to South Africa had proven his skills as an iconic scam artist. It was important to not let the trail go cold with his new friend Juan. If he had the chance, he would phone him from the Frankfurt airport using the phone number on the back of Juan's business card. It was worth a shot. When he returned to Winnipeg, he'd convince his team to take advantage of this new contact to make big money over the next three years. It didn't really matter to him how they managed it as long as they succeeded. Juan didn't strike Hugh as the grave danger Michael had suggested. No, he represented the best prospect Hugh had seen in years.

Meanwhile, Juan was contemplating a bigger deal than even Hugh was plotting. He was looking for new pawns to support his most ambitious plan yet: to draw in his American enemies by building a trap of devastating consequences in their own backyard. At this moment, he had no idea how to do it. But from past experience, Juan told himself, his steady embrace of careful planning and execution would eventually pinpoint the right moment to strike in a way that would successfully provoke the States into a major confrontation. After all, that was what happened after the World Trade Center was attacked. They were still unwinding their expensive, unsuccessful commitments in Iraq and in Afghanistan. If he could contain his own feelings of rage and anguish and absorb all of the advice and information passed his way, he would prevail over his enemy. Distraught people did not win wars, but a calculating recluse just might be victorious. Despite his personal reservations, Juan was open to the possibility that he might find Hugh to be a useful pawn in his first move into the Americas.

WINNIPEG, MANITOBA

Late winter 2008

Annie Palmerston's aunt Susan loved Annie as her own daughter. Several months prior, Susan Armitage had been thrilled to hear that her niece was moving to Winnipeg for her undergraduate education. Searching for the perfect gift for the new college student, Susan settled on a subscription to *The Guardian Weekly*.

"Slightly esoteric for an eighteen-year-old, don't you think?" asked her husband. "Not the sort of gift I would have died for."

"Don't be so judgmental. She's leaving a small, conservative prairie town where her mom and dad still live like their parents lived. Annie wants to be out on her own to do things her way, and she wants to do it without hurting us. We have only one job and that is to make sure that no one takes advantage of her innocence and openness."

"And *The Guardian Weekly*?"

Susan didn't miss a beat. "She has to have access to stories and ideas in a mix unavailable here. Her friends won't know enough yet, and her professors, based on the ones we know, are totally preoccupied with their own narrow expertise. She already has lots of friends in Winnipeg because she is so wonderful, but nonetheless, she will probably leave here lonely, still looking for a soul mate. I want her to know, without my saying a word, that there are a zillion places she can look. I'm late, as usual. See you around three."

Annie was indeed puzzled, initially, when the inaugural issue of the British newspaper arrived during her first semester, as there was no announcement from any donor. She figured it out pretty quickly, however, and thanked her aunt. Since then, she had made it the first read of the morning, choosing an article about places, events, or trends that she knew nothing about, a habit that reflected her determination to consider the unknown issues of life. Annie earnestly and rigorously played back the ideas she read about as she walked to class. It was definitely her most demanding intellectual exercise, as she felt that she wasn't being challenged on campus.

This Sunday morning, cold and still a long way from the end of winter, she broke her own unspoken rule of always leaving *The Guardian Weekly* at home—but was self-conscious, as though she were making a statement that no one else would understand. Aunt Susan had arranged brunch for just the two of them in the impressive, renovated, century-old railroad hotel, The Hotel Fort Garry. The Sunday breakfast room would be noisy, but her aunt always remembered to reserve a quiet corner table where they wouldn't be bothered by the more rambunctious families. Knowing that Aunt Susan could never show up on time as promised—it broke some rule that escaped Annie at her age—she sat at ease, reading her newspaper.

That week's edition did not disappoint her. Annie read about Senegal helping its old trading partner, Iran, despite American efforts to isolate Tehran. She thought about China's new role in South America, recalling that in an earlier article, a journalist suggested that China was looking for increased world political clout by aligning its interests with those of Brazil and Venezuela on various issues. Zimbabwe's old leader, Robert Mugabe, was apparently still taking on Britain, America, and the EU in the same breath. Annie poured over page after page of news about nations she had barely even heard mentioned around campus. She methodically next turned to the book reviews and descriptions of art exhibitions in seemingly far off places.

She felt frustration rising as she continued to read; how was she to keep up? How was she to know everything? Who murdered whom in the Bhutto family, or why the English nurse convinced young people over the Internet to commit suicide, or what hindered UN aid to the poorest countries? How could she start to make sense of new European art? With whom could she talk about these issues?

Annie was thankful that her aunt showed up as she worried that her pent-up frustration was being noticed at neighboring tables. "I want to scream," she told her aunt. "I want everyone in this room to stop and think about what is going on. They should tell me, right now, how they stand it. Find me a microphone!" She finished before Susan had even opened her napkin.

Her aunt could barely suppress a smile. "I'm glad to see you're taking this all in stride. Shows progress. It must be your good old small-town common sense." They both began to giggle. "I'm afraid all you're going to get here is a solid meal to sustain you through a few more classes. This crowd doesn't remind me of a revolutionary scene out of Robert Redford's *Reds*! Let's join that demoralizing buffet line. After that, we can talk up a storm."

Susan's first question was to find out how Annie was organizing her life to nurture her inherent genius. "You're creative. Although you're impatient to bust out, I hope you are also learning to withdraw and hide yourself from the more disruptive aspects of university life. Made any initial steps?"

"As a matter of fact, maybe." They both acknowledged her tentative nature. Susan knew, however, that her niece's hesitation would disappear when she left this college.

"I was reading about a well-known detective crime writer who just passed away in his Massachusetts' home from a heart attack while at his computer," Annie continued. "Every morning he wrote 1200–1500 words for his novel, no more, no less. That story got me wishing I could harness my own creative urges by doing exactly that. I must force myself into a routine; his commitment inspired me. Maybe I could finish both my essays and my own private notebooks, if I scribble something down every day...but I've rarely applied myself to that extent in any artistic dreams."

Annie went on, "Remember my stupid journals? I used to love them. I'm not sure where this current burst of writing will lead, but I want something beyond the classroom. I'm more creative than that. I hope I can end up doing something different, like art or photography. I want to express my thoughts."

Her aunt encouraged her to continue. "What are you looking for?"

"I'm writing each day and leaving my other artistic ambitions aside for now. I'm home some mornings, given my class schedule, so I pretend to be a hidden *artiste* until noon. The writing brings me more fulfillment than anything else in my life. I'm often too distracted in the afternoon after classes, so I go for long walks on my own. It's the mornings that bring me the calmness to face the day."

Annie went on to describe, as clearly as possible, her anxiety as well as her determination to be creative. "I'm too embarrassed to show my writings to others, and to live an artistic life you must let go. I think to be a successful artist you should have a narrative that stretches through your work no matter what medium attracts you at the time. If you want an audience, they have to feel part of your experience. You have to explain yourself.

"There is a tension within me that's hard to ignore. School life can be cluttered and noisy. By that I mean, well, the demands of a university degree are legitimate, but they only make sense for someone on a career path. I'm not. I want to sit and think. I have to protect myself from playing hectic and frantic games. I don't want to be dragged into the chaos that others create for their own purposes. Running around like that would probably destroy the intrinsic nature of which I see myself becoming."

Annie grew silent after this discussion about her artistic ambitions. Susan understood just how exposed her niece must be feeling and continued smoothly onto other topics. They talked about family, gossiping lightheartedly about the wacky lives of as many relatives as they could remember. It was fun. Finally it was time to go. "What do you plan to do in the summer?" Susan asked. "Stay here in town?"

"I think so. One of my professors is already looking for a research assistant. He wants to investigate corruption at city hall. Sounds exciting to me. Maybe I'll catch a crook. I've spent some time with the professor, and we've had some great conversations. I like his gentleness and the way he lets things slide…he gives me all the time I need to debate my latest theories about society. I don't really understand the summer job, but I'm sure it will be okay."

Annie would have been surprised to hear that this same professor, Arthur Crawford, was at that moment telling his wife Brenda that he had no longer had a compass and was, in fact, totally lost even while he was supposedly hitting life's stride as a result of his hard-earned accomplishments in the university world. While Annie's world was unfolding with both uncertainty and excitement, Arthur's was consumed with only anxiety that threatened to paralyze him.

As a bright, hardworking, and successful academic, Arthur was proud of his twenty-year tenure at the university. He carried himself as any midcareer executive would: tall, confident, a good weight for his age, lots of hair, and a ready smile. He spent many happy hours in his small if somewhat disorganized campus office, avoiding hallway conversations about university politics in favor of research and writing, his real joy in life. Unfortunately, he had come to a crossroads that threatened to affect his career and perhaps his life. Today was the first day he was willing to speak about this discombobulating moment in his otherwise perfectly respectable life.

Arthur's initial training reflected exactly how academia prepared the next in line to become professors. Although they made extravagant cases about their commitment to mentoring newcomers, most professors left their protégés to fuss among themselves about their emotional and career problems. The professors helped with intellectual riddles, but that was about it.

This was largely found to be acceptable among the graduate students and young professors, as no twenty-something in their right mind wanted to spend endless hours with an older professor. Usually, the graduate students simply moved on to other universities to climb ladders of success guided only by their best guesses and intuitions about what to do. If a professor realized he didn't know any longer what he was doing with his career—or perhaps more terrifying, with his life—there were no lifeboats. Such was the case with Arthur.

On that evening, after an early movie, Arthur and Brenda went for a walk along Corydon Avenue, a busy street where they could stop for a casual dinner. He decided to open up and talk to her about his next steps.

As he did so, Brenda responded brusquely in her matter-of-fact fashion. "You know, I rarely comment on what you do at work. But you've looked so puzzled lately that I've grown more and more concerned about your confidence in your research and writing. Yet you're really good, from everything I hear."

Arthur spent a long time over dinner taking her through his rather morose sentiments about the corrupt world they were living in. His thinking was, by his own admission, leading him nowhere and probably seriously undermining his self-esteem.

Brenda had heard enough. "Listen, you're not making any sense. When guys hit their forty-fifth birthday—and you're 47—they all start mumbling and babbling like you are doing right now. I certainly don't want to hear about this. We've done just fine building our life here, and you will end up as high up in the university as you want to go. So you're unhappy, or angry, or whatever—that's life. You're a sociology professor. You're not trained to be a political analyst, let alone a muckraker, so I cannot understand your newfound frustrations with the world around you. Nothing has changed since you arrived here. Stick to your specialty, and you'll be okay."

"That's not good enough right now," he said softly.

Brenda rarely became edgy with Arthur, but this time she was ready to challenge him for his apparent stupidity. "I'll make you a deal. Let's get this sorted out in the next few months. I think you're ruining a career for some unfathomable reason. Having said that, here's what I want from you right now.

"Starting tomorrow, write a new research proposal for whatever foundation will have you. Then I want you to consult with those you trust on campus. You're nodding too quickly; I'm serious. I want to know right now who you're going to talk with next month. Let's get this done instead of your usual habit of entertaining countless conversations about the same problem. Here's a pen and paper." She fished efficiently through her purse and slapped them on the table. "Let's get started."

Arthur sat hunched over the paper, staring at it before committing himself to a list of consultations. He pushed it back to her. She read it, shrugged, and said, "I want this to happen soon. I want to know what you intend to do."

Arthur wasn't as forthcoming as he should have been with Brenda. Over the years, no matter how skeptical she might be, Brenda always remained respectful of his ambitions. The lifestyle of an academic couple suited her; she never challenged their relationship. Yet, underneath this vague dinner conversation was Arthur's first threat to their comfortable relationship. Brenda's impatient rebuttals were clear signs that she understood that his malaise could torpedo their lives.

Under such pressure from his wife to focus on his work, Arthur began writing the first draft of his new research project the next morning. He didn't get far. He wished at that moment that corruption had never bothered him.

PHILADELPHIA, PENNSYLVANIA

Spring 2008

The Philadelphia branch of the Brown University Alumni Association always put on fun evenings that kept its members actively supporting their alma mater. This time, they brought in their outstanding president, Dr. Ruth Simmons, the first black woman to head a major American university. There was still a buzz in the Georgian Room ballroom at the Westin when Heather Worthington spotted her old friend, Brent Oliver, standing off to the side. "What, you're feeling conflicted now that you're graduating from Wharton? I want to see you cheering on the old school!"

Brent smiled broadly at the sight of the delightful and energetic Heather. She was perfectly suited to her new job at the Philadelphia Foundation and was working this crowd as well as any professional fundraiser much more experienced than she. "I'll only feel conflicted," he replied mischievously, "when the likes of you think I have enough money to support your favorite projects. Until then it's probably safe to invite you for a quick drink to get caught up. Let's go down the street to Rittenhouse Square—that is, if you still drink beer."

"I do indeed still mix with the likes of you. Let's go!"

They were actually a threesome when they graduated. They had met improbably at Brown University, Heather from small town Pennsylvania, Angel Moreno from a wealthy family in Madrid, and Brent from nearby Boston. They had arrived cheerfully in late August 2001, ready for an elite American undergraduate education, and had become good friends within a wider circle of classmates. They had promised to stay in touch in 2005 when they graduated and headed off in their separate directions. Heather chose to go away to Canada to study the world of fundraising for foundations and had come back with her master's degree from the University of Toronto. The program included time for internships and practical training, so it wasn't hard for her to find a job back in her home state. She loved the excitement of Philadelphia and immediately felt comfortable in the neighborhood around Arch and Third Street, which was going through a successful rejuvenation of new apartments, condos, restaurants, and art galleries. The quick ride downtown on the bus or subway meant she could easily live the metropolitan life she wanted.

Brent had decided to follow the hints of his advisors at Brown, who had instructed him in American and European history, and take a year off before heading to business school. He'd traveled to Brazil for several months to learn how to work and play in one of the world's great emerging markets. When he returned from his stint in South America, he politely ignored his parents, who had enough influence to place him at Harvard's business school and give him a solid start in Boston's financial community. Instead, he chose The Wharton School at Philadelphia's University of Pennsylvania. On his own, he found a job working in a local boutique investment house, Aird Investments.

Angel had returned to Spain after graduation because his dad, Juan, wanted him back to learn about their trucking business. As a final stage in his preparation, Angel entered the prestigious IESE Business School at the University of Navarra on the Barcelona campus. Immediately after graduating, he started his apprenticeship in the trucking business in Europe, North Africa, and the Middle East. His father answered all of his questions about transportation but remained aloof and rather silent when asked about politics, culture, or anything in the daily news. Angel had no idea what his father thought about any of the big issues of the day.

The three alumni stayed in touch after Brown through e-mails, texting, and occasional phone calls. Heather and Brent saw each other periodically in Philadelphia, but no romantic sparks flew between them. Brent always thought that Heather had a fondness for the absent Angel, judging by her questions.

They ate lightly after the reception at the Parc Brasserie, a few blocks from the hotel. This was their first chance to be alone together, although they had been in the same city for over a year. At first they apologized to each other for such rudeness, admitting how difficult and time consuming it was to establish one's self professionally and personally in the new city. As their salads and wine glasses were taken away, they agreed to work together on a special project.

"Okay, how do we get Angel back over here? We all miss him, don't we?" Brent asked. Heather looked askance at Brent, as she didn't want to admit that to anyone.

"I guess so. I stay in touch a little." She hesitated. "What do you think would bring him to Philly?"

Brent had his answer ready. "Leave it to me. I'll have Aird Investments invite him to drop by during his next trip to America. He's smart. He'll figure out what I'm doing. He'll give his dad some story and will come over with his family's blessings. Guaranteed!"

They parted with promises to stay in touch. This time, with the additional chemistry of Angel, those promises would actually be realized.

PHILADELPHIA, PENNSYLVANIA

WINNIPEG, MANITOBA

Spring 2008

Unlike Hugh and Susan, Arthur thought only about young people as students as he had no children in his everyday life. His immediate family in the West was composed of only Brenda, so he had the luxury of indulging himself in a mid-career crisis without having to consider anyone else's interests. When he wrote his first two manuscripts, his thesis and then later his academic book (*Baby Boomers: The Dream Generation*), he wasted very little time during writing sessions; he prided himself on writing quickly and continuously. This time however, as he prepared background notes for his proposal to study corruption, he found himself stymied, spending all of his time building up his old stamina just to concentrate and write critically for a few minutes at a time. Only gradually did he progress from self-pitying personal themes about evil in city life to more coherent thoughts about public problems. He seemed to be getting nowhere, however and took to checking out words in his old dictionary, hoping his expanded vocabulary would magically save him. That's when he knew he had to discuss this project with friends, as Brenda had urged him to do.

Arthur had already heard from two old confidants who knew him from grad school. They offered very different solutions. The first, a fellow teacher and researcher, suggested he give up academic writing in favor of becoming a novelist. He could write about imaginary corruption and not get hurt. The university would likely indulge this change in focus, at least for a few years, as so many of his colleagues were doing nothing at all. He was told that he could venture out from his established voice as an aloof researcher into the writer of fantasy while still dealing with many of the issues he wanted to research. Would a novel in itself coerce others into changing how they lived? He doubted that very much, but if he published, he would survive.

His second friend, now a university president, wanted Arthur to join his staff as an administrator. It was the most acceptable way for Arthur to abandon his research in favor of university politics. As Arthur's friend explained, many academics ended up very happy and well-off in academic politics instead of in fruitless fights to change the world. Arthur could establish himself as a powerful bureaucrat and enjoy perks like travel without the Spartan life of a researcher.

Neither tactic appealed to Arthur. Instead, as he pondered the issue over too many Manhattans, he decided he would hunt down the bad apples he had belatedly come to dislike. He would apply his research and writing skills to vilify pretentious baby boomers, especially those he found abusive to young people. The question was how? Brenda would not be happy, as he had not mapped out his next pragmatic steps as he had promised. If she ever heard him talk like this, she would be furious. He would have to camouflage his intentions carefully.

Despite his friends' appeals that he ride out his current misery and stay with his secure university life, Arthur sat motionless in his home office, discouraged with his prospects. Even though some had offered him viable options that were both concrete and practical, he continued to search for the ultimate solution that promised happiness forever. That's what was driving Brenda nuts.

Days went by. He organized his activities from the time he awoke, promising himself he wouldn't slip into heroic daydreams. Sometimes he woke abruptly, worried sick about potential disasters if he actually undertook the research he was contemplating. Academic life afforded him too much time to think about personal debacles while not giving him the emotional energy to fight his way out of his conundrum.

Reading Canadian morning newspapers, Arthur realized, was not a diversion that could help him in the least. He was on the verge of an anxiety attack before each sunrise. He now spent more time reading international papers found on the Internet, the New Yorker and Harpers and fussing more and more about things he couldn't control or influence. He prepared his usual breakfast, porridge like his grandfather had always made, before he sequestered himself and mentally pushed his way into academic writing mode, studiously avoiding any controversy that might set him off. His specialty as a sociologist was demographic trends, which gave him a platform for talking about baby boomers, generations X, Y, and Z, all of which were the rage last century. This had been Arthur's love in learning since early university years. His professors were quite taken by his analysis, if for no other reason than that they had trouble understanding his peer group. Right away Arthur recognized that baby boomers were going to be his lifetime business.

Arthur understood that his generation came into university life more at ease with themselves than previous ones had. They filled the unfinished new campuses that sprang up across the continent, making the lives of the newly minted professors frustratingly busy. Residences became chaotic as nineteen-year-old kids broke out of their family constraints, against boundaries on all fronts. Burning an American flag was a matter-of-fact activity, one that became no more significant than having a beer in the evening.

Arthur's genius lay in being one of the first to recognize that his contemporaries would dominate for the next fifty years. They filled every school space, from kindergartens to high schools and eventually to universities. When they hit the job market, they created a buzz because of their youthfulness and sheer numbers. Similarly, they transformed suburban and urban life throughout North America, eating up enormous tracts of land to house themselves and their offspring. Unlike their parents, they demanded lots of living space as well as new public facilities such as new roads, schools, and big-time sports facilities.

Ever the jaundiced observer, Arthur had never bought into the enthusiastic endorsement of baby boomers as the vast majority of his academic colleagues had. This was partly because his 1961 birth date put him at the tail end of this generation. He thought that the boomers' innate self-centeredness supported conservative leaders who captured and hoarded power for baby boomers and no one else. What Arthur recognized before others was that the so-called drive to transform and change society was a show entirely supported by a dubious cast: developers, communication specialists, apparel manufacturers, advertisers, the travel industry—an endless supply of self-serving hucksters.

Finally, he'd had enough of this crap. It was time to step out into the community and find out about local corruption. He turned to Brenda, who had seemed increasingly skeptical of him, and announced his decision.

"You'll be happy to hear that I've found my new research project. I'm excited to see where it leads." His pronouncement was not received with the drama he had hoped for. Since, as usual, he had given her no details, she shrugged absentmindedly.

After a few minutes of uncomfortable silence, Brenda pushed her coffee aside and asked, "Is that it?"

"Well, yes, my decision to apply will settle a lot, don't you think?" He was completely ambiguous, telling her nothing.

"Arthur, I doubt it. If it puts you back to work, go ahead. Right now it means nothing to me. What is your first move?"

Arthur did not dare tell Brenda that his life mission had changed: he was about to launch his crusade against corruption. Instead he tiptoed through a convoluted explanation of baby boomer urban leaders: were they that different from previous generations? She suspected he already knew the answer to that. "No surprises there. Nothing changes," Brenda told him, "Nothing."

"Probably true, but how do you prove it? That's the question," he answered. "I'll show everyone what's going on."

Suddenly his voice betrayed a meanness that Brenda had never heard. He continued his rant. "The study of local politics can be more brutal for researchers than for anyone in almost any other field of study at the university, except maybe the occasional anthropologist roaming around in the jungle." Brenda didn't laugh, so he knew how she felt about this: she was bored stiff.

"That's why I'm working so methodically in setting the stage for my denouncements. I want to start completely unnoticed. I will reach my goal by stealth so that everyone doesn't think I'm nuts. I will publish profiles of lousy leaders and expose them through blogs and Internet news sites—who needs the old-fashioned academic journals? Nobody reads them. For years, only a few will know what I'm doing. I want to be recognized as the unknown academic who broke open the code of silence about political corruption.

"I will pounce on some unsuspecting politicians, viciously reveal them, and then destroy their criminal ambitions. This is the dream of every sociologist—to change the world by highlighting those who are to blame for the sad state of our cities. I want to be the first to do this in Canada. Most academics refuse to deal with this reality as long as universities are part of the system." The dark and contemptuous side of Arthur's mind, buried for so long during his statistical research, was emerging with a vengeance.

Brenda tried once more to break into his unclear thinking, asking how her husband was planning to fund this project. She knew money at his university was tough to obtain, even in meager amounts.

"This will take you to a completely different and very dangerous place," she added with more than a little fear in her voice.

"I have my plan. For the next few months, until the end of the term, I will make every effort to establish my credibility. The Jacobs Foundation based in Chicago has a large urban research project. I'm going to approach them for support. If I get a grant, everything will be just fine."

"Okay, let's see what happens, but let's stop the daily moping and the nightly drinking. It's too much for me."

As Arthur walked away from Brenda, he knew that he needed a better cover story, or he would be marginalized before he started.

During his months of indecision, and before he launched his own private anticorruption campaign, there was someone on campus planning her entry into his world. Annie had resolved, as young women often do, that she wanted to know more about her Professor Crawford. Her classes were all progressing exceptionally well, and since she was confident that she'd be graduating on schedule with strong enough marks to be considered a great candidate for the best graduate schools, Annie had time to experiment. She still had a couple of years to think about which program to pursue; right now, it was too early to make those decisions. In the meantime, she was looking for something unusual or maybe eccentric that would assist her in determining what might be next in her life, adding understanding of her own private angst.

She encountered him one day as he was leaving campus on his walk home. This was no accident; she had been trailing him since late last term. She was enrolled in her second course with Arthur this one being large enough to allow her to watch him unnoticed among a wider audience of disinterested students. She liked the way his mind worked through tough problems while he stood in front of a class. He was good at lecturing about the subject at hand while suggesting more complex concepts to the brighter students who listened carefully to his arguments. Above all, he was so self-absorbed that his primary concern was fundamentally not whether they got it; he organized his lectures as vessels designed so that he could muse aloud about his somewhat tangled intellectual agenda. He shrugged off those who found him discombobulated.

Annie's objective was to flatter her professor until he took a reciprocal interest in her; she craved the strength of a mature man who could play the role of the older brother she never had. She broke into her stride as Arthur left campus; she had carefully planned her route knowing that she had reason to be on the same street for the next twenty minutes. By then, she could gracefully exit knowing whether she had made any progress.

"Hello, Professor Crawford. That was interesting yesterday. Oh, I'm sorry. I'm in your urban demographics course. My name is Annie Palmerston."

She knew that he recognized her and was pleased that she had interrupted his daydream.

"Yes, Annie, nice to say hello. What caught your interest yesterday?"

She was ready. "Well, you made the point early in the term that each generation would look at city life in a unique way. You suggested that we would best appreciate your class as a chance to learn how we, as young people, view city life differently than our parents do. Eventually, you argued, we could later claim this city space as our own. We would transform the existing malaise into a new positive experience."

Arthur nodded. That was an impressive recounting of his first lecture. "And yesterday? What stuck with you after that class?"

Annie calculated that she had less than ten minutes before her exit. "You've been talking about your parents' generation and how everyone was new to city life, particularly in these parts, where immigrants arrived from places like rural Germany, England, and Russia and obviously didn't speak the same language of their new neighbors. How did they make deals to build schools and roads, get rid of sewage, or agree to taxes?"

Careful now not to push him, she finished. "I never saw my grandparents as having the skills to deal with these problems, but they must have had them. This leads to the question down the line: what skills will I need?"

Before he could answer her, she stopped abruptly. "Here's my corner. Which way do you turn?" She already knew the answer.

"Uh, straight ahead for a while." Arthur was unsure of himself.

Annie took over. "Well, I hope I didn't bother you. Maybe another time we'll find ourselves on the same street."

He nodded and said good-bye confusedly, signifying that at this moment, he was totally incapable of dealing with any intrusions in his life. Nonetheless, Annie's striking personality and sharpness stayed with Arthur as he reached home. He had never considered any of his students particularly special. He considered it too much work, and he saved his energy for his intellectual life. Yet this student seemed exceptionally brilliant, taking in not only his words but the very themes he believed in and tried to convey in his lectures.

Arthur noticed her in class the next day; he wondered whether her focus and character were as deep as they appeared to be.

For Annie's part, she wondered whether she could convince the professor that it was worth his while to share his mind with her, possibly even invite her into his personal life as a friend. Her plan worked, and it didn't take long before others on campus noticed his newfound confidence. It came at the very moment he craved for uncritical support in his bid to shift focus in his research and to find funding from a prestigious foundation. It took courage to present his overhauled academic mission to be the logical outcome of a careful review made by a substantive mid-career academic worthy of a new long-term grant to sustain his innovative research project. Such blatant ambitions, after all, required energy and smarts as well as resilience to carping from peers and administrators. With his latest admirer firmly by his side, Arthur was ready to battle for his pet project. Annie fit immediately into her role as Arthur's friend and confidant but was careful not to verbalize that their professor-student relationship was becoming something special to both of them. She knew early on that she had made the right choice in selecting him as her friend and mentor. They were comfortable in each other's space just as she had hoped would be the case, and she doubted that she would ever come across such a man again.

Annie was at the stage where working with a man who eschewed a bureaucratic life pleased her. While they may deny it when they are young, she thought most eventually gave up the romantic notion of creating a life where they worked on their own in favor of employment in organizations where the daily routine superseded private time or personal friendships. This professor was her ideal exception.

Editing his applications, Annie watched how Arthur had cautiously incorporated a role for her in his research proposals. After Arthur took the unusual step of applying to the university research office to fund such a young undergraduate as a part time student assistant during her second year of studies, they worked hard together shaping his sketchy ideas on local corruption into an acceptable grant application. Following many hours passed each week in the university library, she came back religiously with articles, facts and questions that fed his curiosity and generated intense discussions between them.

Annie was immediately in her element. She was raised a free thinker and grew up nonchalantly following her beliefs without fear. Somehow from day one, Annie was immune to the criticisms of others as one might imagine an eighteenth-century European queen ignoring the squalor around her carriage by ordering the curtains closed. The isolation protected her proud, confident inner-self in a fashion that never offended any of her family, her friends, or adults who passed through her life. She daydreamed her way unhindered if there were a conflict in her daily routine. Despite coming across rather aloof to her peers, she was often privately moved by their gentle habits and sentiments. Her intension was to project a calm togetherness in face of any temporal agony or confrontation but she was steadfast and uncompromising in her refusal to reveal anything meaningful about her soul. Arthur, like all of her other friends, had a chair in this room but only as a tenant.

It had dawned on Annie that she was destined for a more complete life than her routine days on campus allowed. To attain that goal, she had to protect herself from mean laughter that might unexpectedly tear at a corner, leaving her scarred forever. She resentfully remembered a family dinner table discussion, when they were all chatting about how stupidly cars were being made—ignoring the environment, costing too much, unsafe to drive, a normal dinner conversation for a young family—she announced that she, one day as the first woman president of GM, would end such nonsense. The sibling laughter was instantly derisive although her dad vaguely defended her dream. This episode engrained in her the instinct to protect her lofty ambitions from those who had none.

That was why Annie immediately saw in Arthur a kindred spirit with whom she wanted to spend time. She correctly anticipated that Arthur would be accepting of anything she decided to reveal about herself. Like she, Arthur went about his business on campus as a "singularly unattached observer," quoting back his own jargon. He watched but didn't play. He heard the music start but never danced. No doubt he found comfort in having a young assistant equally disengaged.

While academic pressures did concern Arthur, he passed on any departmental opportunity to speak aloud about the problems facing faculty. He'd rather remain silent during the meetings, daydreaming about baseball or leaving for a half hour solitary walks to mull over his thoughts about the corrupt world that was preoccupying his imagination, anything but the agenda at the many inconsequential university meetings. His demeanor produced the results he was seeking. His contemporaries left him alone after meetings and, eventually, for the rest of the day. Why gossip with him? A person without organizational ambitions was a pretty scary prospect for all of his colleagues.

Annie and Arthur worked well together that first summer. It was total silence in his university office, removed from the hectic swirl of the city outside. This initially appealed to Annie's longstanding goal to be away from the crowd and to mark out an independent life that would feature quietness as its core value. Still, Annie was uncomfortable with the notion of living too quietly: would this be her proper solitude apart from others or an inner peacefulness that freed her spirit from distraction, allowing her to flourish on her terms? To that end, without mentioning anything to another person, she mapped out her life after college knowing that this brief adventure would soon end.

Somehow Arthur and Annie pushed each other to put in the hard work that was required for a foundation proposal. Annie listened for hours, in his office or on long walks together, to his ruminations on the immorality of baby boomers. She felt his anguish about the moral superiority they projected while bringing so much harm to others, particularly to their children.

The proposal submission to the Jacobs Foundation meant a great deal for all of those in the university watching Arthur's progress as he traditionally was one of their busiest researchers; however, they all missed the importance of his revised research agenda masking as it did the most significant digression in his career. Administrators were so happy with the promise of a research program with an esteemed foundation that they barely read the fine print heralding the transformation that the casting of Arthur in the treacherous territory of politics implied. He remained aloof in university discussions about his proposal, as a good academic should do, but underneath the veneer was a surging desire to lash out and demonize individuals whose ideals didn't match his own. This growing aspiration would eventually put him face to face with a neighbor, Hugh Parks, who lived only a few blocks away and whose ambitions and tactics were deeply at odds with Arthur's. At least that was what Annie originally thought.

Annie initially respected Arthur's consultations with various colleagues but she soon surmised that she was witnessing a clever charade to hide his campaign against corruption. It started out as a joke between them except that the more she overheard his conversations, the more she recognized the duplicity in his playful voice.

She remembered that rather early on, during her first month as his researcher, he'd had to line up his university allies to secure more funding for her summer internship. This had required his manipulation of just about everyone on campus, as he avoided telling them the true focus of his research. He had told no one he was launching his crusade, even though he had made up his mind to do so weeks earlier. After all, if they had known what he was up to, they would have abandoned him immediately and blocked any cash for research. Annie was far too young and new to academic politics to comprehend the enormity of this fraud.

She had heard his conversation with his colleague, Jack Hayden, who taught philosophy, that same first month. Jack had a firm view of the university where he had taught for over twenty-five years. "The great attraction of an academic life, when all is said and done, is that you have so much time to get into trouble. You don't have to report to anyone, in any serious fashion, and, if you are willing to hide out in a smaller university where tenure is readily attainable, you can put together a life in which essentially no one knows where you are. Sometimes they do find out, but they don't say anything so that you will return the favor. It is one of the few perches in the world where one meets dozens of people and works with them for a few years, after which they naturally disappear into other worlds. Despite the good times, the objective remains to stay out of real trouble."

"Staying out of real trouble...interesting," Arthur replied, a certain hesitation in his voice.

Jack went on. "Remember what a great reputation you have because of your innovative writing linking demographic trends with changes in North American society. Your writing excites and motivates other researchers. This has all been good. My word of caution is simply based on my experience on this campus. Take care with your goals...remember how much you have to lose."

The next day, despite Jack's warning, Arthur turned his attention to setting his campaign in motion. Annie later noticed from his records in his project notebook that he had already questioned his newly minted local spies, who didn't have any idea why he was probing them with his endless stream of questions about city hall. Two evenings a week during the winter term, Arthur taught an undergraduate class in urban sociology where he pushed his students to think more about cities where they had never lived: could they imagine a different life? Over the years, he had built a solid network within municipal departments; he decided to take advantage of his connections to talk vaguely about his research project and probe how they might help him. As she read his notes, Annie realized that he was slipping away from the classroom and into the back of a police cruiser to observe his new interest in the world of urban crime. He, of course, saw no danger in this.

WINNIPEG, MANITOBA

Spring 2008

When Hugh had returned from South Africa in late January, he told his closest friend, Rob Bennett, about Juan as soon as he landed in Winnipeg. Indeed, he skipped first going home to his wife, Joanne, phoning her with a weak sounding excuse that his plane was late. Stomper, as Rob was more commonly known, was already at Sal's coffee shop waiting for Hugh to tell his story of a fabulous opportunity to make real opportunity. That evening Hugh had explained that without any reservation if they started right away they had an unbeatable scheme. He spent time with Stomper going over every single detail of his latest scam.

As was his habit, Stomper bought in without raising a single negative question. Old dog, old trick, thought Stomper, who relished his role as Hugh's sidekick. They worked every swindle in the same methodical fashion. Hugh always embellished Stomper's mediocre undergraduate science degree so that he could present him as the leading researcher in several new fields of cutting-edge science and entrepreneurship. Their tactic was to circulate reports to their closely guarded list of investors, who had short memories and deep pockets. The two of them had always been able to excite a loyal following who quickly put between $500,000 and $1 million on the table after Hugh promised to match it within a few days. They would register a new venture based on Stomper's research and give it a sentimental name after one of Hugh's elderly aunts (such as Katherine AG Ltd.—a potash mining venture, now bankrupt). Without fail, they always generously offered two of the investors a chance to head up the company. It was the perfect scheme to keep their names off the accounts and away from suspicious regulators. Hugh and Stomper had not once signed corporate or banking papers.

Hugh was beaming that cold, miserable night about his trip overseas. His smile signaled that he had found another way to make a quick buck. This made Stomper grin in his affable, stupid fashion. Given his size—well over 6 feet tall and 240 pounds—and his rough reputation in local Sunday football leagues, Stomper was a natural to be cast as Steinbeck's Lenny, but without any naïve gentleness. A couple of investors from past deals had found out the hard way that he enjoyed protecting Hugh, his only source of cash.

Hugh and Stomper had originally organized this South African trip back in 2007 as a high-profile launch of their nascent information technology company. Hugh was ostensibly in Johannesburg, using contacts from previous trips to land a big contract for supplying software to a government that could barely afford to feed, house, or school its people. The Bison Board investors in Patricia Technologies quickly provided them with the money for his trip, showing their appreciation by issuing Hugh several thousand shares to build them an African business through his skullduggery. Hugh had immediately, without permission and with only Stomper's knowledge, sold off his free shares to other naïve investors to give them a chance, in his words, to be in on the ground floor. Not much paperwork was ever generated for these deals. Stomper had liked how the software deal was evolving. Hugh listed the important cabinet ministers he met, showed his photos from the reception as proof of his access, and reviewed the commitments made to the company. He added in a list of new contacts from the world's biggest contractors. Stomper committed to write a second report about the new African partnership and the exceptional new local shareholders Hugh had attracted. The report would leave no doubt that a multiyear deal featuring many of their products would be signed in the coming months as a result of Hugh's exceptional meetings in South Africa. Even Stomper, however, had no idea that Hugh had simply made up this story and that he hadn't held a single one of these meetings. That's how they did every deal.

When they finished mapping out how they would roll out their plan, they put on their heavy winter coats, a weight found only in Western Canada, and headed for the frosted doors. Hugh remembered one last piece of the puzzle and then asked, "Stomper: do you remember that crazy scientist, Albert Jackson, living here in Winnipeg, who invented a wind turbine to increase the fuel efficiency of trucks?"

"Sure," replied Stomper. "We set up meetings for Bertie with some truckers, but they all shied away from either investing in them or even trying one of these wind turbines on their trucks. I think Bertie was too excitable to win them over, but he had a great product. Remember, I wrote you a report on the science behind it. Still have it saved on my computer." He smiled, tapping his old Dell laptop, which he kept beside him at all times. "What's up?"

When it came to buying into Hugh's stories, Stomper was always, always first in line. That's why they worked so well together—Stomper actually believed his tales.

Without missing a beat, Hugh continued his story to trap Stomper and prepare him for another shoddy deal. "This Spanish guy I've been talking to might be suckered into buying Bertie's wind turbine. Our first priority remains offering a new business for his son but I think we might sneak a second one passed him. We'll show him how our science research on the lightweight composite turbine could, for example, keep his refrigerator trucks cool in the desert without drawing on the truck's power system. I'll put the price at $50,000 per truck; we'll offer him exclusive rights in Europe and maybe North Africa and the Middle East too. What do you think?"

"I still have the prototype," Stomper said. "And it would be easy to ship it to Moreno's company without telling Bertie." They accepted the reality that thieves rarely stop and explain themselves to either inventors or investors.

"No, I want to do better than that. Let's put a plan in motion so that by next Christmas we will have enough money to spend the winter in Arizona. We'll start by calling our Bison Board together and give our buddies a chance to think about how they could make some real change. Remind them about the last deal they missed. They won't know what you're talking about but they'll all show up at the next meeting. So let's work them over again."

The Bison Board was their inside joke. Expert teammates in raising piles of cash, they were quite proficient in convincing their friends to invest in their projects. They always told these fellows that they were like a corporate board of directors: they were the ones in charge.

"What's the angle for our investors?" Stomper asked, now standing outside in the subzero night waiting for his car to warm up, knowing from experience that this was certainly the most demanding question when they initiated a new confidence game.

Hugh unexpectedly hesitated. "This is more complicated than usual. I need the scientific story as a cover for our taking advantage of whatever is Juan's mysterious agenda in North America. Ostensibly, he's thinking about giving his son a new enterprise, and I offered to help. First, I want some scientific ruse for accessing the trucking industry as we really don't know anyone. After we have established some credibility, it will be easier to get closer to his true ambitions. In other words, I think we might have a bigger opportunity but within a more complicated racket. All the nonsense about our scientific breakthrough serves as cover while we exploit opportunities with this Spaniard. I'm not sure where we are heading if you want to know the absolute truth. I plan to bridge Bertie's scientific innovation, Juan's trucking, and the Bison Board's money. I have a few holes to fill in, but that won't stop me."

Hugh, ignoring Stompers restlessness to get out of the cold and to drive home as quickly as possible, continued with very measured comments as he had privately concluded that this chance overseas meeting just might catapult him into the big leagues. "We must achieve our goals quickly. Right now, we must raise money for the production of Bertie's energy-efficient wind turbines as the scientific underpinning of our business plan. Let's call the new enterprise Wendy's Wind Solutions. It's an easy-to-understand picture." When he was on a roll, thought Stomper as he swayed from foot to foot in an effort to ward off the cold, Hugh could be quite eloquent.

"Let's have this play out quickly. I want you to show up at the initial meeting with nicely bound copies of your research report. When you finish your presentation, let's get our expert on the phone, as Bertie will give everyone an enthusiastic update. We can't have him actually at the meeting, telling our investors of his latest conversations in outer space—but on the phone he could work."

Stomper drove off, already engrossed in the preparation for the proposed Bison Board meeting.

Hugh had learned his skills in an odd way. He'd acquired all of his ideas, homilies, little touching stories, and sad-but-true facial expressions at hockey arenas across western Canada and the northern states. He had an unbelievable memory for players and watched as many games as was humanly possible. He knew which kid needed a break and whose father wasn't helping out. Hugh's intensely generous personality made others feel that he cared and made him a reputable spectator in the rinks around town. His way of coming up with one or two twenty-dollar bills when a hockey stick was needed, or more gas for the weekend tournament, ensured he could pepper business conversations with hockey references that he knew would pique the interest of the person to whom he was pitching his latest scheme.

Those who were not so enamored by Hugh's skills completely underestimated the sports connection. As a young man destined to be a salesman, Hugh recognized that the prime common factor among men migrating into Winnipeg was their love of hockey. They all knew who hailed from which small agricultural or mining town, the name of the team, and the profiles of their stars. This knowledge extended far beyond their childhoods—it continued their whole lives, and they passed on these important nuggets to their boys. The same could be said for all of Canada's regions and into the university towns in Michigan, Minnesota, and the Dakotas.

Once Hugh had tapped into one poor soul, he was usually able to find the fellow's trusting network of hockey aficionados. As soon as one signed the dotted line for a new start-up promotion, the rest were sure to follow.

The hockey network had opened the door when he was in his twenties and led to his scouting small Canadian towns for prospects to play for an American college. Even though few players ever received the opportunity promised by Hugh, he was rarely blamed by the parents or the players themselves. They felt good about his promoting one of their sons as a potential star—and for folks outside Winnipeg who loved the game that was enough.

Hugh had great pep talks that he used over and over in front of teenage teams and their parents. Calmly, he described how to defeat an opponent. "Never give him hope. Never let him think he has a chance to win. He must understand that if he makes an effort, you will show a grim determination to shut him down. No matter what secret moves he thought he had before the game started, you know every one of them and will destroy him and break his confidence. He will be embarrassed to be beaten at his game in front of supporters. You will force him to play subdued and diminished as he decides to be complacent and compliant to avoid further embarrassment. After that, you have one focus. At some point, and it's impossible to say ahead of time when that will be, you will experience a game-changing moment. Since you are in charge, that game change will always be yours. You will win the game. They will lose." With a victorious wave of his hand, Hugh would yell out, "Go get them. Seize the game. Be a champion. Win! Win! Win!"

Hugh's surefootedness around the rinks was in stark contrast with his brutal behavior in his own house. The Parks family barely held together. Hugh might have been a public face that projected enthusiasm and goodwill to the community, but overall he was not the personality that his wife Joanne and daughter Emma could bring themselves to love and enjoy. Although their home life was not marked by open hostility, the threat of its disintegration hung over them constantly.

Emma bailed out as soon as she could by attending Brock University in Ontario, 1300 miles from home. Compared to those growing up in more charmed circumstances, the odds were stacked against her success.

Some students were equipped with strong family ties to support their efforts; others relied on the strength of their intellect and charming personalities. But the economic storms late that decade put them all face to face with an impending doom that challenged the gifts bestowed on them. Their fate would be changed by the unanticipated vengeance of more powerful people. Maybe it didn't matter whether they came from Winnipeg or Madrid; their fate was precarious.

Emma's nemesis was her father. On her own, she had no obvious personal or social advantages. Having never been touted as a gifted child, she arrived on the Brock campus in a fragile state. She had no well-wishers to see her off, no checks in her purse, and no trunks overflowing with the latest clothing. Emma was one young, awkward woman. But hidden beneath her nondescript appearance was a steel-like temperament. She had always been exposed to all sorts of danger, simply because she was Hugh's daughter. By moving away, she fervently hoped that she was no longer so vulnerable.

Emma had rarely played a part in Hugh's world since she was a very young teenager, and only once in a blue moon had she participated in family life with her mom and dad in their Winnipeg home. Around the house, she kept to herself, quietly afraid of the world that Hugh had brought into her life. At school, Emma was an acceptable, ordinary student, who in a previous generation would have been applauded and supported for her B grades. Nowadays she fell into no man's land. She wasn't bright enough to be honored at school graduation or to be singled out for her exceptional marks on a history or science project. At the same time, she never gave the teachers any problems. Her homework was done, she stayed clear of the groups looking for trouble, and she had no dates. Maybe it was the same as the experience of ordinary high school girls everywhere. She kept quiet during class study time, preferring to read a novel while others gossiped. Emma lived an honorable existence, one that teachers could acknowledge quickly as they moved on to deal with either the brighter or the more difficult.

Emma's family life left her lonely, despite her mother's efforts to smooth over the tensions. Joanne was a good mom, anxious about her daughter but not sure how to show her love. Emma spent most of the day in her bedroom with the occasional journey to the basement to watch television or into the kitchen for snacks. It was not a life made miserable on purpose; just the life of a teenager trying to find the right buttons to push for her own happiness.

Hugh wasn't one to think much about his family, barely noticing their anger. His wife tolerated his weaving and bobbing through the many hapless business dealings. He shielded her from the worst of his capers by showing up with enough cash to keep the household intact. She worked occasionally in the retail trade to bring home her own spending money and later to help Emma through college. Hugh barely acknowledged his daughter. They had disliked each other from the moment Emma's distraught personality took over the house in her early teenage years; Hugh took offense at her standoffishness and obvious distain for their family life. Not one to reflect on his own shortcomings, he heaved his vindictiveness at her with abandon. He hurt her beyond repair; they barely spoke after she announced her departure for Brock.

Hugh had tried again and again to make this teenager into something she was not—an outgoing joiner or an aspiring athlete. Emma cringed at the thought of doing such things. Often she overheard conversations from her mom's community groups but they never tempted her enough to open her bedroom door and say hello. When Hugh would learn of her behavior, he would berate her afterward for not showing up in the living room, unleashing a long list of her ineptitudes. She found his charming approach to everyone else—she knew this from snooping around—to be purposely false and misleading because of what he did to her in private.

It was not, in the end, a situation in which Emma could seek support from one parent in the hope of receiving sufficient comfort to ignore the awfulness of the relationship with the other. In this home, all of the relationships were completely unfulfilling. Joanne was wise enough, and certainly sufficiently frantic about her husband's business life, to know how uncertain their lives together were. Perhaps she would not be surprised to hear it crashing in around her. Beneath Hugh's bold assertions was the ugly truth of petty white collar criminality. They had enough to get by, and with suburban pretentiousness were able to keep up appearances.

In her last year of high school, Emma made it clear that she would follow her parents' advice and go to university. There was one important caveat, however. She was going away to study; university at home was not an option.

She blurted out her position, figuring that subtleness had never worked with her dad. "I would rather move on and work on as a clerk in another city than stay here. If you refuse to help, it doesn't matter; that's what I'm doing!"

Hearing such a declaration from their timid daughter threw the parents into argument after argument. As Hugh had neither the inclination nor the actual cash to help Emma out, his views threatened to undermine their tense marriage. Joanne's support for Emma was based on the indication from her daughter that if she walked out the door without their support, she would succeed on her own despite them. There would be little communication and no visits from her.

That reality was too much for Joanne to handle. Over Hugh's irrational declaration that they didn't need the money, Joanne began to work again. The pay for her part-time work was moderate. She took Emma aside and for the first time had a major conversation that she did not relay back to Hugh, a clear indication that she didn't trust him to do the right thing.

"Every penny will be for you, sweetie," she said in a quiet, deliberate tone. "I will not abandon you. You will be supported so you can go to college. That will be the centerpiece of your future." The unspoken reality, Hugh's unreliability and his exclusion from this conversation, hung over them heavily. It could not be avoided.

"Mom, I'm worried more about you," Emma said cautiously. "Will you be okay after I leave?"

"Believe it or not, you don't need to think twice about me. This is my town with friends, extended family, and helpful allies. Everyone is always here for me and will support me, no matter what. Your dad looks after me in his own strange fashion."

Joanne continued, "I want you to find a university you'd like to go to; they're almost all good, and you'll find a new group of friends no matter where you go. We'll work together to complete your university applications. We'll hear back through my e-mail or in the mail at my work so that we can keep this to ourselves. I don't want another stupid domestic blow-up. When you do go, I'll send you whatever money orders you need."

For the first time, Emma felt the strength of a parent actively supporting her ambitions by making this commitment without comment or retribution. She was thankful and sad at the same time. The experience came too late for her to choose to stay home, which was the path her mother dearly wished she would follow.

And go she would. By late April that year, they had her confirmation from Brock, a small but competent university in a rather plain city. Once she settled into residence, she gained much more self-confidence in both her academic and social prowess. Since modern campus life in Canada is peopled mostly by young women, they supported each other and laughed about the sisterhood taking over the campus. In addition, Emma's marks improved slightly with the constant encouragement. Although she was never going to be an A student, she had a group of friends who were a joy compared to those of her high school life. Nobody had any money, so they passed their days together contentedly, sitting around, telling stories, and sharing a few dreams. Emma supplemented her mother's money orders with work in the cafeteria and a summer job in a local call center. Although it wasn't much fun working in St. Catharine's during the summer, she treasured the fact that she never had to go home except for perfunctory visits at Christmas when no one else was on campus. She was fully aware that at graduation, she would have to face all the insecurities confronted by so many of her generation who were stymied looking for worthwhile careers.

. . .

Hugh remained sitting in the Frankfurt airport for a long time waiting for his flight to Toronto then onto Winnipeg. He wasn't completely sure of what to make out of his chance encounter in South Africa. Hugh was sure that Juan wanted into North America for reasons he wasn't willing to discuss in South Africa. It was just a gut feeling. What was he really interested in doing? There were several possibilities, but one stood out for Hugh—munitions: explosives, bombs, missiles, or any similar materials. America was a haven for the manufacture and distribution of armaments; in fact, this was the biggest market in the world. Despite the uproar over 9/11, the reality was that North America was a safe continent for over 350 million people. Governments and corporations spent tremendous amounts annually to protect themselves from further attacks. Despite alarmist voices from the many sources who were dead wrong, nothing serious had happened since 9/11. In fact, day after day, most security personnel were dying of boredom.

Hugh decided to find out more from his new Spanish connection, who, it turned out, had just arrived in Dubai on his way back to Madrid. When Hugh called him, Juan was immediately on guard, acting like he barely remembered their casual conversation in Johannesburg. At least Juan now knew who had his cell number. Unfortunately, so did the listeners who monitored calls to his cell, even though he was nowhere near Spain.

Hugh didn't think it was necessary to reintroduce himself except to say, "Hi, it's Hugh," as though they spoke all the time, and started right into a business conversation. At no point did he notice that Juan wasn't saying much.

"If you want some help over in North America, give me a call. I phoned home after we talked, so I know for sure that we can either help buy a company or line up the trucks and drivers for one of your special projects. We can give you whatever you need, as we are terrific niche players. Your son could learn a lot from us."

Juan still had not said anything beyond the initial hello.

"I think we can build an effective partnership." Hugh didn't stop there. Given Juan's silence, he should have.

"Uh, thanks," Juan responded distantly.

Oblivious, the nervously excited Hugh plowed ahead with his pitch. "The economy is really terrible in the States, so trucks are available. It might be best to invest in a small trucking business and your son can gradually build up his capacity to compete. I already have offices in Buffalo and Winnipeg. Our financial advisors work out of Philadelphia. We can help you move whatever unique cargo you want to shift from Europe and the Middle East into North America—or ship overseas to your destination."

Now Juan had heard enough, and so had anyone else listening in to this conversation. It was time to cut this off. "Don't want to get ahead of ourselves. We've only met once and barely know each other."

Undeterred, Hugh had missed every cue to shut up, even when Juan did his best to close down the conversation. He unsuccessfully tried to hide his desperation. "Okay, how should we leave this?"

Juan answered in a terse and noncommittal businesslike manner. "What we have to do here is follow good business practices. I will discuss your overture with my advisors. We'll check you out through our contacts. If you're okay, you'll be called in three to four months to present us with a business plan. I would prefer to characterize our initial conversation as one in which we only outlined in an exploratory fashion an unusual business opportunity. Therefore, I would urge you not to discuss this with anyone. A breach of confidence voids any possibility of our working together. We'll contact you. Bye."

They ended their conversation with very different reactions: Hugh was smiling, but Juan was perplexed about his new contact. "Who is this guy?" he asked no one in particular.

WASHINGTON DC

Spring 2008

Myron generally enjoyed Todd's tales; a good story was part and parcel of his trade; he dragged out the plot while offering endless, meaningless details, which was considered a much-respected skill in his circles. As Todd finished this one, however, Myron was less patient with him, as he felt pressure that this story was overtaking them. Instead of this being a historical adventure, he knew that it was unfolding as they spoke. They were on the phone, so Myron was comfortable indicating that Todd should get to the point. He did.

Unbeknown to Hugh, the American Drug Enforcement Administration, from its European listening post not many miles away from the Frankfurt airport, had had the same questions as Juan: "Who is this? Where did he come from? What's in Buffalo? What's to be shipped to America?" Puzzled, the listener called Washington. "All hands on deck. Juan Moreno is coming over."

Todd had picked up the message from Frankfurt on his BlackBerry later that same night. It reconfirmed his longstanding belief that a good law enforcement organization had to be prepared for very long waits for a new clue to pop up on its radar. Hearing that Moreno had been caught in a strange conversation warmed his heart. He was going to be on his trail again, and this was the first time he'd heard from the elusive armaments dealer since Todd had decided he might be a suspect in the 2004 Madrid train bombings. That suspicion had turned out to be off the mark and hurt Todd badly among the intelligence agencies, but he had shrugged off their criticisms. He was bound to make a few mistakes over twenty years. When a Spanish security officer had passed on the tidbit about his hunch to Juan, the Spaniard simply laughed. "If this guy thinks I'm stupid enough to blow up my own city and hang around to see what happens, I have little to worry about if he's on my trail. He'll never figure out what's really happening."

Anyone could tell right away that Todd operated like a cop. Everything he did had the air of a covert operation. He went so far as to block his cell phone number so you couldn't tell he was calling. He liked creating insecurity and uncertainty, but you always knew that it was Todd calling, because no one else blocked their number.

Todd watched everyone, finding out their patterns, who they talked with, where they lived, what they thought of the president, and so forth. It was a mind game that kept him thinking about others and their motivation. Spying was all about sitting still, waiting for someone else to move. Like Myron, Todd lived alone and had for years. That lifestyle suited him, as he needed peace and quiet to unscramble the problematic files that held his interest day in and day out. He had friends who worked for hours on crossword puzzles; others were fascinated by computer games to keep them busy. He actually had friends who found television to be fulfilling too, although he refused to go there. Todd thrived on solitude, digging deeper and deeper into the lives of others around him.

When he came across a case that baffled him, and that happened more often than he cared to admit, he put aside all diversions. No matter how long he watched, there were cases in which nothing happened; no one made a move—or at least no move that seemed to indicate a sign of a deeper malady. Juan was at this moment such a character. His fingerprints were nowhere to be found, and Todd could never find a trail from him that led anywhere. Spain's standoffish attitude was no small barrier to his studying Juan. A few years back, after the explosions that wreaked such havoc on public transport in Madrid, Todd had found an excuse to spend a few days in Spain. As a member of a special American antiterrorist team put together to help their European counterparts, he had the freedom to walk through Juan's neighborhood in an effort to immerse himself in his quarry's life. What did it mean to be Juan? What did the house, the cars, and his family tell him? Juan's plots were so well-hidden and the transactions cleverly camouflaged under the transportation company. Since Todd's contacts had accessed that company's records, he knew about the Dubai bankers, but he couldn't figure out what else they did for Juan.

Todd shrugged away his frustration when he left Madrid with only part of the story; he couldn't make sense of the facts in front of him. Myron had taught him that good spooks thought like politicians and arms dealers; he learned his lessons watching who survived in Washington. They were the ones who never made a move without waiting for every piece of the puzzle to fall into place. He always lectured Todd: "Make sure you know everything. Learn about everybody: the arms manufacturer, the trucks and drivers, the financial dealings, their targets, and, most importantly, the terrorists themselves. You must know everyone and watch them closely and quietly."

Todd was rarely inclined to discuss his mandate, as he quietly had to operate outside the usual antidrug cartel operations that were the DEA's meat and potatoes. He had rather mysteriously walked into their organization after 9/11. He held his tall, muscular frame in a way that confirmed the rumors about his marine training, but no one could figure out what had done afterward. And he wasn't about to tell. The message to the DEA from Myron, on behalf of the most senior congressional security group, was to put aside their fantasies and create a case file to explain his authenticity. Special investigator Aykroyd's confidential mandate was outlined in the briefest of notes circulated in early 2002 as a way of introducing him. There were neither background documents nor elaborations during administrative meetings. It was crystal clear to those sitting beside him that drugs were of little concern except when they were used to finance terrorist operations. He loved to sit and read everything he could about armaments; he knew where they came from, who sold them, and how they were transported to buyers, paid for, and stored until the right moment. Although Todd was easy to get along with and admired by many, he didn't share much information within the DEA. He played games to arouse their curiosity. For example, he often sent around e-mails asking about the purchasing power of drugs: he was totally fascinated by how much a ton of cocaine shipped from South America to the African west coast could fetch in Morocco, then again in Berlin on the street. He asked rhetorically if anyone knew which sellers took bullets instead of cash or how many tons of cocaine were needed to support a terrorist cell? No one could answer his questions.

Todd had immediately relayed information about the intercepted call to Juan during one of their frequent meetings at Myron's intellectual habitat, the Cosmos Club near DuPont Circle. Myron's take on the situation was that Todd should continue following this lead since they had heard almost no fresh information about Moreno for several months. Todd readily agreed.

"The drug enforcers like their sister agencies receive funds from Congress in a highly camouflaged process; only you and a few elected officials have a complete picture. The DEA has to be pushed to move expediently so their experts can find new names, bank accounts, girlfriends, and home bases. Since the agency now has offices in over eighty countries, its reach is significant. The contacts of each office are different because the drug trade has different alliances in every market. It's improving but I find it painfully slow."

Myron knew that Todd's real victories at the DEA came when they found terrorists at work. They could be buying and selling small armaments, pieces of the nuclear puzzle, or knocking off individuals or small banks; they were usually available to anyone who wanted to buy their services. International assassins weren't partisans but worked hard at keeping their profiles as low as possible. That's why Juan was of interest to both Myron and Todd. He was wealthy, well-connected, protected in Spain, almost always at home when the postman knocked. He'd also been involved in far too many bombings since the nineties.

As Todd explained all the relevant details to Myron, he proudly included the fact that his handpicked, Washington-based duty officer working late Saturday evening instantly knew that the listener in Frankfurt was onto something. This agent had watched too many careers in the security forces go down forever because someone didn't read the first signal correctly, and he moved without hesitation to contact Todd. Once Todd heard the news, he had called in his small crew working the weekend shift and set up a conference call Sunday morning with the European team.

"Myron, we swung into action immediately. It was getting late in the day in Europe, and we had to find out who this newcomer might be as quickly as possible, no matter where in the world he might end up after his flight. My team had recorded the time of the call, so we worked on the assumption that the German payphone was located at the Frankfurt airport—a peak time for passengers in transit back to the States. The caller's accent was definitely North American. That much we confirmed right away. It was impressive."

Myron listened, astounded. "You know that it came from Frankfurt at exactly 11:30 p.m. local time?"

"Yes, it was great. First objective was covered. Second, we got the airport's security people to rewind their video tapes and find out who was on the pay phones at that time. Done, and by this morning we had those tapes. Finally, once we had a few pay phone numbers, we asked the major credit companies to run their systems; they can usually find that charge fast. We thought we would soon have a phone number, a picture, and the credit card info, but that didn't work out right away. It turns out that some credit card operations headquartered in jurisdictions used for tax evasion didn't cooperate as quickly as we would like. But, eventually, late this afternoon, we found our man, "Hugh Parks"—a Canadian hitherto unknown to us.

"Myron, even now, I would appreciate if you share no information except that you've been told we intercepted a call originally thought to be about importing drugs. The truth is, I'm very concerned about an attack on the United States being organized by one of our most dangerous enemies. I recommend that you tell your congressional bosses that we should raise our internal alert status up one level, but say as little as possible. I'll talk to you again tomorrow around 1:00 p.m. with more of an update. I'll phone your office." They finished their conversation more urgently than usual, as both felt their nervous energy and anxieties taking over. The hunt was on.

That Juan was regularly at home and talking on the phone was not news to Todd. The real gem of information was that although Juan rarely used his cell phone, he did this time. He almost never mentioned anyone of any value, so who was this Hugh fellow who was dumb enough to introduce himself? Todd smiled, as he could only guess how confused Juan must be by this amateur.

"Hello Darkness My Old Friend" played gently on the old rockers station as Todd drove home with a song appropriate for his spook personality. He was recounting every detail possible about recent developments. He tested out different scenarios as he speculated about the European news. An unknown business associate of Moreno was somewhere in Canada thinking about getting involved with one of Europe's great scoundrels. The agency had previously speculated that Juan was in the Spanish countryside for a few days, a subterfuge he often used to throw off his invisible but constant watchers. Through their informants, the DEA usually heard from one of the airlines if Juan was leaving the country—a courtesy that the Spanish government itself rarely formally extended to American agencies. When Juan realized how he was being tracked, he switched to Middle East airlines. Finding out where Juan had been traveling since then was difficult, particularly as American agents had to be quick and quiet without alerting Spanish authorities.

With regard to Juan's background, although Todd could not approve of anyone helping out any terrorist, he begrudgingly understood the circumstances. Juan's family had risen in importance only at the end of the Second World War by helping allied forces deal with traumatic civilian problems in the late forties. Juan's relatives had danced reluctantly with Franco's people, transitioning into the more democratic environment with greater ease than the rest of Madrid's business establishment. Authorities knew about his armament deals, but Juan meticulously stayed away from any domestic problems. Todd now guessed that Juan had turned the tables on him by giving Spanish authorities the good tips they needed to find those who blew up Madrid's trains. In doing so, he smoothly foiled Todd's attempts to link him with domestic terrorists.

The next day, Todd phoned Myron on schedule, right after lunch.

"Do you have any connections in Canada?"

"Why?"

"Well, I'm now 100 percent sure, as I suggested yesterday, that the phone call came from the Canadian, Hugh Parks, out of Winnipeg. We're carefully putting a surveillance operation together but are leery of not having any Canadian engagement."

"Is there a financial angle? Because if there is, I have a contact."

"There is. The caller expressed interest in helping Moreno set up a transportation business somewhere on this continent. We now suspect that Parks has no money for such a business, so where does he come up with the cash to impress his new friend? We are assuming it's someone in Canada. They may unsuspectingly end up investing in an American company that may be involved in exporting and importing armaments. Tell your contact that we know for sure that they will be transporting Mexican drugs north and probably into Canada." This was more than a slight exaggeration, but Todd was determined to find a Canadian operative.

"You might be in luck. The Canadian Embassy always tucks away a senior finance official down from Ottawa on a rotational assignment. This one, Shelly Spicer, is exceptional and has spent time in their security agencies before coming to Washington. My speculation is that she is here as a friendly spy, but that's okay. What would you think if I fed Shelly the story that we were worried about Canadian funds supporting terrorist organizations? In return, she would help us find out more about Parks and his friends in Winnipeg."

"Sounds like a perfect deal."

WINNIPEG, MANITOBA

Late Spring 2008

For the past few days, Hugh had spent his time readying Bertie and Stomper for their meeting with the Bison Board, his favorite first stop in fundraising. He had little doubt that he would be successful in convincing everyone that now was the time to finance this scientific venture. As he walked out the door, Joanne reminded him of the community meeting at their house after lunch.

"Will you be back in time?" she asked, knowing how much Hugh hated such events. "We like as many as possible to show. Sounds like the mayor is sending out his assistant to hear our complaints."

"What complaints?" he responded in a mumbled, disinterested tone, failing to hide for a moment his genuine dislike of the more pretentious neighbors.

"Well, you know." Joanne hesitated, as she had enough issues to fight about without starting up here. "We've been talking about ways to stop all these noisy trucks roaring down our streets as a shortcut. This is a pretty good group we've put together."

"I've an important meeting. I might have to pass. We'll see."

Hugh could teach the better educated university types living in his neighborhood a thing or two about organizing a campaign, for or against anything. This Sunday morning he was connecting the businessmen who had the cash with Bertie, whose invention would give the project scientific credibility.

In addition to ensuring that Bertie was ready with his commentary, Hugh had instructed Stomper to compile a list of points he should be making to ensure the meeting was a success. Their minds were already leapfrogging ahead of Bertie's scientific explanation of his wind turbine to the problem of closing the deal that morning. They loved to take preposterous ideas, such as this, make them sound reasonable, and milk friends and family with the lure of a quick fortune. They were hard-core pump-and-dump pros whose understanding of the weaknesses of small-time investors had to be admired. They set up this room the same way they worked every scam. They singled out one of the participants to be their lead cheerleader and to sign on first. That always worked out well. Hugh had previously arranged so much money for one fellow that he was put on the spot yesterday by Stomper and cajoled into being the first to stand up and support Hugh's scheme. It was orchestrated like a revival meeting. As soon as one volunteered to be an investor, Hugh knew that the rest would follow. It happened every time.

Hugh called Stomper from his car phone to review in detail their strategy. They had to be on the same wavelength and he knew from experienced that he had to prep Stomper on every nuance. "As much as we might not want to be known by the friends we keep, we fully understand that sometimes our friends keep us. Let's make sure everyone joins in with their money. I think Bertie is crazy with this invention, but we can make a buck out of it. If we succeed this morning, I can phone Juan back and make sure he doesn't hang up immediately."

Although several regulators were dying to put these two out of business, Hugh and Stomper weaved through the entrepreneurial world sensing who was desperate enough for a quick and easy deal to take yet another chance with them. Hugh was the smoothie who could purr about his sporting mates and the guys he brought up from St. Louis for hunting in northern Saskatchewan. There were always very important people around, according to Hugh; others just never met them. When one skeptical investor asked his lawyer, who specialized in financial fraud, about Hugh, he was told: "My office is filled with well-spoken security sales people who claim directly to my face that their offering was crystal-clear and that the other side did not read the deal carefully enough. To call in a regulatory investigator is insulting and unfair to all of my clients, if you listen to them. That's how guys like your friend Hugh get away with whatever they decide to do. Nobody is chasing them."

Stomper, a regular, tough con-artist, claimed great success in many fields, although he still could only afford to drive around in his mom's 1989 Chevy Malibu. He was a brute of a sidekick who did not hesitate to come across the table and wreck the face of a naysayer. Hugh was lucky. It was not often a guy could meet his protection in a university pub and have him by his side for the next twenty-five years at no obvious cost. Exactly what was the deal here? Bertie, who was dragged out more than once to present a strong case for a marginal scientific innovation, answered somewhat bitterly that they were classic scam artists who could not be trusted under any circumstances. But he was trapped by his own admission that their strategy worked. They had probably helped every person at the table in some fashion; including him so the loyalty was undeniably strong. Although it was easy to knock them by calling them thieves, they had rescued most over the years, forcing the skeptics back into their arms. They saved one by taking money from the others. It was not necessarily the best arrangement, but members shrugged and accepted the rules of their club.

When the Bison Board came together at Hugh's lawyer's office, Stomper carried in freshly bound copies of his old report. He described in them Bertie's invention: miniature wind turbines for trucks. The report outlined the financial and environmental significance of these innovative wind turbines for the North American trucking industry. His presentation took half an hour with few interruptions; he then placed the speakerphone at the center of the table so that all could hear their favorite scientist.

"All of the research has now been completed. I was over at the university using its wind tunnel aerospace testing site late last month. The results are great, as the turbine produces all of the energy needed to keep any truck's electrical system going, including the big refrigerated units. This means enormous savings to the fleet owners. Listen, I've figured out exactly how much they will save."

As Hugh had anticipated, it took no time at all before Bertie was off track from his agenda. He prided himself as being one of the few inventors who understood the business of his buyers. After a few minutes, Stomper coolly directed him to talk more about the science behind the turbine, not the business.

"We'll discuss our business plan later in the meeting, if that's okay with everyone."

Hugh saw what was going to happen next. "What makes this development of yours such a good product?" he asked. He hoped his intervention would keep Bertie in a good mood, as his endorsement of their project was critical to their success. They needed his product to raise funds. Luckily for them, at this moment, Bertie was also in dire need of substantial cash.

"Good question," Bertie responded, with a nervous laugh. "Composites, my friend, composites. A decade ago, engineers had no idea of what to do with new composites being created in the big R & D labs, as most of them are trained in metals; they love to feel the weight and thickness of aluminum, steel, copper, nickel, and so on. The truth of the matter is that they don't trust the lightness, the almost weightlessness of a composite part. Hughie, did you bring a turbine into the office to show your friends?"

Timing was everything when a swindle like this was unfolding. Hugh rose, went to a side door opening into his lawyer's adjacent office, and picked up the turbine in one hand. It was polished and shiny, about two feet high, and less than that across its base. As they had rehearsed, Hugh casually threw it to Stomper, who placed it on the table for all to see. They could literally hear Bertie's proud sigh. He was indeed their very dear "mad scientist."

"Look at that baby!" he exclaimed. "I tell you, it works like a charm." Although he wasn't in the room, Bertie could imagine their looks of pleasant surprise.

"Who's using it now?" asked one of the Bison Board members.

Ignoring the question and moving quickly, Hugh signaled to Stomper that Bertie was about to be history. "If there are no further science questions, let's thank Albert Jackson for his time and move on."

"That's all?" said the scientist. "Okay, that's fine with me. I want to catch a program on the History Channel that starts in five minutes about the residents of Bridgetown down in Barbados, who saw a space craft land on a big cruise ship last month just off the south coast."

"Oops," Stomper exclaimed abruptly, breaking the connection, "I cut him off without a proper good-bye. I'll phone him back later and apologize."

Hugh now took over the meeting. "We're developing this project at exactly the right moment. Bertie has finished his work as the scientific developer, and a local composite company now has the tools to build as many as we can sell. In the last decade, oil spiked as high as $150 a barrel, and it looks like it will settle at $100, from what I hear. This makes trucking an expensive business. Stomper has drafted a marketing plan, and he calculates that sales will be about five hundred this year and probably one thousand by the end of next year. After that, as everyone notices these wind turbines on so many trucks, our sales will be at least two thousand annually. I would cautiously predict, without much trouble, that sales will approach five thousand in less than five years. Because there's a good patent on this invention, no competitor one can get in. Since no one else except a local manufacturer knows how to make these at profitable price points, we will have an easy ride into the market. They'll come out the door at $10,000 and will be sold for $50,000, including batteries that will be shipped in from Japan. Do the math, boys. The local manufacturer gets his fair share, as his real costs are negligible. If everyone at the table is in, we'll put aside the usual amount for my management fees plus some for Bertie. We will build twenty of these units valued at $1 million in sales to get started. Dividends will commence next year, and I'll have you an IPO in four years. We'll price our first shares into the market at $100 each; anyone buying in today will pay $5 with a minimum buy of 10,000 shares. You will make some real coin here."

"Everyone good?" The designated board member chimed in on cue, and Hugh moved to end the meeting.

"Okay, Stomper has the paperwork, and you can each leave a check."

Hugh wound up his show smoothly and no one seemed to notice that only fifteen checks were collected at the table from the seventeen individuals in the room. The two names missing were those of Hugh and Stomper, who argued that their development and management work would constitute their contribution. With $750,000 in the bank, a bigger take than normal, the new venture was up and running. Hugh and Stomper would each receive a monthly retainer of $5,000 plus expenses while they promoted the project. Since the last deal, a class action over an obscure patent owned by Bertie, brought in triple the original investment, Bison Board investors were ready for more action; all signed on the dotted line. Hugh stood back and let Stomper do his job. On Monday, he'd ask his accountant to set up the company books, deposit the checks, and otherwise "look after the details." As usual, neither Hugh nor Stomper had their own names on any paper. In fact, according to one disgruntled regulator, when Hugh went on a mission, it reminded him of the photo stories about European pigs looking for truffles. What actually appeared on the plates of foodies dining out in fine style in Toronto began with a large, snorting animal rummaging through a forest. This was his image of Hugh.

Hugh was indeed such an animal. He could smell a good find long before the best of con-artists. He could see the game developing and put his allies in the right positions long before others knew what was happening. He was now ready to go. He had a coherent narrative, an invention easy to promote, a team of equally determined individuals who knew their roles from past heists and, above all else, cash to play the game. Hugh was very confident that he could make a lot of money in this deal. More importantly, he had what he wanted for his next pitch to Juan.

WINNIPEG, MANITOBA

Late Spring 2008

Arthur wasn't making much progress with his project. Sullenly, he sat down during coffee break beside the two police officers who were students in his evening class and talked about his research proposal. "How do you define corruption?" he was asked pointedly.

"Good question," he responded, playing for time. Finally, he responded, "Everyday life for public servants like yourselves has ethical moments, times when you just don't have the energy to do the right thing. It may be a decision to not pick up a criminal at the end of a shift when you know it has to be done—or like a situation on the television show "The Wire," where a cop was sleeping night shift so he could work during the day selling real estate near his suburban home away from the dangerous inner city. There must be lots and lots of daily decisions that color the overall character of city hall."

The second officer brushed this off as too moderate a view. "Aw, but your examples are all bullshit—there are big-time problems that you're missing. Like who gets the lazy desk job or whose butt is covered after an accident. Those are real decisions we face every day."

Arthur listened to their frustration and added a final comment, as it was time to return to class. "I know, I know; we all can find examples of how life in the city drives us nuts. I'm proposing to show how good leaders respond to voters who demand different results. Taxpayers want to have their money spent on different and more ethical priorities. It is corrupt to not respond. I already have lots of examples-but now, back to class."

"Yeah, well, you still haven't told us what it means to be corrupt."

A frustrated Arthur realized that he had to refine his approach if he were to be successful in his campaign against city corruption. It was also important for the rewards that academics love after they receive funds for their research projects. He had heard the story of a University of Chicago professor who headed a European study group and kept an apartment in Paris paid by an American foundation. Arthur was readily willing to fudge for that perk. He, too, preferred that seminars and consultations take place in London or Paris. All he required was a competent research plan lasting for three or four years that dovetailed with the aspirations of an unsuspecting foundation. The travel alone was worth the conniving, although he denied to Annie that he was being disingenuous in his application to study abroad.

He had to create a compelling argument for the funding of his anti-corruption campaign, especially after he calculated the rewards of international research compared to his current work of studying computer printouts in his pathetic university office during Canadian winters. Concluding that he would be foolish to pass up the chance of free overseas travel, Arthur still had the formable task of convincing important people on campus and at the Jacobs Foundation to support him. He had to be a risk taker, almost like the politicians he wanted to attack, but since he had never organized a campaign before, this was turning out to be hard work. Since his academic friends were not in the habit of approaching foundations by hiding their true intentions, he had no one to turn to for help in mapping out his next steps.

It wasn't until the next morning after he finished a cup of strong coffee made in his small Bodum press that it dawned on him what he had to do to make a mark for himself: tackle the corrupt ways of a whole generation. His self-imposed mission was to prove beyond a doubt that the most revered generation in western civilization was fraught with public thievery and fraudulence. He would begin this crusade by exposing baby boomers as untrustworthy city hall politicians bankrupting the coffers on every continent. Arthur intended to be fearless in his attacks. He'd write his research papers in a popular and anecdotal style to capture the imagination of a wider audience. He might even stitch together a popular book exposing payoffs across the States. Boastfully, he predicted that the Internet was to be the new forum to showcase his campaign and soon study teams from Barcelona to Burbank would join in battle for world reforms. He could sell himself as a blogger. The more he thought about this, the more Arthur became a victim of his own self-aggrandizement, losing all sense of practicality. He hurriedly headed off to the office. The urge to undertake this mission was driving him to the brink of insanity, although he effectively hid that from Annie.

His proposal was finally taking shape, but one problem remained. He couldn't answer Annie's straightforward questions asked repeatedly that week: "Precisely what is your prime litmus test of corrupt baby boomers? Do you plan on using Winnipeg as your lab? Is there someone you're secretly watching and loathing in the local scene? Can we really launch this world campaign from your office here on the prairies? But why are you suddenly so hyped? Am I missing something?"

With a deep breath, he again consulted at dinner with Brenda, who was by now only vaguely interested in his chatter about research. He toned down the more radical elements of his holy war. Undeterred by her indifference, he asked his wife, "What cities should I include from the Middle East? Iranian and Iraqi cities are out, since no baby boomers are still alive there. I love the idea of Alexandria -not really a major city, but it has a great library that I've always wanted to tour. That would make me look very, very serious."

Brenda responded skeptically. "Frankly, some American and European travel with you would be great. I'm not sure about the Middle East. Have you talked to the Jacobs Foundation yet about this project? Is anyone going to support you? The best strategy would be to ask the funders for direction on this point. Go where the Foundation wants you to go."

After dinner, Arthur looked down at his list for the consultations he had long ago promised Brenda. Although he unfolded the page as if expecting a secret note, he knew full well the first name: Professor Howard Goldsmith.

Arthur took his chances in phoning his doctorate thesis advisor, who remained at McGill University, where Arthur had completed his studies. They'd had a good student-mentor relationship, fondly appreciated by both. Professor Goldsmith had slowed down as he neared retirement but still immediately answered all communications from his former students, spread as they were throughout the continent's six time zones. Whenever Arthur had faced a difficult decision regarding his academic career, he always turned to the advisor who had shepherded him expertly through his dissertation and helped find him his current job. Goldsmith was an animated, enthusiastic, and outspoken teacher, famous for pushing his protégés to the limit. They repaid him in the best way possible for a scholar: They found excellent positions in North America's best universities, funneled the brightest of their undergraduates to his department, and, most importantly, stayed in touch.

As Professor Goldsmith cleared his throat and readied himself for the familiar mentor-student discussion, Arthur was regretting his decision to call him. He had thought this would be such a good project, as it would allow him to spend time in Europe, but he tightened at the thought of now having to defend his ideas to such a wise man.

The accomplished Goldsmith was not surprised when he heard Arthur saying hello. Since neither one was keen on or adept at small talk, Goldsmith soon asked, "What's up?"

"I'm changing my field of study," Arthur ventured, almost nervously.

"Never a good idea," Goldsmith interrupted before Arthur could explain himself. "Researchers rarely have the time or the skill to pick up the nuances of a new field, nor are they able to find the right contacts quickly. Sometimes we all forget how much we depend on friends, spread throughout research facilities around the world, to bail us out of our own initial, misguided instincts. Although collectively we might be bright and our research might be pushing the limits, we can make huge mistakes individually unless our friends intervene and protect us. Without that network, you are at risk. Having said that, what are you thinking of doing?"

Goldsmith grunted through Arthur's recitation of his preoccupation with the rise of baby boomers and with the widespread assumption that this marked a sudden and positive transformation of Western societies.

"Could be an interesting project, but don't set yourself up as a grumpy old man. As you're still in your mid-forties, you're far too young for that. Don't start slogging men and women who have chosen careers different from yours. They have innumerable reasons for doing what they do, and not what you do. That in itself does not make them evil." Professor Goldsmith was in an argumentative mood.

Arthur pushed on with his mantra about corruption, but he wasn't convincing this perceptive master.

"Look," Goldsmith butted in, unapologetically, "this all sounds both childish and vindictive. I would prefer that you stick with your existing, broadly accepted research. You are well-respected. I'm told that your regular contributions are widely read and appreciated. Stick with it, and you'll retire, whenever you want, with glorious commendations."

"Okay, I understand your viewpoint. I promise you that, if it doesn't work out quickly, I won't waste more than one summer of my research time. One last quick question. Do you know of a major research organization that will give me a fair hearing if I use your name? I'm thinking of the Jacobs Foundation, but I'll follow your advice."

This time Goldsmith laughed at the plight of his former pupil. "Not enough that I oppose you and think you're wrong to go in this direction; you also want me to help, do you? That, that takes the cake. Sure, call Robert Clarke at the Foundation in a few days after I've had a talk with him. He'll give you a chance to explain yourself, and he'll decide if he wants to support your work. Cheers."

The next day back on campus, Arthur sought out Wendy Jones, who was really the only genuine urban studies specialist among the faculty. She came to the university with her academic husband, a brilliant biologist trained at Berkeley who was interested in the purity of northern lakes. They were one of the more engaging couples in the city. Totally comfortable with herself, Wendy was the heart of a disparate band of faculty and students who dabbled in urban studies. She had an impressive degree from a respectable university and worked in a matter-of-fact fashion on research projects in which the work was completed and successfully submitted to funders—on time! That's what made Arthur completely determined to get this conversation right and to come away with her support. When Arthur contacted her, she immediately said she'd be happy to sit down with him and talk about his proposal.

Wendy started the conversation by making as much eye contact as possible. She was obviously unsure from his call whether Arthur was solidly together. Even though she was junior in rank and younger in age, she was smart enough to see his uncertainty. She decided to probe gingerly without risking a social disaster. Besides, she had a soft spot for Arthur as she watched him walk around campus, never harming a soul. He was a rare personality and one she thought should be cherished in a university setting.

"What are you trying to accomplish in this project?"

"I don't really have a precise research question. All I have is anger and anxiety." Arthur talked hurriedly and openly, much to his own surprise. He was instantly very comfortable in revealing his private uncertainties to Wendy.

"All my life, I've studied the baby boomer generation. I'm a younger one myself, obviously. I wrote about the transformation hype found in the media, and my research program was openly welcomed by my department. That's why they hired me. They thought of me as an up-and-coming star with great academic and media potential because of my baby boomer agenda. It was very overwhelming at the outset.

"This generation is now entering its final years of creativity, moving ever so slowly into the dependency years. They think that they've looked after the younger ones, and they fully expect that their children will take care of them. At least, that's the theory. My question is: how well have they really taken care of this world for the next generation? Looking around, I'd guess we now have more messed-up families, for example, than ever before. I'm no expert, so I'm loath to comment as to why. I'm just thinking that their legacy isn't all that terrific.

"The big picture interests me. I've written extensively about their views on education and neighborhoods. Some of what's happened is pretty positive, but I'm left with this hollow feeling. Baby boomers aren't any different from the millions and millions before them who have come to North America for over four hundred years, who supported families, bought what they could, fought off sickness and starvation, and battled in terrible wars all around the world. It's been the same for every generation, and each time they generally came out ahead, making life better for the next."

Wendy abruptly interrupted, "You're probably right about what's gone before us. What about the here and now? What's your question? You're still not focused."

"Here's the problem. We look back at people who settled here before us, mocking their stupidity and belittling them for the corruption of previous times. Bootleggers, mining companies, railroads, landlords, bankers—anybody you want to list.

"Wendy," he broke his monologue with the smile that she loved, "I don't think we're any different. I do think we hide our dark side much better, but that in itself creates huge difficulties in our society. We think we're better, so we play along with the idea that corruption died in the Second World War. Was everyone after that born a saint? Maybe we've read too many times that the war was a generational benchmark, one where clear-cut good fought off the bad. At least in North America, we baby boomers never stopped thinking that all communists, Africans, Asians, Mexicans, and Russians still don't count. The gift of the good life came from our parents, and we believe we deserve all of the rewards.

"I have one big project left in my career," he declared. "I want to document corruption. Nothing has changed; it may be different than it was in the nineteenth and twentieth centuries, but it's still there. I want to talk about the ethical questions around the lifestyles of baby boomers—not just the rich and famous but more broadly. This is important."

"Wow," she responded quietly. "This is so big to think about that I actually don't know where to begin. Urban research teaches us to think small and locally. We are dependent on a few grand thinkers, like a Jane Jacobs or a Louis Munford, to swoop by with the big question of the time. Then we reshape our research projects to help students think about how these grand questions impact local lives. For instance, can we actually build a neighborhood based on fewer cars, local food, neighborhood schools, affordable housing, and low crime rates? The big thinkers say we have to do so, but I can only think of a neighborhood like the west end here by the university that actually does so. Can I work with a group here and suggest what we could do together? What can I say when my husband refuses to live anywhere close to this neighborhood? This is my way of asking you, after you wrestle with this big question, what, if anything will it mean to my west end? Can you bring yourself to focus locally?"

They sat there together but alone in their thoughts. "You might be too far from your home base to understand this," Wendy suggested gently. "Baby boomers did not all flock to the folk festivals or to the playing fields of distant universities. Most stayed at home and carried on proudly with what their moms and dads started. You'll have to decide whom you are talking about and why anyone should care."

"Where does that leave me?" Arthur asked anxiously.

"That I don't know, but based on my experience, we all require a very dispassionate eye to be good academics. Right now, you're sorting out plenty of anger and frustration relatively late in your career. After twenty years of teaching, is that what you think it's about? Be careful, Arthur; you should be taking a proper sabbatical; move away with Brenda for six months, get us out of your mind, and concentrate on what you can tell us about where our cities are heading based on the dramatic demographic changes that only you understand. We need your insights. You're highly respected for your work. Don't fool around as though time isn't a factor. You probably have only one good book left. Don't waste it."

He left Wendy on warm terms, as she was always supportive. Wendy observed his vulnerabilities as though she were watching an awkward buddy growing up during his miserable teen years. As both a professional colleague and a friend, she supported Arthur like few others did at the university. But she was careful to remain aloof.

He was hesitating, but after a couple of conversations, Dr. Clarke, head of the Foundation's Creating Vibrant Cities Project, convinced him to proceed. The director was excited that one of his team would be out there asking about corruption and perhaps making sensational comments. The Foundation's board loved publicity; more money would roll in for more projects.

Arthur couldn't shake off his uncertainty. He hated to think he might be unsuccessful. It was going to be hard to uncover new information. Come to think of it, he wondered, what was it that he could find out about corruption that others didn't already know? Turning to his computer screen, he glanced over web pages documenting previous studies. There was scarcely anything written. Senior academics rarely delved into questions of corruption. Maybe they loved their wives and children too much to investigate such topics. Or was it the nonchalant avoidance of tough social questions in the university world, ones that might be meaningful but are more controversial than anyone cares to confront, that kept them away?

Annie saw that he was still perplexed that afternoon. "What's changed so much for you since you started teaching?" That was her roundabout way of asking him to open up and tell her what was pushing him away. He ignored her question. Sitting at Bar Italia, he felt like talking about the lighter side of life and avoiding daunting work issues. He dismissed his young friend with a fatherly, "Not now," he pleaded. "But I will promise to consider your question during my walk home." They both laughed aloud at his stoic professorial answer.

True to his word, Arthur worked through his quandary as he returned home, concluding that his abstract ideas on corruption in urban life were unlikely to hold the attention of anyone for very long. He put his ear buds on and turned his music player to a classical public radio station as he made his way home. "Nice look," he caustically muttered to himself, as other pedestrians glanced at the preoccupied professor ambling by, listening to his music. As he ruminated about their imaginary corrupt lives, Arthur speculated which passersby were thieves.

He took out his notepad when he settled next to the fireplace before dinner with Brenda and scribbled down ideas to get back on track. He was no further ahead but it was now close to seven o'clock and time for Arthur to turn on the barbeque. Before doing so, he phoned an old friend from the tennis club, Don Davidson, one of his few acquaintances outside the university. As a lawyer long engaged in real estate and corporate deals, Don knew a lot about the dark side of local politics.

Arthur's initial joke was an error. "I'm surprised you'd still be at the office!"

"Why not? Not everyone is a university professor."

Arthur chuckled quietly at his own stupidity and explained why he was calling. "I'm starting a research project to see how our city hall has changed in the last fifty years. Any thoughts based on your work?"

"It depends. It's a lot bigger and more bureaucratic, harder to stay in touch with those who can help move things along."

"Do you think it's more corrupt nowadays?" Arthur flinched, waiting for a hostile reaction.

"I wouldn't know how to answer that. No one pays me to do corrupt things. You should talk to my partner, Neil Thompson. He's been on the scene forever and doesn't actually practice law anymore. Around here, we call him the rainmaker. He's the one we go to when we need something done with governments. None of us has a clue how he does it, but clients love him. He pays the bills here by bringing in a good chunk of our work. He's the only one with an expense account. We ask no questions, especially in an election year."

"Are there younger lawyers helping him out, learning the ropes or perhaps doing it differently?"

"Not that I can think of, except that he did hire the mayor's niece, Jessica Brown—she's about 27 or 28—as a special adviser. She's not a lawyer. Neil thinks she can help out by putting together public-private ventures for local infrastructure projects. There is plenty of legal work closing big deals, and we're hoping she'll be a good addition to our team." After that, the harried lawyer gave a quick good-bye and returned to his files.

The following week, Arthur searched out Wendy for another coffee. "Listen," he started up cautiously, "I know you think that this won't work out, and I'm getting the feeling that I'm driving my colleagues crazy."

She interrupted him, laughing. "Right on both counts."

"Nothing has changed since I last talked with you. I'm told that city hall is the same as always. Hardly a book in it for me. Maybe not even an article. But in each of the cities I'm selecting for travel and study, I am convinced I will find academics, lawyers, and fixers who will talk to me. I'll build my story around them. I'm determined to get this show on the road."

"This is perverse," she retorted. "When everything is said and done, when your research report is finalized, you will still be left with your disappointment that for most of your career, you watched society not changing into what you want. That's the life of a social scientist. Sadly, you probably dreamed as a young academic that you would be the hero in a project finding out exactly the opposite phenomenon. Maybe you should test drive your proposal in tomorrow's faculty meeting. See what your colleagues think."

The next morning, Arthur settled into the cramped meeting room of the campus's Centre for Urban Research. Arthur was never inspired to raise controversial questions with them; he feared that if he did so, he might end up in the president's office having to explain his proposals. Today's agenda, finished as quickly as the Tim Hortons donuts brought in by a hard-working research assistant, featured the typical mumbled exchanges about department curricula, status reports on the few active small research projects, and, of course, the incompetence of university administrators. Not an original intervention was uttered, but conversation filled the one-hour time slot that had been set aside. Arthur spoke up, figuring he'd better start practicing his research questions on people who didn't matter to him.

"I'm designing a research questionnaire for a new project, so can you help me with a few insights? I'll read you a few of my questions, if that's okay."

Some tended to be very suspicious of anyone working in the morning, but others recognized this could be a good way to pass the time and report back later to colleagues that there was actually a brain movement on campus. Lunch at the faculty club would be dynamite.

"Thinking about our city and the neighborhoods you live in, do you believe the baby boom generation has changed much in the past twenty to thirty years?" He started deliberately with a broad question to gauge their interest.

"How old are these baby boomers right now?"

"Say, fifty to sixty," came his first response.

"How long do they have to have lived here?"

"It doesn't matter," he responded.

"Are we talking about the women or the men?"

"Whatever comes to mind?"

"Are you looking at the positives or the negatives?"

"Both."

"What do you mean by change?"

"New. Different from the past."

"Are you thinking about personal relationships—like family, kids, parents, neighbors, and friends?"

"Right now, everything."

"Are you trying to get at their shopping and saving habits, how they consume and purchase cars and homes?"

"You tell me what comes to mind."

"Are you really trying to ask about political and social change? How do you plan to ask about topics this big?"

"I've just started to think about it."

"Do you want us to include reading habits, watching TV, going to movies, smoking dope, careers, affairs, using us as examples, drinking white wine instead of beer, organic food from local farms, bicycles and small cars?"

"Start anywhere you want, guys."

"How can we start this with four minutes to go? Why don't we come back next week, same time? We can all come in with a page of notes and help you out."

"Maybe that would work better."

On Arthur's way out of the seminar room, a colleague from the political science department asked, "Do you have a draft questionnaire yet? It has to go through that new ethics committee before you can ask anyone a single question. If you want, you can let me see it first. I know someone on the committee who will make this easy for you."

"Great," he thought to himself, "a back door to the committee responsible for ethical campus research."

Arthur was completely exhausted. Every one of the urban studies professors had checked him over with their own bias, based on their training in political science, nutrition, sociology, history, psychology, or geography, but no one had attempted to suggest any answers. More unnerving, he had made a terrible personal mistake by revealing what he was thinking about and that maybe he was wrestling with a big question. He had brought this to the attention of his colleagues while admitting that he had no funding. Arthur was now totally exposed, with no allies except Annie.

Back in his office, Arthur opened an e-mail from Dr. Clarke. It read:

"Thanks for your note; you've chosen cities that interest us. Some on my team are still not quite sure what you think you'll find out in this project. Consequently, we have a problem that must be addressed now. This is important to us, as we like to settle on clear research questions and methodologies before we give new team members any funding or encouragement. I'm sure you'll agree that this is the best way to proceed. We would appreciate your sending a few more pages, providing better definition of your research hypotheses, preferably later this week. We will commit to responding quickly, and we'll go from there."

Nice academic note: chatty, informal, and brutal.

Shaken by the morning's events, Arthur tried to revise his project proposal. Several hours later, after lunch, casual hallway chatter, and a few phone calls, he stopped staring out the window and returned to his computer screen. He was falling far behind schedule. He had promised Brenda that he would get this right so he had to revamp his application as quickly as possible; there was no more time for daydreaming.

While Arthur fussed, Hugh, for all his faults, knew how to address his problems right away. He wasn't tortured by Arthur's anxiety; he hustled from one scene to the next while the professor sat immobilized. Hugh accepted the reality that he could always find someone willing to take a shortcut, so his search for corrupt allies took no time at all. When Arthur finally decided he would look at Winnipeg's politics to tell his lofty tale, he shouldn't have been shocked to stumble onto Hugh. A good con-artist was always first in line. Without having spoken with each other, both had concluded that truckers were the common thread tying their projects together. Hugh's conclusion was based on his experience; Arthur simply imagined that at least some of the men running around like crazy all day must be up to no good—just a lucky guess. Juan could have told both of them that the same held true in Europe. That was how he covered his deals.

Arthur was forced to hurriedly provide a story for Clarke. With a rhetorical flourish, he e-mailed back the following:

"Local truckers are forced daily to accept politics as it is; their questions revolve around how to make it work in their favor. Their customers end up being the least of their worries. Just think of all the intricacies: finding drivers, training them, getting them proper licenses, learning city truck routes, fuel costs and location for filling gas tanks, knowing parking regulations, figuring out how the police monitor speeding and related violations, zoning for large and small terminals, special municipal operating licenses and union rules at various delivery sites. When they deliver to public buildings, such as city, school, and hospital cafeterias, they are watched by more health inspectors than normal, especially if they have frozen goods. Those bureaucrats, in addition to the regular vehicle and tax inspectors who cruise the streets constantly looking to ticket violations, add complexity to the relatively simple assignment of getting someone to drive a truck to the next stop."

It sounded straightforward. Surely, Arthur thought, no one would oppose his snooping around the truckers. Arthur continued with his typing of his revised application.

"Truck owners are at the heart of urban corruption. They carry goods everywhere in the city, taking short cuts whenever they can, demanding cheap fuel, buying trucks that feature commercial advantage over environmental controls, and fighting off parking restrictions such as designated driving lanes and speeding zone restrictions. Drugs, alcohol, stolen property, guns, women—you name it, they move it. These guys all require old-fashioned city hall allies for their survival. The likes of Jimmy Hoffa ran American truckers fifty years ago for this very reason, and current owners and union shop leaders still do the same deals today. This is not only an academic matter but a concern for all of us. New leaders are talking about rebuilding and reshaping cities—but who is winning in the streets? And how and why? Those are my questions for this study."

The next morning, he quickly resubmitted his revised research proposal with an additional note of clarification. He wrote:

"For each city, I will present a historical overview of how cities deal with corruption. Take, for example, a city like NYC: why do they have an internal Bureau of Investigation to review local corruption in their police force? If there's work for these agents, why don't other cities have similar bureaus? I will then put together a list of the three biggest problems facing urban truckers; I will analyze how the five cities handled these problems, over time, through regulation and financial penalties. Once the case studies are documented, I will highlight what happened when our generation took over city hall politics, both in the bureaucratic and political ranks. This will not be too difficult, as most cities keep good records. I have found a senior student, Annie Palmerston, to assist me."

Arthur was studying what Juan and Hugh already had established for themselves. He would find that the old ways continued everywhere. Arthur suddenly realized that he was creating a real problem. If the Foundation saw that the likely outcome of his research project was the accusation that the liberal reform movement of the baby boom generation was as corrupt as previous urban administrations, they would quickly decline his application. It would be as simple as that.

Arthur e-mailed Warren Agger, a former McGill classmate now at Washington's prestigious Brookings Institution, a think-tank fully experienced in winning grants and with close ties to the Jacobs Foundation. "Warren," he wrote, "Can we talk right away? I have an urgent question unsuitable for e-mail traffic."

His phone rang almost immediately. "Your timing was perfect. I just submitted my research proposal on American social security and will be heading off to Germany for a round of interviews about European pensions. What's your focus these days?" Without waiting for an answer, Warren continued. "I've shifted my own pension research away from sustainability into questions about governance. We'll leave it for now, but there are some Canadian pension investment organizations playing with fire. No one knows where the cash is really going. In fact, there's a big public pension fund in Vancouver that has all the social activists up in arms over its private investments. But you didn't call to talk about my work. What's happening?"

As soon as Arthur had described his research project, Warren expressed the view that he was not the least bit surprised at the difficulties Arthur was encountering at the Jacobs Foundation.

"Well, it's time to stop writing your self-serving application and to start thinking more like an academic entrepreneur who really wants the support of this Foundation, which has always been close to the Democrats. Their board believes that the 2008 presidential election will result in a mandate to do things differently. No longer will there be politics as normal, so goes the mantra. All they talk about is the "new politics," whatever that means.

"The notion that a liberally minded foundation with a great track record in urban issues would back a guy from a mid-level university outside the States to study whether baby-boomers are reformers at heart goes unbelievably far beyond their imagination. I would suggest you stop the application process immediately. I cannot tell you strongly enough that they will not support their enemies. Their interests are bound in a coalition of academics, think-tanks and all sorts of union and voluntary association leaders. They all want a new Democrat president. They love this candidate Obama from their hometown, Chicago. They think the election is the battleground to determine what America will look like in the twenty-first century. In this environment, I can't imagine their funding an academic who talks like he's a crusader. Your research findings would definitely be used by their political opponents. This is war down here. Don't get in the way."

Arthur sat silently. He had no response. Finally, he asked Warren, "I know you have to go now, but is there another angle I haven't thought of, to get to the same point?"

"Sure, but your heart will have to be in it. The problem may be that baby boomers underestimate the depth of moral and transactional corruption in politics, no matter whether you're in Europe or in North America. It's the intransigence of these interests from one generation to the next that overwhelms reformers; they try, but they succumb to the realities of everyday politics. This is why liberal foundations sympathize with those who try. Instead of looking for villains, go and find fighters; search out leaders who are taking on the old fashion political rulers. Support reformers and don't trivialize those who fighting the good fight. Make them heroes! This is what they will fund and they would probably be very generous with your proposal. It's definitely ground-breaking work. If you want, I'll help you write a more attractive proposal and float it into the foundation. While I'm away for the next two weeks, think about this strategy. You're a sociologist; this world is political. Be careful. All the best to Brenda. Bye."

Arthur made a rare Saturday call to the rather innocent and inexperienced Annie and replayed the conversation. "Gee," he added. "Was that callous or what? Does this mean I now have to like these baby boomers? Or just say I like them? Or do I simply decide to travel at their expense? At least, that's a relatively easy question for an academic to answer. We all take the money and fly away." They said their good-byes, with her sweetly adding, "See you Tuesday after classes." After she put down her phone, Annie realized how disconcerting she found Arthur's behavior. She regretted having said nothing.

Arthur was perplexed after his conversations with his various academic friends and really didn't want another round of consultations. But he absolutely could do with some help from those he trusted, as he now fully comprehended that he was disturbing so many friends, perhaps unnecessarily.

It was too quiet of a Sunday afternoon. Incapable of working through his own personal contradictions, Arthur wanted to engage someone else. Brenda was smart enough to visit one of her friends. He chose to start up again with his philosopher friend, Jack, who could be counted on, in his blunt fashion, to hammer home his worries. Buying drinks at the faculty club, Arthur sought to win over Jack, who pushed back with a folksy tale of his own.

"My story for you does not come from the rigorous application of logic as I teach it to undergraduates. No, it comes from the wild fantasy of a crazed Canadian daydreamer. Follow my daft thoughts about your life as told by my imaginary, aging hockey player.

"To start with, hockey is one of the very few sports you can play on your own, against yourself, making brilliant moves against an ever-changing opponent. I know some will say that you can play basketball or golf on your own, but you can't really. You need a court or a course that someone has built for your pleasure. You are constrained by their design and their rules for success: for instance, in both games, you have to sink a ball at some point.

"Not so with hockey. You find a clean lake, freshly frozen, and you can skate for miles and for hours, changing the rules as you go. There is no harm done to anyone. You imagine you are faster, stronger, and more athletic than anyone else playing the game; there is nothing except silence around you.

"As long as you can tie up a pair of skates, find a stick and a puck, you can win your own Stanley Cup.

"That's what a great academic thinker is. As long as he can lace up—we call that getting a tenured job—you can skate with the best of them, with the sparse tools of the trade, like pencils, pens, paper, a library card, and, nowadays, a computer.

"Our hockey player is in perpetual heaven as long as he skates across the empty lakes. He stays happy unless, for some reason, after doing this for so many years, he thinks he's bored with this solitary activity and seeks out something more thrilling. He decides that he has developed his skills to the point that he can keep up with any player on the ice.

"Without further thought, he stops by a local rink, laces up his skates, and jumps over the boards to join in a game of shinny. Suddenly, he's missing passes, finds he can't really shoot the puck properly; he gets body checked so severely that he loses his balance and smashes hard into the boards. He's been hurt and has to go home. He realizes that he could have been permanently injured, because he really didn't know how to play with others. He is so disillusioned that he gives up his skating. The daydream has been shattered.

"So, Arthur, what will happen to you, our innocent academic, when he decides he can play in someone else's game? My guess is that your fate will be the same as that of the solitary hockey player. He could certainly skate circles around himself, but what could he do in a real game situation? I don't want to belabor this image, but I trust you are intelligent enough to grasp the parallels with your own situation."

"I haven't thought of it that way," was the only mild response Arthur could master.

"Give it some thought. You're a wonderful colleague who is widely admired for your academic work. Your vantage point should not be eroded away without good reason. So far, you haven't given me one virtuous justification for your venture. I'm curious. You are revealing to me and to others on campus who like you a fundamental character flaw that we missed. And this flaw just might hurt or even destroy you.

"Do whatever you think best, my dear friend. You are substantially smarter than I. In the end, you'll nurture this project into groundbreaking research, and we'll all forgive you."

"Forgive me? Why is forgiveness even a question? I don't understand at all."

"Well, since I've been a philosopher teaching the same courses in the same small university my whole career, I must forgive others for asking the identical questions their parents asked. Some things can't be taught, only learned through experience."

"Such as?" Arthur's question had almost no friendly undertones.

"Oh, a good example is decamping the academy. Arthur, what are you getting at? What are you trying to say, fellow? And, no, I can't stand lunching or drinking with you again until you straighten out your life. Sorry, I have to go."

With all of the conversations behind him, Arthur decisively put aside his ambivalence. He would march ahead with the assistance of the Jacobs Foundation to dismantle city hall corruption. Arthur's worrying had ended; he was done with his circular and repetitive arguments. He was ready when Clarke told him he was the first social scientist they had come across committed to the study of corruption.

Dr. Clarke's response was positive. "You have a great reputation as a teacher and as a researcher. You may be a little way from home, but you're certainly not the first to change. I personally welcome it. You'll create a new niche. If you do well, your career will take off, and a more substantive campus will welcome you. It is really important that you get it right. Before you head off to your five chosen cities, let's start this year in Winnipeg. Find a hero fighting for liberal reforms. That's what we are interesting in. See how it goes close to home. Since you're probably setting aside the next five years, you'll have to get this right from day one. We're prepared to stay with you and support you for as long as it takes."

Arthur had anticipated after his conversation with Agger that he would be put through the hoops. Surely no foundation would suddenly place itself in the forefront of such a study, risking its credibility and scores of friendships among the urban leaders whose networks crossed over several countries.

He took a deep breath before he responded to the director. "I can start this in Winnipeg." He shuddered at the thought of making his mark by exposing corruption so close to home. And who in heaven's name would be the hero fighting the system? No one came to mind.

"That's fine. We won't skimp on your resources. We'll give you what you need to travel, to support a research assistant, to publish your findings, and to get you some time away from teaching."

Ah, music to his ears. A university job with no students.

He sat very still after the call. Winnipeg actually was probably the worst place to start. Suddenly, he realized the whole idea was about to bring paralysis to his very person. He had no idea what his next call should be. Who could he possibly turn to for help? He actually knew nothing about his own city. Arthur had never faced this problem before; his grandiose musings about the world were about to be tested. Could he actually demonstrate the corrupt ways of Winnipeg's city hall? His original objective was to take down public figures in faraway cities taking literary license and creating a great new story. But to start right here in Winnipeg was a scary challenge. He went back to Wendy one more time.

When he told her that the project was accepted and fully funded, Wendy was not impressed. "Your research proposal takes you away from your established academic life into something completely different. It's a big change. I cannot emphasize enough that I don't think you're catching onto your problem. Let me elaborate. You will be dealing with political operatives on their turf. No one's going to come here to see you in your office like your students do; you have to go to them. That might mean meeting them in their office, talking to them on the phone, walking with them, or even going to events with them. They will tell you what they think is going on; you'll have to take copious notes or bring along Annie, your rookie assistant if they even let her anywhere near them. You can't go back to the office at the end of the day, open up your computer, and expect to find e-mails supporting your search for corruption."

"I had thought about that, at least superficially." Arthur's intervention was defensive. "I've never designed a research proposal that would initially be so focused on this city. The director gave me no choice about this approach. Hopefully, he'll be able to guide me."

"Guide you?" She was incredulous. "From his office in the States? Alone or along with the Foundation board members? Tell me you don't think he's coming here to help?"

Arthur didn't bother to respond, as he was far too uncomfortable to push back.

She was angry with him for the first time. "Well, I sure hope not. You have to think about your new role. What will it mean to be an academic when your focus is crime, corruption, or, perhaps more softly put, unethical behavior? What defenses do any of us have when someone lets us into their world, a place in which they quietly and privately admit that they are not perfect? You interview them. They tell you more and more each time you chat as they begin to trust you.

"You don't even think about your passage into a different space. I liken it to a long, enjoyable walk along a path in the woods that has no crossroads and no exit signs. As long as the weather is good and you have lots of energy, it's great. When you want to find a way out, it's difficult. How do you tell people that you are no longer interested in their lives? What do you say: 'Thanks for talking with me during the past two years; all the best to you'? Do you think you can get away that easily? If you don't find baby boomers standing up for a new politics what are you going to tell the foundation? They won't be happy campers."

"Once you leave academia as you have experienced it since your undergraduate years, you move into a world where everyone is struggling. People do make mistakes. At certain levels of abstraction, who is to blame them for their mistakes? Are they corrupt? That may be for you to observe, but is it yours to decide? I personally don't think so."

Arthur was taken aback by her comments, both engrossed and lost at the same time. "Keep going, please," he pleaded.

"A good academic like you, Arthur, brings intellectual integrity and moral superiority to any political arena. Key players will defer to you, and gradually, you'll find yourself giving advice and maybe taking a stipend for your efforts. Nothing wrong with that, I suppose." She noticed that his face was becoming more remote and dark. "It's just that every time they ask for your advice or help, the problem will not always be straightforward. It will make you uneasy; you will then have to decide if you are comfortable and if you can accept what is going on. That will mark a big change in your current impeccable life. You will have to be strong to manage these new moral contradictions.

"Be sure that you understand this deep down and that you know what to take and what to refuse. If you don't know what you can't take before you start, you will be badly hurt. This much I know."

Arthur smiled feebly, rose out of his chair, and left her office, offering her only the briefest of good-byes. He was now completely on his own. Notwithstanding the honest advice proffered by his wise colleagues, Wendy and Jack, Arthur took the path they warned against. Later he told Annie that he had received the research grant but would be changing their focus in the short term; Annie was supportive but watchful. The reception that evening at home was no better as Brenda was obviously disgusted.

Arthur faithfully glanced through the local newspapers to familiarize himself with local characters. He could not have fathomed how boring this was; however, Mayor Patterson was renowned across North America as one of the more aggressive elected reformers who led a reluctant city council into his new way of doing political business. He was winning major council battles for a more artistic and environmentally friendly city while keeping tax hikes to a minimum, thereby staying under the radar of the newly arrived Tea Party-like crazies. He socialized with the best of Winnipeg while finding time for beers at the union center; he was a welcomed guest at every table. His strength was taking over Winnipeg at a time when the Depression-born crowd was running out of steam. Although he was always courteous and full of questions about their lives in retirement, no one doubted that he was determined to change the way the city was run.

Arthur had observed from the press that the mayor's style was just what political observers expected from a new boy in modern politics. Council meetings were open and televised on local cable. The mantra of no surprises nourished the feel-good atmosphere that the city was experiencing under his leadership. Obviously a potential national star, he made a point of publicly claiming his current job was the height of his ambitions while simultaneously accepting calls and dinner meetings to hear offers for his next step. The professor immediately let the foundation know he had found the champion they were wanting. Meanwhile he started looking for hidden faults.

Arthur found out from his city hall students that beneath the surface, not much was changing. There were very few new faces making it easy for the old gang to carry on as if nothing had changed despite the mayor's rhetoric. Arthur's first thoughts were that this familiar landscape reminded him of his own university life, which was based on a long career without much outside scrutiny.

But he had to find someone who knew at least a little about the details describing how local deals were made. It would be good for him to have an experienced informant who might share a little gossip about city hall, maybe one who would consider joining forces with him. Arthur broke his long silence by asking Annie whether she had told her Aunt Susan of her plans to work with him. Smiling, she responded, "I'm a step ahead of you with this one."

She recounted how she had told Susan about the research. In fact, Annie decided her aunt would be a perfect source for Arthur; she was a combative, smart leader who had written several position papers, press releases, and pamphlets to effectively push her views into the local media. She reached out aggressively to other groups across Winnipeg via Neighbors Against Trucks, or NAT—the acronym for her group of activists. Two years previously, NAT had unexpectedly hit a responsive chord across the city. As its tireless leader, she had worked hard to avoid being considered just another self-interested, local interest group working solely to protect the value of its members' homes. She was a perfect fit for this role. Susan had trained as a speech therapist but had veered away from her original ambitions. Now she was constantly on the go; she dressed stylishly but modestly In youthful Club Monaco attire, attending meetings across the city and fighting for her agenda while simultaneously endorsing others who had their own fights with city hall. Susan represented the type of engaged citizen Arthur needed to connect with, at least that's what Annie thought.

Arthur passed on the initial prompting since he was feeling confident that he had his crusade underway. He was as organized as he had ever been in the academic world. His modest budget for the first summer included money for Annie. While Arthur set out to learn firsthand about the key people around city hall, Annie dug into the library to help prepare for his initial meetings. They worked well together, and the days passed quickly.

He subsequently took a tentative step to learning more about Susan if for no other reason than Annie's frequent calls to her aunt meant she knew more about him than he cared to admit. Arthur ended up sitting in the back row of the council chamber, listening to her presentation during one of his sojourns into his new world of political skullduggery. While waiting for the action to begin, he took stock of his rather pathetic efforts to transform himself into a political insider. He hadn't yet suppressed his intense internal misgivings. He was determined, some would say naïvely so, but he wasn't willing to admit defeat before he had even started. He would march on as planned.

When he finally telephoned Susan for an interview, she hesitated but agreed to it. What started out as an initial, standard interaction between an activist and a social scientist moved immediately into a comfortable collegiality that surprised him. They went through his list of prepared questions quickly;

she offered a pile of documents so that he could continue his research back at the university.

Encouraged by Annie, Arthur asked Susan to meet for a second coffee. "You know, I live in the neighborhood you're concerned about," he said, after he took a sip of his nonfat cappuccino. "Is it possible for you to let me know when your next meeting might be? I'd love to stop in and watch how your group operates."

Susan froze. "You'd come as a spectator and not as a neighbor concerned about our traffic problems? That's pretty intrusive."

Arthur had only an awkward answer. "First I have to get to know everyone; that way I can better make informed suggestions." There, he had made his first move out of his academic chair and into another world.

"Fine," Susan responded without the enthusiasm she had displayed at their first meeting. "I'll check with my volunteers to see what they think. If it's okay with them, it's okay with me."

The next time Susan called, she left a brief message on his home phone. "Arthur, this is Susan Armitage. You are invited to our next meeting, Sunday at 2 p.m. at Joanne Parks' place at 854 Grosvenor Street. Hope to see you there." Although Susan sounded like she was more open about the research undertakings of her newfound professor friend, she was actually more interested in the future of Annie given the potential for the project to blow up. She trusted Annie to do the right thing, especially given her roots in small-town Manitoba, but she was very young and inexperienced in these matters. Susan resolved to keep an eye on her niece.

In preparation for his first foray into a community meeting, Arthur had asked Annie to sketch out profiles about significant local leaders who might show up. She phoned her aunt for names. It didn't take long for him to appreciate that he was about to be introduced to some pivotal players in Winnipeg politics. One character whom Susan was hoping to show was the mysterious Hugh Parks. He normally avoided NAT but she told Annie that his attendance might be obligatory because it was his wife's turn to be the hostess. "See," she teased Annie," If your boss is smart enough to figure out the good guys versus the bad guys!"

Hugh had his own reasons for joining in that afternoon. Initially it was against his better judgment that he had driven directly home after the Bison Board had agreed to fund his proposal. He was hoping he could quietly move from the garage to the entertainment room for his regular Sunday afternoon nap in front of the television. As Joanne had warned, his living room was populated by NAT members at their regular get together, staying in touch and mapping out their next tactics. Despite this month's event being at his place, Hugh had no intention of joining the neighbors scattered throughout the front rooms of their bungalow. He had almost reached his sofa when the energetic and nattily dressed Susan spotted him. Her immediate inclination was not to engage Hugh in any discussion about city politics, as she found him a rather contemptible person, but rather to see if she could coerce any tidbits of information out of him.

Seeing that he was trapped, Hugh didn't even attempt to turn on the television. Bracing himself, he turned back on the charm he had used earlier to raise funds. Joanne came over, squeezed his hand, and thanked him for joining them. She explained that he had walked in at the very moment they were exchanging information about truckers and the local politicians who supported them; these were their political enemies at city hall. She and Susan took turns explaining that politicians were pretending to turn truckers into the leaders of the new urban politics and how frustrate they were with this. Joanne then turned to Andrew Keselman who was there in his official capacity on behalf of the mayor. She quieted the crowd and introduced Andrew. "This young fellow from the mayor's office has some more news for us."

He thanked her and said confidently, "Councilor Johnnie Ambrose gave me a call yesterday. I know he consults regularly with all leaders interested in good public policy in and around this city. The mayor does too. They both wanted me to be here-they have other commitments-so that they'd have a better understanding of your views."

Arthur was sitting comfortably on the edge of an oversized sofa, hanging on the sidelines. No one paid any particular attention to him, as everyone assumed that they were all at the Parks' house for the same reason: to stop the trucks from driving on their quiet streets. Grabbing a coffee, he picked up a copy of Susan's latest letter to the local newspaper. As he surreptitiously watched the crowd, Arthur could see smirks and suspicion around the room while Andrew attempted to spin the mayor's message among these skeptics.

Andrew smiled back and with great effort avoided picking a fight. He continued, "To our surprise, the truckers wrote the mayor last week, asking to be more involved in our new green city plan due out next month. It was good to hear from them. The mayor immediately asked me to call Susan and arrange a few minutes to discuss any ideas NAT might have for us. This conversation opened up a cascade of ideas, thoughts, pet projects, and complaints just as any political meeting does. Susan, in turn, suggested that I come to this afternoon's gathering to give everyone, and not just her, a chance to ask questions and to promote their ideas. Fair game. Love to hear from you."

Arthur was curious about these activists; this session was worth attending, because it could give him a better idea of the ways in which these people wanted politics to be different and how they were willing to work to change their city. Without citizens such as these, nothing different would happen in Winnipeg. He smugly guessed that the foundation would be excited by this little story about baby boom do-gooders.

Hugh was on the exact same page as Arthur, only his perspective was that of a man who had something tangible at stake. He eschewed the moral ambiguity of the laidback, observing academic opposite him. On the other hand, Hugh recognized that the unfocused emotions in his living room could easily spiral out of control. If that happened, he would suffer an unnecessary setback. The truckers had to be his first buyers so that he could launch the next stage in his campaign to entice Juan into a business venture. He clearly saw what he had to do. He stepped forward with the assurance of a fellow who knew he was among his own and spoke above the din.

"Right now," he declared, "our local truckers are disappointing a lot of people, including most of us in this room." Several quiet cheers encouraged him to continue. "We have the car companies either taking our tax money or taking the lives and health of friends and neighbors. Right here in our neighborhood, we have problems so frustrating that we often don't know where to start to make things better."

He was on a roll, although his wife looked away with embarrassment. This certainly was not the Hugh she heard yelling rubbish at the evening news. Emboldened, Hugh proposed his solution. "The transportation leaders should be asked to finance a few research projects. Put money back into the community by supporting innovation in the green economy. They should be forced to do it right away. They should respond to us and be part of the new green plan. We need to hear about their commitment, and now is the time."

It was the perfect touch and resulted in lots of applause and back-slapping. Afterward, Andrew came over and handed Hugh his business card. "Let's talk tomorrow," he suggested to Hugh. Arthur watched this initial meeting with great curiosity and then turned his attention to other participants lest Hugh catch him staring. He sensed that Hugh did not enjoy being watched.

Close by, Joanne and Susan were discussing NAT's next step, as Hugh's diatribe had derailed their earlier plans to make an announcement about their new environmental plan. Hugh quietly joined them as he sensed their frustration. They couldn't say much with him standing there beside them. Joanne, who now loved being an activist, was bewildered by her husband's performance. Hugh would never have guessed that fighting truckers would become the cause of her life, but he had known that stepping into the living room was the right move, if only to please her. Overall, he preferred she keep busy with community work so that the topic of their daughter, Emma, wouldn't resurface and renew their bitter quarreling. Susan and Joanne drifted away to avoid Hugh's eavesdropping.

Late in the afternoon, Susan was still in the middle of her debrief on recent events in front of the dozen women and two men who stayed for the entire meeting. Hugh took advantage of her talk to check out the small crowd; he knew all the wives from the neighborhood and recognized the professor who often walked by their house on his way home from the university. Susan worked through her notes, outlining the police response to their complaints, and she received much praise when she asserted that the truckers were on the defensive. She ended her talk with her usual admonition that everyone keep working together.

Andrew came over to Hugh a second time just as he was leaving.

"This meeting has been great. I never thought of some of the angles you mentioned. Is there a way to make your plan happen quickly?"

Hugh waited several seconds, attempting to look as though he was having trouble answering. "Andrew, I just might have a way out for your boss. Talk as soon as you can with him. Tell him about the positive spirit of this meeting. Tell him we chatted afterward, and give him my cell number so that he can talk to me directly." It was Hugh's turn to hand over his business card with a telephone number scribbled on the back. Just like Juan did. "I'll offer him some ideas of what to do, and if he likes them, we'll have a deal by next weekend. Tell the mayor I'll do my best to keep Susan on the sidelines for the next two months."

Once most of the neighbors had cleared out, Hugh helped tidy up so that he could hide in the kitchen. Between stacking plates of leftover humus, carrots, and crackers and rinsing out cups of coffee and diet Coke, he noticed Arthur huddled in the corner with Susan and Joanne. He couldn't say why, but Hugh didn't like that at all. Susan finally announced her departure, as she had to be home to prepare dinner. She returned to Arthur on her way out.

"It was good to see you again. I hope we're of help to your study. I always hear so much about you," Susan said warmly. Arthur bowed his head. She continued: "Annie said she's spending a lot of positive time with you and enjoying the first weeks on the job. Says she loves your teaching so much that she's hoping for another seminar next year. I didn't know that sociology was still so fascinating. You must be an exception!"

Before Arthur could say a word or recover from her teasing, Susan was out the door. He was befuddled; it seemed he almost needed a psychologist to explain to him why he kept missing crucial moments to establish the supportive relationships to make his new work a success. Oddly, Arthur distanced himself from Susan, even though she embodied the spirit he was looking for: she was a genuine warrior against corruption and might have been his best ally. Instead he chose to pass his days with the likes of Annie who, although she was a clever student, lacked the savvy of the older Susan.

Hugh came over both to introduce himself and to say good-bye to the last of the guests; however, Arthur had other plans. "I saw you talking to Andrew. Did you enjoy his speech? Did he want to respond to your call for action?" Arthur knew that he was coming across as a nervous questioner.

"Hmmm, that's getting into it pretty quick," Hugh responded. "Nice to see a good kid involved in politics."

Uninvited, Arthur sat back down. "What're your views on Mayor Patterson? Do you think he's making progress in his reform agenda?" Hugh did not, at the best of times, like being peppered with questions, especially ones that required thoughtful, careful, and honest answers. He begged off as his text message signal went off in his sports jacket pocket.

"Politics isn't my field. As long as they're straightforward and they appear to be trying, I'll give them my support. Excuse me; I've got to deal with a business issue." Hugh was off, just as Arthur's own text message signal sounded.

It was Annie. "My aunt is wonderful, yup." Too much collusion in real time was all he could think of as he made his way out the door as quickly as possible. As he scampered out, Joanne stopped him to say good-bye. He couldn't resist mentioning that that he walked by frequently on his way home from the campus. He refrained from adding that he had stared more than once at her attractive silhouette as she worked in the garden.

"Well, stop by sometime," Joanne responded with the casual air of a woman not expecting him to do that. "I'll show you my new plants."

After everyone had left, Hugh went back to scheming. He turned his attention to the text message from Stomper, now doing the heavy lifting of his scams during the next few weeks. The feedback from the morning sales pitch was outstanding, as he heard that even more funds would flow their way. This was what Hugh enjoyed about his life—he wasn't reporting back to any organization, wasn't building something he hated, and wasn't working with those he disliked. No, Hugh saw himself as a deal maker, as good as they came. The focus of the transaction didn't matter. It never did. The story was the same each time. Hugh watched for the greedy, the naïve, the eager, the inexperienced, the wannabes, and the needy. Emboldened by how frequently he could find these people, he wasted no time roping in small investors willing to be conned into yet another deal. Hugh was bright enough to know from the pool halls of his teenage neighborhood that the sharks never totally dominated. Opponents always came close and sometimes won, except when big money was on the table. The sharks never smiled at the loser, but they always commented on how close the game was and how lucky they were to win the match. "Next time; you never know," was the perennial farewell.

Hugh now had three, maybe four con games going on simultaneously. Juan, his Bison Board, the mad scientist, and now maybe the mayor and the truckers could all be tricked into helping him succeed. Hugh had to be careful and work fast this month to nail everything down. Moving parts were always trouble. And what exactly was that professor watching?

When Hugh later explained his apprehensions about Arthur to Stomper, his henchman didn't hesitate. "In this game, nobody can be a watcher. Everyone has to have their hand in the bucket of blood. Let's keep an eye on him."

Arthur still hadn't sorted out all of the possibilities. Susan's coalition didn't include the business community, although she and her allies had reached out several times in futile efforts to gain their support. The Chamber of Commerce committed itself to maintaining a dialogue but that was blatantly a stalling tactic. Susan was their enemy, so Arthur should have understood that this reality alone made her a friend.

He couldn't untangle the plot lines on his own. Annie was no help, although she threw out suggestion after suggestion. He attributed his and Annie's lack of understanding to their inexperience. The more they watched, he thought, the more successful they would be. He couldn't accept that the truckers were smarter than he was. Once, as they sat after lunch in the faculty club, taking advantage of the furniture that was so much more comfortable than that which the university provided for his office, Arthur reassured her that "it's only a matter of time before we hone in on the gang leaders." Annie looked back in surprise: What gangs?

It was not solely Arthur's inexperience that was working against them. He had never in his life had to scramble for a paycheck. Starting back in graduate school, his income, albeit modest, was always there. Some organization even regularly deposited his monthly check into his bank account. This project, by contrast, put him smack in the middle of a world where so many characters were fighting for more money. They had learned to control their game long before Arthur came along. Chances were that they weren't about to share this success unless they trusted him, until they determined he was one of them. It was Annie who first saw the problem. She pointedly asked her professor if they were looking in the wrong place, "What's at stake? There's a swarm at city hall. We're not invited. Right? Talk to you later. It's definitely not a green plan."

If he paid more attention to Susan, Arthur could have found a big clue to his puzzle. She had pointed out to Annie that one of the councilors was far too close to the truckers. "Councilor Ambrose is a weak politician who openly prefers the company of truckers over us. Johnnie is a hefty fellow who really enjoys his steak lunches and the fellowship of men. They all know how to treat each other, share experiences, and keep the camaraderie very, very private. We found out that the mayor keeps an eye on these lunches but personally stays away. I'll never be at that table."

Annie then told her that Arthur had asked for an invitation the first day he heard about the lunch meetings. He thought it should be open, like a faculty meeting. When he called his tennis friend, Mr. Davidson had reacted with incredulous skepticism. "You're not in any way part of this, Art. If I put in a call, I'd be blown up for my stupidity. You belong at your faculty club for lunch, not there."

Annie further described for her aunt that Arthur was not deterred by this reaction. He had shrugged and told her, "I'll find another way in; you can count on that."

Arthur proceeded to call another friend, this time a former student, James Barber, now the city planner. "I'm curious about the lunches. How do they play into the mayor's strategy of changing this city?" Barber changed topics by congratulating Arthur on his research grant as an announcement had appeared on the university's web site. They talked on for another five minutes about the city but James assiduously avoided anything controversial. The conversation ended with Arthur convincing James to visit his class before the term ended. That's as far as it went.

Immediately after this call, James was on the phone to the mayor's office asking for a private meeting before the day ended. Andrew set it up immediately.

"We may have a problem." James started in right away, as his time with the mayor was limited. "The old guard is thinking that Susan Armitage is causing them grief. Susan is about to send you a letter accusing city hall of corrupt practices. She'll state openly that the deals are set monthly over lunch at Sam and Benny's steak house. On top of that, a local professor has decided late in life to observe how newcomers like us deal with old-fashioned corrupt politics. He wants to sit in on one of the lunches. Our lives could unravel and leave us more tarnished than we want."

The mayor nodded, agreeing completely, and quietly thought over his options while he gazed out onto the rather depleted civic park. Suddenly he remembered the call from a Mr. Parks arranged by Andrew. Maybe he could steal a role for his own gain. "We can't abandon our plan to humanize this city. I'm sticking by that. But we could use a little smoke and mirrors right now. I want the truckers to come forward with a green agenda that we'll endorse and support in our new city plan. Then they can go back to business as usual. I'll get one of my political staffers to speak with councilors.

"James, you stay away, and I will too. No traces here, none at all. Andrew's a good kid who knows how to deliver a message cleanly and far from us. Your job is to give him suggestions for the green agenda. Andrew will pass on the suggestions. Johnnie will have to use the next lunch to do the dirty job of telling his co-conspirators what I want to happen. Nobody will be happy, but that's life. In return, I will help him out with his son, who is searching for work in the engineering world. I just wish I could be at that lunch, don't you?" They laughed and parted company.

When he was told of the scheme, Andrew was a little unsure of what he should say. "What exactly am I supposed to tell the councilor?" he asked. James simply shrugged as he handed over a single page of suggestions.

Andrew delivered the mayor's message as Johnnie drove over to Sam and Benny's. The councilor was more than a little perplexed. "What kind of green project? My friends are already committed to making the city a great place to live and work. That's nearly all we talk about at lunch." They both chuckled. "I wouldn't know where to begin with this pitch. What am I asking?"

Andrew waited a minute. "Oh, you're quite right. I know it will be difficult, but we'd appreciate it if you give it a shot. By the way, the mayor and I were talking about your son Toby—you know, he and I went to high school together before he went off to engineering school. We talked yesterday, and I told the mayor how crazy difficult it was for young engineers to get a break. He took the initiative right away and phoned Bill Jennings over at Smart Engineering—did you know they're managing the expansion at the stadium? Bill's calling Toby for an interview, I think, tomorrow. Maybe you should give your son a heads-up. It'll improve his spirits. I'd be surprised if he doesn't get the job. Call me later to give me your take on the lunch meeting so that I can report back to the mayor."

The councilor sat still in the car after arriving at Sam and Benny's. He hadn't been snookered like that in a long time. This kid working for the mayor talked a good game of reform but knew exactly what to do to put the squeeze on the rest of the crowd. He dreaded going home later and facing his wife Marjorie and son Toby, knowing that he hadn't made an effort to help. "Well, here goes," he murmured as he shut the car door behind him.

As the lunch wound down, they did their business quickly by making their points directly to those who could rectify whatever the problem might be. This time the owner of one of the largest local truck companies led off. "Somebody's putting pressure on our drivers over in the Heights. Now, you stop us, check our papers, and even give us tickets. What's the deal, Councilor?"

"Good question." Johnnie nodded for the deputy police chief to respond.

The deputy chose his words more carefully than normal. "At our last community policing meeting, we were confronted by a well-known activist, Susan Armitage, who showed up with ten friends. They more or less took over the session. With videos and maps they showed us the routes your drivers are taking to get to the airport. We had no defense against their original research, and we told them that we'd be right on it. Also, some professor who lives in the same neighborhood asked a whole lot of questions about our relationship with you guys. I'm guessing he knows about the lunches. Susan and the rest of her gang just loved the way he confronted us. I had to put some officers out that way to show the flag."

Jonnie saw that he had only a few minutes before the group finished their coffees. "I have a proposal from our mayor. We think you fellows should be front and center in the city's new green plan." Guffaws were heard all around. "No, seriously, your companies have huge energy bills and are always looking for ways to save money. Why don't you show us a high-profile project and be part of the mayor's most important policy parade next month? Everyone will be competing to be the 'most green' in return for favors from city hall. You're saying nothing. It doesn't have to be big—just an experiment or something; that would do. It would certainly help us."

One of the regulars finally responded to Johnnie's thinly disguised threat. "We're always thinking along these lines and have had a few meetings already. Give us a week or two, and you'll have more than a few ideas. A local businessman named Hugh Parks phoned me last week with a solid idea. He's quite the character. We'll be back to you shortly."

Everyone nodded in agreement at this genial lie.

"I've a final item of business before you have to go, Councilor." One of the more sinister-looking truckers moved him by the elbow over to a corner. "I was talking to the national office about our annual meeting. This year it's in the Phoenix area at the Fairmont Scottsdale resort. Right now, the agenda is being drafted. The organizing committee wants a panel discussion on the municipal issues that we are facing as an industry. I'm going to call the chairperson back after lunch suggesting that you sit on the panel and give us an overview of Winnipeg's new green plan. If she likes the idea, and I think she will, you'll get a call. You and Marjorie will join us for the four-day meeting, and your presentation will be finished by 11:15 of the first morning. After that, the two of you can come and go as you please. Remember that in addition to golf, you'll be in the middle of baseball's Cactus League. We have tickets to the Cubs games, and you'll stay as our guests. We pay expenses and a modest honorarium that should cover Marjorie's airfare. Sound good?"

"It sounds great!"

. . .

When Hugh prepared his regular breakfast of oatmeal and blueberries, he was conscious of his beginning a special day. Over the past several weeks, he had successfully maneuvered his investors, local politicians and finally the major trucking companies into his mishmash scheme. He was the only one who had the whole picture; everyone else only knew the role he had sold to them. Since no one worried about being a loser, they were all committed in the belief that Hugh would deliver because as, as he repeated many times, they were special to him. He left no doubt that he would make good on his promises. He lazily placed the dirty dishes in the sink as he always left the responsible step of putting them in the dishwasher to his wife. Totally fixated, he moved to the den and picked up the phone.

Juan heard his cell phone ring and cringed when he saw a North American exchange flash on his screen. It was Hugh implementing his European plan. Speaking quickly, the Canadian nervously moved into business mode right after Juan said "hola."

"Just wanted to say hi, let you know the family was happy to see me sit still after our trip to South Africa. I've completed a round of meetings with trucking specialists and sent my research team out across North America. I'm simply phoning to say I haven't forgotten your curiosity about the market here and will phone again shortly with a few options for your consideration. When I call back with more details, I assume I can use this number, or is there an office number you prefer? Is there anything to report from your side? Probably not, as you don't strike me as one who makes decisions on the spur of the moment."

"No, everything is fine."

"Bye!"

"Salute," Juan stared at the phone. "What the hell is going on?" he asked himself. That was the same question Todd was asking back in Washington when he read the afternoon report from Europe.

At eight the same morning, Hugh phoned Bill Brown, owner of Cando Composites, a small but very profitable aerospace repair shop. Hugh was apprehensive that this hard-edged Scot might see through his promoter-style gimmicks but he had concluded before the call that he would make a Cando Composites a legitimate winner. That's the way it was with all his schemes. He wasn't personally convinced that the wind turbines would save the truckers a nickel but either way they were not likely to find out for years. Hugh's task was convincing investors to buy into his plan. The gist of his business proposal had to be repeatable, with ease, by an investor to his family and friends as proof of his own acumen. If Cando Composites were the manufacturer, then Hugh had instant credibility in the city's tiny financial community. Hugh did not care for a moment if the wind turbines actually were a fascinating and innovative use of green technology to increase energy efficiency; however, that was his sales pitch.

"Bill, Bertie Jackson told me the other day that you made the prototype for his wind turbine. Is that right?"

"Yes, several months ago. Haven't spoken to him much since. He probably couldn't find the money to continue. It's tough being an inventor these days," Bill said stoically.

"That's normally the case," Hugh said, "but I've just met with an industrial investor group who likes the product. One of my associates undertook a research report that's entirely positive."

"Doesn't surprise me, as we all liked it and thought it would be a huge hit, especially for the long haul and refrigerator truckers. They'd save big money."

"This week," Hugh began to warm-up to his pitch, "I'm signing up a major customer right here in the city. Did you do any costing? I thought I'd better chat with you first."

"That's hard. How many would you like to build in the first order?"

"Let's say a hundred to be done as soon as possible." Where that number came from was anybody's guess.

"I'll think about a price. You'll need 50 percent of the money up front," Bill added, as a way to test the authenticity of this unexpected phone call.

"Let's meet. I'll have a check, and you can begin next week, if your schedule permits."

As he impatiently reached for his Blackberry to punch in the next number, he checked Brown off his list written on the back of an overdue electrical bill which Joanne had handed him on her way to bed last night. His next step was to contact Councilor Ambrose at the suggestion of Andrew. Knowing something was afoot, the councilor promptly called back. Hugh knew him slightly. Johnnie had helped a mutual friend at city hall and Hugh had subsequently donated two grand to his last campaign. Johnnie obviously hadn't forgotten. They arranged to meet in a nondescript bar inside an old Chinese restaurant far outside of Johnnie's ward.

"Councilor, how's the engineer in your family doing?" Hugh began, staying on top of the personal lives of even his most casual acquaintances.

"Pretty good, and you asked at the right time. My son has finally landed a great job with Smart Engineering. What's doing at your end?"

"Lots. I've joined an investment group, exciting local money wanting to see economic development right here, right now. But they invest with a twist. They're being advised by a guy they call Stomper whose mantra is "go green." He's a good guy who found them a solid proposal for the trucking industry. It's a locally owned patent that saves energy, and the actual component can be made here, starting next week if we want. I am truly excited."

"What's the catch? Why are you calling on me?"

"Now you're talking my language." Hugh chuckled out loud as he maneuvered the politician into position. "You are well-respected, not only at city hall and within your ward for all your work over the past twelve years but, interestingly enough, also for your efforts in helping the transportation leaders get what they need from government. It's a rare guy who can do all of that."

Johnnie was pleased. "Thanks. I appreciate the compliment. I'd like to get a better understanding of how I can help you."

"That would be wonderful!"

Before they turned to political business, both ordered a beer and a combination plate of nondescript Chinese food. Hugh fretted that the councilor's jovial mask of geniality hid the calculating personality of a small city dealmaker, so he proceeded carefully.

"Our local inventor is looking for support in his hometown," Hugh continued. "Because his personality and lifestyle are a little crazy for the average conservative businessman here, he's had to fight hard to be taken seriously. Bertie, I must point out, has won several small victories over the past twenty years, but none until now have been game changers. You know what it's like. Everyone puts you on the sidelines because you're a little off, and soon it's nearly impossible to get the attention of the players who can raise cash and open the right doors. I've done the first part. We have cash for him to build his invention into a commercial success. What you can now do is what a politician does best: open a few doors."

The councilor, proud of his reputation, was attentive to Hugh's pitch.

Sensing this, Hugh started into his game plan by describing the invention. "The wind turbine has previously been built on old technology but this time our friend, Bertie, has developed expertise in composites, the lightweight material that substitutes for metals. Aircraft manufacturers such as Boeing use it more and more in their planes. You know Bill Brown over at Cando Composites?"

Johnnie nodded, knowing that Brown was well respected in business circles.

"Brown made the prototype and had it inspected by Stomper, who's not only our great researcher but somebody used by every investment house north of Chicago."

"Never heard of him or of composites; it's not really my field."

"That's okay, and it's probably true of most of us. We don't know anything about composites. That's why Stomper's reliability is the key to investor confidence. When I get the approval of my colleagues, I'll slip you a copy of his confidential report."

The councilor was growing impatient to hear the bottom line. Hugh decided it was time to close the deal. Leaning forward, he dropped his voice.

"The inventor figured out how to put his small turbine on the top of a truck, connect it to the truck's electrical system with special batteries he found in Japan, and, presto, you have a low cost, no carbon source of power for the trucking industry. They will, for those who care, leave less of a carbon footprint starting next month when we install them."

"What's the catch?"

"Finding trucking companies to test Bertie's turbines. It's a rough industry, with no one spending a nickel these days. The current economy has put everyone up against the wall. There is little cargo, lots of unemployed drivers and high cost diesel fuel. On top of all that, local political activists like Susan Armitage are demanding that they invest in new equipment with less fuel consumption, less pollution and greater noise controls. These activists are winning battle after battle in every North American city. Whatever we do or don't do, your green plan could be the standard for other cities. This is a great opportunity for Winnipeggers to show other North Americans how sophisticated we are in solving major problems. I want trucking executives to step forward and publicly announce their partnership with our city and local companies to produce a new green technology, our very own wind turbine. One of the truckers told me that you went to one of their luncheons with a message from the mayor. I say, bravo, let's start a new era."

The councilor still didn't connect all the dots. Hugh took a deep breath. He understood how vague and obtuse he had sounded up to this point but it was all part of his grand international scheme: he had to find a way to put Winnipeg on the map so that he could set up Juan in a bigger game. He recognized that this overweight and over indulgent councilor was his best hope as a local champion.

Hugh zeroed in. "Our research is too weak for us to raise big money. Our invention is ineffective in city traffic. These wind turbines are lousy on city streets. They don't work like they're supposed to: Drivers spend too much time idling at red lights and in traffic jams. Or they are constantly looking for a proper parking space. Their trucks move too slowly and stop too frequently to replace the power from fuel-guzzling engines with wind power. So investors just shrug and turn away. Any questions, or can you see your opportunity?"

"Will you be able to see these turbines?" was the councilor's only question.

"Like a hat. We can do them in the city's blue and gold colors, like the football team, if you want."

The councilor leaned back, looking at nothing in particular, except his empty beer glass. Hugh picked up the blatant signal and ordered another round. Hugh was in a quandary. His proposition so far was lost on the politician. But if he had to finish his pitch by going into more detail than he originally wanted to in this meeting, he ran the risk of exposing his scam to the wrong player. In a rare moment of self-doubt, Hugh entertained the proposition that he had selected the wrong guy at city hall. Desperate for more time, he let Ambrose ask his questions.

"Let me see if I understand all of this. We start with a mad scientist of an inventor who has a product that will help the trucking industry reduce energy costs by using wind power instead of fuel. Correct?"

"That's right."

"You then put together some investors who will make money if truckers buy these new gadgets and put them on the top of their trucks. Bertie, your investment group, Bill Brown, and you, presumably, make a lot of money in this deal. Right?"

"Correct again."

"Now for some reason, your buyers are reluctant, and you are trying to wrangle a deal through me that will cause truckers to buy lots of these gadgets in spite of their misgivings. You even tell me that the turbines probably won't work in the city. I honestly don't get this deal. It sounds outrageously stupid, if you want to know the truth."

Hugh pushed back as hard as he could. "Why not give the truckers, if they help the city's green plan, a high-profile designation, maybe set aside special routes so they can move around more quickly or find decent parking spots right away. You, as chair of the most important city hall committee, could issue special stickers so they don't get stopped unnecessarily. You might even convince your colleagues to waive proposed restrictions on cell phones just for them. Your job is simple but key to the future of our city. You must keep the trucks running on time. It will be great politics for you if you support the green economy."

Now the councilor saw the deal, and so would the mayor.

Later in the afternoon, at the Velvet Glove, a more prestigious and social lounge in the Fairmont Hotel, the proposed arrangements were laid out for the trucking bosses. "Here's the deal," the councilor started up as soon as the usual pleasantries over their ryes and ginger ales were finished.

He told them in blunt language, "You are going to sponsor a special project to protect the environment by testing equipment based on wind power to decrease fuel consumption and noise levels. Hugh Parks, a friend of the mayor, is behind this and has already spoken to some of you. It will cost you a few hundred thousand dollars, but when I give you the details, you'll love it."

The deal was sealed by six o'clock. Both sides knew what they had gained. After the mayor was debriefed before another one of his recruitment dinners, this time with a visiting federal cabinet minister, he was totally committed and excited by the shrewdness of how Hugh put this together. It was the mayor's hope that he would be viewed as the genius local leader who finally pulled off a deal that both truckers and environmentalists could live with, across the continent.

Hugh had finalized arrangements so he could proceed with his deal. Like a skilled chess player, his precise moves were rewarded. His first customers were guaranteed by city hall's collusion. He had everything in place. The political deal had been tricky, but it, too, had come together. City hall's support meant that Hugh had a green light to make side deals with those truckers who were most anxious to participate. He would set his price once he had a better lay of the land as to their motivation. As the councilor had initially surmised, it was preposterous, at least on the surface, that anyone should be the least bit interested. Yet he had a profitable deal in place; the sooner he mastered the money flow, the more quickly he could skim off his share.

A few days later, he witnessed the first political payoff. It wasn't cash being stolen; it was a commodity more precious to politicians: free, positive publicity. Mayor Patterson leaked the deal, claiming it as a centerpiece of his green plan; by stealing the information and making the news, he cashed in his chips early. Behind-the-scenes, truckers were sitting down with everyone who counted at city hall, getting assigned the special passes that elevated a driver beyond everyday traffic restrictions. The bureaucrats quietly worked out the value of these new passes for the truck owners. That was the easy part. It was more complicated to replace the side income for those no longer with the opportunity to fix tickets. Where were the public servants to find their extra cash? The trick was to organize kickbacks so they made as much under this scheme as they did by cancelling traffic fines. They settled with the truckers on a fee for each permit far in excess to the posted price. In addition, the truckers agreed to finance a new fund to support local projects recommended by a committee of city hall veterans. As Hugh watched from the sidelines, he marveled at the collective ingenuity of these gangs of petty thieves. Under the banner of a green environment, Hugh had brought together those who had convinced themselves that small thefts were an acceptable part of government. What he understood from his many deals was that once individuals explained away their small time corruption, they were natural accomplices when the stakes became more significant. He knew that Juan would be smart enough to check him out. Since he had everyone locally in and around the trucking business in cahoots with him, Hugh reasoned that this meaningless little game was worth every minute of his time. As he insisted with Stomper, this was the way to set the table for a bigger scam.

WASHINGTON DC

Summer 2008

The first several weeks after the original intercept were pretty quiet for those watching the Moreno file as there was little contact, at least as far as Todd could discern. That was fine with Myron as he and his cronies were largely preoccupied by the intense political season featuring the election of a new president. Every security meeting ended up as gossip about the internal politics of the national parties. Myron's life didn't allow much time to check out the Internet, although he read all he could in the *New York Times* and *Washington Post*. He had a nagging suspicion that older executives like Todd ignored the new communications network simply because it didn't gain prominence until after their own careers had already settled into rigid routines. There was no room for newness in work habits; all of Todd's space was occupied. Despite being acutely aware of his friend's reluctance to endorse change in his particular style of spying, Myron phoned Todd and prodded him to think about the Internet as a tool for watching this file more completely.

Todd listened skeptically, but Myron pushed his case until he relented. At the end of the lengthy telephone call, Myron thanked his favorite lieutenant for going the extra step. "You understand," he chided him, "you'll be glad you made this decision. Who knows, you might even bump into somebody under forty for the first time in a decade. Thanks again."

A month later he reluctantly admitted that Myron was right to force him to deal with web sites, emails, blogs and text messaging. He found the agency's lead Internet analyst, the down-to-earth Mona Brigham, and mandated her to find out all she could about Winnipeg and the crowd that Parks hung out with in that city. She was calling today from the agency's Atlanta office to present her findings. Myron was bang on in one important respect: Todd was now at least talking with a woman significantly younger but equally competent. As her training at the University of Georgia involved learning about the early skirmishes between Europeans and Muslims over the future of Jerusalem, she found out that there was never much uptake in the southern American job market for historians specializing in the crusades, Despite this handicap, Mona did luck into espionage work as her competence in research and writing were appreciated by those who thrived on reviewing detail after detail in supposedly unrelated files.

"Mr. Aykroyd, let me explain something," she was saying, "blogging is mostly a man's world; there are only a few women who make big bucks from their commercially designed sites that drone on about their family life. My women friends prefer to pick up the phone or go out for a coffee if they have something to say. Men like to think of themselves as genius observers of all humankind, so they sit down in front of their computers and bang out silly thoughts. Bloggers believe they're the new messengers of truth. Although angry and vengeful men have always been around, I think blogs are their newest playground. This is especially true, ironically, with scientific blogs. Even though science is supposedly all about truth in research, the lack of referees allows too many vicious character assassinations. I want you to understand this context for what I have discovered."

After listening to her pent up opening commentary, Todd reflected on his wise predisposition to avoid younger women. While he normally was too busy to read blogs, he had to go along with Mona to hear what she was she pressing him to review. His analysts regularly followed Internet discussions, particularly in languages heard and read outside North America; in fact, as Mona had explained, English had long been left behind as the online language of choice; most threatening writings were now posted in Arabic, and in the not-so-distant future, she predicted, Chinese would dominate.

Since Todd knew how thorough Myron's questioning would be, he asked Mona to explain how her corner of the espionage world worked. "Western intelligence agencies share Internet surveillance techniques and pass the findings on to colleagues whom we never meet but understand that they, too, pass their days staring at computer screens. Agencies frequently exchange information about obscure names, topics, or writings in a language understood by only a few linguists, on the outside chance that this could end up meaning something important to another specialist." As he listened, Todd thought to himself that they all must have loved the Rubik's Cube puzzle as kids.

She was now ready to discuss one blog that was central to Todd's work. "A NASA analyst specializing in scientific blogs forwarded to me a particular e-mail of interest. I'll read it to you.

"We've had your request about Hugh Parks out of Winnipeg. Take a look at my attachment. Just saw this blog from two days ago. The blogger calls his column 'The Mad Scientist' and signs it Pinawa. That's an inside joke; it's the name of a small Canadian prairie town that once housed one of the most powerful nuclear research communities in North America. He's had a solid following for many months. I read him all the time. Because your alert signaling the DEA's interest was in our system, I'm forwarding his blog to you."

She paused. "Keep in mind that scientific bloggers are brilliant but frustrated men," she told Todd. "Without the usual university niceties found among scientists, they can be difficult personalities. We already know his real name; he's Albert Jackson. Currently, he's been vetting his frustrations about an invention he wanted to introduce to American and European markets three years ago. He describes building wind-generated turbines for power cooling and heating systems in transport trucks and claims his invention would be particularly well-suited for extreme climates in places like northern Canada, Mexico, and the Middle East. In one column, he suggested that Europeans should also be interested because of the high cost of fuel there. So far, this may or may not make sense to you."

Todd didn't take the bait and let her continue.

"We're not sure, but we think someone took an interest some months ago and arranged for a Canadian firm, Cando Composites, to produce at least one prototype. We haven't made any calls to confirm the veracity of these claims in the blog. Although the price he quotes is high and he ignores the fact that trucks have to be driven for years for this investment to pay off, he's only a scientist and doesn't claim expertise as a businessman.

"This week he reported that he had found a new savior. A local businessman had raised money to produce a hundred of these and claims to have a market for at least a thousand more. But Bertie's not happy. Bloggers are crazy that way. No good news is accepted at face value. I think they are always angry about something.

"The investor's name is Hugh Parks. Bertie doesn't trust him one bit, nor does he have time for Parks' sidekick currently known only as Stomper. You might think it a little odd to read such direct references to these characters. Keep in mind that this fellow is one angry, frustrated scientist who is out to impress his audience. He's probably completely unaware of the danger he's is creating by exposing Parks if he's up to no good. I've talked this over in our shop and we really don't think he has a clue that something big might be happening. Of course, we're not too sure either what that might be but you must be looking for something. We think that Mr. Pinawa is discounting Hugh's street smarts. He's emboldened to speak about his own scam as if Hugh never searches the Internet. That is nowadays a pretty risky assumption." She stopped dead, realizing the irony of her words. This was Todd's first online search. She gulped at her stupidity. "You can read the key paragraphs in the attachment and let us know if you want the search to continue or be expanded as a higher priority."

Todd quickly read through the blog, searching for references to Parks. Bertie had written the following:

I know I should be happy about Hugh Parks, but I'm not. My good friend Bill, who runs Cando Composites and did the only prototype several months back, called me to come over and meet Hugh. Another guy, Stomper, came along as his engineer/scientific advisor. Bill's voice over the phone was noncommittal, but he thought a first meeting would do no harm.

After the call, I checked around because all independent inventors know every scam artist, so-called investor, and so-called investment advisor. We recognize these characters quickly for what they are. For a start, an order of a thousand of my wind turbines would be several millions. In this market, who's kidding who when they claim an order of that magnitude?

I sent an e-mail that reached every scientist and inventor in this region, including university researchers who normally don't like to deal with independent inventors without their ticket. Our lack of PhD's offends them.

A pile of messages ended up in my computer written by some pretty angry folks. I digress. At the meeting, I listened carefully to Hugh and watched Stomper pretend to take notes for yet another report for their investors. While Hugh was the consummate smoothie, Stomper was the opposite. A disappointing football player in college, he had moved on to taking out his aggressiveness on reluctant investors and inquisitive regulators. He loved to drive up in his mom's old beater, get out with a sour frown, plunk himself down in the middle of the meeting room table, and menace everyone within reach.

Bill and I had set the room so that Stomper was seated in the corner, taking notes. True to form, Hugh pulled out a certified check for $50,000 to make the first payment on schedule. He even attached a schedule for the next nine payments. The check was signed by two investors; Hugh's and Stomper's names appeared nowhere.

There wasn't much talking until Bill said, "No money, no production. One check does not make a line of business." Hugh proposed that Bill proceed with the construction of the first wind turbine and promised he would return with an extra $100,000 to cover the initial expense of setting up the process. He would be there later tomorrow. They would then draw up production and payment schedules, just the two of them, and I would see cash starting in sixty days. Bill, being the owner of a small business in a precarious industry, had no choice but to accept the risk of doing business with these two characters.

For a moment, I didn't know what to do. Then, it hit me. I had to dangle another opportunity to trap them in their own scheming. I had to play their game, only be much better at it. I intervened with the following impromptu speech.

"Hugh and Stomper, I thank you for your interest in this. We will do very well together. Thanks for the recognition, and thanks particularly to you, Stomper, for your very professional approach. The payments are important to me, as I'm ready to start my next project. These initial payments will keep me having cash flow for the next few months."

"Great, great, happy to help," offered Hugh.

"Is your project another breakthrough in transportation?" asked Stomper, ready to absorb information in preparation of the next proposal for unsuspecting investors.

"Not really. This time I'm having fun with rockets, life in space, and travel to other planets. This is mostly what I read about every moment I get a chance. This started years ago when I worked here in the old rocket factory. The owners left everything behind in storage. I've been thinking: how can I put these to use? What is their value, and who would buy them? Could they be reconfigured to carry climate change monitoring equipment and launch new science into the skies? Right now I don't know exactly why, but I want to study this. All I know is that the rockets are sitting close by in storage. No one else seems to remember them. If I don't think of something new, all they are good for is killing people, lots of people. There's no value in that, is there guys?"

There is no doubt they bought into that story right there and then. They basically think I'm crazy and that they can go around me. Sure enough, Stomper started his research that afternoon by calling me with an innocent list of questions about propulsion.

Here's the background. You can read more if you want in Wikipedia Winnipeg was the center of rocket production in the 1950s when a British aerospace company used its facility here to produce several generations of the Black Brent, a specialty item originally used to study high-power solid fuels. The Americans, including NASA and the military, loved these rockets and encouraged their development. At first they held the tests in Churchill, Manitoba, where a World War II base still conveniently existed with perfect conditions for launching rockets. That was okay with NASA, but the American military wanted privacy to modify some of the rockets for its own uses during the Cold War. They kept a stockpile in storage in Kansas but haven't used them in years. We built several hundred here in the city.

One modification I explained to the boys really caught their fancy. Our research team configured a process using the highest-performing solid fuels then available. They created the first rockets capable of penetrating standard Warsaw Pact aircraft hangers. Now, depending on what you wanted to do, you could stuff the space reserved for scientific equipment with explosives.

Stomper phoned a second time, as he clearly wanted to know where the rockets were stored. I was open about where they were stored in Winnipeg, since they'd probably find out from someone else anyway. Kansas was a different story.

Technology changed. The rockets were now described as too unreliable by Pentagon planners, who had shifted their priorities to the design and building of their next-generation weapons. The 10,000-acre test site just outside of Wichita was sold to an ambitious, successful business leader from outside the state who wanted wide-open space instead of suburbia. He kept the existing buildings and cement launching pads tucked away in the most unattractive acreage of the ranch, and he allowed Eagle Aerospace and the military to store parts for the old rockets there as they centralized the small inventory from more active bases. They would check it out occasionally, but since the new owner assigned the facility a minimal value for land, building, and contents, it was the least of anyone's worries at the time.

I piqued their interest. Stay tuned. There is a lesson on respecting inventors.

Pinawa

As he absorbed the meaning of the *Mad Scientist* blog entry, Todd realized that a very important piece of the puzzle had fallen into place. At the same time, he couldn't stop thinking of the rockets: what was this all about? Was it the first sign of another plot that he hadn't anticipated? He thanked Mona and instructed her to get in touch with him if anything else popped up.

After he hung up, he grew worried while checking his morning e-mails. The European listening post had heard Hugh's second call and had traced his cell number to Winnipeg, not a usual location on terrorism radar. His records would soon be available to other analysts in Washington, who would generate a list of potential co-conspirators based on cell phone calls. Myron would be updated over a drink. Soon DEA office walls would be covered with yellow Post-its showing possible connections within this newly discovered terrorist cell. The savvy analysts already knew from the roaming charges that Hugh traveled extensively, mostly to the States but also to South America, including Ecuador, which wasn't located on any major drug routes. At this point, the government had no idea what he was doing on these trips. Hugh was now being actively watched, not yet in person, but in the electronic world.

With this in mind, Todd walked out of his office and took the escalator up to the library. A hefty file, quickly put together by one of the bright young interns looking for a way into the agency, was waiting for him at the secured front desk,

The stories about Hugh that had been gathered from the usual police sources showed a successful, small-town con-artist suddenly connecting with a wealthy European businessman who was likewise being tracked by several agencies. Juan was known to be engaged in the support of terrorism through financing their gangs, special operations, and munitions supply chain. All of this took millions of Euros. He was a smart operator. He wasn't always looking for the proverbial big deal; he simply didn't want to get caught. The watchers knew Juan's success originally stemmed from a family transport company that shipped manufactured goods from Europe to the Middle East. His father had had a good run after the Second World War as he witnessed the growing need for fresh food across Europe. The near starvation of civilians in several nations in the late 40s and even into the early 50s gave the family firm a rare opportunity to expand while others suffered. They cheaply bought or promised to buy surplus army supply trucks, turning them into makeshift transport trucks for carrying fresh produce north into Europe. The loads were small, but labor and petrol were dirt cheap. What wasn't available on the regulated markets was readily available for cash throughout the continent. Notes found from the Allies after the war showed that Juan's father tolerated the Americans in those years, as they understood they had to house and feed millions to keep the embittered and emboldened Russians at bay. Family trucks carried foodstuffs into airports, where huge planes ferried load after load into Berlin. No one much cared about quality; the battle was to get supplies to Berliners and stop Russia at that border. Moreno made it easier for the Western alliance to get the job done.

Not many trucks were filled on the return trip to North Africa and the Middle East, as Europe was slow to rebuild manufacturing capacity. Besides, only the leading Arab families had any money. It was left to them to decide what was to be purchased and transported in these empty trucks.

Those moneyed and powerful families who dominated the trade routes decided to buy armaments to settle scores across the region. Political boundaries defined in Paris in 1919 were up for grabs, as European colonial powers were completely destabilized and could not enforce any borders without allies on the ground. Although coalitions were fragile, if enough munitions were supplied, the Europeans could retain some semblance of influence on post-war nations that were being taken over by local toughs. And, certainly, no local powerhouses liked seeing European Jews arrive at the new Israel, an affront to the Palestinians and Arabs of the region. As every side sought munitions, business boomed for the Moreno family.

The Spanish Civil War had created deep-seated animosity among leading families, and everyone paid a steep price for maintaining the Franco regime for so many years. Memories are long in Madrid, as they are throughout Spain. Families were formed, broken up, and then reformed for over 600 years of conflict. These battles covered not only the lands of modern Catholic Spain but also old Muslim Spain, Morocco, and even Algeria. Families came from everywhere, stayed for generations, and were forced out, only to migrate back. Internally, the Spanish leadership continued to be undermined by Basque nationalists, who bombed both governmental and private sites with impunity. Juan's father lived through this and warned his son to stay out of domestic politics. He took that advice. The government knew full well of the Basque Diaspora in South America, particularly expatriates living in Venezuela who kept funding brutal attacks killing innocent bystanders. They were willing to pay big money to ship munitions back home in support of the rebels. Juan's transportation network stayed out of this terrorist front, and he warned all employees about using his equipment to settle old family battles on Spanish soil. His loyalty to Spanish governments over the years was returned to him every time the Americans tried to grab him for his support of terrorism elsewhere.

Juan learned from his dad who by the late 50s had established himself as one of the most successful trucking interests linking Europe, North Africa, and the Middle East. He kept up his own clandestine trafficking of munitions by tipping off the Spanish government about any shipments that might harm its interests. Officials chose their spots carefully but passed on a few messages to allies, particularly the Americans, when something dangerous might be in the planning stages. Everyone kept their job and looked as though they were on top of their files, and the family continued to make money. Although at first Juan was surprised that his parents never traveled much outside of Spain, he soon recognized the danger of supplying rebel groups with munitions. The family lived well within Spain and encouraged their children to see the world before settling into the life of a transportation executive. In those days, the sins of the fathers were not visited upon the children, so everyone left the young ones alone while they traveled and attended private schools in Western Europe and universities in England and America. They were well connected by the time they turned thirty. The expectation was that the new friends would come to visit them, as the Moreno family often found it dangerous to travel outside Spain.

Juan's university specialty was international finance, supplemented by an English degree that showed how serious and smart he was. He learned how the family business could benefit from the evolving European integration and why they should avoid American and British banks, which were parading themselves as the wizards of currency trading and corporate financing. Juan's entrance into his father's finance department coincided with the oil crisis of the 70s as well as with later inflation scares. Middle Eastern banking interests, flush with new money, offered to help the family weather the storm. Funds were arranged for new vehicles, despite inflationary pricing, and for scarce diesel supplies for the trucks. Juan never knew quite what was going on until many years later, when his father explained whose side they were supplying during the various wars. The Americans and Israelis watched and heard everything but could do nothing.

When Juan took over in 1981, just about the time his only son was born, he was well-schooled in the operation of the entire fleet of trucks. His father's counsel had been the same over the years—stay out of what you don't understand. If they want to move something and are willing to pay whatever it takes, then charge whatever they'll pay, collect ahead of time, move it with care, and quickly get out of the way. The businessmen emerging on the other side were also changing. Czechoslovakia was back into the armament business in a big way, as was Russia, whose former bureaucrats were intent on selling off stockpiles of military equipment and pocketing the proceeds. China decided that Sudan was a worthwhile ally requiring military support. They bought their way in through a Canadian company, Talisman, replacing the energy company's support of schools with endless shipments of armaments. The Americans were making an effort to control the flow of hardware into the Middle East, but their moves were instantaneously countermanded by families who had controlled territories within the region since the Crusades. Although this was no longer the Holy War, it was still a series of religious and tribal battles intensely fought on several fronts year after year.

Weapon trips required complicated camouflage, as there are many border crossings from Europe to Iran and into the West Bank or further on to North Africa. Cargo planes were one option, but pilots grew scared of the Americans' habit of using unmanned aircraft to knock out clandestine cargo planes as it was relatively easy for its military to pull off these operations. Few governments are capable of properly tracking planes in mountainous areas or even a short distance off their coastal waters. These episodes often went unreported in the *New York Times* or *The Guardian*, both of which thrived on finding such nefarious incidents. Since it served no one's interest to record these attacks, the agencies from various nations had kept the lid sealed shut on any rumors. Planes simply fell out of the skies or crashed on takeoff.

Juan's clients preferred to truck munitions onto the edge of war zones and then break up the loads into manageable sizes for smaller carriers. According to agency reports, Juan's trucks had stopped in the oddest places, sometimes two hundred miles from the destination on the trucker's manifest, and then unloaded in the darkness, with their cargo carried off by animals, jeeps, SUVs, or whatever was available. Juan's trucks then carried on as originally planned, picking up a wide assortment of agricultural products including fruits, vegetables, olive oil, and unusual goat cheeses, turned on their refrigerators, and returned to Europe via the most direct routes possible. All trips were organized in Juan's Madrid headquarters to be executed without interference and with minimal delays. The company apparently preferred Dubai-based banks whose executives enjoyed their weeklong trips into Spain. They preferred talking during walks through parks, picnics in the vineyards, or dinners in dark cellar restaurants. Anywhere that made it a chore for the Americans to watch and listen too closely.

The librarian, in his preparation of all this information, had lived up to his billing as being among the best recruits seen in many years. Although Todd had taken very few notes, he returned the file intact and understood its significance for Myron. Over dinner, once he had reviewed the dossier, the two of them would sit quietly asking each other why they were so unsure about where this was all going to lead.

MADRID, SPAIN

Summer 2008

Juan's bankers had flown in from Dubai, making their regular trip to settle accounts, amicably and on time. They never brought a check; they simply opened up a file folder that gave Juan a review of bank transactions in faraway places. The bank accounts had grown appreciably, particularly since the early 90s. These savings accounts were not intended to produce much income for the present but instead were available for a rainy day. The entire family maintained a luxurious lifestyle from duly reported income for transporting foodstuffs into Europe and manufactured goods into North Africa.

The bankers had phoned ahead this time to suggest that they wanted to introduce potential investors who were bringing an important proposition for Juan to consider. He agreed, although without much enthusiasm; he recognized the reality facing his bankers, as they, too, had to make deals. Aside from the regular advisers who knew him well, the other four were from the National Algerian Fund created in 1997 and operated under the auspices of some of the most distinguished Algerian families with the discreet support of the national government. It was Algeria's brand of a sovereign fund. The head of the group, Amar Benaissa, definitely understood the true value of Juan's operations. His bankers had, with the utmost discretion, made the point that Juan had fostered the perfect environment for covering up clandestine operations while making good money in the family's legitimate business. The sovereign fund was looking at establishing a European presence for the first time and had decided that Juan's company would be a superb vehicle for its new initiative. At this point, no one was discussing money; the idea of establishing a new working relationship would take months, if not years, to nourish.

Juan hadn't known much about sovereign funds before the NAF approached him. He had taken the unusual step of phoning and asking his son, Angel, for more information. After he contacted a few friends who were working in the financial world, Angel phoned his dad back.

"As part of the global shift of wealth to resource rich nations, super funds were created to meld state power and private interests," Angel explained. "Despite being opaque beyond the imagination of Western observers, the funds in oil-rich countries are highly sought after as investment partners. After you called, I did a little reading but then decided to phone an old school chum. Brent is just learning the ropes in Philadelphia, but he's quick and will do well. He told me almost in a whisper during a late-night call last week that sovereign funds are the best clients. Big numbers are thrown around casually in marketing meetings, as these funds invest $100 million to a billion dollars without any hesitation. They all joke about why all the money now comes from outside the States. The reality is that these are the new vehicles driving most investment agendas. Everyone is chasing them. It's all about their wealth, concentrated in a few families who count, being applied to their historical mission to get Europeans, Americans, and Russians out of the Middle East. Sovereign funds are a remake, a new vehicle for the old goal of power, dominance, and purity in race and religion. And these guys know how to play tough.

"Listen, Dad, this is all new to me. I think America is fantastic; you know I love it. But there have been so many changes in the last decade that I doubt it will again dominate the world as it did in the twentieth century. The sovereign funds in the Middle East and in Asia are signs that others are working at building walls to buttress themselves from a collapsing power. I think our family would be smart to align at least some of our assets with a sovereign fund. Otherwise, they might think we're too European. I'm sure you'll share your views of the world and convince them that you're just like them!"

Juan loved the way Angel privately and spontaneously shared his insights about the family business. Juan had long ago concluded that his son would do well in life.

Based on Angel's hasty but competent research, Juan was well prepared for his Algerian guests. Juan slowly left his office and joined them for nonalcoholic drinks on the spacious poolside patio. They all exchanged pleasantries, but he could tell that the delegation wanted to say something important. They shifted uncomfortably until Amar outlined their offer.

"We would like to present you with a unique business opportunity. We're putting this on the table for you to think about until our next visit. Our fund managers want to buy a majority interest in your company by creating a new share structure that would leave your family dominant in the transportation business for the next few decades, covering your interests as well as those of anyone in the next generation already in the company. No one else will be allowed in, so that by that time, your customers and European governments will be comfortable with the new management people and our style of doing business, When NAF completes its buyout, that final settlement will provide more security for generations of your family, although, frankly, they will be without positions in the trucking industry."

When Juan didn't flinch at the broad strokes of the deal, they moved on to talk about market developments as the NAF saw them.

After listening for close to an hour, Juan took his turn to explain his company's strategy. "I've shied away from building a more integrated company, because for generations we've been taught to 'stick to our knitting,' as the English say. We don't build trucks, we don't source our own fuel, and we don't buy companies whose goods we ship. We have excellent information about these activities, but each business, according to my father, requires a particular genius to be great. Ours is the genius of getting goods from point A to point B better than anyone else, decade after decade. We've made a lot of money along the way. Your executives and the directors are probably aligned with other businesses. You may be able to bring in new customers and perhaps even integrate some functions, creating new symmetries. It could transform the company entirely."

The delegation quickly offered ideas about how they might expand Juan's company through their networks in North Africa. Fair enough, Juan thought; they'd done their background research before meeting him. They probably even knew that his travel was restricted, and that's why they came to him, no questions asked.

"I'm convinced that Africa will grow very quickly over the next twenty years; there are over fifty nations, and some will get it right. There are resources, including farmland, minerals, oil, and even rare earth elements wanted by others around the world. The fight will be with the Chinese, not with the Americans."

The room was quiet as the delegation absorbed Juan's analysis of Africa's huge potential as a frontier market. NAF had come to the same conclusion.

"My problem is that at each meeting in Europe about Africa, I have to listen to the histrionics of the representatives from countries that ran various regions of Africa into chaos and poverty. Of course, Spain's track record is not much better. Every European power in charge looted Africans and their resources. Nothing was sacred. It's no different from what happened in the Middle East dating back to the Crusades. I don't have to lecture Algerians on this point, do I?"

Everyone nodded. The dark history of European dominance was a core subject in their education.

"To be fair, the job of a Spanish politician is very hard and different from that of the politicians you know back home. Your friends have public funds for their projects in health, welfare, education, infrastructure, and defense because of your oil money.

"Here, it's complicated. Politicians have made commitments for over sixty-five years, since the last great continental war, and now their countries have run out of resources. They literally borrow from each other and force their banks to loan them huge sums of money. It's crazy, and it's no longer working. Our cities are flat broke. You'll see the deterioration around you in the coming decades. On top of that, Spaniards refuse to acknowledge that you, the Chinese, and maybe even the crazy Russians are wealthier than Europeans. They continue to demean the immigrants we desperately need to work for us, whether they be from old Russia—the Poles, the Romanians, and the East Germans—or from Africa and the Middle East. They are totally freaked out by Muslims walking around dressed as they have for centuries. In the meantime, they turn a blind eye to the Catholic Church, a most corrupt institution protecting its own priests who quietly, sexually attack their own believers. It's amazing! It's disgusting!"

The delegation was silenced by this outburst. Juan had bared his true character. The listeners were surprised to hear such a rigorous attack against Christianity. Looking up, he caught their skepticism.

"Listen," he added, "my own family was not religious. We were generations of small town merchants staying away from powerful forces that regularly destroyed our communities for whatever was the cause of the day. At some point, we were probably Muslims, but that wasn't a sin in North Africa. Once my grandfather took our business back into Spain, we found ourselves in a deeply divided country where the Catholics dominated many institutions. We begged off all conversations about such ecclesiastic standoffs and made our reputation in business. The establishment came to us, but lessons taught to us as children have made us wary. Life can change suddenly and be very cruel to the unprotected. That's why my family accepted my marrying a Catholic girl: it would offer us protection. Her family merely tolerates me, the nonbeliever, because she has been so well looked after here in Madrid. We never talk politics or religion, but she knows my deep-rooted anger against intolerant regimes."

His story revealed why he was in the armament business. They now understood why they could trust him and his family without further questions.

"You have enough to mull over and to make recommendations to your board. Let me know when you're ready to continue this dialogue. I would welcome your return."

When he did call them back to suggest another meeting in Madrid, they politely said they would enjoy returning to his beautiful country. There were not sticklers for business protocol, as they were briefed by Algerian security about his travel restrictions. This time he would take them to the beautiful sites his people once owned hundreds of years ago before being driven out by the Christian Spaniards at the end of the fifteenth century. Many Spanish families still had this memory in their blood but had quieted their predisposition to fight back against northern Europeans. Juan enjoyed the company of these families, shared their frustrations, and helped out where he could.

Juan suggested to Amar that on one of trips he'd like to introduce his son. "I want you to meet my boy, as he has an interesting plan for expansion. Angel won't be in all of our meetings, but I hope you find him over the years to be a convivial host and companion."

"I'm sure we will," Amar quietly responded. "Please tell him that we look forward to hearing his thoughts and helping him become a success." He rang off as quickly and as politely as he had picked up.

"Ah, there's nothing like calm and confident wealth," murmured Juan to no one in particular on his way to another evening out at a Madrid restaurant. As he walked through his beautiful neighborhood, Juan thought through his next steps. He was still not ready to tell the NAF everything; however, he would take the time to go into more operational details that gave them a better handle on how he combined the two businesses. When they arrived back in Madrid, on the first day that was mutually convenient, they quickly huddled and turned their attention to Juan's business. Both parties were ready for a deal much sooner than originally anticipated. He explained how he operated.

"We make sure that our truck manifests for our return to Europe are clean, as we don't want unnecessary scrutiny. We usually stay away from drugs, although the trade out of Afghanistan through Iran is tempting, based on rumors about volumes being shipped. I'll give you one example of how dangerous that world is. We had one fellow in the early 90s operating as our wholesale agent, putting together loads in Tehran that combined stacks of dates, caviar, raisins, onions, potatoes and tomato paste—all fine, except that he added in a few kilos of opium. Luckily, we found out before the truck left Iran. When we finally found him, we made the driver return with the contraband, and another fellow took over the truck. Sure enough, he was pulled over just outside Germany by drug cops with dogs. We obviously smelled of opium, but none was found. However, the tip about us was taken seriously by authorities, and the next thing I knew, the American DEA was all over our government wanting to question me. I was protected, so there was no interview.

"Subsequently, I found out that the DEA has a broad mandate, and their agents don't let go. I've been told they are still after me almost 20 years later, although I suspect that it's an excuse to hunt me down over bigger issues. We remain totally clear of the drug trade, and I personally oversee regular sweeps through the organization to search out any small-time criminals with their own agenda. More recently, we heard that Mexican and Columbian cartels are landing drugs on the West African coast and looking for safe ways north into Europe, maybe through Algeria; who knows? You should know that we stay away, and I want to continue to be cautious and avoid the easy money."

As Juan had the undivided attention of Amar and his two colleagues, he pressed on. "There are undoubtedly many opportunities for us to truck valuable stolen property across borders. Russians gangs that specialize in high-end jewelry robberies approach us all the time, saying that their small packages would never be found in our trucks. They're probably right. We decided, however, to stay away; these gangs are too dangerous. We would always be anxious about their turning against us one day. They are quite capable of using their money to force their way in and take over our company. The Spanish authorities like our distance from common thieves, as it makes it easier for them to push back on the Americans: they tell them that their friend and good citizen Juan is clean of drugs and does not compromise his credibility by facilitating money-laundering operations where the proceeds end up with anti-American terrorists. All southern European governments have failed to keep the Sicilian gangs at bay. Because they failed, they now have to defend themselves against criminals from new places such as Serbia and Russia. Those guys stop at nothing to corrupt a government. Look at what the gangs have done to the Italian police. It's far too dangerous."

One of Amar's colleagues picked up on this point. "That's what we've heard, and that's why we're still interested in your company. You're right about the Americans. The DEA has stayed on top of you, looking for a way to entangle you on charges that eventually will reach past trucking to destroy the heart of your business and you personally. Luckily, they refuse to share much information with other security forces across Europe and probably give very little to their own colleagues within their sister agencies back in Washington. We have friends who watch the Americans very closely at their listening post in Germany, so we all know their longstanding interest in you and their frustration at failing to bring you to justice. We've heard what they think you're doing. We, too, are of course curious but are waiting to hear your story directly. Maybe in our next discussion, you'll give us a better idea of what you do to help your friends."

Juan stared at the questioner, whose presumptuousness bothered him. He decided not to challenge him then and there, as any personal embarrassment would likely end the negotiations far too quickly.

Instead, he offered a way of moving to the next stage of negotiations. "We've accomplished a lot this afternoon, and I'm truly enjoying my time with you. Now, it's time for a break. My driver will take you back to your hotel. As is my daily routine, I'd like to have my usual pre-dinner drink with my wife at 8:00 p.m.; after that, she'll go off to a restaurant with friends. Amar, come back and have dinner here, followed by good Cuban cigars outside in the garden. My driver will happily pick you up at 8:30. Your colleagues will find plenty of great restaurants in the same quarter as The Westin Palace Madrid Hotel where you are staying. Amar and I will be on our own here."

Before there was time to object, Juan repeated: "Only Amar. I want everyone to respect the privacy of this conversation."

After dinner, during which the two men jousted over business, politics, and sports, like any other male strangers, they retired to the patio and gave the wine a chance to loosen up the storytelling. Amar sat patiently waiting for Juan to relax and detail the dark side of his life. Since his guest had declined further alcohol beyond a perfunctory glass at dinner, Juan put aside his own wine. He picked up where he had left off in front of the others.

"We have close to two thousand truckers working out of six depots in Europe and four in the Middle East and North Africa. We have trucks and containers available for special assignments such as the recent one in South Africa. We made a conscious decision not to create a widely recognized brand for our trucks. Instead, the depots and drivers who have been with us for a long time are encouraged to choose their own paint colors for their buildings and cabs to create their own brands. The casual eye does not notice us everywhere. We are not on the watch list of any police forces; nobody is following us vigorously as far as we hear, except one crazed guy in Washington. We give to local charities sufficiently to keep community leaders thinking positively, and we recruit where we own terminals. Drivers come and go, as long-distance hauling is definitely not for everyone. We look after them as much as we can. Accidents happen; a driver rams a local car, and someone has to help him get out of that country in a few hours. Or his wife goes missing with another man because of his being away too much. So we fly him home to look for her!

"If I had to give a sense of the size of our real business, about thirty to forty trucks are set aside for sensitive loads. They are not always on the road, nor are they always filled with contraband. Each load is picked up and packed by the factories, and the partially filled transport moves on to a second terminal, where a special consignment of smaller items—maybe five hundred kilos of this, three hundred of that, all legitimate freight that finds its way to North Africa and eastward into Lebanon, Syria, Iran, Jordan, and Egypt—awaits. Our special cargos cross your country unimpeded.

"It's up to the factory owners to keep local police in northern Europe out of our trucks so that we can pick up quickly. Sometimes we send along two phantom delivery vehicles while a third carries the payload, just to see what's happening. The watchers are there from time to time, but finding the right truck at the right moment is more difficult than you think. We have learned ways of confusing watchers. We use every trick."

Juan went into more details about how the family trust operated apart from the transport company. He made it quite clear that Amar was to not repeat operational details but simply to explain to his superiors how his function as an armament dealer was disguised by the trucking company. He was committed to covering all of the specifics later, as their partnership built up trust. They would be invited to watch Juan issue his thorough operational directives. He went over his major sources for armaments; he reminded his visitor that it was crucial to know who exactly in the manufacturer's firm could be trusted to deliver the goods.

"We wait a long time before placing orders if there is a change in ownership," Juan continued. "You just don't know what newcomers are up to until you watch them; sometimes it takes many months, even years before we return. Most of our original dealers disappeared with the fall of the old communist regimes. It took until the late 90s before we were sure again of our suppliers."

"Where do you deliver these shipments?"

"Wrong question, I think, at least for tonight. Amar, you've directly asked me about the murky world I must keep to myself. There will be answers to all of your questions, of course, and I will eventually tell you about the buyers. I'll skip those for tonight, in favor of explaining to you more generally why I do what I do. After you leave me to return home for meetings with your colleagues, I hope you will be able to endorse the corporate culture I have created and the commitment we must undertake in support of our friends."

Juan paused until this message had sunk in. His listener looked at him to acknowledge the significance of the declaration. It effectively meant this enterprise was built to do more than supply income. It was driven by Juan's fierce desire to punish his enemies.

Juan waited until he was sure Amar was completely attentive to what he was about to say, and very curious. "Spain is more interesting than an Algerian like you might think. Its modern character reflects long, bitter struggles during which Jews and Muslims alike settled in this country to flee disruptions and battles in faraway places. After these immigrants had settled in what we now call Spain, they were kicked out by the northern Catholic forces supported by the Church. Most were slaughtered, but some escaped and were scattered around Europe and North Africa. As best we can determine from scanty records, my own family ended up in Morocco, which is where they probably came from in the first place. We stayed there for many generations. We fared well in the nascent Muslim community, mostly as traders. During those years, Spain turned out to be a major world power through its dominance of sea trading lanes and many overseas colonies. It stole everything in sight and built great fortunes for the leading families.

"We gradually reintegrated into Spanish life through migration and business relationships. There has been considerable movement over the centuries between Spain and North Africa. Many more sensibilities are shared than is generally recognized by those who don't know us. Americans certainly have no understanding of this, since we are viewed with distaste as the point of entry for so many illegal migrant workers. We are perhaps a little more sympathetic to their overwhelming urge to get away from their miserable roots.

"My dad taught me how to be quiet and sympathetic at the same time. He urged me to think about where they came from and what their families had to endure. It was not necessarily God's will that they be impoverished. Rather, corrupt regimes that lasted for generations forced these people to live without anything at all, including hope. It may be tempting to welcome as many here in Spain as can sneak across the water at night. That will eventually end in disaster by shifting the conflict between rich and poor, Muslim and Christian, north into Barcelona, Madrid, and Valencia. My father passionately believed that these battles for justice and fair play must be won in their homelands. Our obligation was solely to help them back there but not in Europe. So when rebels came calling for help in challenging corrupt regimes, my father was ready to lend a hand, as long as he made good money at the same time.

"To go back to your comment about the customers of our family trust, we don't think of these people as customers. I've never heard that term used in family meetings. These are leaders who explain what is going on in their country and ask us for help. As long as they have the cash, we help them. My own commitment to these struggles is obviously deeper than that which I have to the trucking business, although I'm very proud of how it sustains everyone in the family. I expect my new partners to approach my embattled friends in the same spirit. Indeed, I imagine you, too, have friends in similar situations.

"Your colleagues will likely want more details, but none will be forthcoming until we make a deal. Take back whatever financial information you need. After you have had a chance to review the documents, feel free to present us with a list of questions from your analysts back in Algeria. Transportation enterprises change hands all the time, so your valuators will give you a price range that probably won't surprise us. We'll deal or we won't deal; it will be a speedy, simple process. You'll be astonished how quickly you'll know my answer.

"The rest is more complicated. Further discussions will involve only a few people. I certainly won't meet with more than one person at a time from this point forward. The only question for NAF is this: if you want to be the major player in the munitions game, certainly in North Africa, the Middle East, and probably elsewhere, this is your opportunity. Are you ready? We can strategize about that. How I got there, the risks I have taken, the rewards brought back to the family, my contacts, suppliers, buyers, protectors: you personally will never know those details. Your leaders will have to decide if this is how they want to work. If so, tell one of them to contact me, and we will continue our private discussions. These will be arranged as I see best to protect my privacy."

As the host rose after his cigar, Amar asked a final question about a different topic. "I forgot to ask this afternoon about America. Do you ever see this company expanding into the U.S. market?"

"It's a tricky question, as I personally probably could not guide us into that market, although it's very tempting. The DEA is still stalking me; besides, I don't like Americans. If that agency finds one mistake, one tiny aspect of the business out of order, they will come after the entire company. I think Washington could even force European governments into action against us. American law is quite extra territorial, so I must be careful."

"Would there not be an upside?"

"Of course. The whole continent is crossed each day by thousands of trucks, so getting a share of the business when you are capitalized and experienced would not be difficult. We also hear that their munitions market, particularly small arms, flourishes there. Once you design and implement a way to export safely, you'll be a hero and paid handsomely by folks wanting your wares."

Juan paused and then added, "Keep in mind that Americans don't like sovereign funds. They're crazy about their private capital markets but fend off overtures from Arab funds that want to buy American property, businesses, and infrastructure. They now even have legislation ensuring that big funds like yours are scrutinized more closely than those of private investors. A few years ago, Congress blocked the sale of east coast ports to Dubai World, and my son told me that another fund was investigated because it wanted to invest in a run-down toll road in Pennsylvania."

"What's the best move in this environment? America is a priority focus in NAF's world strategy."

"Right now, I'm thinking of buying a small, niche-player trucking company with routes across North America so we can better know how the business really works for operating logistics and costs, border crossings, union shops, taxes, reporting to regulators, and access to critical supplies. Angel is very smart and in love with the United States. He studied commerce, organizations, and entrepreneurship at Brown University. He just finished at IESE Business School, which is closer to home. I wanted you to meet him tonight, but his mother had other plans for him. I'm arranging to have him travel back to America to scout out possible investment opportunities.

"And one more thing," Juan added as the driver opened the door of the waiting limousine. "Tell your team that we've heard about the new highway being built along the coast of Morocco and Algeria. Can't imagine it happening without wealthy nations such as China and Japan competing for the right to throw money at it; we have many customers around there. A better highway always helps the delivery man. Do a good job, and tell your government not to take too much on the side." He waved good-bye to the excited passenger. None of the day's events surprised Amar, nor would it surprise Said Ghoul, the chair of NAF to whom he would be reporting as soon as he returned to Algiers. Ghoul had always assumed there would be two deals, with the first buying access to the second. Amar's mission was to arrange the purchase of Juan's trucking company. That was not going to be a problem. When asked about the armament business, he outlined the second deal as best he could without notes, as Juan had instructed. He was sent away with a noncommittal nod and wondered if he would ever hear again about this proposal.

The next morning, Juan called in Angel. "You're finally going to get your chance to go back to America. I'll spend tomorrow afternoon sharing my take on the strategy we might follow, but in the end when you return you'll have the task of researching and presenting a proposal of what we should do in America. You've probably heard I had some important visitors yesterday." Angel acknowledged the family gossip.

"They want a deal with us sooner than later. That's fine. I told them they had to follow whatever plan you have for America. You will be in charge. That's where you want to be, right?" Again, his son acknowledged how much Juan understood.

"Okay, start by calling this guy." He handed his son Hugh Parks' business card. "This wacko is not in our league. He's definitely a throwaway, but he wants to run with us, so you should use him as a sounding board during your first few visits. You have to start somewhere, and I can guarantee that none of your friends from Brown are truckers. Be sure to phone Mr. Parks from a land-line outside our offices. Tell him that you're the contact and that he is never to phone me. Offer to have lunch with him as soon as you get to America. Say you're excited to work with him. I personally don't want to hear from him again. Make that clear."

After a quick hug, Angel left to organize his first trip to the United States on behalf of his family. His dad sat back down at his desk to ponder his next move. Juan was an expert at setting up a successful attack long before anyone was watching. This time he was putting his longstanding ambition to target America into action. He would soon have a new financial partner equally interested in the States; the Algerians were excellent cover as well as a good source of money. With his son acting as his personal scout, Juan could check on characters like Hugh to determine whether they were for real while snooping around for a new business. Most importantly, Juan was accomplishing all of this without ever leaving Madrid. He was ready.

WINNIPEG, MANITOBA

Fall 2008

Life was not moving along smoothly for Arthur. Lacking the experience of Juan and the brazen opportunism of Hugh, he had no roadmaps for his dilettante adventure into local politics. He was hoping against hope that his academic training would once again pull him through, but as classes were resuming in a few days, he was losing confidence in his ability to cope with the most familiar of tasks, the simplest of which weren't being done properly. For example, he knew the absolute importance at the outset of a new research project of writing down everything, but he wasn't doing it. Arthur had strong, clear memories of Professor Goldsmith mentoring him through his doctorate program and readying him for a tenured teaching position—the one still in his possession twenty years later. He bombarded all of his students with the same message. "You must take notes daily. Your detailed information has to be recorded perfectly. You're no different than a rookie policeman. You'll only be trusted if you write down everything. Otherwise your memory will trick you." It was good advice. His new study on corruption demanded that he pay attention to every factor he observed. When he didn't get around to his writing task every day, Annie was most curious as to why he'd stopped his obsessive routine of detailing events and outlining his speculations. Eventually, the increasingly Spartan entries in his notebook turned out to be Annie's best guide to his erratic behavior which she thought was more pronounced after their summer working together. He was, indeed, in the process of changing from his traditional role as a disinterested academic. Yet this transformation begged the question of who he was expecting to be when the new Arthur emerged. It was eerily, according to the quizzical Annie, unclear to either her or the few others still paying attention to him what was driving him.

Meeting with her aunt over comfort food at the Pancake House Annie talked about her professor in somewhat ambivalent terms. "Can't figure him out. Yup, that's the problem. Is he a modern day bitter campaigner against corruption that he alone uncovers in his research or is he an eager recruit who is excited that the local establishment welcomes his advice? He sure likes to lunch with the wheelers and dealers."

Susan shrugged as she took tiny bites of her strawberry-covered waffle. "I imagine it's daunting to paint the mayor as a villain while his friends are suggesting ways the professor can help them. Does it have any impact on your work?"

Annie had no compunction about eating such an unhealthy mixture of sausages and pancakes. She kept shoveling it in as she answered her aunt. "At first, no. Originally, he was so preoccupied with his notes that he didn't realize no one else was jotting down a single word. He saw that Hugh what's his name didn't even carry a notebook with him. This made Arthur very self-conscious of his role versus theirs; he is supposed to be there to take notice and record their moves while I think they want everyone to forget everything. I've been tracking this change of heart, as I don't believe Arthur can magically recreate conversations for his story simply from memory. I wonder what he is thinking."

Susan's parting advice was simple. "Ask him directly"

"Sounds good." With that sunny response from her niece, Susan picked up the tab and they went their separate ways.

As usual, Annie was not one to let such questions hang in the air, unasked. She questioned him directly at the first opportunity, "Why are your notes so meager? I can't follow what you're doing every day as I did originally."

His first instinct was to avoid her. He paused, searched for an excuse, and then answered her with complete candor: "Because no one else does."

When the Foundation had readily agreed to fund a summer student, Arthur had been quick to tell his wife Brenda that Susan's niece would be the perfect candidate. Over the summer she had proved that she was, indeed, the ideal choice from almost every perspective. She was a good ambassador on campus for him and his work. She was a cheerful assistant who brought smiles to the faces of the most hardened academics. She was a competent researcher, using both the old-fashioned library and digital devices with equal skill. At the outset, they worked smoothly together. She would hand him notes and questions to prepare him for his interviews and meetings, and in return, he was to hand back copious notes for Annie to file. When the note taking ceased, her suspicion, later confirmed, was that he didn't want her to know the whole picture. Now that classes were about to start, Arthur suggested to Annie that she'd be spending her time searching library documents.

She shrugged and responded, "It would be helpful to have your notes so that I know what to look for in the archives." Why had he stopped taking notes? It was still unsettling for her and his brief did not help matters.

Annie had read Arthur's earliest observations, which included his Sunday afternoon at Joanne and Hugh's house. His most vivid notes were about Hugh. In his margin notes he pondered—why had Hugh taken Andrew aside? He had also noted how excited Andrew had been by the older man's attention. Obviously, something had been set in motion, as Arthur had tracked this meeting and concluded that the subsequent public announcement about the first environmentally friendly initiative from the trucking industry was somehow born in that living room. The *Winnipeg Free Press* reported that truckers were purchasing locally made wind turbines to attach to specially designated trucks as part of Winnipeg trial runs to measure their effectiveness in low-speed, high-density traffic conditions. Everyone interviewed including Bertie, talked enthusiastically about a bright future for Winnipeg in North American and European markets. That was the last elaborate and speculative entry in the dossier for Annie to read. She did find out by accident from Susan that Arthur surreptitiously sought out his students who worked at city hall. One day, she snooped around his office until she found the contact name of Arthur's student working as a clerk near the mayor's office. She phoned Sheila Banks with a farfetched excuse that the professor wanted Annie to confirm some facts. She parlayed that opening into a detailed recounting of Arthur's time away from campus.

Apparently, he was always asking her and other students to stop by for a drink after their evening class at his faculty club, sometimes even cutting his lecture short to give him more time to find out what was afoot with the mayor. He had first always to tolerate their banter about municipal jobs compared to the good life of a professor, a fact he good-naturedly acknowledged. The second time out he casually slipped into a discussion about the latest green plan being championed by the enterprising Mayor Patterson. They were all supportive, as the media coverage had made them proud of working at city hall. Annie took notes based on her informer's expressive memory.

"The only deal that I don't understand yet is why truckers are so keen. Any ideas?"

Two police officers, who were quiet in class, hesitated, looked at each other, and then laughed. "Let me take you through the story of how your city hall really works," began Detective Leslie Reynolds.

"First of all, we think it's a great initiative, and so do the parking patrols. Trucks with the experimental equipment get a special tag on their license plates that we can easily see. This designation means no tickets and no violations, except, of course, for accidents and very high speeds. There are no route restrictions for these trucks. This means a lot less work for us; truckers are a real pain to stop and ticket."

Arthur looked surprised, so the detective quickly added, "This new order from the mayor's office is being implemented under the guise of allowing the trucks to stay in motion as long as possible without stopping so that the wind contraptions can be tested. As part and parcel of the green plan, we are experimenting with new methods to move traffic and conserve energy. We are told to ignore these trucks, so the drivers love us, at least for now."

Her fellow officer, Bob Sampson, joined the conversation. "We heard there was quite the scene before the program was announced. Someone suggested a lottery to assign these permits, and that's still the official word. It turns out they arranged a confidential list drawn up by Don Davidson, a downtown lawyer who is assisted by the well-connected Ms. Brown—you know, the mayor's niece—who followed up by presenting it at the usual luncheon meeting at Sam and Benny's. Apparently, she highlighted the exemptions the truckers were expecting. It was agreed that they would finalize the deal at city hall on the same day. Pretty good service, don't you think, Professor? Well, we'll never know, because you can be sure that no one took notes and that there was only one copy of the list. They'd make lousy cops. We're always taking notes."

To Arthur' surprise, according to Sheila, a single parent, who by her own account spoke most bluntly right then, after downing a beer. In class, she never said boo. Working hard on her university degree after being in the trenches at city hall as a secretary for close to two decades, she was now assisting committee chairs with their meetings. Her university degree was her ticket if she wanted any more promotions.

Sheila tried to fill in as many details as possible for Annie as she assumed that this neophyte researcher knew very little about city hall. She continued, "I was unusually animated in talking with Professor Crawford, especially in front of the policemen as they're always so snoopy. I explained that after one of those famous boys only lunches the shit hit the fan. I heard that Councilor Ambrose, being worried that he might be jeopardizing his cozy relationship with local truckers, apologized for new fees being levied for the special environmental licenses. 'Are you okay with our new fees? You know, we had to compensate a little for the ticket revenue we just lost.'

"Apparently, the trucker just laughed and told Ambrose, 'Compared with what we are paying Ms. Brown for the two-year break from fines and parking fees and the dream of being left alone all day long, this is nothing!'

"Councilor Ambrose subsequently found out how the truckers had sorted out who the winners should be. His committee was to rubber stamp the deal while the mayor took the credit for Brown's new community fund. This raised many eyebrows around our place, given her close relationship with the mayor.

"I heard more details secondhand from Andrew, a new kid in the mayor's office, who attempted to fill in the blanks for the councilor. It was to no avail. Ambrose returned in a huff just before his meeting. Clearly something had dawned on him because he loudly yelled at me. He feared that they were leaving him out in the cold. The truckers were stickhandling around him. Instead the new community fund will be run by the niece."

Sheila was now in full flight as she described what happened next. "The councilor pounded my desk in frustration. Boy, was he crazed. He took me aside and asked about the status of the wind turbine deal. I told him, 'As you instructed me, sir, if there is nothing negative, let's do it as soon as we can. It's set for approval today.'

"'Take this proposal off the agenda,' he barked. 'It will never see the light of day.' He walked down the hall to yell at Patterson, and that's how we later found out what happened.

"Andrew heard a little more from the mayor afterward but chose not to repeat the details of the conversation. He's too loyal to do that. We know about Andrew's suspicion of the councilors and his worries about the wheeling and dealing that he hears about secondhand. At first, Andrew didn't appreciate why Ambrose was upset; in fact, I didn't catch on either. So Andrew and I huddled after work to play out a few scenarios to support a more coherent story. Nothing was making sense.

"We reconstructed what had happened. City hall was very cleverly bamboozled. We thought the idea that came originally from Hugh Parks was small potatoes but unknown to us it took the truckers a nanosecond to see how much it was worth to them. Not only would their drivers instantly save time and money, but also they could save themselves a lot of trouble. We didn't have a clue about the level of corruption in the police ticketing and parking department. Guys were getting away with serious kickbacks. So when the mayor presented this offer to get the truckers onside, our staff made a fuss and, to our face, only grudgingly agreed to help make the deal work. Meanwhile, behind our backs, they were cranking out their own schemes to keep themselves in extra cash.

"Andrew and I were sitting there, puzzled about Brown's new community fund. Like, what can possibly be at stake? Winnipeg is a small city. There's not much happening here. What are we missing?

"It then hit us. There could only be one answer: the drug trade. Who else is in and out of traffic, looking to stay ten minutes at a restaurant or a café while a deal is consummated? And they are typically the same gangs that move stolen goods in and out of trucking depots, rail yards and airport cargo buildings? They want to move fast and not be hassled either downtown or on neighborhood streets by the likes of Susan Armitage. They want to be invisible.

"When a truck is tagged with a ticket, the vehicle is put in the computer system. If it's a driving offense, of course, the driver's license is always recorded at the same time. A good cop can use this information to pick out suspicious behavior. Annie-at this moment the two cops looked at each other then away from the conversation. Andrew caught on right away and exclaimed, 'That's why they've had to pay off the ticket guys; it's to keep out of the computer. It's not the money; it's maintaining a clean record so the narcs don't see a pattern.' At that point, I stopped talking to let it all settle in. Your professor friend said nothing so I didn't know if he got the drift of my story. The cops sure did.

"After a brief silence, Sampson looked at the others and added, "Sheila, you're right from your end. I hope the mayor sees what he might have stepped into. There's a second issue I personally think is even more insidious. You know that cell phones are being restricted for use in vehicles in most of North America. Well, local truckers are asking for a long-term experiment in which professional drivers get a waiver from this restriction. They are lobbying to combine this with the mayor's green plan to enable the designated truckers to move about unfettered. We all know how the criminal world depends on cell phones, especially by using quick text messages to avoid us. And don't forget that when parking tickets are given out nowadays, photos are taken of the vehicles and the location. Visual images like these are very helpful to detectives dealing with organized crime. The gang leaders know how we operate and are behind this scheme to make our lives more difficult.

"After that outburst, everyone grew quiet, looking at their watches, wondering if they could politely leave. They had already shared too much information, and nobody wanted to leak more to the overly curious professor.

"Since I had enough beer in me to pose one final question, I asked the professor if he knew this Hugh Parks as I personally found him a little too evasive for my liking. I checked him out after he asked to be a witness in front of our committee. Lives in your neighborhood, so I thought you might know him.

"Professor Crawford quickly detailed his limited exposure to this neighbor, including the afternoon neighborhood meeting and asked why Parks wanted to be a witness. I explained briefly that he claimed that he wanted to express publicly his support for the green plan. Our professor mulled over this information; I think he recognized that Hugh had put together a reasonable half-story. Now it's interesting to speculate if either Parks or Crawford had contemplated that they were on the edge of Winnipeg's drug trade? I doubt it. There was a heavy silence as we got up to leave when the professor made the strangest revelation to us. Pretending to check his watch, he commented that there was a story about Parks but he didn't want to start up so late in the evening. Apparently, he claimed, he had been tracking this character who put in many hours downtown with local leaders to ensure that this green plan experiment goes ahead. Then he asks us to come back as his guests at the faculty club to keep him in the loop. Can you imagine that? I think he saw us as his spies. A little crazy! As proof, the embarrassed cops, putting on their coats, didn't say anything more. From their perspective, it was much better to nod wisely at any further recounting of events at city hall as though they were happening across the continent in faraway Atlanta or Miami, but not here at home.

"Okay Annie, I know I've talked your head off but the story ends with you so hang on another moment. They were hurriedly on their way out when Leslie stopped to pull the professor aside offering a private story so I hung around to eavesdrop on their whispered conversation. She explained she was part of the community liaison branch of the police department and that his name came up in their last meeting in the Heights, mostly in a light-hearted fashion. The group was talking about university life; Leslie told them about her evening courses, as suburban wives always approve of this. She mentioned the professor's class and his new urban research project. I heard her say the following: 'I joked that I actually didn't understand it, but this Susan Armitage piped up: 'Don't worry. I can fill you in completely. My niece, Annie, is there as my spy.' So there you have it. Your own mole! Love to hear more about your work.' She was off before he could offer anything to rebut her unsolicited information. So, Annie, I wasn't surprised to hear from you but you better be careful if you're free-lancing many calls like this."

For the record, when Annie went looking for his take on the evening, she found that he must have been too tired or distracted to write out his notes when he returned home.

PHILADELPHIA, PENNSYLVANIA

Fall 2008

Aird Investment Limited, a Philadelphia-based private investment firm, operated a two billion-dollar fund based on monies raised from six North American
pension plans. Their smart, aggressive managing director, Marsha Hendricks,
kept an eye on both the performance of the portfolio as well as the satisfaction
of her clients. Usually this wasn't a problem. The investment advisory committee, consisting of a single representative from each fund, met by conference call
once a month for updates and performance reviews. She was wary heading into
their first meeting after the summer break.

This hands-off approach was best suited for good times; by 2008, Aird's
fortunes had declined dramatically. Marsha could no longer sit back and count
on generous fees and bonuses from her earlier investment decisions. There
was trouble everywhere. She had been intrigued by North America's aerospace
industry, for example, and believed she could make money where others had
failed. It turned out she was wrong, and her investors were not at all happy.

One man in particular, Theodore Williams, the director of private investments for the Vancouver-based Cascadia Employee Pension Plan, confronted
her repeatedly about her decisions, as they were both causing him embarrassment and costing him cash.

"I'm not sure," he warmed up, "how you managed to get us into the airplane business just as the market died. This is quite the investment without any
income. Any thoughts, Marsha?"

She replied in the most deliberate, uncompromising voice she could bring
to the conference call. "No one anticipated such a downton. You are right,
Theodore, it will take a few years to get back your original investment. But we

all said we were patient investors and planned to wait at least five years, and this is only year three. So we'll see what happens. Already air cargo and passenger traffic is picking up in Africa and in Asia. We're very actively looking for new contracts. I urge you not to worry."

"I am worried, and so is my organization. What else can you report on for the aerospace sector?"

Marsha continued smoothly now more confident with that exchange behind her. "Fortunately, we own a large aerospace storage facility in Victorville, California. We're parking dozens of the planes that the airlines can't afford to fly. It's not a complete trouncing."

If she were simply wearing the hat of the firm's chief investment officer, Marsha would have had to admit that recent investments had seriously undermined her funds. As president and the public face for Aird, she needed good news before she went back into the market for another one or two billion dollars. After the call, she returned to her office in a reflective mood. Although she never liked the confrontations with Theodore, he did have a legitimate point. She had made some lousy investments. She came to believe that as long as she held on to the monies already raised and brazenly went back into the market for more funds, she would be okay. Her ambition was to grow her firm rapidly by attracting new capital within a few months. To do so, however, she would need a better story than the one she had.

With that in mind, Marsha called in Brent, her new hire, a young but very bright investment analyst out of the local Wharton business program, where he had made a strong impression on his professors. Now she was about to put him to work on a very tough assignment: saving her business.

"Brent," she began over an office desk lunch meeting, "I've decided to put you in charge of finding a way out of this aerospace mess."

Seeing the look on his face, Marsha laughed. "Don't worry, I don't expect miracles. It's just that we've found ourselves in a terrible market with very little warning. I have to get us out of this untidiness, or our whole firm will collapse. And don't think I'm exaggerating. One failure like this can mean a loss of confidence among pension investors. After that, I won't be able to raise a dime. Once investors already in the fund watch me come to a standstill, they'll begin to cancel their commitments and withdraw their monies. When everything is going great, no one asks questions. When it turns ugly, they're out the door. Let's talk about how you can help me save this mess."

Brent was anxious to please her. "Where do I start?

"Brent, I think we have to dig deeper into the aerospace industry. While others retreat, let's work as contrarians. Let's find out if we can build up the

California operations. If that won't work, keep looking around. I'll always support you, don't worry. Let's finish the cookies and get back to work."

Two weeks later, after his research report was drafted, he left it with Marsha to read over the weekend. "This was quick, but I do explain why the company will likely thrive. We should keep most of it," he e-mailed in his cover note. Saturday afternoon she sat down and carefully read Brent's analysis of Aerospace International Systems.

"Over twenty-five years ago, some ex-pilots started to repair aircraft almost as a hobby. Active pilots have much time on their hands due to their union contracts, while those who retire early typically have the energy and interest in running a small business on the side. This opportunity was ideal for them. They started by opening a Cessna aircraft repair center in Texas, where many ranchers, oil men, and regular, wealthy guys own planes. Because pilots can fly free of charge on their airlines, they organized their flights to give them time to drum up business. They soon had three repair centers strung from Texas to Montana. These pilots are all nuts about planes and quickly attracted a group of supporters willing to build them a bigger business. It was about a decade after they started, in the mid-90s, that they found a great niche that makes this property valuable.

Apparently, the American government during the Clinton years was fiercely determined to close military bases wherever possible. Local congressmen and businesses always fight back, demanding outrageous funds to build new enterprises, when bases are being closed. This was happening all across the country.

These pilots bid on a proposal to turn an air force base in Victorville, California, an unattractive community northeast of Los Angeles, into new airplane storage and repair facilities. They looked into it, talked to their investors, and made a successful bid. At the sight of those pilots, their successful track record, and the availability of private capital, governments couldn't wait to throw some real money their way. The deal was struck, and Aerospace International Systems was created.

What only the pilots knew (keeping the investors and governments in the dark), was that they were entering a whole new ballgame. The customers were no longer the dozens of single aircraft owners but rather were big airlines that were actually working day jobs: United, Northwest, American, Jet Blue, and so forth. Behind them were the big aircraft leasing companies, which carried considerable clout in the maintenance business. Because of the environmental movement, most planes were no longer quiet enough or sufficiently fuel-efficient to meet North American and European standards so the company anticipated that several hundred aircraft would soon be mothballed. They would need some very big parking lots. Their new company would start the engines, fix up the easy composite parts like damaged floors and walls, and then repaint these dolls. Planes came in and flew out in dark skies, making it impossible to know what was going on. Cash came in, and the business of parking made a good return on a modest investment. It was the same idea as using empty lots downtown for parking cars. This is why Aird made its investment and took out the original investors.

The repair side, however, is a bit more complicated than expected. Management coped by bringing in cheap Mexican labor and setting up a trucking company to support their feeder system for inexpensive parts across North America, including Mexico. That made the men running the trucking company more important than most would assume in the aerospace business. At the same time, our investor group fights regularly with you and our president out there, Gordon Hutton, to keep the operations profitable. You've kept everyone happy until recently. Unfortunately, we didn't really understand the stealth behind the statistics.

As you well know, about two years ago, the bottom fell out of the world aerospace industry. At first, Aird was happier than anyone else in the airplane business because we were paid to store planes others couldn't use. We ended up having eight hundred aircraft parked there on the long military runways. But then reality hit us too. Airlines were in desperate financial shape; some merged, and most cut back capacity and borrowed money, trying everything to stay afloat. Cash was disappearing. No one was repairing any aircraft, so our business for North American customers came grinding to a halt.

Here's the key to the story. While the industry imploded in our country, others were doing just fine. Airlines in Asia and Africa were still flying and looking for more and more planes. The quickest way for them to acquire planes was to ask Aerospace International Systems to bring a plane to them, ready to fly.

The lead times are tight. To move a plane back into service quickly means you have to have everything completely under your control. You have to bring parts from the airplane chop shops in Louisiana, the composite repair businesses in Canada, engine components from all over, including Mexico, huge quantities of paint in different colors, perhaps new material for passenger cabins. Trucks would roll in at various hours and drop off their cargo at the planes far away from where others could see. That's why Hutton wants to keep his trucking company.

I think otherwise. I recommend we get rid of it and free up some working capital. How Aerospace International Systems in Victorville came to own and operate its own trucking company of over a hundred vehicles of all shapes and sizes escapes me. Apparently, when Aerospace International Systems was first formed, it dealt mainly with military planes stored at the end of the runways. The U.S. forces insisted on a remote location to keep out the vandals and the curious who stalked old planes. At first, Hutton took over the surplus military vehicles that came with the deal. This made it super convenient to drive down the miles of runways, check out the planes, ferry security guards back and forth, and move parts and machines to the planes as needed. Because the managers were all nuts about planes and not trucks, they created a special operating group for transport, found a newcomer who knew nothing about airplanes but loved trucks, gave him a budget, and told him to make it work. From board notes, I've read that Theodore, among others, loved this story when he first heard it. It probably appealed to his romantic notion of helping poor immigrants. This mechanic, Caesar Rodriguez, a first-generation Mexican-American with a large family locally in Hesperia and back home just across the border in Ensenada, expanded this business over the past decade. As long as he did what Hutton needed and did not ask for any money, all was fine. He found all the drivers he needed for his real business: moving illegal migrants into California by hiding them in boxes marked "aircraft parts." The first boxes in the truck were always so heavy that no one at the border wanted to move them to find what might be tucked away behind them. Soon he had trucks for everyone and used the company's name as a shield for his own business. I suspect that there is other contraband being transported.

I think this operation is dangerous to your reputation, and I recommend selling AT but definitely keeping Aerospace Support Systems. You can use the proceeds from selling the trucking business to build a badly needed paint shop."

Marsha concurred with this analysis and immediately sent Brent a note thanking him for the impressive research completed in a very short time frame. However, Brent was dead wrong to assume that her embrace of his research note had secured him a place in the firm.

When Brent at last tracked down the rest of the story about AT, he reported to Marsha that she could soon sell the trucking company. The story line for potential buyers would be that AT had an experienced, bilingual workforce with both domestic and international customers in Canada, the United States, and Mexico. When Brent's analysis made it to the investment committee, however, the only comments that came back were Theodore's margin scribbles: "How did this happen?" "What is going on in California?" "How did we get into this mess?" "Who's in charge of this file?" He determinedly undercut Marsha whenever possible.

Marsha worked out her frustration with Theodore by hurling her impatient questions at Brent during their next review of the file. Marsha's reproaches weighed heavily on him, as he wanted her blessing in this, his first job in the very difficult investment world. Most of his college friends were still looking for employment; he didn't want to be back out in that job market. She reviewed her own notes and asserted aggressively: "We need to put this behind us, or we'll look too shoddy for any future investors. What are my options?"

Before Brent answered, he glanced at Marsha while she answered the phone about another problem. Her slender face magnified the lines of anxiety that appeared in every discussion with her. Today was no different. Brent had the option of giving the typical answer rehearsed over and over at business school. His common sense instinct told him not to go that route.

"AT is not working out. All of us sitting here in Philadelphia with you are frustrated by management out in California," he answered as soon as she finished her call. "I've checked this out the best I can, but I don't see how we can make a profit in the trucking business. What struck me in preparing this report was that no one could answer my repeated question: what exactly did all these truck drivers do every day?"

He knew what Marsha was thinking. She responded with a very bitter voice. "My investment firm is not in business to tread water; it is there to increase value in every single operation."

Brent feared that she would set him up by leaving him holding the bag on a failing enterprise. It would be just like her, if he believed office gossip, to dismiss him without warning, telling others that he couldn't help the firm solve this problem. Instead she coldly let Brent know her misgivings and then abruptly left the room without giving him any real instructions.

Frustrated, he phoned Caesar Rodriguez, AT's manager, who responded coolly to this invasion into his turf. "Check the books. We do not cost the company a single penny year after year. I pay my expenses; I upgrade the fleet when I have to. Everything is perfect, and on top of that, Aerospace International Systems has no transportation issues. Everyone is looked after."

Undeterred, Brent pushed on with his list of questions.

"Do we carry cargo for anyone else?"

"That's not in our license with the state of California. We are allowed to carry only for the company."

"My question was slightly different, Mr. Rodriguez."

"There are times we pick up some parcels for families back home in Mexico. We bring back boxes to them, but the cash is between the driver and the family."

"Do all of the drivers have proper trucking licenses?"

"Nobody goes on the highway without my supervisor keeping his records perfect for the authorities. Everyone has the right papers."

"What about the base?" Brent was listening carefully to the half-answers.

"Sometimes, if we're in a hurry, we ask one of the young guys to run errands. Some of the new staff hasn't completed their training. No big deal."

"Are they on the highway sometimes?"

"Not normally. There are good back roads if they are staying in this area."

"What's our busiest route?"

"Probably equally into the Midwest, from Wichita, Kansas, over to Arizona. Lots of stops when the repair side is busy. Also into Louisiana and Georgia, where there's a business in dismantling old aircraft. We pick up used parts there."

"Mexico? Canada?" He could see his business school professor nodding in approval as he dug into Rodriguez's business.

"Mexico, we go at least twice a week. Canada, maybe once, twice a month. We supply composite material to a few small aerospace businesses in Winnipeg and return with their finished products."

"Are the trucks filled both ways on most routes?"

"Usually. Lately we've been on the phone looking to pick up more cargo before we head off. Pretty tricky. If the state finds out, we could be in trouble. Sometimes we give a lift to family and friends so the driver can make a little extra cash. Like, last week, my cousins wanted to move to Chicago, with their furniture."

"Thanks for your help, Caesar."

"No problem, Mr. Oliver."

Once the call was over, Brent stood there staring out the window, watching the fast-moving, well-dressed crowds on Market Street in downtown Philadelphia. He imagined life for those in Victorville whose best views were abandoned air force buildings built fifty years ago across the street from Caesar's garage. What was this guy up to? No good, but at no apparent cost to Aird. Nevertheless, these truckers were moving around across North America with impunity and with the company logo plastered on the side. The brand was supposedly there for everyone to recognize and to help build trust in the aerospace industry.

Brent understood why no one questioned Caesar's operations. Gordon Hutton was getting unbelievably good service, so he decided to leave it alone. Hutton particularly liked that when he called Caesar to ready a plane to fly out of the States, trucks raced to supply the departing aircraft. When Hutton did ask any questions, Caesar pushed back, lowered his voice, and spoke more Spanish than English until Gordon backed off. Hutton had offered Caesar the chance to buy out AT, but he'd scoffed at the suggestion. Caesar took the president through the hoops of what it would be like if a Mexican-American owned the trucks: the regulators would shut them down through endless paperwork unless he was able to offer some payouts. Homeland Security would be very slow in reviewing the ownership structure, custom brokers would ask for a lot more, and so forth. The list of problems was unfathomably long. It was much better for everyone if AT remained as it was.

Gordon begrudgingly defended his support of Caesar when Brent called again about the trucking division. He explained his business strategy as though he was speaking with a kid brother he didn't much like. "Look, the truckers are so different from the rest of us at the base. We know civil and military aircraft—how to park them, repair them, and send them back into service. That's our specialty. Caesar Rodriguez looks after what we really don't know anything about. When we need a truck, there's one immediately at the door. We need a part, it comes in on schedule. That's what counts for me. Because of that, I ask few questions."

Brent had his suspicions about Caesar Rodriguez's real business, but he had no proof of any insidious activity. It was clear, however, that unreported cash was flowing to Caesar, and everyone was turning a blind eye. Questions lingered. What if he suggested to the investors that they were probably a cover for an illegal operation? They would be furious. These high-status pension organizations did not muck around in criminal activities and might even exit Aird if they felt unduly exposed. Brent found himself with many questions but no answers. To find out what was really going on, he would have to ask for more time and travel to Victorville. As this would be a surefire red flag to Marsha, this wasn't going to happen.

His final and very private hand-written note explained his strategy for dodging future legal problems. If Aird could find a buyer, he recommended they sell it off for whatever price they could get in an extremely weak market. A few million would do; Hutton could use the money to build a new airplane paint shop in Victorville. This would be a much more profitable business, as planes were changing owners so fast that everyone needed paint. The bottom line was that AT and Caesar had to go. He tied his immediate success to Martha's risk adverse personality. If she took his advice, he imagined that she knew his instinct was to protect her at all costs.

WINNIPEG, MANITOBA

Fall 2008

It had been a whirlwind time that a dealmaker like Hugh loved. Although he had set his investor scheme in motion as planned, the local political game turned out to be more complex than he had anticipated. He had to recalculate his moves a dozen times as the bit players divvied up the money the truckers put on the table. He acknowledged ruefully that this was small change for the Juans of the world but potentially lucrative in wholesale Winnipeg. At first Hugh's plans had a rough ride with the hostile councilor, Ambrose, beyond the management skills of the panic-stricken Andrew. Hearing this Hugh swung back into action.

Hugh could tell by Andrew's reluctance to talk openly that it would continue to be up to him to find solutions, not just for the mayor and the councilor, but for everyone.

"Now, Andrew," Hugh said, starting into his side of the telephone conversation very, very cautiously. Hugh was better than most at putting together deals that made him money, but taking on a politician was all new to him. "It's important that we chat and discuss all the issues in detail. Now that summer has past and everyone is back into the swing of things, a lot can quickly happen in important files such as this. I want the mayor to be prepared for every eventuality. I'm actually expected shortly for an important presentation,"—a total lie—"why don't you come by at six for a chat? You remember the house... That's right. See you then."

Neither Andrew's student days as a political science major nor his current brief career as the mayor's political assistant had prepared him for the likes of Hugh, his boss, or even the professor. Andrew had made his mark in university as a solid B student; he was accepted by his friends as a hardworking, genial fellow who would always help out those he knew. His eagerness to please was quickly recognized by the older guys opening doors for him and offering him a start in life. He worked diligently for the mayor and enjoyed running errands and being described as "the young Mr. Fixer" around city hall. Previously, given his youthfulness and inexperience, Andrew sometimes naïvely misunderstood the motives of the mayor's supporters, but they always appreciated his efforts to come in, make a deal they could all live with, and pretend the hiccup hadn't happened. His misgivings about this visit were based in the lessons he was learning on the run; a particular good one was not to trust anyone.

He arrived at Hugh's house a few minutes before six. Hugh offered him iced tea and sat him in the office with the door half-closed so as not to be unfriendly to his curious wife while also ensuring that it would be difficult for Joanne to catch even a few words if she happened by. Hugh knew she was innocent enough to pass the information about this meeting to Susan; he didn't want her to be left filling in the blanks on her own. He glanced outside, at first smiling at the sight of Joanne wandering around the garden away from his office, but then he caught a glimpse of the professor talking beside her, feigning interest in her hobby as the justification for his stopping by after work. Hugh frowned, troubled by Arthur's sudden interest in begonias, and mentally reminded himself to deal with it later. He would have to tend to this young buck first.

Andrew found Hugh's explanation of the summer's events to be somewhat odd, although he listened without interrupting. Hugh had opened their chat with his own brand of political truths. "We, the Bison Board group of investors, have been lobbying the truckers to test an innovative technological experiment. City hall loved it, incorporated it into the green plan, and then made a rather strange side deal with the truckers, which, frankly, I don't understand. Apparently, the proceeds from a private auction for the environmental experiment permits were turned over to some sort of community affairs trust fund controlled by the mayor's niece. We assume that your mayor has heard about this. Can you confirm that Mayor Patterson knows the details of this arrangement?"

Andrew had to protect the mayor, so he shrugged an ambivalent acknowledgement but was careful not to say anything. He was just about to respond when he noticed Arthur. Pointing to him, Andrew remarked, "He certainly asks a lot of questions. He phones me and makes a real effort to draw out information. I'm not sure I'm comfortable around him." He hesitated, eyeing his host for clues as to how best to deal with Arthur.

Hugh acknowledged his own discomfort so Andrew hurriedly wrapped up their conversation. "The mayor is good at his politics within the business community; we don't worry about elections. There's a full year to go before voters have their say. The immediate danger is that we've accidentally broken up a racket we didn't initially know existed. My guess is that we have city hall employees who the truckers no longer have to pay on the side. The question is: what do the truckers intend to do to keep everyone happy? Where are they going to spend that money?"

Not a bad analysis for a kid, decided Hugh. "Where can I help?"

"We need to gather a lot more intelligence so that none of our political allies gets hurt. We need to hear from the green plan supporters that this is a great idea. If we blink, we all lose, including your investors."

Hugh paused, as if to think about it, and added, "Okay, you'd better go now. Take this draft copy of the green plan and tell those two outside that we had a great talk about the local environment. I'll watch from here to see whether they believe you. And you had better give me your cell number."

After Andrew left, Hugh watched him cheerfully greet the two watchers, who seemed to be observing him closely. Hugh's guess was that whatever Andrew said did not dissuade them from wanting to know more. Soon they moved into the living room and waited for Hugh to appear.

Initially, he ignored his wife and her new, most excellent friend, the professor, begging off a drink. "I'll join you in a few moments," he promised, returning to his office to sort this out. It was the sort of puzzle that intrigued him. His instinct was to take risks and to get into deals no matter what was happening among the other players. He was always confident that he could manage whatever surprises came his way. Besides, since in the end he never paid up in any deal that went sour, his absolutely worst position was that of losing time, which could have been spent daydreaming about another scheme, with a few lunches and cigars to impress other ne'er do wells.

The baffling twist this time was the political shenanigans. His original proposal was straightforward: he'd take the investors' money, fabricate a few turbines, sell them locally, build up a huge success story with media coverage everywhere, and take the opportunity to Juan—there; he'd make a really successful deal of lasting consequence. It wasn't difficult, he thought, but now it might not happen. And so far he couldn't decipher the second game that was happening simultaneously with his. He had originally assumed that his scheme was, from every angle, such small potatoes that he could exit in a few months and still be under the radar. Frustrated, he called Stomper and told him to find out as much as he could from their buddies on the streets who owned their own trucks. Hugh knew how guys gossiped at the Tim Hortons across the city where truckers stopped regularly. Stomper's networks should overhear unguarded conversations that might provide valuable information not available from more calculating characters. He kept to himself the information gleaned on his own at city hall.

He plaintively explained his frustration. "What's happening here, Stomper? I cannot for the life of me understand what's at stake. My best guess is that we have stepped into someone else's game by mistake. I don't want to pay the price if they are pissed at me. Listen to this scenario. The city has a limited capacity to write traffic tickets each day. Let's say they write one hundred daily at an average cost of $100, for a total revenue of, say, $50,000 each week. If they stopped issuing tickets to all the participants in the wind turbine project, it would no doubt cut back their revenues. But, I ask myself: by how much? Don't know and no one will say. The mayor's niece has $300,000 in her kitty. I was told that by an insider; I have no idea if it's true. Does that mean the truckers are skipping three thousand tickets? Doubters. No, that still doesn't make sense. Something else is at stake. What's really going on? What's the real deal here? I want you to go to the hockey game tonight, as the Moose are at the arena. Find out as much as you can from our buddies there. Between them and our trucking friends, you should hear something by late tomorrow. Talk to you after supper tomorrow."

As Hugh ended the call, he considered that Stomper had not said a word, but that was always the case. Hugh talked, thought, and planned all their moves; Stomper simply grunted and executed as instructed. It suited both of them.

This time, Hugh bolted upright after the call; his heart was racing. Their guest would have to wait. "One more minute; pour me one of your great vodka martinis and put out some chips or whatever nibbles we have, dear. I'm starved. Honestly, I'll only be a minute," he shouted in as friendly of a tone as possible to his wife and her snoopy guest. He was totally distracted. It was criminal activity, probably a combination of drugs and stolen goods, which was the basis of all of this. Some of the truckers must be moving contraband around Winnipeg. One or more trucking firms most likely had a sideline in drugs. The fewer times they were stopped or their vehicles ticketed, the cleaner their records. They would pay big for this cover and in the end would probably still shell out to those at city hall who knew the scoop. Hugh grinned. He had just discovered a way to make a lot more money. All he needed was a foolproof strategy to get in on these deals. He again decided against phoning Stomper to give him this angle. Instead, he went to join the others.

His drink was waiting for him in the living room, where there was an alcove perfect for seating the three of them. Arthur was never the master of social chit-chat like Hugh, who took over the conversation as soon as he sat down. He steered it to university affairs, the new school year, urban studies, and the job market for graduating students, giving each topic a round of three questions and comments, making sure Joanne was engaged and talkative. It was now 6:45, and all visitors should be on their way home, thought Hugh. As he looked at his watch, he caught Arthur responding positively to Joanne's signal for another round of drinks. Hugh quickly got up to pour, but Joanne took control of the scene.

"Stay put. I'd enjoy making another Manhattan for Arthur and, of course, a second martini for my husband. You guys chat, and I'll be right back."

"Andrew's quite the young man." Arthur's comment was intent on getting the conversation focused immediately on city hall.

"Could be. I barely know him. First met him in person here at the house, although we had talked before," Hugh responded nonchalantly.

"What about?" Arthur's sharp question caught Hugh at a loss. He had forgotten that inquisitive academics could be off-putting.

"The green plan. He had heard about our work with one of the councilors. Was following up to make sure his boss was in the loop."

"Was he good on the telephone? He was effective here last spring, right? And he was smart enough to come back and talk further with you in your house. Must be pretty satisfying for you personally to start off so quickly and smoothly in a new relationship."

Hugh was fully on guard. "If you know politicians at all, the answer is no; this is the way it is. The big guys like the mayor send out one of the aides to snoop, to make false promises, and, later, to ask for help. Standard MO. That's why I stay away."

He had just outmaneuvered Arthur and bought time as Joanne returned with drinks.

Arthur soldiered on. "I'm a sociologist by training and spend my life inside the cloister. I don't get how political business is done; I'm like you, full of questions, not answers. Like, for instance, what sort of 'false promises' did Andrew make on behalf of the mayor?"

Persistent, but definitely not as bright or devious as he might think, concluded Hugh. I'll give him a little joyride, but then he's history.

"He was curious to hear of any other private or public initiatives the office might take on to promote the green plan. We talked in very general terms, but I'm not connected with much here in town. I'm on the road every month, with interests in places like New York, Toronto, Chicago, and elsewhere, mostly the Midwest states. I told him I wouldn't have the credibility to act as the mayor's special advisor on the environment and the economy."

"You were offered that? Why, that's a great perk to be given a position where you can suggest what governments should be doing."

Joanne had distributed the drinks and placed a bowl of nuts on the table as she settled into an armchair. "What's this? It sounds like a fabulous offer."

Hugh was uncomfortable. Once again, he had gone too far. "Well, I shouldn't put words into Andrew's mouth, as he wanted to talk some more with the mayor. However, he asked me to help out with making sure things went okay with the new initiative. I certainly will do that. Now they'll talk it over and see what's best for everyone. Me," he put his hands in the air, "I don't like meetings. I like to walk around the yard with a drink, a cigar, and a close friend or two."

"Like you do all the time with Stomper," Joanne chimed in. "You guys are always huddled away in the back corner, whispering your men's fantasies. When I look out from the kitchen window, I just laugh. Why so many secrets?"

If Hugh didn't look uncomfortable, he sure felt it.

Arthur sat there surprised. Another new name—Stomper. Who was he? How would he find out? Not today with Hugh; that much he knew for sure.

All too casually, Arthur posed his final question, after thanking his hosts for the couple of solid belts.

"Do you think the politicians will continue to support this green initiative?"

"Wouldn't have a clue. That world is beyond my comfort level."

"That's odd. You should be more vocal from what I've heard. The mayor likes you. We could all benefit from your leadership skills."

Hugh batted him away. "That's politics. You offer them five minutes of your time, and they try to take over your life. I told them I'd say a few words of support. I must get back to work before dinner. Watch for dogs. It's getting dark. Good night, Arthur."

Both men, first Andrew and then Arthur, ended up making the same mistake after chatting with Hugh. Arthur, having had a few drinks, took refuge in his home, reflected indecisively on the evening, and went to bed without jotting down any notes. Although Andrew rarely took notes, he regretted that he could not detail to the mayor's satisfaction exactly what was said at Hugh's. Later in the evening, he had spent time back home revisiting the conversation. Politics was a life tough on memories of every conversation. For once, Andrew wished he had a clearer recollection of his time at the Parks' home. He felt uneasy about Hugh for the first time. He went over every nuance of their conversations to dig deeper into Hugh's questioning. Undoubtedly, Hugh wanted to understand the money trail. This was something new to Andrew, as he was always much more interested in politics. Was he missing something? He thought so but had no idea what it might be.

WASHINGTON DC

Fall 2008

Myron was having difficulty determining what was coincidental and what was deliberate, as Hugh was turning out to be a more skillful rogue operator than originally appreciated. He phoned Todd while reading his latest briefing note and offered his take on Hugh.

"He might be thinking he can run in and out of Juan's life, snatching a satchel of money on the way through. Thugs like Juan who dress expensively and enjoy public respectability do not appreciate hit-and-run characters. From what I've observed over the years, they operate in tightly knit circles where outsiders are vetted for months before any deals happen. Hugh better be careful in making deals with the likes of Juan."

Todd agreed. "That might explain why Hugh keeps pushing the wind turbines. It gives him cash while he waits for a big score with Juan. Not a stupid person. I'm watching too many unknown places to find out all I need to know. Take Canada, for example; they don't have anything like the DEA up there, and their national police force is in a tug-of-war with a civilian security office."

"I know. Our embassy despairs of it. They don't know who to talk to when there's something serious on the table. Our guy is on his way out and Canada's prime minister is a pipsqueak. There is one option if you have a message for me to deliver."

Todd was intrigued. "Who? I have to know more to tailor the message so he understands it."

"Well, for starters, it's a she. I mentioned Shelly Spicer to you some time ago. We've been talking regularly about this file and the angle that draws in her country. She's officially tucked away in Canada's embassy on Pennsylvania Avenue as a representative of their finance department, which runs the show back in Ottawa. Shelly is senior, down-to-earth, and spent part of her career working on security issues for her government. She's great, straightforward— could be from Fargo, North Dakota."

Todd had heard enough. "Alright. Here's the story. Tell Ms. Spicer that her life is getting more complicated. We've uncovered a major Canadian investor in a fund that's supporting international drug and human cargo trade stretching from northern Mexico into western Canada. We've intercepted communication about a sleeping terrorist cell here in North America getting their hands on rockets to ship to either North Africa or the Middle East. We don't yet know the exact destination. For reasons we don't understand at all, the Canadian city, Winnipeg, has become a hub of activity relevant to our surveillance mandate. We need more local info right away. Will she get it?"

"I'll talk to her tomorrow to up the ante. She'll decide on her own what to do next. My guess is that all hell will break out in Ottawa, their tiny, quiet capital city. It might take a while, with how clued out they are about security issues. To call them complacent is a grand understatement. Sit back and enjoy the fireworks. In the meantime, I'll talk to you no later than Friday."

After they hung up, Myron poured a glass of water and returned to Todd's briefing note.

"We have gradually been increasing our surveillance activities, as we fear Hugh Parks might enable Juan Moreno to establish a cell here in the States. Yesterday I called a brief meeting between his headquarters' team and one of our best listeners in Germany, Wolfgang Patsch.

According to Wolfgang, our listener in Germany, there was not much new on Juan's file. He had heard no more calls from Parks. We've been thinking that a brief family call to Juan from Angel might have alluded to Parks, but we're not at all certain.

I asked Wolfgang to elaborate. 'Nothing much really. Just the son boasting, that fellow shouldn't call you again. I'm meeting him in a month when I go to America and will make sure that he doesn't get in our way.' For the rest of the brief call, they talked about watching a televised football match at home after a light dinner earlier than normal. Juan usually likes to get out around town as much as possible so that nobody thinks he's trapped in Spain.

I brought the meeting back into focus by tasking everyone to find out more about Mr. Parks and to start sending e-mails with every tidbit they could find.

It turns out that Parks is a local con-artist who takes advantage of unsophisticated investors. Parks is known to the Canadian securities enforcers, but nobody is available these days to help us, as they're all working hard assisting each other with the banking scandals. Right now Parks is in the middle of a business venture to sell dubious environmental equipment to the trucking industry. Although we originally thought he'd be easy to catch as a huckster breaking several laws, somehow his mayor has been brought in and wants to sell the wind turbines around the world. It's given this fellow instant credibility in Winnipeg, and everyone has forgiven him for past failures. Your Canadian friend has been instrumental in explaining all of this to me; as a further precaution, I've put a higher level of alert than we normally have for the border crossings just south of Winnipeg.

The next day, Wolfgang listened in when the young Moreno left a message for Parks. Below is the entire exchange.

A.M.: "Hi, this is Angel Moreno. I think you've met my dad Juan, who asked me to call you and to establish a more active line of communication. My dad is into a very intense week of meetings out of the city. He really wants the two of us to connect so we can know a little more about your businesses. Look forward to hearing from you. I'll call you again in the morning."

Sharply at 9:00 a.m. the next morning, Winnipeg time, Angel began the call using his best Ivy League school English with a pleasant Spanish accent to his advantage. Wolfgang describes him as sounding young and rather sure-footed, as one might expect from the boss' son. He also shows exceptional maturity in dealing confidently with the unknown North American whom Juan had turned over to him.

A.M.: "I hear you met my dad in South Africa. Are you in the same industry?" He jumped right into the business at hand with a loaded question that required a careful answer.

H.P.: "I'm an investment manager working on several projects, including one in transportation. That's how we began talking at our hotel bar. Your dad seemed a little regretful that he'd never extended his business into North America. That certainly piqued my interest. When I came back here, I asked my director of research to profile your industry and highlight a few options for Juan. I phoned your dad to let him know that the full research report would soon be completed."

A.M.: "My father instructed me to take over all communications with you. He's long thought that any expansion into North America would be the mission of the next generation, headed up by me. That's why I went to college in the States at Brown and why I stay in touch with my friends over there. It's a good network, lots of reliable connections. How about you,

Hugh? What's your Canadian university done for you? Has it given you all the right people to network with as Americans like to do?"

Wolfgang reported in a side note that he could feel Parks' embarrassment, as he probably did not have a degree—notwithstanding many years of hanging out on campuses. As expected, when confronted with such inconvenient facts, any con moves on to a new topic.

H.P.: "Our investment firm always starts with a solid proprietary research paper; then we ask questions in a variety of personal and professional networks, depending on the sector of the economy, to test our investment ideas. We are good at calculating where money can be made. Works well, most of the time, which is all any of us can ask."

A.M.: "I don't understand. Your networks are not based on your college? Surely your business school has helped you."

H.P. (sounding desperate): "Of course, of course, I always golf in the Carolinas and sail off the East Coast with my buddies. We stay in touch, and occasionally we're in deals together. Yet my real work turns out to be with the owners of small businesses. These owners, now in their sixties, are looking for a solid transaction as a way out of their enterprises. Few of them went to college; they left it for their kids who hate the businesses that pay their way. In some cases, we end up phoning engineering schools in boring towns and cities where guys know their work world inside out. Not everyone loves truck drivers, for example." Listeners picked up and noted the uncertainty in his voice.

Apparently A.M. got the message from Parks and moved on to another topic.

A.M.: "Sounds reasonable. I'll organize a trip in about a month. I'll send you a draft itinerary, and we can figure out where to meet. I'm sure you're in New York and Chicago on business frequently."

H.P.: "Mostly Chicago. Every month. That will work best for me."

A.M.: "Chicago it will be, in a month. Look forward to meeting you there. If it's not too difficult, e-mail me a copy of your resume and a profile of your investment firm. Here's my address. I'll send you more details of my trip once I have your e-mail address."

"What is this all about?" Myron asked Todd during their second call. They went back and forth considering various options until Myron was reassured that Todd had everything under control. His instructions were to spend the next three weeks preparing a watch over both Angel Moreno and Hugh Parks and increasing surveillance once the DEA had ferreted out Angel's itinerary. Although Todd decided not to send an agent to follow Angel to each individual meeting, Myron wanted to know what he was doing and whom he was seeing. Reports were to be phoned in immediately to Todd so that he could judge the level of coverage required that day. Most of the trip appeared to be innocuous, a young man showing his dad that he could succeed by growing the business in America. Nothing was wrong with that. Again, the most difficult character was Parks, as they had yet to fit him into the overall schema. If he were simply there to hustle up a new buyer for wind turbines, they could live with that and pretty much ignore him, but if he was snooping around to find bigger action, they were concerned about where that might lead.

With their plan settled, Myron and Todd became more reflective of the two men they were watching. They bandied about several scenarios until Myron ended the conversation with a final observation.

"Both fellows would have spent time after this initial call assessing where they might fit into each other's lives. The young Moreno thinks like a rookie: he has time to explore all contacts and will later tell his dad what might work in America. He has the luxury of an experienced family business to back him up in case he misjudges someone. There's no way he's being left out in the cold unprotected. Parks, by contrast, has no such support; he is forced to read the situation accurately and immediately make up his mind whether he can deliver a winning proposition to the Moreno family. He knows he will not grab the role of dealmaker unless something falls into his lap, and soon. Yet he instinctively understands that one good play with this Spanish family is far more valuable than anything he's doing in Winnipeg. Our job is to find out what that play might be the same moment he does. Good night, Todd."

PHILADELPHIA, PENNSYLVANIA

Fall 2008

Lunch would be a good start with Angel, thought Brent. He understood how much his school chum enjoyed the American-style business lunch with its fancy restaurants and oversized portions. Neither drank at midday, but even without that indulgence, Angel had coached his colleagues on the European way of eating late lunches. Talking a mile a minute and making the occasional deal was far superior to grabbing a Subway sandwich. The real benefit, he said with a grin, was returning to the office only after the most hectic time of the American workday had passed. More leisurely calls to others would be followed by a few preparations for the next morning and then off for an evening with friends or family. This Spanish lifestyle was obviously passed down in Angel's family from one generation to the next. Brent wondered if all Europe's moneyed people spent their days in the same fashion. It was one of those rhetorical questions he would never be able to answer from personal experience.

Their lunch was to begin promptly at 1:30, so the young Brent surprised his workmates, who rarely took a two-hour lunch break and never in the middle of the afternoon, with his jaunty and carefree departure. Angel's lifestyle preferences had prevailed, and Brent was delighted when his old classmate was shown to their table at Davio's, a second-floor, high-ceilinged sophisticated establishment located on South 17th Street across from the Sofitel Hotel where Angel was staying.

They gossiped about others Angel had visited since his late August arrival, after his family's annual summer retreat to the Ritz Carlton Abama Gold and Spa Resort in Tenerife, Canary Islands. He had already visited New York, Boston, and Washington, where other fellow graduates were establishing their careers. Not everyone was doing well; hard times in many financial institutions had taken their toll on even the best and brightest of their generation. Angel spoke passionately about how difficult it was for their friends.

"I was pleasantly surprised to hear how many have found their likely marriage partners, but the reality is that few are anywhere near settling into family life. It's both too early in their careers and too unsettling in the economic malaise here in America. The idea of marrying a lover, building a career, buying a house, and having a family is fast disappearing among our friends for all the wrong reasons. They can't find traction in the job market. It's very, very sad."

It was hard at the outset for both Brent and Angel to keep the conversation optimistic and light with so many concerns, ranging from the endless number of business failures to the large, unrelenting government debt that was accumulating. Brent decided to change the subject and thought the best tactic was to engage Angel in talking about his own life.

When Angel spoke defensively about his lack of accomplishments at Brown, Brent offered a gentle reminder of how much he was admired. "You were not, by any means, ignored at Brown. It's just that no one thought they would see much of you after school. You were always reticent to talk about your family. I think you also knew that operating a trucking company would be considered déclassé at our school. Everyone wanted to be investment bankers, lawyers in big metropolitan firms, lobbyists learning their trade by working for a senator from their home state, or university professors, if they could find a very wealthy partner to support them.

"It dawned on me the other day," Brent continued, "that all this excitement about succeeding in one of America's great eastern seaboard cities is pale in comparison to the potential of your life in Madrid. Nothing overstated, but everything perfect. Like right now: No cell phone on the table, just a small notebook holding a modest Mont Blanc pen!" They both chuckled. Angel thanked him for such a complimentary view of his life, but as he had many questions about Aird Investments, it was his turn to shift the conversation.

"Well, your assessment is ironic, as I came on this trip to scout a new life for myself on this side of the Atlantic. I have to convince my dad that this is doable and in the best interest of our family. Seems like all I do is ask questions of everyone I meet; it's your turn now. What does your firm do? How does Aird raise its funds? What is the fee schedule? What share can you get in a deal? Do the investors actually control the investment decisions? Who creates the opportunities to make such high returns? How do they consistently make a profit? Are there ways to end up in serious trouble? Are you making a pile of money?"

Brent was taken aback by Angel's barrage of questions. He did not respond immediately, as he speculated that Angel might be looking into Aird Investments as a solid place for some of their Spanish assets. Brent recognized his opportunity and put himself into play. "In answer to your subtle but most important question for me personally, it would take bringing in an investor like you for me to make big money."

Angel didn't miss a beat. "So where do we start, and how do we make you a hero?"

Brent chuckled. He barely had time to eat the oversized veal chop, let alone the mountain of sweet potato fries, while answering all these questions, yet Angel switched topics again. "I love lunches like this. It's the only country I know where you are expected to eat so much steak at midday along with huge portions of everything else you order. Afterward, you're supposed to act like a well-fed gladiator and go back to the office energized for another deal. You can bet that I'll react differently. When I finish a huge lunch like this, I want to go back to the hotel for a nap."

They both laughed at their different approaches. Angel then brought their business discussion to a close. "This is one of the more thoughtful sessions I've had on this trip." He explained in vague terms why he was in the States without offering too many details about his family's business plans.

"I've been thinking about firms such as yours, Brent. We continue to rely on our European bankers, including those who have helped my dad for decades." Angel thought it best to skip over the Middle East banks that were the backbone of their financial dealings. "As you might imagine, they are well established. We could certainly continue to rely on them without much difficulty. However, that's not my plan. The Spanish banks, particularly the *cajas*, are too small. I'm out looking for something different, probably a bank or investment house that can help me expand what the family does.

"I would like a financial partner of a different sort. We aren't really looking for a business partner in Spain, as the family operates on its own with all of the deals and details of the business shared with almost no one outside the company. Here, it's different. I can see that. America is so dangerous. The laws, the characters, and the very size of the economy all conspire against family firms, whereas in Europe, generations of hard work that created wealth certainly are respected and honored. If you're not abusive, you are taken care of by the system. It's an easier life. That's why our governments are so different: socialists in the minds of Wall Street; caregivers in the minds of Europeans. We really don't care what's written in the *Wall Street Journal*. Business and governments are inclined to work together.

"I want to grow our business slowly in America. My dad wants me to spend my time looking at opportunities while absorbing how Americans think through business opportunities and problems."

Brent was excited. "I have an immediate, modest proposal for our working together."

Angel nodded encouragement, emboldening Brent to lay out a plan he had thought of only a few minutes ago.

Brent made his move, totally unrehearsed, but he wanted to seize the moment. "We have decided to force one of our companies to sell off a trucking operation. We don't think it fits with the management focus and style of the parent aerospace company. From what we can see, it doesn't lose money, but who knows what the crafty general manager is really doing with our trucks? He's built up a solid fleet, but this is not the market for selling trucking firms. Nobody is moving much by truck, as our big-city consumer markets are flat. Costs in transportation are high, and revenues volatile. It may not be the greatest time for our investors to sell, but for you, it could be a gem of an opportunity."

Angel's interest was definitely piqued. Brent moved to the next step.

"I'd like to arrange a day for you with the firm before you go back to Madrid. If you agree, I'll put together a package for you as a potential investor. That'll take a couple of days as well as management's permission. You'll be given a standard nondisclosure agreement to sign. If you can circle back in a week or ten days, I'll arrange meetings with the firm. That way you'll see how we operate. No obligations. It will give you something to talk to your dad about. Show him how hard you worked." He ended his pitch with a wink.

"Sounds good," Angel responded without any hesitation. "I'll e-mail you my itinerary so that you know where I am when you're ready to send me material. I'm staying here tonight, as I have an evening with Heather. Tomorrow I take the train back to New York. After that, my only obligation is to meet some fellow—I believe you might use the term "nincompoop"—in Chicago."

Brent looked puzzled.

Angel finished his story cryptically. "A Canadian, Hugh Parks, met my dad during a business trip in Africa and is attempting to parlay this brief encounter into a commercial deal. Sounds like a wacko." Brent noticed Angel's penchant for up-to-date American slang. "Dad told me to get him out of his life, permanently. That's the first priority of a son learning the family business: looking after the father. So I'm going to Chicago—that's where we're meeting."

Always the gentleman, Angel paid for lunch, waving off Brent, who saw this as an easy expense account item. After saying their good-byes at 3:30, Angel returned to his hotel to place his regular late afternoon call to his dad. He would discuss today's events as he did each day, only this time would be his first real opportunity in the family business. He followed this conversation with a nap to rest up for his old friend, the enticing Heather, who always prepared for a fun time with her European lover.

Sure enough, Heather was able to break away from the foundation well before her normal departure time of 6:30. No one in the office commented out loud, but they all guessed correctly the likely reason for the young woman's hurried departure. The phone calls from Angel that led to this date were exciting, as she'd had no other romantic companion since her days in Toronto. Heather anticipated that her parents, who still lived in Huntington, would not be enamored with the idea of a Spanish boyfriend whose family home was in Madrid. Yet, she had months before she needed to consider signaling anything to them—maybe never—so why pick a fight from the outset? Spending an evening with Angel intrigued her. She was always balancing a contradictory personality. On the one hand she was precocious and ambitious, while on the other, she was overly cautious. Mistakes as a single professional woman could cost her dearly. Despite her misgivings, she sat in the bar patiently waiting for Angel curious to see if this was to be her new life.

In contrast, Brent almost ran back to his office, eight blocks away, as exhilarated as he was by what had just transpired over lunch.

WINNIPEG, MANITOBA

Summer 2009

Arthur had always encouraged Annie to listen in on his calls so that he could show off his wheeling and dealing. His unspoken presumption was that he could outwit any of those he was bargaining with, from the academic power brokers at the Jacobs Foundation to the local politicians at city hall. He wanted Annie to appreciate just how good he was at winning skirmishes over the phone, right in front of her. He airily dismissed others as simple pretenders as he pointed out how baby boomers worked the political scene in the same corrupt fashion as their parents had, and their parents before them. He was particularly proud of staying beneath the radar so that no one caught on to his raging madness to destroy their careers and personal lives with his research findings.

Annie watched and listened, not so much in fascination, as he had hoped, but in an agitated emotional state that initially surprised even her. It would be months before the scene played itself out and her revised perception pulled her out of his orbit. Meanwhile, she was mesmerized by the changing character of a man totally unaware, from any perspective, of what was festering inside him.

Arthur had little appreciation for the fact that his personal commitments to a peaceful existence were made possible by his wholly protected lifestyle. Outside the original employment issues he negotiated to secure his teaching position, and later his tenure at the university, Arthur pretty much remained aloof from university politics. Others respected this anomaly if for no other reason than that it gave them more room to expand their own careers.

His brilliance in analyzing academic problems was largely possible due to his detachment from daily life. Nothing that he was committed to and spoke passionately about with Annie was garnered from deal brokering, political campaigning, or promoting urban change. Rather, it was borne out of his life as an observer. Sitting beside him as he thought out loud about this project, Annie began to appreciate that he was untested in moral matters and that he had little idea of what it took to make something good happen in the world. Although Annie struck Arthur as an inexperienced undergraduate whose judgment wasn't yet backed up by experience, that wasn't actually the case. She had been raised in a talkative family where dinner table conversations featured her dad and grandfather arguing about their gravel business. Most of it was boring, all about trucks, contracts, and making money the hard way to maintain the family. They lambasted local politicians who wanted free truckloads of gravel at the cottage— although, of course, they delivered it without the slightest complaint. It was from their nonstop conversations that Annie learned what happened in the real world of her family's business. Her dad taught her explicitly:

"Everyone steals something, even if it's the tiniest of things; nearly every-one gets away with it. Always be careful of these thieves. Pay attention to those who think they can get away with stealing small amounts and never be noticed. I've found them to be the most dangerous."

The first signal she caught of Arthur cutting corners happened when she overheard Clarke confront him directly about having changed his original approach. "You have your research hypothesis upside down; you should be arguing that new leaders—including, we think, the candidate Obama—are anxious to change the moral equation of modern politics. It's been so hard for them to succeed because of previous intransigent interests that have been nearly impossible to disperse. That's why I think, and so does this Foundation, there is little purity in Western political life. Our task is to show how frustrating it is to win critical ethical battles in this environment. New faces promising change are the most important dynamic today. We want narratives supporting this. We will fund your research project, and you can design it to accommodate this perspective. You would naturally be accepted as a full participant in eighteen to twenty-four months, with a significant budget consistent with our support for major academic participants. You should contact us when you have rewritten your proposal."

The quickness with which Arthur had modified his proposal, just as Professor Agger warned he would have to do, had alarmed and then informed Annie about her new academic friend. She had gauged their relationship in a different context from that point forward.

As Arthur wasn't normally available in the evenings, Annie often hung out with her peers, just as every undergraduate did, for endless evenings of chatter. People came and went as their own schedules and moods dictated. Some brought pizza; others could be depended on for beer and the occasional joint. She was dismissive about most of their conversations. Too many were the bravado of the young and untested. "I would never do that" was a refrain you could count on hearing any given evening. She was never challenging or offensive in these debates, but she privately believed they would all change and do the very things they were currently rejecting.

Young Annie had failed to notice any consequences from this same weakness during her first six months working with Arthur; she simply enjoyed his companionship and could feel herself growing right there beside him. She had her own mental mirror in which she checked herself out every morning; it was all good. Undermining this wholehearted commitment to her professor, however, was the fact that Annie lost her initial youthful innocence about his objectives. The longer she worked beside him, the more ambivalent she became about their relationship. His phone call with Clarke and the subsequent revisions to the proposal she helped draft caught her off guard. She paused emotionally to take stock: what did this step imply?

Annie was smart enough to absorb the obvious answer. When faced with an opportunity, Arthur took the same step everyone else did and moved into a more advantageous position. Was this the end of the world? Was he ruined forever? Certainly not, she reasoned, as such a small decision had little consequence, hurt no one, and probably would aid both of them.

On days when she didn't have to go to the university, Annie sat for hours at her apartment window viewing the world going by her as though she were a bystander. She wasn't picking a fight; she was just staying away, curious if she would feel this way all her life. She had shown strength in uprooting herself from home to move into Winnipeg. She nurtured a positive, committed friendship with her professor in a way that would have likely evaded most young women. The internship would be a highlight, for sure, but she was not confused about sticking around this campus.

He had irked her greatly over the summer as he had allowed himself to be drawn into the local political world—or perhaps more accurately, he had ingratiated himself into this small world of Byzantine intrigue. His former brooding about higher philosophical questions had been replaced by the more pedestrian "who does what to whom," with the occasional "why" added in. Arthur never excluded Annie in any fashion; he continued to talk at length about what was happening and always asked for her opinions and thoughts. Yet he had changed. He had once haughtily described newspaper reading to Brenda as a worthless waste of time. Now these characters in the local media were his new best friends. He always commented on what the mayor was doing—yet for the longest time,

Annie could not comprehend this interest in local trivia. She knew that the Jacobs Foundation had wanted the project to start in his hometown; that way he could get his story right before heading off to Europe. Annie had resolved not to fight him but to learn more about this strange man. She decided to probe Arthur without giving any clues about her own misgivings.

"Do you need any help with your interviews?" she asked one day after class.

"No, I think they are going okay."

"Should I be typing your notes and filing the results?"

"No, not yet."

"It would be good for me to meet some of these people, don't you think?"

He froze. In his new world, he knew that they would take one look at the young, engaging Annie and instantly believe she was a girlfriend, and he wasn't prepared to open himself up for such gossip.

"I was thinking of having you befriend Andrew in the mayor's office. He's a solid young guy. You could volunteer; find out more about their politics. What do you think?"

After a long and deliberate pause, Annie finally came back into the conversation, carefully choosing her words to mask her disgust.

"Classes are busy. I can easily help you here on campus from time to time. Going to city hall on a bus is a big deal for me, though. It chews up a lot of time. Maybe later, after the semester is completed; spending time at city hall will give me a break from your office ." She could be ruthless, but he was oblivious.

"Okay. Whatever suits you. See you Tuesday. We'll go for a cappuccino." He finished off the conversation absentmindedly.

"Sure." Annie was seething at his aloofness. She was furious. When she was alone later, she mimicked his tone: "What did Annie think? Did you have to ask, Professor Crawford? Really, you need an answer?" Annie vividly remembered when Arthur had first met that Hugh fellow one Sunday afternoon last spring and later described what a bad character he was. She had immediately supported this judgment when she'd heard Arthur's accounts backed up by her Aunt Susan's negative reaction to Hugh. She was, as a result, confused when she found out that Arthur and Hugh had lunched together recently at Sam and Benny's to talk about Hugh's views on local politics. Instead of the copious notes Arthur had normally taken during the first round of interviews, she found a single page underneath a couple of phone numbers, obviously scribbled down hurriedly several hours after their lunch meeting. To top it off, he agreed in late winter to act as an academic consultant to the very people he was supposedly studying. She couldn't help but be puzzled.

As Arthur repeated over and over, his job was to ingratiate himself to the leadership of Winnipeg politics by parading the pretentious research project so favored by his academic funder. After observing the decision-making process in the untidy world of urban politics, Arthur was not at all as sure-footed as he was supposedly trained to be about the gray areas where ambition met morality. Once Annie recognized and accepted what was happening to Arthur, she began to disengage. She was as unobtrusive on the way out as she was on the way in. Arthur never saw the changes; she listened as she always did.

Occasionally Arthur asked her opinion about the people he was dealing with, but more often than not, he left her out of his deliberations. It caught her eye that he was always thinking narrowly about which relationships should be pursued because he could imagine their tactical importance to the success of his project. That made him very reluctant to open up to Annie when he knew at the outset that he was about to make the wrong decision—yet persisted in doing so. Completely unaware that Annie was becoming increasingly disillusioned, Arthur retreated further from partaking in any reflective conversations by building walls around his new world.

After work and on weekends, Annie was experimenting with her free time, looking for different ways of expressing her inner spirit away from the busy, frantic world she disdained. She attended art classes and showed up frequently alone at an artist's emporium to finish her projects. It was new to her, and she wasn't particularly good at any media except glassware, a competence that would take her years to master. This talent, combined with her exceptional skills in writing short stories and a little poetry, was one Annie was cultivating so that it could later help her move seamlessly ahead to the next stage of life. The prospect of failure didn't occur to her.

She was nearing the end of her first year as a research assistant and was reflecting on her experience with Arthur. She obviously had misgivings after seeing his behavior up close but was reluctant to abandon him; after all, it was hard to find such a good position on campus. She concluded that the only approach to maintaining warmth in the cramped atmosphere of the professor's disorganized office was for her to ask him endless questions about his life.

In that spirit one afternoon she questioned his decision to teach university. "When did you first know you needed the sanctuary of a post at a university?" she asked Arthur

"I only vaguely thought about it in those terms," he answered her evasively trying to anticipate where she was taking this conversation. "I was in my mid-twenties largely consumed by a romantic notion of spending my life thinking of world issues. I honestly never pursued any other career. It never crossed my mind that there might be another place with the opportunity to think about whatever problems caught my attention. Once I settled in here, however, I realized that university life was actually structured to block one's freedom to think. Academic friends fret that they don't know what they should be thinking about or which big questions should govern what they do, every day, all day long. If you read European and Middle Eastern history, say from about a thousand years ago, it was the mission of wealthy, learned, and powerful men to establish libraries, monasteries, and publishing houses that afforded good philosophy thinkers an escape from the authoritarian recklessness of the Catholic Church. Our goal here is not that noble, but we at the university represent the freedom to think. Leaving my post for a bureaucratic one is a great threat to my opportunity to research what I want. That's why I chose to remain aloof."

"That's why I think so highly of you." Annie pushed herself to say the right thing. "You've exposed me to your world, where you've managed up to this point to retain your innocence while demanding a better place for my generation. You have truly inspired me." She ended sadly without any further elaboration. There was such purity in that explanation of his life that she began to cry. Soon she was sobbing uncontrollably; he did not understand it. She knew with absolute clarity that she was really crying for the lost soul of Arthur, the one now shunted to the corner of his existence while he pursued earthly pleasures. Annie realized that although Arthur had started out later than others, he, too, was responding to the many pent-up desires found in a more earthly life. Making himself more comfortable late in life was turning out to be a full-time commitment. Everyone else was on the sidelines.

That evening she made a short entry into her notebook.

"Where will my professor, whom I so admired when I started working in his office, fit into my life? He will certainly disappear physically by the end of August. Spiritually he will stay with me forever. If I were painting his picture, I would do it twice. The first would be a grand, colorful one of a thoughtful prince imparting wisdom to a young student. I would capture the beauty of his innocence. Beside it would be a smaller painting diminishing him by age and color. His clothing and the backdrop would be exquisite, but his face would not be serene. I will cherish the first and learn from the second. I will not leave him feeling victimized but rather will view him as the person who taught me the supreme lesson that will govern my life. I will be true to my belief in myself and to my commitment to be free, always and without impediment, to live the life I want to lead."

She kept this passage with all her writing that dated back a decade. Some stories could never be read again without embarrassment. This one, however, became a cornerstone.

WASHINGTON DC

Fall 2008

Out of the corner of his eye, Myron kept track of the afternoon baseball playoff game. While he had no particular love for the Minnesota Twins, he generally begged every franchise to beat the Yankees. Today was no exception. Since the New York team had a significant lead in the late innings, he was relieved to take a call from Todd. This diversion would also delay the tedious regular weekly meeting with inexperienced congressional aides who were mandated to prepare notes for their bosses on the latest hotspots in funny-sounding places.

Before Todd could utter a single word, Myron was well into expressing his fears about the Winnipeg caper as he despairingly called this case when talking about it in private. He sounded more jumpy than normal as he expressed his frustration. "Frankly, Todd, I'm lost. We simply don't have enough information on which to base any reasonable interpretation of these two characters. One's from a remote city in Canada's Midwest. The other is from Spain. We aren't sure why the Canadian, however you'd like to describe him, is on the road to meet the young Spanish scion about business opportunities in trucking, are we?"

When Todd hesitated, Myron took over the conversation. "I need you to brief me daily until the situation is clear enough for my reporting up to the congressional leadership. There are too many loose ends for my own comfort level. I'm up to speed about the Moreno boy's visit to Philadelphia but now you tell me that Parks has left Winnipeg and is crossing into the States today or tomorrow. Call me regularly and send send notes daily so I can assess for myself what dangers might lay ahead."

Todd didn't waste a minute. He was on the phone instructing agency people in Buffalo and Chicago about the importance of their surveillance operations during the next few days and the absolute need to stay in touch hourly with him.

Todd made his first of many calls before Myron left for his office "I have to bring you up to speed on the whereabouts of Moreno and Parks, as they will be meeting in Chicago tomorrow. Everything has been quiet with Angel's travels, as we had expected. Yet he recently called home to say that he was interested in purchasing a small West Coast trucking firm, mentioning no name. I know FedEx delivered a small package to the James Hotel in Chicago this morning; I had no idea what its contents were until Wolfgang's summary of the daily call home arrived a short time ago. Wolfgang's simple précis was: 'Son likes the look of a small trucking company. Father thought any purchase was years away. Conversation drifted to his imminent return.' Wolfgang noted that Angel was now planning to return to Philadelphia after his lunch with Parks to meet again with Brent Oliver, returning home later this week to Europe."

Todd repeated for Myron's benefit his instructions to his team: "We'll have to contact Aird Investments about their possibly bringing a transport company to market. Someone should call on Mr. Oliver next week after Angel leaves the country. Find out if one of our agents or researchers knows people in Philly connected with the firm. Once we know the name of the company for sale, we'll assess what dangers lie ahead. In the meantime, for Chicago, ask for any agent floating around without any big sting scheduled in the next few days. Let's see if we can get close enough to find out more about this Hugh Parks, as he's now the wild card; maybe for the first time, we can learn what he's up to on our turf. Everyone: plan to send me daily activity reports."

Myron expressed his support for the Chicago operation. "This should keep us in the loop, but what do you make of Parks showing up in Chicago? I know we expected him, but what's the latest scoop? Fill in all of the details, as my political bosses take a special interest in the threat posed by Canadians wandering around as if it's their country, free of charge."

Todd acknowledged Myron's request, looked over his notes, changed some minor points, and sent over his detailed brief outlining the past week in the life of Parks.

"It was a busy week for this Canadian. After he had settled on a date for meeting Angel in Chicago, he spent considerable time planning his trip to the States. As conditions for border crossings become more stringent, we're told that Parks apparently prepares for every contingency by, for example, rehearsing his answers to ease his crossing the bridge into Buffalo. Homeland Security is typically not interested in the likes of Parks, but any hint that he was up to no good would fetch a team to go over his rental car and browse through all of his personal belongings. He definitely does not want that to happen.

"He inherited, so to speak, a comfortable condo in Buffalo several years ago when he was tangled up with a sophisticated smuggling gang involved in crimes from Canada down to Mexico. He learned a few habits, such as crossing borders safely, that still come in handy. Parks was obviously also taught how to stay invisible, sometimes for years at a time. But before I tell you more of his peculiar trip from Buffalo to Chicago, I'm attaching a copy of a report on his activities from our local agents there. As soon as you read this, call me back, and we'll continue this saga."

It took Myron a few minutes to digest the implications of the agency report now in front of him. While Angel was busily preparing his trip to the States by openly talking to friends and potential business associates, it appeared that the more important activity was Hugh's careful preparation for covering his reasons for crossing into the States at Buffalo.

Myron suddenly turned the sound of CNN commentators down as he needed to concentrate. To his way of thinking, Hugh had enjoyed a good couple of months of making money. By spending the last several weeks fixing city hall, selling a few more wind turbines, and taking several advances from the second wave of investors, he was sure that Hugh thought he had stumbled onto something that could run a long time. According to conversations that were wiretapped, Hugh was suggesting to close associates that his greatest achievement in many years was tracking down the story about a cache of unused rockets. Yes, they had been manufactured in Winnipeg, as Bertie had described, and there were storage facilities both right there and in Wichita, Kansas, where he would do a quick reconnaissance on his way to Chicago. Hugh spent time on the internet finding universities that boasted about their rocket propulsion courses, which gave him several clues about the rather secretive world of military rockets. He found one campus, Niagara Regional University, close to his Buffalo condo and made arrangements to visit.

Hugh had huddled with Stomper before he left Winnipeg; this conversation was closely monitored by Canadian authorities who had been pushed through Shelly's clandestine activities to monitor Hugh more closely.

The coverage was spotty, as the connections between Hugh and locally powerful leaders, including the police department, made it tricky for the national security operatives to record much without offending those whose cooperation was essential on other pressing files. This time one agent was close enough in Bar Italia to capture the conversation between their two targets. Myron read the transcript carefully and more than once, looking for clues as to what was happening in Canada. It featured a damming conversation between Hugh and Stomper that was included in this backgrounder:

Parks: "I have no idea what I want to propose to Angel. He sounds like my junior probably by twenty-five to thirty years, as he's a recent university graduate about five or six years older than my Emma. Juan struck me as a guy who knows how to make a deal and when to turn a blind eye. Juan is out of my league, but my 'hail Mary' play might just produce some cash. More importantly, there's no doubt our Bison Board was most impressed when your marketing plan included a profile of Juan's company along with the detailed marketing overlay of the European and Middle East trucking industry. We now have to put in motion a strategy that won't arouse the curiosity of any astute watchers, at home or elsewhere."

(Of course, if he had looked across the café, he would have had his answer: The antiterrorist police were already curious enough to have him under surveillance. They had caught every word.)

Stomper: "I also have no thoughts about what you can put forward to Angel directly or to Juan indirectly when you meet in Chicago. I should prepare a one-page summary so you can give him a proposal to see if they will buy fifty of our wind turbines. The beauty of this is that it will show our investors how serious we are about making them some real coin. This will impress them. If nothing happens by way of follow-up, that's life. Your success will be measured by the commitment this Angel makes to host a second meeting in Madrid. Doesn't matter if it's real. You will be able to say that's what Angel promised. One of us will travel to Europe as a marketing ploy to keep everyone happy."

Parks: "Sounds good to me. I admire your ability to build a good story around an absolute lie. You have amazing skills." The transcript noted their laughter, and as Hugh stood up to leave, Stomper asked him to sit back down.

Stomper: "I want to pursue the other story about the rockets. I've picked up your interest in Bertie's story. From what I gather, you've found rockets in our city stored by the same company that owns a facility in Wichita. What's the scoop here?"

Hugh: "I have no idea at all. I just think it's interesting that we found the rockets that our friend, the in-house mad scientist, briefly described in passing. My question is: 'since they exist, how do we make a buck?' Before my meeting in Chicago, I'll check out Wichita."

Myron was back on the phone with Todd. "I've read what you sent. Take me through the next steps. I have to know every detail since this character is now wandering around our country. What a nightmare!"

Todd calmly continued by bringing him up to speed on recent activities. "We picked up the trail when Parks left home a week before the scheduled Chicago meeting, flew to Toronto, and crossed into the United States at Buffalo. It was definitely a roundabout route, but Parks had a clear agenda and was very methodical in its execution. He brought with him a considerable sum of cash to leave at his apartment, as was his habit. When asked why he was entering the States, he joked with the border guard that he was a sucker for NHL exhibition games even in early September.

"The scanning of his license plate announced his arrival in the States; that news was relayed to our waiting DEA agent, who had been tipped off by Hertz after Parks had left its Toronto's Pearson Airport rental office. We followed Hugh to his condo, not the hockey game, which was perfect for us. From that moment on, Parks was there illegally for giving Homeland Security false information about his trip. Our agent passed the address back to our operations people, who were to find more details the next day. If we had to enter his apartment, we had our excuse—he should have returned to Canada after the hockey game.

"The three-story walk-up, converted from a warehouse into condos, is twenty blocks from the HSBC Arena. We've been interviewing as many people as possible to learn more about this condo. Parks apparently disappears from Winnipeg and ends up in his Buffalo condo when the pressure is on because of a deal gone sour. It's best to think of it as his hiding place. He tells his cronies that he has a great apartment in New York; all of his buddies naturally assume he means New York City. Whenever they ask to stay there, Hugh tells them he's sorry, but a friend from an important Ecuador oil project or an African mining operation recently arrived in the States and needed a place to stay. Situated fifteen minutes from the Canadian border, the Buffalo unit was originally purchased by criminal friends who have since disappeared from his life, leaving him with the keys. We're not sure why, but we're doing our best to find his connections in this country. They're more extensive than we first thought.

"A light on the third floor turned on just after Parks entered the locked building. No guarantee, but it was a start for the agent below guessing where he was going. Once inside his residence, Hugh took out a few cryptic notes that wouldn't make any sense to a casual reader who happened upon them. He turned on the small, old computer that he kept there to make the place look occupied and opened up Office Word, where he typed out his two proposals based on the few handwritten notes he allowed himself to carry into the States. The first described the wind turbine project for Angel, using most of the page to introduce the inventor, the scientific premise, the production facility, and the implementation of the prototype project back home as a civic green plan initiative. He used the bottom quarter to present a suggested list price based on volumes, as well as his own contact information for Moreno's engineering department.

"He must have printed out extra copies and typed out the second document, also to be presented on a single page. He didn't risk carrying the papers across the border; hence, he had to stop at the Buffalo condominium before heading to Chicago.

"The document we found described he existence of rockets available for delivery overseas within a month of an order, to be paid in American dollars in advance. Each one was originally sold by the manufacturer for $15,000 plus the costs for explosive devises but Hugh was smart enough not to name his price-yet. The specifications were detailed with test results from previous launches suggesting the range and accuracy. It was a clever document, as there was neither price nor any suggestion of how the rockets could be used. Instead of his usual business coordinates, he included his American cell number and a Hotmail address.

"We think he then printed out a copy, looked it over, and realized that he shouldn't list his cell number at this point. He threw it into a waste basket, redid it, printed it out, found an envelope, folded the document, put it in the envelope, and sealed it. Done, he thought.

"The next morning, we watched as he went out and ran his errands, making sure that he stopped and talked with the few who knew him; he included a visit to the First Niagara Bank on Fountain Plaza to use his safety deposit box. Over coffee at a Tim Hortons, he read the *Buffalo News* to check the scoring details and attendance figures of the exhibition hockey game that he'd supposedly watched. After that, he drove toward the campus of the Niagara Regional University, where he had arranged to meet the dean of engineering. On the way, he stopped by O'Connell's Clothing to buy a few items appropriate for a university visit.

"Parks was carefully exploring the university's interest in surplus rockets, positioning himself as the facilitator of a possible gift for its program. The university, anxious because of the region's economic uncertainty, was aggressively positioning itself as a leader in new engine technology, perhaps because of the early presence of the auto industry in and around Buffalo. They loved the idea of receiving the rockets as a gift, although they found Parks' vagueness slightly unsettling. Parks' objective was to secure an address for shipping rockets out of Winnipeg without causing too much suspicion.

"By late afternoon, our agent recorded that Parks was back in the condo and out again with a small suitcase the next morning at 4:30 a.m. Our Buffalo agent confirmed that Parks had arrived at the airport. We initially thought he was departing a day early on a cheap flight for his Chicago meeting. Soon after he called in, our agent headed back to the condo to look through the place and let us know what he found. It took an hour or so to get in, but it was worth the effort. Since Parks had decided to leave his condo as though he were still in Buffalo, table lamps and the computer were left on. Our agent traced his itinerary through a Google travel website left open, and much to his surprise he found that we had a problem. Overnight, Parks had made airline reservations, first at 6 a.m. from Buffalo to Chicago and then on a separate booking, from Chicago to Wichita. So the Canadian information was correct; we should have suspected this side trip to Kansas. After searching for Bertie's fabled rocket storage facility in Kansas during the afternoon, he was to fly back to Chicago and stay at an airport hotel close to O'Hare. In the morning he would travel into Chicago on the 'L' for his lunch meeting with Angel. Once I heard this, I arranged for our people to be in Wichita to watch Parks.

As much as Myron wanted to continue this briefing, it was time to return to his tight schedule. He asked Todd to send more documents over for his late night reading. Todd spent the next several hours checking every detail as it was dawning on him that Myron's fretting meant that this file was front and center among very senior but invisible decision makers.

His team had done a splendid job of keeping track of Parks despite his heading off to Kansas. The first real clues were not from his computer, as Parks was smart enough to delete whatever he was doing as soon as he finished his work. But Todd's agent rifled through the wastebasket which appeared to be filled with flyers, with one exception—a note describing the rockets they overheard being discussed back in Winnipeg, along with Parks' contact information. Todd followed up with a quick call to confirm as many fine points as possible. He questioned in a staccato fashion:

"You have found a page describing twenty rockets available—are they for sale?"

"Doesn't really say that."

"Is that the only copy? You think he's distributing it to terrorist groups around the world?"

"Impossible to tell. Might be something else on the computer, but, no, I didn't find anything else."

"Are his travel plans for real? Is he on his way to Chicago and Wichita?"

"I confirmed the itinerary this morning. I also saw a bill for his American cell by his bed. We can get the details from the service provider."

"We better increase our coverage starting this afternoon."

Todd called a late morning Washington staff meeting to make sure his immediate reports appreciated the implications of what was found in Buffalo. He spoke at length to open the session.

"This guy is hawking rockets to the Moreno family right here in our country! Unbelievable. I'd like to beat the crap out of him right now! I want to know more about this guy by tomorrow at noon. We're missing something. When we meet next, we'd better include Wolfgang so that our European station understands what we are listening for in Spain. Let's plan for the day after tomorrow, when we have all of our reports. Whether Parks knows it or not, he's got our attention, that's for sure."

Two agents picked up the trail in Wichita as soon as Parks landed. Parks was watched while he sat in his rental car outside the Eagle Aerospace complex, which is where Bertie told him to anchor his search. Since the inventor was constantly scheming of how best to screw Hugh, this time by passing on the wrong directions to Stomper. Not surprisingly, with his ultimate goal of thwarting and embarrassing Hugh, his map gave Hugh few clues keeping in mind how the surrounding areas had changed so much since Bertie's last visit a few decades ago. He insisted that the practice range and storage facility was no more than a half-hour's drive away from the plant based on his understanding that local plant managers would never move newly built rockets very far down any back roads. Given Bertie's sketchy information about the plan's operations, Parks' best guess was that the rockets would be stored close by and wouldn't take him long to find.

It was difficult following Parks on the outskirts of town, as the flat roads and wide-open spaces of Kansas made it somewhat easy for an observant driver to see a car trailing him. But since the road system was laid out in a pragmatic way around large farms, there were not too many routes to patrol. The sign on the other side of the interstate intersection indicated that Wellington the next town was forty miles away. That would be his outside boundary.

Parks was followed as he drove for a half hour, counting the number of roads, large and small, that crossed this highway. The watchers fell into a pattern and kept an eye on him without actually seeing him for more than a few seconds at a time. They were in direct contact with Todd's office throughout the afternoon. It was simply reported that it was not necessary to go over all the details of Parks' search, but it was important to note that he was very methodical and intelligent in covering the most likely options.

In yet another note from Todd, Myron had it explained for his eyes only most clearly what was happening in the field.

"Our agents concluded that their target was looking for something, and not someone, but he didn't know where it was. The directions that he kept glancing at were obviously of no help. Their frustration was compounded by my

164   WINNIPEG, MANITOBA

decision not to pass on all the relevant information, as I was nervous the rocket story would be too good for agents on a search to keep quiet. Instead, I told them that the suspect was looking for drugs lost en route to Canada. I could hear their disbelieving conversations over the police radio. Here's a small exchange to give you a flavor of what the officers were saying as they watched Parks.

From the state policeman: "I can't think of much out there of interest to an outsider."

Our agent, the one who wasn't buying my drug story, responded. "I have a few questions. As far as you know, these are all active farms except one?"

"Right."

"This is true down both sides of this highway for at least three to five miles on either side?"

"Right."

"Your records show no major marijuana-growing operations out here?"

"Right. No prosecution, and as far as I can remember, no charges, no warnings, for years."

"Many troubles at the schools with drugs?"

"In the town, yes, like the whole country."

"Do you know how it's distributed?"

"Pretty hard to track down. Lots of people shop in Kansas City, so who knows what comes home. There are a few stories out of the Eagle Aerospace operations that truckers show up with cheap liquor and drugs from Mexico. Boy, that may be true, but how do you break it up? No government spies in there."

"Okay, so something out there interests our man. You don't think there are any drug operations. If something is hidden on a working farm, or if a regular farmer that everyone knows is living a secret life, then we're looking for a needle in a haystack. We agree?"

"Certainly agree with that."

Another state trooper working in the fully marked cruiser cut in. "Just talked to your man."

Everyone made startled noises. "Yeah, I wasn't planning to, but I pulled off the highway to get a good look at him as he was stopped on the side peering at a map. He waved me over. We talked for a minute. Gave me a story that he was searching out his family history. His dad apparently worked around here, probably at what is now the Eagle Aerospace facility. In those days, after the war, they modified rockets made up in Canada and tested them in the countryside. According to your man, his dad always told the family that he loved testing rockets and could personally beat back the Russians, even if they came over the North Pole! Usual Cold War boasting malarkey, he said. "It was a long story, but he wanted to see if this testing ever happened. Parks told me he stopped by the plant, and they knew nothing."

"He didn't stop there."

"I know that. I let him continue. He asked if I knew of any research facility out here. He thought it would be like a big garage, boarded up by now, away from traffic and homes with a fair-sized cement apron around the garage. 'Beats me,' I said. He thanked me again and drove off."

"It's the blind leading the blind," said the agent with frustration. "Where's he now?"

"Down the highway another mile, turn north. I have to go. I'm of no more use to you. Good luck," he said, signing off.

"Our agents got a break from an experienced local policeman several miles away, standing in the office beside the dispatcher; he took less than ten minutes to solve the puzzle. He guffawed that their quarry was practically having a picnic beside a boarded up rocket storage garage. He suggested that either Parks was searching for drugs he thought were being stashed there or else their Washington bosses had something else in mind. "Wait a few more moments and you'll have your story," were his sign off comments.

"Parks finally found the cache one road over at the rundown site that obviously hadn't been used in quite some time. Walking carefully, he managed enough of a peek into the dark storage building to confirm his prize rockets. Carefully, he left no evidence for the perfunctory monthly security visit. Again, he was as smart as any good petty thief in covering his tracks. But because he was no longer on his own, having moved into the big league of international terrorists, he didn't have the smarts to decipher who exactly had been watching him."

Todd listened to his agents reporting back late that afternoon. It was apparent that they were unhappy with being told half a story. He grumbled back but didn't apologize. He still needed complete control of this operation.

Back in his quiet apartment, with a west coast baseball game on his small screen television, Myron read over Todd's hastily written report on the last few days of following Parks. Myron thought the information provided was very thorough and didn't require much conversation. Together they knew full well that they were onto something of international consequence. They had agreed to keep their key people in the loop but cautioned them to remain silent. While it was indisputable that they could arrest Parks at any time and put him away for twenty to thirty years, it was an exercise that would yield precious little, though, so they had to be patient. They understood that spying was waiting and watching. Myron reminded Todd to send along the agency reports about the lunches in Chicago and Philadelphia as soon as he could.

CHICAGO, ILLINOIS

Fall 2008

Brent's package outlining the operations of the trucking division arrived at the ultra- modern James Hotel on East Ontario Street in Chicago a day before Angel did. He set aside time in the early morning to read Brent's report and to talk to his dad who given that it was already noon in Madrid was pre-occupied by other business affairs. It turned out that Juan didn't say much about Aird's proposal as he heard from European investment houses every week describing deals he should jump into without further thought. He brusquely told Angel that this idea would have to wait until his return. Juan was entirely fixated on Hugh and pushed his son to listen conscientiously so that he could later enhance their appreciation of this intruder.

He bluntly told his son. "This guy is still a problem that I want to go away. I know you like the idea of a green business but don't get carried away with this stranger. Find out all you can and fill me in when you come back." Finally he lightened up for a final joke to end the conversation. "In return, I'll protect you from your mom for the first week you're back. I'll tell her you're too tired and concerned about the business to meet new Spanish women."

Angel took advantage of his free time to take a boat trip on the cool, beautiful October morning to gaze at the city's famous architectural landmarks before meeting Hugh. The lunch actually went much better than either anticipated. Angel chose to eat at his hotel's restaurant, the well-respected David Burke's Primehouse located off the lobby. Both were better prepared as to what they would talk about than they had been during the initial call when Angel was simply fulfilling an obligation to his dad. He had read several articles about the greening of urban public policy and how it was impacting the trucking industry.

Spain itself was heavily invested in wind power, taking advantage of its geography and natural weather conditions. He was able to find a few engineers to talk to about Hugh's wind turbine, and they didn't laugh it off as a wild proposition.

"If it helps cut the cost of fuel, it would be great," added their chief dispatcher, thinking about their drivers who carried fresh produce and had to burn so much fuel to keep the trucks properly refrigerated traveling through the Middle East and southern Europe.

Hugh worked hard over their steaks to avoid portraying himself as a small-town clown. He asked questions about the European industry, showing he had read enough to not embarrass himself. They talked about North American politics as interested spectators and avoided venturing into anything too controversial. Despite the age difference, they enjoyed a congenial afternoon and went their separate ways with a deal in place. The understanding was that Hugh would ship five turbines over to the family's general manager once their engineering department gave the go ahead. They would exchange documents covering non-disclosure agreements about the technology, schedules for shipping, and other details normally covered at the outset of a new business arrangement.

As he headed for the door, Hugh pressed a sealed business envelope into Angel's hand.

"I realize your family is busy and that I misstepped originally in talking directly to your father about highways in North Africa. I know nothing about these things, as he spotted right away. I am perfectly happy to work with you, and my board will be as well. However, I have an unrelated matter to ask of Juan, as he struck me as one with exceptional business connections and judgment. A friend of mine came across a business opportunity in the Middle East, but he and I, as well as his associate, are unsure where to begin. If you can hand your father the letter, you can be sure I'll accept without question his assessment regarding our overture. I won't phone him or try to contact him. No matter what, we'll work together on the wind turbine. Okay?"

The letter disappeared into Angel's suit jacket pocket before they reached the doorway that took them back into the compact lobby. The exchange was completely missed by the local DEA agent who sat nearby munching on an oversized hamburger but who had been dreadfully bored by the lunch conversation. Hugh thanked Angel for hosting, as there was no confusion as to who could easily afford the meal, and strolled out of the hotel. The agent's bungling left a huge hole in Todd's analysis. What was the significance of the express package from Aird Investments? Was there nothing for Hugh in this delivery? If that was the case, then the story had divergent subplots.

Angel glanced at the letter up in his hotel room and decided it was none of his business. His dad might show anger over a stupid proposal from an untested and unknown source, but his anger over a violation of his privacy would be greater. Many times over the years, Angel had seen this annoyance surface when large envelopes arrived and everyone wanted them opened at the dinner table or together in the living room. Whatever was in those envelopes, the family never knew. This, too, would be delivered as is, to be opened by his father on his terms.

PHILADELPHIA, PENNSYLVANIA

Fall 2008

Angel flew back to Philadelphia late that afternoon, arriving in time for drinks and dinner with Heather at the funky Continental restaurant where they enjoyed each other's company. The next day he lunched at Aird Investments. Checking his luggage through the Sofitel Hotel left him with only a small satchel for his meeting and a book for reading later. The note for his dad was tucked away safely in his luggage to avoid the madness of America's hyperactive airport security. Angel had reviewed Brent's package a second time while Heather showered; the young Spaniard was ready for a serious discussion.

The surest sign of her worrying was Marsha's attendance at the lunch meeting with Angel at 1:30. Lunch was far beyond sandwiches, but it was modest by Wall Street standards. The point was to make Angel comfortable. He might be taking back to his dad a recommendation to the most ideal investment partner if he decided to build a business in North America. Aird, by putting together a deal with the trucking company, could emerge a winner. Although she suspected there would be no transaction for months, Marsha would parade this meeting in front of her investors as a sign of just how good she was.

"Your offer was sanitized of any problems," Angel joked as food was served, tapas-styled in an effort to impress her guest, in the alcove beside Marsha's office that was reserved for intimate, deal-making occasions. "My dad and his advisers are probably going to demur and read your report as a "wishful thinking but doesn't fit" proposal. They'll do so just out of principle, because you left out any discussion of problems. They think it's hard to find a business without its own difficulties. I'll tell them you got lucky."

"Yes, I can imagine," conceded Brent, "You thought it was cute but not convincing?"

Angel shrugged in response and to show Marsha that he had read the dossier carefully he engaged Brent in a spirited discourse about business strategies in international transportation. Their showing off didn't faze her in the least.

Brent's insightful report skipped over what Angel liked most, the all-important complementary cultural attachment—the language built into this deal. If he kept the general manager, the two of them could instantly speak in Spanish intimately about business matters. He'd know more in a week than Brent and Marsha had discovered over several months. Angel's family experienced enormous benefits by working in the several languages of their managers. It had helped them avoid trouble on distant highways since their employees understood the subtleties of everyday English, Spanish, Arabic, Italian, French, and German.

Angel was a long way from making a recommendation to his dad, but the meeting was significant for both him and Brent. His college friend was treating this as a coup, a chance to show early in his career that he had connections. Perhaps Brent could parlay today's success into drawing more potential clients into Aird's boardroom. He knew that was about the only way to impress Marsha.

Brent's management team had agreed to sit in on this meeting only because they were also looking for a quick fix to their own problems. The morning investors' conference call had not gone well, especially when Marsha had reneged on her earlier commitment of regular quarterly distributions as per the investment deal.

"I doubt you'll see any cash for another year or so," she had told them matter-of-factly. "We've done better than most funds have over the last five years. Certainly better than the stock market. However, it is what it is for the present time." She tried but was unsuccessful in heading off criticism from the irate investors.

That exchange triggered an acrimonious review of Marsha's portfolio. Committee members led by Theodore had obviously done their homework and were under instruction to find out more. His own boss, surprised to hear how superficial past monthly calls had been, was demanding greater care in analyzing the viability of Marsha's strategy.

Marsha realized as the meeting deteriorated that she was now being put on the dreaded watch list by at least two of her investors. If they decided not to place money in her next fund, scheduled in a few months, it would be devastating and probably crippling for Aird Investments.

She had aggressively interrupted the naysayers and taunted them. "I like this robust discussion. It's the first time I've heard about your concerns. Hopefully, all of your issues have been raised here today. Now, we will be better able to keep you posted. If you agree, why don't we schedule weekly meetings? I'll send out agendas, going through the portfolio, one investment per meeting. If everyone is okay with that, I'll close this session."

Her investment group nodded with relief, while those on the phone signed off curtly. Marsha looked around, shrugged, stood up, and berated her staff. "Do something. Clean up this mess. Use your brains for once." She sent them upstairs to join in the meeting with Angel. It was all hands on deck, as she could feel the firm slipping into oblivion. Brent slogged his way through the whole presentation, as no one except Angel had read it beforehand; The Aird crew was still eating and worrying about the steps that would follow the morning fiasco. As he lamely finished up, Marsha quickly jumped in before she had a second fiasco.

"Thanks, Brent. Angel, you're our special guest, but I'd like to put you to work for five minutes. Could you describe your company as it now operates and where North America would fit into future plans? I must say, before you start that, although we have a significant footprint here and are knowledgeable about the trucking industry, we have absolutely no presence in Europe let alone the Middle East. When I read the excellent notes Brent prepared, I suddenly realized the deeper symmetry that might be possible. But I'm getting ahead of myself; please, Angel, tell us the story of your family." Marsha was on her game; it was easy to see how she raised hundreds of millions whenever it was her turn to perform. Today she was working hard.

Angel smiled as he began speaking. His years at Brown gave him a pretty good ear for the American salesman. She was good for sure, but he was not tricked into thinking that Marsha was his new best friend. No doubt his dad would enjoy besting her in a deal. Angel gave a rudimentary review of the family's business empire as he had been instructed by his dad. Since he really didn't know what was going on in Madrid, he could be forgiven for passing over the most salient details.

Brent walked him out after the meeting to a side street, where a waiting limo took him to the Philadelphia International Airport for his 6:40 p.m. flight back to Madrid.

Angel later told Heather that he had spent most of the overnight flight conjuring up reasons to return to America as soon as possible. He had to be careful, because his dad was both smart and cunning; he would spot an exaggerated tale in a second. Angel would advance his case prudently by suggesting he had the makings of a new team for the company. Their job was to build his father his first North American company. He put assignments against the names of his new contacts: Marsha, his financier; Brent, his advisor and dealmaker; Caesar, the trucking operator; Hugh, the visionary, networker, and jack of all trades, and, finally, his lovely Heather providing social and philanthropic introductions into the old Philadelphia establishment. He had no doubt that if his dad sent him back to America this would all come together very speedily.

WASHINGTON DC

Fall 2008

Todd had it confirmed for Myron that Hugh returned to Buffalo and left the next day for Canada. Nobody followed him across the border, but his check-in time with Hertz signaled he had stopped somewhere between Niagara Falls and the Pearson Airport for a couple of hours. Hugh was far too self-absorbed to notice that he had set off so many alarms in Washington. Once Todd's colleagues had digested the news about his pushing the sale of rockets to a family active in various weapons market, all eyes were on him. The DEA pulled together scads of information so that Todd had a pretty good idea of the old rocket stash in rural Kansas; agents were sent back to comb the area and were busy tracking details without disturbing the site. While improbable, it was not impossible that the rockets could be moved somewhere else, fixed up, and then used. It was a sobering finding for Todd's team.

The Buffalo DEA office had quickly moved to find out more about Hugh's apartment while he was away. The agency was curious to know whether this was a safe house for unknown terrorists slipping into the United States. In the context of the agency's daily work across America, the Parks file was quietly taking on the character of a high-priority terrorist plot. At some point, Todd recognized he would have to bring in other agencies to assist him, but he knew that the greatest mistake was moving too soon. "No good deed goes unpunished" was his mom's exhortation, so he decided to continue on his own for the time being.

Meanwhile, Hugh spent the late evening in his Buffalo apartment going over his Gmail account, checking out hockey scores and news about the Bills in case he ended up in any random conversations at Tim Hortons or the border. He changed the SIM card in his cell phone back to his Canadian number. On the flight home, he mulled over the likelihood of the Moreno family buying these rockets. He guessed yes, but if he were wrong, he'd use his access with Angel to entice Juan to buy several wind turbines. He still had no feel for Angel's relationship with his dad, and in the end, that would definitely be the most important consideration.

Over the following month, the regular morning phone calls between Myron and Todd took on an air of increasing tension, disturbing their long, warm relationship. Although Myron appreciated all the information presented by Todd, who passed along every detail he came across, the insecurities and anxieties festered by so many unknowns ate away at their friendship. Despite his being more junior, Todd actually was handling the pressure better than Myron. The former enjoyed the solitude of lone projects like this; the latter preferred the sharing of risk among colleagues. Sooner or later, they would have to make a move that was counterintuitive to their comfort levels with each other: sit down face-to-face and have a long, difficult chat.

WINNIPEG, MANITOBA

Fall, 2008

Arthur had seriously lost focus. He didn't know why he was so mixed up in local politics. He was in over his head decoding what was happening at city hall. He'd remained suspicious ever since the day he had stopped by to talk with Joanne and had seen Hugh and Andrew deep in conversation. Yet, instead of using this information to further his research, he had allowed his undisciplined curiosity to drag him into complicated and unrewarding circumstances. He was, simply put, bogged down.

Because Arthur didn't know what he really wanted out of his project, he had learned nothing from Hugh when there he was, sitting across from him in an empty living room. Most interviewers, who were skilled in their craft, would have drained Hugh of all relevant information. Instead, Hugh had shut the door on any likelihood that he would play the role of Arthur's informer. These days, Andrew was almost always too busy to talk. Setting aside her dislike of city hall types, Annie followed through with Arthur's request that she volunteer to work in the mayor's office every Friday morning as part of her internship. Andrew was thrilled to have such a good-looking young woman who cared about civic politics working there and asking questions about everything she saw or read. Arthur had to admit that with all he was involved in, he had left little time for private and creative thinking. Thus, Annie's Fridays at city hall were a welcome break, as in theory the time alone offered him time to bring his notes up-to-date and to prepare his foundation progress reports. It all sounded good when he explained this to Brenda and Annie, but in reality, he rarely wrote a single word. Instead he sat there. On a particularly bleak day, he wrote one word in his notebook: immobilized. Beside the phone was a pad with the words *Things to Do* stamped across the top. The page was blank. He was as close to depression as he had ever been, but he avoided acknowledging that analysis by portraying this stage of the project as one that demanded deep introspection about wading in uncharted academic waters. The truth was impossible to cajole out of him; this inertia practically begged for something to happen. A moment of transformation might propel Arthur into a better space, but he couldn't do it himself.

Despite Annie's dashing back and forth to city hall and running errands for both Arthur and Andrew, somehow she managed to retain her first-class academic marks. She hadn't been suffering the way Arthur had. With a deliberateness that was hidden beneath her easygoing demeanor, she quietly prepared for her future entrance into any grad school she wanted, although lately she was more certain that she should take a year off, far away from Winnipeg, before tackling another academic program.

Time was not on Arthur's side. Nothing was making sense. He reviewed his earlier writings again and again. They weren't much help, but he couldn't admit that to anyone, including Annie. He was stymied and unable to explain what he was watching. Besides, he had hardly made any notes in the past several weeks, a sure sign that he wasn't making any progress. To find out some new gossip, Arthur lazily called his student, Sheila, who could always be relied on for an honest update. She was not very helpful as by then she too was worried about his motives. She filled the uncomfortable silences with chatter about events already widely known by those following local politics.

"The mayor made sure that he had lined up all the players to approve his environment plan including the trucking project." she told him. "I know Mr. Parks comes by all the time to drop off concert tickets but I've no idea what else is discussed. The door is always closed. Jessica from the law firm, you know, the mayor's niece, apparently has dinner with Hugh and some of the councilors. All I know is that the truckers have everything they want as I've had to arrange all the approvals based on a list that Jessica's law firm sent me. Andrew gave Hugh the list of trucks, their business, and the timetable for installing these devices. We've long since issued the special permits and notified everyone concerned. A lot of guffaws when I went around with the news. What can I say? That's normal from what I call the 'men only' club around here."

They went on to discuss university life and agreed to get together so he could help in her studies.

The next day Arthur found himself on the phone responding to questions from Dr. Clarke, whose responsibilities included keeping track of the work of his international academic team. The only two signs of life that Clarke was sure of were the hiring of attractive young research assistants and applications for travel to far-off places. Although his persona was gentile, his questions were always direct and disturbing to those being called for updates.

"What's to report? I'm not sure," was Arthur's unguarded response to the unexpected caller. "I still can't break the code on local corruption. Plenty of small stuff, for sure, but nothing worth writing in a research paper."

Clarke continued the conversation with a broader observation on the state of politics. "When you watch Obama, you feel his passion for doing politics differently. His point of departure is his declaration that the current American political discourse excludes far too many working people. He argues that no matter what the subject—health care, financial institutions, national security, environmental calamities—nothing changes as those opposing reforms fight aggressively behind-the-scenes to make sure nothing happens to their interests. That was truly an important contribution to his narrative. Are you getting at the same point?"

Arthur picked up on this. "Here, the mayor never speaks out about issues of exclusion. Patterson talks only about specifics such as a tax freeze, a new business for the city, or an environmental project. Underneath it all is politics, as usual. The narrative isn't bold—it's stuck in the old style of politics and is diametrically opposed to Obama's."

"Very interesting," commented the director, who was working today from the Foundation's headquarters in Washington. "I'm sure you can show a solid understanding of the ethical dilemmas facing our incoming president and present us with a well-documented report on the continuing malaise on the local scene, not just in the United States but also in Canada. That is a significant finding. Canada becomes a proxy for all Western democracies. After less than six months on this project, you're making good progress. We were right to start out this way.

"Here's what I would suggest. I'm going to send you the names and contact information of our best project researchers here in the States and in Europe. Spend the next few months reading about them and their published studies. Check our website for their papers on this project, and talk with them. Send me a list of whom you want to visit, and arrange a trip just before your fall term starts next September. We'll pick up the tab for your travels. If you're ready for preliminary field interviews and first-hand research, I'll try to find a little more money so that an excellent student researcher of your choice gets the proper exposure away from the home campus.

"Keep up the good work, Professor Crawford. Stay in touch."

Arthur promised to keep at it and to submit a progress report sometime soon. When Annie came in, he lightheartedly repeated the phone conversation.

She was proud inasmuch as the Jacobs Foundation obviously thought highly of him. Almost as an aside, he mentioned the strong possibility of her, the student of his choice, traveling in August as well, to meet with these famous academics, all paid for by the Foundation. She was delighted. This might be the first step in her year away from Winnipeg.

The phone call served as a reminder to Arthur that he had to immediately turn his attention to the task of bringing greater clarity to his perplexing research problem. He no longer had stacks of computer printouts and research journals to bring him comfort. Learning about the pattern of local corruption was an on-the-job training exercise, and he had to master connecting the dots on his own. Nothing much was happening, and if it were, no one was talking even casually with him. He had no leads.

One fact that did catch his attention as he flipped through his pile of unsorted research material was an item from a local construction industry online publication about the recently launched Community Investment Trust. Jessica Brown was indeed the chair of the trust, confirming the story he and Annie had heard several times at city hall. According to the article, she was quoted saying she was pleased with the opportunity to listen to the community on behalf of the truckers. "Our fund will provide timely support to those seeking to improve local transportation in an environmentally friendly and innovative fashion."

Two questions struck Arthur as he immediately sent an e-mail to Andrew. "How is her mandate linked to the Mayor's green plan? Do you have any idea if some of her funds are from governments?" He never did get a response; this was another pivotal signal that he didn't catch.

Later at home, Arthur stood there at the edge of his garden, as he often did, with his Manhattan glass tipped slightly away as if he were about to dump half of it on some unsuspecting insect. Finally, his long brooding thoughts pushed him into action. Putting aside all caution, he again phoned Don Davidson at his law office.

His acquaintance answered briskly speaking in clipped tones, as if he were prepared to say good-bye before any real conversation could take place. Fearing he was about to be cut off, Arthur quickly asked for an introduction to Jessica.

"For you, of course, Arthur; as soon as I hang up, I'll ask Jessica to take the call. I've spoken casually to her before about your project, so she shouldn't be surprised to hear from you. Here's her direct phone number. All the best." The phone was back down in its cradle before Arthur finished saying thanks. He waited less than ten minutes before calling.

"Hi, Arthur, I was expecting this call, as our mutual friend Donald just spoke of you. It's not the first time he's mentioned your name. I think he's proud of your accomplishments at the university. How can I help you?" Jessica got right to the point.

Arthur weaved a credible story of his interest in demographic shifts. Many in Arthur Crawford's generation X wanted something different from city hall to deal with all the massive changes around them, but he couldn't yet put a finger on what they were looking for in their community leaders. That was the focus of his research. He abruptly shifted topics, as he soon bored of his own voice. "I noticed the recent announcement of your new role—congratulations!" he finished. "I wanted to ask if you had reached the point yet of identifying priority projects?"

"No," she answered. "Not yet. I could certainly use your help. I might even be able to find a stipend for your time. Profs always can use that, correct?"

Arthur couldn't find an answer right away.

"That's what I thought," she said. "How about lunch Thursday or Friday, and I'll take you through this and pick your brain."

"Uh, okay. Make it Friday."

"See you at noon at Sam and Benny's. I'll make the reservation. You show up with the ideas. Cheers."

Arthur answered her earlier question as he said his good-byes, a little quickly but entirely honestly. "This is indeed a world where additional income is welcomed. Look forward to meeting you Friday."

MADRID, SPAIN

Fall 2008

Angel's trip back home to Madrid was uneventful. He was a little surprised to be pulled aside at customs for a fuller discussion about his trip to America. Since he had never returned home as a business traveler, he shrugged off the inconvenience as a function of his new status.

"Just routine," added the supervisor, while watching his junior go through Angel's briefcase.

"We randomly pick out returning Spaniards to see what we might be missing in the outside world. It took us years, for example, to appreciate why there were so many repeat trips between our country and Venezuela until we found out more about the local Basque enclave over there. Briefcases were coming in loaded with U.S. dollars to help out the Basque terrorists fighting us here in Spain. Not that we think of you as a political terrorist, of course, but every once in a while we cast out our net randomly to see what we find."

"No problem," was Angel's short response.

The customs officer had finished his perfunctory search of his briefcase, and both officials had waved off any further search of his baggage. "It's your briefcase we're really interested in. Thanks for being courteous and welcome home."

Angel thought nothing more of this, as he knew a little of the customs world from many conversations with his father. What he didn't know was that the search was a result of a phone call placed by Todd himself to the Centro Superior de Información de la Defensa—CESID—with the request to pull Angel into the investigation room. He used the excuse that they were watching the money trail of those who might be financing domestic rebels. Even though the encounter was brief and the check of the leather briefcase casual, everything had been recorded on an overhead camera and would be transferred over to a DEA operative. Their analysts would examine Angel's reactions as well as the contents of the briefcase as captured by the camera and heard by the microphone. Every DEA analyst would later conclude that Angel appeared disinterested in the search and didn't seem to be laden down with suspicious papers from Hugh or anyone else.

Juan was excited to see Angel, as was his mother and the rest of the family. They had a late breakfast together to bring him back into the Madrid space, a ritual they had created when he returned home on visits from Brown. He would next shower and sleep for three or four hours and get together with his dad around 7:00 p.m. At that time, alone, they would quietly review the trip. He knew there would be several questions to answer.

Angel had taken the time on the long flight to prepare notes, as Juan demanded immediate and meticulous reviews of events to capture every nuance that would later disappear from memory. He had naturally tucked them between pages of his novel. His handwritten notes were easily missed during the border inspection.

"The only meetings of consequence are the two meetings with Aird Investments, where I was presented with an opportunity for our family to get started in America. We could probably close the deal sometime early next year. I'm not sure how much of my own time it will take over there, although it's safe to say definitely some.

"For the sake of argument," he suggested to his father, "I will make a positive recommendation that we move ahead, and on another day, you and your advisors in the company will take me through all the steps to make sure I can defend my recommendation for this investment in front of our bankers. I'll probably be on the floor begging for mercy, but let's give it a shot, at your convenience, of course."

His father chuckled, knowing how brutal these internal committee meetings had to be to protect the family's fortune. Not many proposals from the younger generation survived beyond this review process. Maybe, he thought, they should show the financial discipline of those before them.

"Not a bad idea. We'll give you a couple of days to rest and maybe another trip to America to look more closely. Tell your friend we will do our due diligence, reminding him, as I know you will, that this is your first independent assignment in the firm and there will be a rigorous review over here. We're a long way off from a decision, so you have to manage expectations so that he doesn't get hurt in his own firm. Okay?"

Angel, hardly able to contain his excitement, promised his dad the world. "I'll do whatever it takes to get a terrific proposal in front of you. If the team of advisors decides that, based on their experience, you should turn it down; I will respect your final decision. It makes no difference how badly I might want this as under no circumstances will I disrespect you or threaten to quit."

They hugged each other. Angel was preparing to leave, suddenly overcome by a wave of jetlag. Juan put up his hand to indicate another subject to discuss.

"Incidentally, your mom was very curious about your time with Heather. She remembered the name from your university days. How's she doing in Philadelphia?"

Angel had to look out the window to avoid blushing as he remembered the time with her at the Sofitel.

"She has a great job at a foundation working in the development office. She is becoming well connected throughout the state. I'm sure mom would love for me to hook up with a good Protestant girl from there. She could visit us every year."

Both were now laughing out loud at the prospect of taking her that news. Mom was definitely going to present her own short list of good Catholic Spanish women.

"A final question. Angel, your trip to Chicago, what did this fellow Hugh want to do with us?"

"I can explain one proposal. It's an environmental initiative and may not be crazy." Angel reviewed the concept of the wind turbines, the costs, and the potential savings for part of the fleet, mostly the large refrigerated trucks.

Juan listened disinterestedly albeit politely, as his son was doing him a big favor. He passed on offering an immediate response.

"Oh yeah, I also have this sealed envelope that I carried back at his request. I had it in a side pocket in my baggage; the customs guys never saw it, for what it's worth."

Juan was never sure afterward if the shock showed up in his face. The proposal was carefully worded so as not to embody a proper pitch, but clearly, two catchments of rockets were sitting inactive and forgotten in North America. They would be worth a fortune if they were brought over to Europe on their way to the Middle East or North Africa. He knew of three or four clients needing such weaponry immediately.

It was almost as if he was unaware of Angel still standing there. Juan quickly realized he had underestimated Hugh's cunning. Angel had deliberately been kept in the dark. If the note arrived opened, Juan would be forced automatically to walk; if the authorities had seen it and opened it themselves, Angel would survive their investigation. There was total deniability, no fingerprints, no DNA, nothing to hang Angel. At the same time, his son was smart enough to guess at some unknown danger and to stow away the envelope. It was good news on all fronts. Perhaps he could trust Parks after all.

Juan spoke to Angel more guardedly than usual. "Let's not lose track of this fellow. He's gone out of his way to personally encourage our interest in the environment. I appreciate that. He is also totally committed to working with you and promises to leave me alone. Tell him we're interested enough to lock up Europe for three years to give us a competitive advantage. Get him to arrange a visit from his scientist to meet our people in the next couple of months, and we'll show this contraption to the operations managers for review."

The meeting was over. Angel begged off dinner, using his exhaustion as a pretext. Both knew he probably was too burnt-out for his mother's questions. Her list could wait until Angel gathered his strength to fend her off once again.

Juan poured himself a Campari while he mulled over the letter, which he soon put away in the safe. This might work, he thought, envisioning the specter of assessing and buying a new business while securing the rockets. There would be no reason for Angel to know for months, maybe years, as both parents were determined to shield their only son from international intrigue for as long as possible.

OUTSKIRTS OF MADRID, SPAIN

Fall 2008

Moreno turned Parks' letter over to his most trusted lieutenant, who came into Madrid from London via Beirut. As far as anyone else knew, Martin Belanger was there to offer advice about the potential changes in the trucking business once the new Morocco-Algerian highway project was opened. He had an innocuous agenda in his coat pocket just in case he was stopped along the way by curious authorities. Belanger camouflaged his covert activities finding that by using his ongoing consulting contract as a government relations specialist, his way into Spain was always without any complications.

They went over the deal, questioning and detailing every angle, as the prospect of buying rockets in North America for delivery next summer somewhere in the Middle East or perhaps North Africa was intriguing. Yet the list of unknowns spooked both of them. Belanger's assignment would be to make it happen once they both had reached a comfort zone concerning their ability to manage the risks.

As they headed back to his Mercedes, Juan stopped to wrap up the conversation; he never spoke of these business dealings in front of his driver. His immediate anxiousness could be heard in his voice; he was embarking on a risky foray into America. Talking as forcibly as he dared with his longtime collaborator, he warned, "Martin, you'll have to take over all the preparations. I think you'll find the most reliable information will be close by you, as the manufacturer is still headquartered in London. If I remember correctly, you have an old friend from your days in Ireland who still works with them. My guess is that we'll find the propulsion system ready to go but the radar and munitions too old-fashioned; we both have people for that, as you know. We will help many friends if this all comes together. Twenty of these rockets fired rapidly will totally unnerve the enemy; more could easily tumble an unstable country even if the army is loyal. These will be worth a lot. Let's put aside what we will need to prepare properly for our first North American job; we'll find a way to put the cargo on a boat landing somewhere in the Mediterranean at a busy container port, and then our prized rockets will be off to war. We'll split the proceeds as always, keeping in mind that we may have a third partner with lots of money to bankroll our future operations. I've decided to test a newcomer."

The visitor waited for more details about the mysterious partner, but Juan only added a final word of caution as he handed Martin the note from Hugh. "Here's his business card and his one-page offer—you now have the only copy. I know so little about this fellow; you must be very, very cautious, as he strikes me as a clumsy neophyte. He knows about the goods, may or may not have a plan, we'll see—but take every precaution in contacting him. Be devious, as I can't vouch for Parks, having only met him once.

"Now let's have lunch. Angel will join us. Remember, he's only learning about trucking. Absolutely nothing else. After that, we'll rest, you can catch up on business calls, and I trust that we'll have time for another walk before you return home."

LONDON, ENGLAND

Fall 2008

Martin's call to Hugh in late October was the first step in determining whether he would be of any use in this deal or if there was any deal at all. Juan wasn't at all prepared to go ahead with this complex venture until he knew a lot more about Hugh. It was senseless to approve any activity without agreeing on a detailed plan to transport the rockets from two locations that neither Martin nor Juan had ever visited. Martin had laid out his strategy for Juan's approval several days before he placed the call.

"The mystery is why he wrote that note in the first place. Is he fishing for an armament deal? If that's the case, how did he anticipate your interest? Assuming for the moment that he's not an undercover agent of some sort—and we can't rule that out—then he's guessing. A few articles written about your business success are on the Web but very few journalists have dared to implicate you as a supporter of terrorists by delivering armaments. So what's he thinking? I bet he has an untested plot as a minor league huckster. He wants in on the family action except he's not sure what you all do. Furthermore, he doesn't know if Angel is entirely in the loop. His only option is to play us straight as a legitimate trucking company. He's offered a viable environment product worth testing, and he's keen to set up Angel. I think we have to play out his story of the hidden caches of rockets. Our angle is that we truck armaments for legitimate authorities and understand all of the regulatory hurdles in our part of the world. What we don't understand is North America. I'll ask Mr. Parks how he can assist you. Then I'll report back."

As usual, Juan smiled and warmly thanked his fellow conspirator.

Martin made the opening conversation as innocent as possible, avoiding familiarity in his references to Juan. "Hello, Mr. Parks. My name is Martin Belanger. I represent a major Spanish transportation company run by the Moreno family headquartered in Madrid. They asked me to call you. I understand you've already had a meeting with Angel, who's been selected as the leader of their new American initiative. They are understandably most proud of him."

"Yes, we met in Chicago. Nice young man. We might work together on some environmentally important investments. He was taking a proposal back to his dad." Hugh, curious about this caller, hesitated to say more. Both men had danced this way before.

Martin responded, "That's great. We all need better ways of doing things. Truckers feel strongly about environmental issues. However, today I have some other business to discuss with you."

"Really? That's interesting. I sent along my own proposal to the owner, at least I presumed he was the owner, but never heard back. What's yours?"

"Well, it's actually about that very suggestion. We have a special assignment for you, if you have the time."

"Go ahead. Let's hear what you want me to do."

At this point, Martin was advancing the conversation in an incredibly slow fashion, like a trucker heading onto a frozen lake for the first winter drive. He was testing whether Hugh could handle obtuse instructions over the phone, having no intention of being openly precise and possibly tipping off a listener. He dangled the dangerous assignment in front of Hugh. "We were most appreciative of your writing about the opportunity to transport some hazardous goods you have in storage. It's very sophisticated work, requiring a very competent enterprise with years of experience; this company can handle this assignment.

"Mr. Moreno ordered me to talk with you and to research this opportunity. Because of my own niche as a consultant here in England, I know the company that owns these hazardous goods. To say the least, they're more than happy to get rid of this stockpile. They understand that they have practically no value in the North American market. Their only costs will be to pay us to ship the goods to a more appropriate site.

"We came away very pleased. Based on your original note, we'll have an extremely sophisticated and lucrative project for Angel's proposed new venture, AT, right off the bat! It's perfect for everyone. Angel is pleased you are helping him build an international network as he takes over the company."

Hugh shrugged into his cell phone. "I don't understand yet. Where do I fit in? Are we talking about the same dangerous—?"

Martin instantaneously cut him off.

"Yes, of course. Well, first of all, you'll get a finder's fee for this job if the family decides to go ahead. You'll have lunch money for a few months. Sound okay?"

"It's a start," was Hugh's measured, cool response. "But it's not quite a relationship, is it?"

"No, it's not, so let's take this a step further and discuss your mandate as our first North American consultant. The seller is interested in hearing if there is an American university interested in taking these goods for teaching and research. We know for sure the government will demand to know the final destination on the travel documents."

"Do you have any suggestions?" Hugh passed on talking about his visit to Niagara Regional University.

"Yes, of course. But someone still has to do the deal. We'll negotiate a fair contract with you. We'll see where this takes us over the next several months. What's your initial reaction?"

"Count me in. I'll cancel plans for another client and focus exclusively on this."

"Great, I have your e-mail coordinates from your business card. I'll contact you. Maybe I should get your cell phone number in addition to the business number I've used today."

"This is my cell number."

"You mean we've been on a cell phone for this entire conversation? Goodbye."

Martin couldn't believe Hugh's carelessness. Neither could Hugh's new regular listener. Todd would have to send Myron a fresh note before the day was over.

PHILADELPHIA, PENNSYLVANIA

Early Winter 2008

Todd's next mission was to call upon Marsha. This would be his first time doing so, so he had asked Myron to help gather as much soft information as possible. Everyone could read her bio in Wikipedia; he was looking beyond the typical self-aggrandizing profile of a star investment manager. Not surprisingly, Myron was able to help out. The feedback was summarized succinctly: be careful of trapped animals. Todd's message to Marsha would likewise be to the point: the sooner she finalized her transaction with the Moreno family, the sooner he would have the Spaniards working in his backyard where he could watch them more diligently and more freely. It was an occasion when national security overrode Marsha's having the luxury of playing out the role of a reluctant camper; he too was hesitant to include her as part of his weary existence. He was tired just thinking of her future calls to him and anyone she thought would know Todd complaining of his intrusiveness.

Taking the 9:25 a.m. Amtrak train 184 from Washington to Philadelphia was the easiest way for Todd to get there by noon, especially with the uncertainties associated with November storms along the Atlantic coast. As her visitor requested privacy, Marsha had a hardy lunch of oversized sandwiches—she imagined all policemen to be large, starving hulks—prepared in the same small dining room beside her office where she had met Angel. She always strove to make sure any senior federal investigator from Washington or New York felt comfortable in her office. She thought it put her in control. Under her instructions, staff had gathered all of the documents about AT and laid them in front of her. Todd's appeal to include Brent was declined; unless he wanted to up the ante with a formal request, it wasn't going to happen. Marsha made sure that the purpose of his visit was totally hidden from her colleagues.

Todd listened to her proposal to sell AT— and Aird Investments' anxiousness to get on with it—as Marsha outlined the new ownership structure backed by her investors.

Todd was curious to find out what Marsha knew—why was she in a hurry? He asked her, "Why not a publicly promoted competitive bid process to bring out more buyers? Why are you selling to the first suitor?"

She replied, "Doubt that there are others, not in this market. Our potential buyer is pure happenstance, brokered by an old university relationship. It turns out that his family is serious; I'll let them have it at any reasonable price just so we can move on. We know its value and can live with a price that reflects the reality that trucking companies are suffering in a big way."

Todd girded himself to deliver the real message regarding this transaction, having been briefed about Marsha's explosive personality. "You have landed yourself in the middle of a security operation of the highest sensitivity to your government. I wish I could fill you in on the details, but I can't. I have no choice here but to engage your business even though you might not be comfortable with it. We are intimately aware of the identity of your potential buyer. We are currently entangled in a complex investigation in which your European friends owning this company would be a big positive for us. I would characterize our operation as being no less than highly and unusually relevant at the highest levels in Washington. Your cooperation will be seen as a real positive in these circles."

Marsha began to look nervously at the reports on her desk. Was there some value she had missed? Why was this company more important to the U.S. government than to her investors? Should she keep it to profile it as an excellent example for potential investors in the next fund? Should she push back and force up the price, again demonstrating her skills and savvy?

After she fiercely worked her brain for new options, Marsha shrugged, hoping to buy more time. "I'll have to wait and see what my investor advisory board would like to do."

"You'll give them a recommendation?"

"Not really, just options at this point. It makes for better consultations and decision making."

Todd knew a stall when he heard it. "Would you like our analysis of what this truck company really carries across borders? Homeland Security will be surprised to learn about it. So will the Federal Aviation Authority as they watch the transport of highly regulated aerospace parts very closely before they go back into planes carrying our moms and dads. There are probably ten guys in Washington who would like to review these briefs for their own take. I can have my legal department draft up a proper document for circulation at your next advisory board meeting to make sure there is a full and proper consultation. I can even come back here. Where is the next meeting?" He was defiant.

Marsha spoke hesitantly. "I'm not sure that I know what you want me to do. Sell or keep AT?"

Todd gave her clear direction. "We want to use AT to set a trap for a buyer we are pursuing as best we can. That's all you need to know for now. It would be best if you didn't let your meeting flounder without recommending a specific course of action. You should state confidently you're recommending the sale of AT to this Spanish interest as soon as possible. Before you close the deal, I want you to talk again with me. This is all moving very fast."

Marsha knew when she was beaten, and this was a real thrashing. "I'll check with my team. If they can get a proposal in writing from Spain, I'm sure I can convince the investors to sell. Next week at the latest."

"Thanks," and he was on his way, scooping up two cookies for the train ride back to Washington.

Marsha called her investment committee together immediately after Todd's visit. Aird's investors dragged out the meeting intend on punishing Marsha for her ineffective leadership. Ignoring their carefully veiled taunts, she hung in to make her points. Marsha was thoroughly engaged in the session, bringing the full force of her argumentative personality to bully them into approving Brent's recommendation. She pushed back on her critics. Since this was a telephone conference call, she could not read the group as was her usual accurate habit. The noise of papers being shuffled close to the various phones, however, told her that each committee member had at least one analyst beside him. Everyone was being extra prudent in what they said, obviously following someone else's script.

"I'm not sure if I understand what this deal is all about, Marsha, since you usually don't engage us in such small transactions. Is it a sign that your aerospace sector strategy is at risk and that we can expect more sell-offs?" asked one skeptical member, who was the top investment strategist of the influential Cincinnati-based union fund, The Ohio Carpenters Pension Fund.

"No, not at all. We're at a point to once again align our interests more rigorously with our objectives. Each of our asset managers, whether in charge of a food processing plant or an aerospace company, has to reflect our discipline. They are tasked with contributing to above-average returns as discussed here at the advisory board. If assets are unproductive, they are sold as soon as we can find a willing buyer. We don't give away assets at bargain basement prices; we just keep the better ones and remain focused on our success stories. That is Aird's core value: productive and profitable investments. That's why you're all here."

Regrettably, for Marsha, the questioning didn't abate. Marsha's voice revealed only a little of her frustration; she managed to keep her cool in the presence of her adversaries. She understood how this would turn out; this decision was to serve as a lesson to her that her financial backers were unhappy and wanting to increase their control over her.

"Is there anything else you want to review with us now, before we make our decision?" asked the representative of the City of Seattle Pension Fund.

"I don't think so," she replied, but she stalled for time, flipping an imaginary coin as if to decide her next move. She chose not to tell the advisory board about the illegal activities Brent had found in the course of his due diligence. "Everything else is as you read it in the report in front of you."

In the end, the advisory committee didn't entirely buy into her strategy and told her to retain 25 percent interest, wanting to protect Aerospace International Systems with a dedicated transport company. They saw a value in that. Cascadia's Williams spoke. "Turn it into a positive for the new owner. He'll have us as an experienced investor helping him in North America. I'm speaking for the rest here. Our major asset in this play is Aerospace International Systems. Why would we put it at risk? It needs trucks every day. Besides, some of us want to keep a window into the trucking industry, and this is our only holding. Why start over again?"

They had obviously been talking to each other and wanted to show her who was in charge of their money. "Teddy, will you serve as our special representative on whatever governing structure we come up with?" The conversation was so brief and mumbled that Marsha and Brent weren't sure who spoke. The agreement to have one of their own there added insult to injury. "Sure," came back the prearranged answer.

Brent didn't know what to say when Marsha later told him to convince Angel to accept their change in plans. The two of them had spent several weeks going over the books together and settling on a price. He knew Angel had liked Caesar and that they had spoken together frequently on the phone, in Spanish of course. Angel had only one concern. He didn't fully grasp why there was a trust company set up in Caesar's name, but his father understood and told him not to worry. Juan's unspoken assumption was that Angel would soon learn from this local guy how to hide his money the same way his father did.

"In due course, we will know more about the manager. For now," Juan advised, "it is probably no different than the way our family sometimes has done business." Angel was no wiser but deferred to his dad.

Angel had come to Philadelphia hoping to close the deal that week. He was resting in his suite, again at the Sofitel, the phone on one side, Heather on the other. When Brent called and explained the situation, Angel's face showed his disappointment.

"How can we sort this out? I'm not at all sure my dad will want your firm to remain as a partner," was his initial response.

Marsha had scripted Brent using her quick wit to guide him through the upbeat sales pitch he would have to make. Brent told Angel that this strategy would reduce the entry costs for his family and that the 25 percent retained ownership reflected internal issues he wasn't authorized to discuss. He reassured Angel that the board member who proposed to keep an eye on the business would not be a problem. "He's a Canadian with lots on his plate. You'll never hear from him."

Angel said his good-byes to Brent, not at all sure of what his father's response would be later that afternoon.

Again, Juan surprised Angel. "Not a big deal. It will help us a lot if the firm fails for any reason. Knowing these people and how they dismiss families like ours, they won't do the necessary investigations to find out how we are changing our own ownership at this end. We won't volunteer that. Soon they will be in business with NAF. That will freak out the American government," he chuckled. "When that happens, we'll have a great dinner in Madrid to celebrate. Your next step is to tell your friend Brent that the purchase is still on if, and only if, it can happen fast. The changes are at their expense. My job is to keep NAF onside."

Brent responded with audible relief when he heard back from Angel. He put Aird's legal team on notice about the changes and advised them to hurry up with closing the deal. He thought Marsha would be ecstatic with the news, but she waved him off with an abrupt thank-you.

She was preoccupied with the deepening crisis in the firm. When she later briefed Todd to bring him up to speed, her worry was apparent. "If your sting works, I trust we're not to be part of any public story. We are solely a minority shareholder in a firm that turns out to be committing serious crimes. Without a doubt, that will in itself bring us bad publicity. You can't imagine the damage."

Todd acknowledged this was a serious problem. "I don't welcome your decision to stay with this investment!"

Marsha countered, "I know. That's a new twist. I swore to you that I wouldn't tell them about your operation. Now that they've decided to ignore my recommendation, I fear I've lost a significant battle in securing Aird's future. This is very dangerous for my firm. What's your timetable?"

Todd took a deep breath. He hesitated before answering Marsha's straightforward questions, because he had to be careful about telling her too much. She was not subject to any security restrictions. If she lost her temper, as she frequently did, this would be a disaster. He could only imagine the mess she could make.

"Let me respond within the bounds of my authority," he offered slowly. "I have been given clear but very restricted guidelines as to what to tell you.

"Hopefully, this security operation will be over within ninety days, six months at the most. In addition to buying your truck company, we think Juan has sent his people to scout out two potential jobs, one here in America and another in Canada. I cannot under any circumstances tell what they are planning except to say that it's to help their overseas terrorist friends. The contraband they are after is not likely to be used here in the States, thank God. I don't expect any violence; more likely there will be a couple of break-ins as they disappear into the night. We'd like to follow them as far as they go, back to the Middle-East or North Africa right up to the battlefield. That could take another few months, depending on the terrorist group, and on the season. The good news is that we hope to catch big time operators in the armament business. The bad news for you, Marsha, is that our regional offices will decide on drug prosecutions while we hand immigration cases over to Homeland Security. Criminal charges could easily involve AT employees."

Marsha's mind was racing. Todd's plan could ruin her. She wanted to raise money for her next fund right away, but in reality, she needed at least four months to cajole and bully investors into committing their funds. She was running out of time. Aird Investments was under siege, running out of time and out of money. She knew full well that in the investment business, you either brought in new money or you disappeared.

"I know you can't say much more at this time, but I need a very good communications plan supported by Washington if I'm to get out of this alive." Marsha did not plead like this very often.

Todd heard her entreaty. He shrugged at the phone. "No promises. We'll do our best given that you cooperate. Just don't forget that for the longest time you owned, operated, and profited from a transportation company that moved illegal goods, including drugs, and you've smuggled migrants across two international borders. When I came to see you in Philly, your initial reaction was 'not me, no way.' You were dead wrong. We don't permit lack of knowledge on the owner's part as a defense. I'm pretty sure you'll avoid jail if I support you in front of Justice, but I can't promise you what the *Wall Street Journal* might print. I'll keep in touch."

VICTORVILLE, CALIFORNIA

Fall 2008

It was not long after Angel's discussion with his dad that the deal for AT was completed. Marsha thought it was too good to be true. Once he heard that the "for sale" sign had changed to "sold" for his trucking company, Caesar Rodriguez started considering his options. Hutton had not given him any encouragement. The owners in Philadelphia decided to exit the trucking business and their change. Management turned from benign neglect to outright hostility. He was surprised that they decided to keep a minority share but passed it off as some internal struggle beyond his understanding.

Hutton did phone to encourage Caesar to stay with his trucking company. "I had already reported back to the young whippersnapper that we wouldn't find a buyer here in California given this economy. They wanted to sell this asset but they're all smart enough to understand that if they simply walked away on you, they'd get next to nothing from the sale of old trucks. I suspect Brent has been successful in convincing his friend from Spain to buy your outfit, but we're a long way from Madrid. Come to think of it, it may be a good fit for you. He might trust you more because you share the same language. He will definitely not meddle on a daily basis.

"In any case, you're likely to get at least six months out of this before this new owner understands you and AT. You're a fantastic manager, Caesar. You'll come out ahead. You know, no matter what happens to the ownership, I'll only use you."

Back in his own office, a hundred yards away across the dusty parking lot, Caesar was contemplating how he could keep this going under a more watchful owner. An experienced transport analyst would ask pointed questions about the load factor, income streams, driver training, truck acquisition and maintenance records, and so on. At what point would the new owner catch on to the fact that there were two sets of books, with the lesser-known fueling the legitimate side? Caesar decided he'd better take the next several weeks to dress this doll the right way for his new owner.

Fidgeting at his desk, Caesar finally connected a brochure in front of him with a Web article he had come across weeks ago. He called his dispatcher over to talk. "I've heard about these wind turbines for trucks. What do you think? Could we ever make use of a contraption like this? Is this for real?"

"This is a new invention by a Canadian scientist. One of the drivers brought back the brochure from Cando Composites, one of our customers in Canada. They have some local buyers and next year hope to export into Europe. When you have five minutes, I'll explain how these can help us."

"Sure. Let's talk now."

"Part of our business depends on refrigerator trucks, as you know. When we go to Mexico, we first stop in El Monte, just outside L.A., about three hours from here. We load up on composite aerospace panels—looks like drywall. Before we leave, we ask what else is heading south. Usually our families know what's happening and point us in the right direction.

"We drop off freight both in Sonora and Baja California, pick up new loads, and then head north, usually through Arizona but sometimes straight back here. If on that day we have one of our refrigerated trucks, we pick up some specialized aerospace products, like resins that quickly lose their value unless we keep them in a freezer until we deliver them. It adds profitability for the airline maintenance shops that we service.

"In addition, I'm told," at this point he winks, "that the 'Caesar Trust Company' shares space with us. The truck stops here and there, unloads some of goods owned by Caesar Trust, usually a family and a big box of dope. It never shows on our manifest. The Caesar Trust is paid in advance and in Mexico. I'm told that money ends up in the Caribbean."

Caesar offered no reaction, so the dispatcher continued with his thoughts.

"Sometimes we have trouble with air quality. Not very often, but losing someone due to asphyxiation is dangerous. It hurts us back home in our own villages and threatens to undermine the whole business. I think it's happened three times in the last five years. We gave out lots of money silencing the newcomers who survived the bad trips by buying them cars or trailer homes. We give them jobs to get started.

"I asked our mechanics if this wind turbine from Cando Composites could work. They think so. We might be able to circulate better air into the cargo area, keeping everyone alive. If it works, it will eliminate losses and make the Caesar Trust Company more profitable."

"I like the idea. Let's do more research. Maybe I should go to Canada and make a deal. We could help them market in return for a discount. I'll bet there are as many trucks here in California as in all of Canada."

Several days later, Caesar was on the phone with Bill Brown. After introducing himself, he thanked Bill for frequently using AT and said he looked forward to meeting him. Bill cautiously acknowledged this flattering overture.

"I'd like to visit your factory, bring a small thank-you present, and look around, if you don't mind. My driver picked up your brochure last month promoting your new wind turbines. I'd like to see one in action."

"That's easy enough. They have a sizable urban demonstration project right here in the city. You can talk to any driver or owner you want. The politicians will love the visit and take you on a tour. You can also meet our inventor, Bertie, and Hugh, his financial champion."

"Perfect. Sounds great. I'll make it soon and work with you on some options to purchase if we like what we see."

WINNIPEG, MANITOBA

Fall 2008

The lunch with Jessica Brown was one of the most anticipated meals Arthur had arranged in weeks, if not months. Jessica's arrival caught the eye of the other diners, who recognized her as one the city's rising stars. She was known for many things, but lunching with academics was not one. After some awkward chitchat, they ordered the easiest menu item (Friday was fish and chip day) and only then did they tiptoe into the arena of community politics.

She took over the conversation by reviewing the fund and its mandate. Jessica was very precise in her description of her trustee role, in which she was well protected by the documents drawn up by Don Davidson. They both smiled at this, as she made it clear that their mutual friend would not tolerate questions about the propriety of the confidential trust arrangements. Once again, Arthur was confronted with a situation he didn't quite understand: why was she making this point at the outset? Without a sidekick like Stomper or Martin, he had no one to warn him of the impending danger implied in being associated with such funds.

Jessica listened politely as the professor talked on and on, putting forward his ideas of what cities might look like in twenty years. Arthur was carrying his monologue with too much nervous energy, his tone approaching that of a condescending lecturer. Jessica took the first opportunity she had to save the luncheon. By her standards, Jessica was finding Arthur a little too esoteric, especially over a lunch of fish and chips. She wanted to steer him back to immediate life in Winnipeg, if possible.

"Neat thoughts, but let's focus for a moment on your current research project."

Now he looked puzzled; Arthur had thought that he was doing a great job ramping up to this subject. He accepted her caustic mannerism as the personality of a superficial society gal. He responded by offering Jessica a barely adequate précis of his work but did manage to drop the tidbit that he was sponsored by the Jacobs Foundation. Judging from the blank stare, she had no idea of what this meant in his world.

She pushed him. "I understand the creative focus and energy this must generate, but what's your turf? What will be your contribution to life in our city?"

Ah. He knew this next part of their conversation was to be the turning point. How was he going to portray himself? Jessica would either think of him as someone she could trust on the inside, complementing her ambitions, or he could scare her off with one of his diatribes about corruption. If he did that, he knew Jessica would leave him writing alone in his study. His mind was not processing his options fast enough; he almost lost her. Finally, he made his move.

"This is how I've described my project to the Jacobs Foundation." His obtuse explanation, he remembered later, had begun without purpose or focus except that he was determined to avoid the word corruption. "I think that the young generation yearns to distinguish their lives beyond the beliefs and ambitions of the baby boomers. They itch to use their own resources, including their careers, even their spare time, to push their cities to grow and function properly like never before. When they take over both public and private organizations, or spearhead voluntary groups and campaigns, they will bring different results. They are committed to making that happen."

Then he finally said what Jessica was waiting to hear. "I want to be there to help show others which changes are likely to happen and how negative and destructive life forces can actually be brought under control."

He was connecting with Jessica, he could tell. She encouraged him. "How do I fit in?"

"When I read about the generosity of the truckers, I thought, here are the resources to get the ball rolling locally. By your funding some new groups, the message will be clear: get out there, do something different for your community and we will support you. It is possible to do things differently."

"You know, you're right. That's why I took on this role as trustee—I want to attract change, and I want to get my message out there that this is a good place to live and to do business."

Jessica continued. "When my colleague called to introduce you, Don described you as one who was both thoughtful and easy to get along with—a rare combination, I might add. I could use some tutoring myself, background, as you suggest, that will enable me to make more coherent decisions, ones that we can defend with confidence. I'd like you to come onboard, publicly, on the fund's letterhead, as my academic advisor. I can pay you only a $1,000 monthly stipend, to start. Will that be okay?"

Arthur nodded his acceptance.

"Great. I've talked to a couple of other families in the business world here. They think this is a useful way to spend money in the community without inviting controversy. As they sign up and send us cash, I'll add to your honorarium. There's a good chance that by next summer, you'll be making at least $2,000 to $3,000 each month, which probably makes it worthwhile on a professor's salary. Once we get going, I'd like to travel with you to meet others on your study team, particularly in Europe, which is likely to be more advanced than our tiny Midwest habitat. It will be good for both of us." She stopped there with a flirtatious grin.

They had turned to small talk for a few minutes when she asked: "You're totally onboard?"

"Yes, this will be good. I'll enjoy it. When do we begin?"

"Well, actually, I've had to make a couple of quick decisions that we'll talk about next time."

"Such as? Give me an idea of what's doing."

She hesitated; she did not want to lose him.

"One was a proposal from a local business leader, Hugh Parks, who I don't really know. He came by with a suggestion that we—with the help of his investment group—support a neighborhood project being promoted by Councilor Ambrose. It sounded great, so I said yes right there on the spot. Unfortunately, the transportation issues were pretty far-fetched, but as long as we don't make too many exceptions, we should be okay with our mandate.

"There's a second proposal from a group at city hall who know all about Winnipeg's transportation problems. Their proposal for change sounds a little more complicated. That can be your first assignment. Now that you're on our team, we want a leader like you to give us advice. I look forward to working with you."

The walk back to the university took about an hour, but that was fine as Arthur wanted to gather his thoughts. In his gambit at the outset to sell his proposal to other academic researchers, he had pitched himself as a pioneer in the art and science of simultaneously being the clever participant and dispassionate observer. He wanted to be known as the best social scientist who had access to the most skilled politicos, first in Winnipeg and then elsewhere. He was to be the intellect that pulled back the opaque curtain that camouflaged the petty ways of small-city corruption. Now, he asked himself, how did today's decision to help Jessica fit in with that?

On his return to the office, he told Annie that the lunch went well. "This is way different from where I started. It definitely changes what I intended to do initially. One might ask: Where am I now? Where did this lunch take me?" It was a mistake to think out loud in front of Annie, but he was forced to do so because he didn't dare ask any of his peer group for their thoughts. It looked as though his job was now to reward and not to punish those very thieves he had been watching. His research reports could never tell the whole truth. As for Annie, if this was what was happening, what could he possibly say to keep her onside? Arthur turned away from her and ended the conversation somewhat abruptly. He silently thought of ways to look after everyone at the same time. His dream solutions were to give his wife a better allowance, Annie the trips, the foundation a good report—and Jessica...perhaps he could work her in somewhere. Bliss everywhere, he madly and naïvely hoped.

While Arthur was busy changing course, Hugh kept his team in line and readied Stomper for another scheme for easy money. They met again for coffee at Bar Italia, which was always empty mid-afternoon.

Hugh opened their conversation by vetting his frustration. "Yesterday I was staring at a line of trucks downtown parked outside a bank tower. More than a few had installed our wind turbines. I stared and stared and stared but still didn't get it. What is the real deal? None of the official stories make sense. The truckers and politicians are not all goofballs, so what is happening? Apparently, the mayor uncovered a new Ottawa program for green energy. According to Andrew, all the mayor had to do was phone the minister of finance, who came running to help. Our bureaucrats have chosen, for some reason, to pay most of the truckers' bills with Ottawa's money to install these contraptions. But this largess really doesn't explain much."

Hugh paused, shook his head, and then gave Stomper his take on the situation. "The city and the truckers will receive money out of Ottawa, because the mayor knows the prime minister, who, in turn, wants him as a candidate in the next election. If they use the money to buy more wind turbines, they'll have a problem few will mention. For the next six months, the wind turbines won't really be attached to the trucks' mechanical systems. Our dear friend Bertie can't secure his Japanese batteries. That means the truckers are driving around safe from police interference while displaying phony wind turbines. Does that sound decent to you, Stomper?"

"Doesn't sound too good, if that's what's happening."

"While others might react to a story like this with outrage, I took it in stride. To me, it looked like a new business opportunity. I didn't waste a minute when I uncovered what was happening. After talking with a few pals and with a helpful introduction from Johnnie, I've arranged for you to sit down for a meeting. It will not take them long to understand our message. I'm going to tell them you are an excellent scientific researcher. You have the skills to evaluate their program, because you know about the technology. If the press calls, you can explain why nothing is really hooked up at the present time. You'll tell them that this terrific, federally funded experiment requires reams of accurate background that only you can gather. In this phase, they are testing equipment before activating the critical equipment with specially designed Japanese batteries. Before you leave the room, I'll suggest that your study will monitor everyone's progress. I'll recommend that they give you a five-year contract to do this evaluation. Since they have little choice, away you go. Treat it as a $500,000 protection plan. Enjoy."

It was several days later that Shelly Spicer, quietly working the Canadian front, heard these stories from her varied sources and realized that there were several connections that had escaped her attention during her first weeks of helping Myron. The commander of Winnipeg's air force base, Howard Kerr, a colleague of Shelly's in an earlier antiterrorism interdepartmental working group in Ottawa, was kept abreast of local politics and freely passed what he had gathered to her. Since he was both an engineer and a pilot by training, he had followed local media accounts of the science behind the wind turbines. He couldn't make up his mind whether they were for real; however, he did know Bertie, who was a pesky character always wanting to share his experiences of sighting spacecraft above prairie communities. Since the region was threatened almost annually by widespread flooding, the military was drawn into emergency planning exercises. From those meetings, he learned the ins and outs of the trucking industry, as they were on call to provide help in emergencies. The police quietly told him which firms were reliable and which could not be counted on. They eventually let him know that they could not explain for sure why the most unreliable truckers had the largest share of wind turbine licenses. All they knew was that these were the same folks under constant surveillance by the drug squad.

Commander Kerr voiced his frustrations in a late night call to Shelly. "How did you get me mixed up with such devious lowlife?"

In response to her questioning, Kerr offered his opinion on what was happening, regretting that he wasn't on the local scene enough to sufficiently tie it all together. "Parks is talking with Mayor Patterson and keeping his sidekick totally informed. Patterson traded favors with Ottawa to get money for Parks and Bertie. I hear this Stomper character is on the truckers' payroll to protect their story. The mayor's niece is running a small foundation to pay off the usual suspects at city hall and in protest groups. For some reason, she has brought in a prof to cover her butt. His name is Arthur Crawford. He came to interview me a few weeks ago, and I was totally underwhelmed. Hope none of my men end up taking a course with him." He paused and then went on. "Do you ever play board games?" He didn't wait for an answer. "This reminds me of Rummoli. Once the game heats up, it's quickly over. Something's happening here, because there is so much motion. All I know, since our job is to protect the country, is that the prime minister should stay away from the mayor."

WASHINGTON DC

Fall 2008

Shelly passed her latest intelligence on to Myron as soon as they could get together at the Cosmos Club. Sitting at a table by a window overlooking the patio and garden, they were able to talk quietly but openly as they deliberately took seats several tables away from anyone else. As Myron had absolutely no compass for understanding anything about Canadian politics, he had to ask question after question of Shelly.

"Myron, in the end, these are pretty unsophisticated people, but since they are looking for their big break, several will jump at the first opportunity to fulfill whatever dreams they have."

"Give me a few examples."

"Bertie would love more respect as an independent scientist and would harm Parks without giving it a second thought. That's why he blogs and bad mouths his benefactor. I doubt if an international audience would necessarily give him much credibility beyond another disgruntled researcher. In turn, it sounds like the same Parks wants a deal to put him on the map. All this minor league thuggery could, by sheer coincidence, bring down a government. What do you have from your end?" she asked.

Myron explained in detail what he had been told about the Moreno family. "We finally got a break when, on closer examination of the pictures of Angel's briefcase, we found the title page of the presentation made by Brent Oliver from Aird Investments on the purchase of a small company, AT. Todd immediately put out an advisory asking DEA agents, particularly those in California, to give him a quick briefing on this unknown enterprise.

"Not much came back. It seems to be a small-time trucking company that occasionally picks up more than aerospace parts needed by its current owners, an aerospace repair and storage business. Caesar Rodriguez, its manager, is known to the police in Victorville but is not viewed as a major problem.

"I'll show you the briefing note that alarmed us. Best to skip down to the note's concluding paragraphs that raised concerns for Todd."

Shelly took the briefing note prepared by different California law enforcement agencies and skimmed the first sections but read the final one with care.

"Two things bother us, but not enough to do much. Sometimes local police agencies have come across one of his drivers who had committed a minor traffic violation. It's the California business model. They don't have a license nor do they speak English. Caesar Rodriguez probably pays them next to nothing. When the officers interview Caesar about the trucks, he claims they must have accidentally wandered from the airport to get family groceries, offering a whole long story, as you can imagine. Nevertheless, we think AT uses illegal immigrants to drive their trucks.

We are also worried about his trans-border shipments. The trips into Mexico are mostly legitimate, since the parent company has a wide network of established and well-known suppliers in the aerospace business. We suspect Caesar has brought in illegal immigrants, and probably drugs, tucked away in behind the heavy boxes of aerospace equipment. None of the Homeland Security inspectors want to move the heavy engine parts, so if the dogs don't pick up a scent outside, the trucks get through every crossing. They also ship cheap alcohol and cigarettes right up through the Midwest and into Canada.

"Here's how they operate. A truck comes in late to a factory, say in Kansas or in western Canada. Workers from the facility take out all the legitimate material, usually starting mid-evening, and in the early morning they're left with boxes in the back. Anyone who is not part of the deal is sent home. The rest divvy it up, paying cash on the spot, putting whatever they've asked for into their pickups and into their vans, and away they go. Next day they phone friends and family, like Amway salespeople working from home, finishing deliveries before their next shift starts. The contraband is all gone by three in the afternoon. We hear about these operations and keep notes if the file includes drugs. These guys definitely stay under the radar. Often, if a Mexican is big and tough, he goes with the driver ostensibly to learn the driving business—but in reality, to ride shotgun. After a few trips he also helps drive, without any permits of course, but we never catch that. The Mexicans are so happy to live around Victorville that AT's general manager, Rodriguez, is like an old-fashioned grandfather from a crime syndicate. They'll work for him for nothing to get started. He takes advantage of it and looks after their going legitimate when they've paid off all favors."

When she finished reading, Shelly handed the document back to Myron. Neither spoke of the reference to Canada; instead, he continued to describe their activities. "Todd found out from other sources that there were rumors of dead bodies when trucks return from Mexico, especially in the summer.

"According to one of his best agents, whom he called about this rumor, they chase these stories, but everyone is too scared to help. They've never seen a body, but there's lots of room further east of Victorville to bury someone without ceremony. All they know is that suddenly a Mexican family is doing better with a new car or home, and the best guess is that they've been paid for a dead relative.

"Todd also asked his source what didn't make it into the report. The agent admitted they had intercepted some e-mail traffic to Canada about a new, interesting wind turbine for trucks. They couldn't figure it out at first and thought it was all malarkey.

"Todd remembered, of course, that Parks was out hustling these same wind turbines in Winnipeg. Without telling his colleagues why this interested him, he asked what the agents there were speculating. I'll repeat the answer verbatim as best I can. 'I think I finally understand why they're planning to attach those new wind turbines. They generate air circulation to keep people alive and the dope smell to a minimum. If you're pulling in an extra $10,000 a week, it doesn't take long for Rodriguez to pay it off. I bet Caesar will unload the cost on the unsuspecting owner as an innovative, cost-efficient, long-term capital investment or some baloney like that.'

"There you have an intelligent analysis, and we can thank our much-abused local agents for contributing important information to our investigation. Todd loves talking to these folks, admiring how much they know and understand about their communities. They often don't get their man or save as many lives as they should, but that reflects their limited budgets and the inadequate recruits working with them. The DEA is lucky more bad things don't happen."

Shelly ignored the usual sermon from high-level American intelligence circles; every agency perpetually fought budget battles. They talked for a few more minutes and agreed to meet again soon to coordinate their efforts. Myron returned to his office and quickly phoned Todd. After summarizing the lunch meeting, he asked Todd to outline his next steps.

"Up to this point in our investigation, local police chiefs and our own networks have found us details on Parks, the California transport group in the aerospace sector that can move contraband, their hiding places of the old rockets and, from overseas, a limited but useful profile of Angel, despite Spanish reluctance to help in our investigation.

"I'm of the view that it's still far too early to make a move. The evidence is all circumstantial, and we would very likely fail to convince any American jury how this all fits together. After huddling with my senior colleagues, some of whom are more than a little dubious given the resources I continually request, this game plan was approved. I've quietly brought my own team together, including the European listening post, and outlined how the trap would play out. I've promised everyone a big success story and even bigger personal career rewards. I most certainly need your help, Myron."

The response was gruffer than Myron meant it to be. "You have it," was all he replied.

MADRID, SPAIN

Early Winter 2008

"Angel," Juan was broaching a new topic carefully. "I'm thinking of taking the family firm to a new level by making it a truly global transportation company, perhaps even with a new name. Our own staff has been reviewing a proposal for many months and is recommending we accept an offer from NAF, the Algerian group who want to invest substantially in this firm. They are proposing to buy an equity interest and to invest several million more into all forms of transportation—land, sea, and air. We will eventually have an integrated system to compete with the likes of FedEx and DXY. It's probably a thirty-to-forty year project, way beyond my business horizons but well within yours. Our expectation, both from the family side and from theirs, is that you will become the world team leader building a grand business. It will be marketed as the Middle-East/European answer to American interests. At the end of your term, I'll be long gone, and it will be your deal with NAF. The agreement, as drafted, will give them complete ownership in 2050. The family will have money; you will have had a great career, looking after everybody as I did and my father did before me. Underneath all this good news is the harsh reality that most family firms have a short shelf life. Alas, few governments like the prospect of any Middle East or North African sovereign fund taking over a major business on their own turf. We will do this slowly and quietly. It will take decades for this to work out properly. However, everyone will be patient and will give you the support you need."

Angel knew he had no choice: he had to take the offer or leave the business. There was no middle ground.

He answered quickly. "This all sound like a great deal. How do we get started?"

The discussion continued for another hour, and it was decided that now that he had concluded the deal for AT, he had a low-cost, low-risk start to doing business in America. Angel could test his skills and learn the ropes without bringing chaos to the whole family firm. Juan shrugged off questions by describing the purchase as a business to watch other businesses. They would use AT to spy on America, Juan's hated enemy. Interestingly enough, Todd saw it the same way.

After Angel left, Juan turned to more serious matters. He phoned his new confidant, Amar, who was at that moment on the road in Paris. "Angel is very excited. We'll let him work on the American side while the two of us put together a succession plan for this company.

"For our more confidential business discussions, let's see how Angel develops. His mom is keen for him to avoid the life of restrictions I've endured. You'll be better aware of these dangers all too soon. The big picture is that this deal is good news for your investment house. We'll withdraw slowly as discussed, leaving you the contacts and an in-depth understanding of what I've been doing. Our company will support you wherever you must go for the best deals. We'll tell Angel what we have to, but not a moment too soon.

"I understand how much you and your countrymen want Algerians to be more important as leaders in regional politics," Juan continued. "I accept that, and I'm happy to help. You also share my distaste for most Europeans, which is reasonable, given your nation's history. I decided years ago I would be helpful in settling old scores only if I could stay out of jail in the process. I've worked hard at that and am happy to say that I have a clean criminal record and, surprisingly enough, many friends in high places."

Conscious of the possibility of being overheard, Juan took a chance with a final message for his listener. "To reiterate, I want you to leave Angel out of this for several years and maybe forever. There is no reason to bring him into every aspect of our dealings when in the end you will take over. The Algerians will be the new force for change in the region; my family will bow out gracefully."

Once Amar agreed to these terms, Juan returned to his life's work by giving more detailed instructions to Martin.

After negotiating the American deal, Angel didn't yet have the authority to sign all the documents. That changed when Juan returned the documents, naming him, and him alone, as owner of the 75 percent interest, CEO and president, and sole signing officer for AT. The family's own legal and financial advisors quickly understood the signal. The changing of the guard had begun.

Angel spent several months immersing himself in the day-to-day operations of AT. He shared his newfound passion in transport with Caesar, who had many ideas for improvements. Angel had a little inkling about the so-called side business, but as far as he could determine, no harm was being done to their company. It would have been more practical for Angel to find an apartment in Victorville, but the thought of living there was oppressive. Instead he used Philadelphia as his temporary corporate office, learning how to conduct business in the investment world of America's eastern seaboard powerhouses. He felt comfortable within his new network of business associates, as it was mostly based on connections from his days at Brown. Although too young and inexperienced to immediately be taken seriously, he believed he could eventually find support for his ambitious plans for AT. Heather played an important supporting role in his plan. She made sure that Angel was seen at all the right fundraising events as well as the most prized social evenings in Philadelphia; she was naturally astute at showing him how best to use family money for the best seats in the house.

WINNIPEG, MANITOBA

Early Winter 2008

Winter was settling in, as usual, far too soon and far too abusive. If you weren't feeling good about yourself by the first of November, the first snowfalls along with brisk, brutal west winds would secure your foul mood for the next six months. This was at the back of Arthur's mind when he considered his predicament. There shouldn't have been any doubt in his mind what he had stepped into, nor could he claim, as he often did later, that his quandary was entirely by accident. By the time Arthur had finished his first afternoon at Jessica's office, he had been presented with all the evidence required to judge his helping her as a bad idea. Jessica had already given the green light to the first application he was reviewing based on a councilor's urging its immediate approval. The councilor had boldly recommended that, since the applicants were still waiting for their appropriate legal status as a charity, a check from Jessica's new fund be issued directly to his constituent, a Mr. Gerry Packard. Councilor Ambrose assured her that the proper documents would follow. A yellow Post-it attached to the note indicated that Mr. Packard was married to the councilor's daughter.

Andrew had supposedly submitted the second application he was reviewing but it had really been sent over by the mayor, who had asked Jessica to sign off on it immediately if her colleague, Arthur, had no strong objections. This, of course, meant the mayor knew immediately that the professor was their cover. The proposal provided for the hiring of university students working on transportation issues during the winter months. They would interview participants such as James Barber and Susan Armitage, write profiles of their concerns and contributions, and hopefully have a chance to submit their research projects for credit in one of their urban studies classes. Arthur noted that his own seminar was one of the suggested courses on their list. He paused to think about that coincidence, passing on any side notes that might leave the impression that he found this odd. Andrew's handwritten note supported the proposal, as it had come from "young people he had known for a long time." They were described as politically astute, having already participated in major campaigns. Since he was such a neophyte, Arthur realized far too late that these same young people would later emerge as the mayor's core reelection team, giving him a head start unavailable to competing politicians. He was not being particularly smart to approve that one with just his signature, as normal procedure was for Jessica co-sign all checks; nevertheless, he signed off, put it in an envelope to be mailed to Packard, and was about to walk down the hall to hand the file back to a secretary when he heard her voice.

"I've just learned we are going to receive thousands from other donors who like what we are doing. Their view is that their families cannot effective pick out projects that city hall wants them to support. I think the politics befuddle them. They certainly know that they have to be seen as more engaged, particularly if their business focuses on problems related to real estate. They heard I had a good sense of what would be appreciated. Everyone is totally impressed that you're helping out by making sure every project is legitimate. Saves the donors all sorts of problems. We'll get paid, of course."

She hadn't stopped talking since she'd seen him. Finally, she sat down in the small office that her law firm had set aside for him so that he would have a place to sit and review files from the applicants. This way he could offer his suggestions and advice without the firm worrying about any paper leaving the office.

"Where's the new money coming from?" he asked.

She ignored his question, believing that he was already too snoopy. "By the way, here's your first honorarium. You're being a big help."

It was a long walk to the bank, but Arthur didn't want to leave any evidence of his dark deal in his university office, especially as it was inevitable that Annie would come across it. And when she did, he knew he would not be able to answer any legitimate questions from her. As he continued his walk after his quick trip to the bank, Arthur didn't need to look into a mirror to know how miserable he was. By accepting Jessica's offer to help her by vetting proposals, he had moved clearly to the other side. One month on the job was all he needed to understand what she was doing for her uncle and just about anyone else on his team. His stamp of approval was all they had to show their critics to gain credibility. The fund was openly parading its support for projects enriching a cast of characters that only weeks before would have suffered the despair of Professor Crawford. They had no worries now that he was on their payroll.

The possibility of purchasing a small cache of rockets from Winnipeg evoked a positive response from more than one of the entrenched dissident groups in North Africa. Their leaders were experts in aged weaponry; the prospect of using these during the following fall campaign for the usual assaults on their capital cities was appealing. Their military operation could turn out to be more than the usual hit-and-run tactic of past campaigns. If Juan delivered as promised, and they had, over the years come to count on him as one of their most reliable allies, there was a reasonable chance of gaining control of the region around the capital. This would in turn allow them to safely transport more drugs from South America, arriving weekly on Africa's west coast through those hills to waiting smugglers traveling north into Europe.

The new United States Africa Command, only formally active since October 2008, likewise recognized these opportunities for the insurgents' success. While the rebels saw promise in this chaos, the Americans worried about a more destabilized region. It wouldn't take much, a senior officer from America's Africa Command suggested to Myron during a telephone debriefing. The same shrewd analysis was being proffered by both Juan's and Todd's contacts but from completely opposite positions. AFRICOM's special operation experts, who were sitting uselessly in their German facilities—no one in Africa wanted them—predicted various rebel groups galvanizing against American national interests, but no one in Washington was answering their request for support. Their sole ally in Washington was the DEA, whose mandate gave them access to an entirely different set of confidential sources than were normally available to military, diplomatic, and CIA watchers. The drug trade historically attracted thugs from all political stripes, so those interested in punishing them worked with the DEA's eighty offices that it had opened around the globe over the last twenty years. With drug profits increasingly being diverted to support political alliances, the DEA's role had suddenly become pivotal in spy work: their operatives knew where the money was coming from to support both governments and terrorists. To the drug kings, it didn't matter where the cash came from as long as it made their lives a whole lot richer.

Myron had discovered years ago that the DEA was a gold mine of information. It was also the prime reason he'd placed Todd in that agency by giving him an airtight but remarkably vague mandate. Once Todd had reported in detail on the rocket trail back to North America, Myron had contacted AFRICON so they could start listening for a destination. "Too bad you don't have an office south of Germany," he teased the chagrined commander.

Myron suspected that the Chinese would interpret the political unrest differently and would react quickly to any news about Western rockets showing up in rebel camps. That was their turf. Since the early nineties, they aggressively sought to establish control of mining exploration and future transportation routes across North Africa. Their strategy was straightforwardly applied in every situation. Myron's sources told him the Chinese set aside roughly the same amounts of money for so-called community development assistance as did Western governments through their aid agencies. The Chinese were brutally aggressive in pursuing their national interests. They make no pretense that they only finance their openly supportive political allies. Their intelligence services knew full well that frequently social development monies ended up in the hands of local officials who publicly offered the Chinese no budgets, no receipts, and no formal acknowledgements of who had their largess. Western observers were inclined to snicker that the Chinese had no idea where their money was spent. In fact, they did, and in great detail. They knew who they were buying off and why. No sums went out the window without questions being asked by the Chinese. Instead of engaging in countless discussions about the relative success of social development projects, which the West loved to do, they zeroed in on how funds designated for armament purchases would win the day and destabilize American relations, discussing this with whomever they had determined would be their allies. In response, NAF's own political advisory group, keeping track of these events, was tasked by powerful Algerian families and their government with immediately arranging a meeting with Juan, moving quickly with their first deal, setting the purchase price, and finalizing transportation arrangements. If they didn't move hastily, the Chinese would soon be strangling them. It was an awkward triangle for all involved. For a spymaster like Myron, the duties were to sort out who hated which other party the most and was on the brink of doing something about it.

When the commander finished telling Myron all of this, he shook his head in dismay. Did Juan and Todd ever stop to think that they might have a common enemy? All the shenanigans among the likes of these two, as dangerous as they might be, paled in comparison to the ruthless ambitions of the Chinese. They worked as a single-minded force, as they didn't stop to worry about old elites in small societies as did the Algerians, or the strengths of European nations versus America. No, they carried on with the powerful dogma of satisfying united Chinese interests. Africa was not prepared for such an attack.

MADRID, SPAIN

Early Winter 2009

By the time the chatter about the rockets was making the rounds in various rebel camps, NAF was signing on as Juan's partner in the armaments business. Although they accepted his assertion that a first client was ready to purchase rockets from them, the Algerians only reluctantly acceded to his stance that he kept the identity as his own information. With that settled, Juan worked on the endless details. His first step was to find Martin again and fly him back to Madrid. His very special ally had worked out of London for years but had remained unknown to most international security operatives. When Juan had first contacted him back in the fall through the elaborate network they had used many times before to stay in touch, Martin had flown indirectly to Jordan on Middle East Airlines and onto Madrid on a Royal Jordanian flight. This time he took close to a week to arrive, double checking at each airport and hotel that he was not under surveillance. It was laborious, but that's how he remained under the radar. When he landed, he updated Juan on his progress in North America and approved the nitty-gritty business details with Juan's people. He returned early the next day via Paris on two different airlines. Once back home in his neighborhood, not too far from Vauxhall Bridge Road, Martin quickly arranged the few appointments he would need to get the job done. The primary target was the British aerospace corporation, which still owned the rockets. Martin's past military contacts would be invaluable for arranging a transfer of assets to another entity without anyone noticing.

It was slow, but Martin had taken the time in Madrid to explain to Juan how this mission would unfold. He had drawn up a rather sophisticated proposal involving the purchase of weapons at a greatly reduced price. "I will tell the current owners these few remaining rockets will be made available for civilian and military training for propulsion. I will suggest a symbolic purchase price; keeping in mind their wider corporate objective is to sell sophisticated engines for American military programs. This London-based aerospace conglomerate abandoned its rocket business many years ago; all of the executives from that era are long gone. There is no corporate memory of what they did with any unsold rockets. Since the weapons are now simply small inventory items from bygone product lines, my corporate contacts will sign over their ownership, happy to see them taken off the books. The two companies on whose property the rockets are stored will be happy to see my proper corporate and regulatory documents and to have their problem go away.

"We found an American university in northern New York State, Niagara Regional University, interested in surplus equipment. This campus has a propulsion research center where students learn about rocket systems. Each year, twenty aeronautical and mechanical-engineering students get eight months to design, construct, and fly a rocket to a height of exactly 5,280 feet. Students enter their rocket in a NASA-sponsored rocket-launching competition. Our new partner, Hugh Parks, has already been there for an initial discussion. The engineering department was very excited and quickly announced a special two-year study program initially featuring the rockets for training and later launching them at their nearby facility."

Juan had a question. "What will they say when we don't deliver these rockets to the campus? Won't they send the authorities after Parks?"

"You'd think so, wouldn't you? But no, I will set the deal up in such a way that we will have several months lead time before the university is ready to receive the rockets. We will be paying for a good chunk of the university's initial expenses, so the administration will be happy with the money we supply them. That's enough cash to keep them busy and quiet. When the rockets disappear, we'll have a good news story for them on some other front. I don't have it yet, but it'll be ready when you need it."

"Okay, let's get on with it. You know how to access whatever funds you need. What about Parks? Can you use him again?" asked Juan.

"Actually, believe it or not, yes. I'll just be really careful."

Martin was pleased a few weeks later when his proposal was quickly accepted by his old friend, Danny O'Keefe, at British International Engines. Danny had spent years in Northern Ireland helping the British ferret out shipments of explosives and was aware of what it took to cover up what really was happening. In those days, Danny had an excellent record in Belfast intercepting shipments along the coasts by deploying Martin as a double agent. This time he immediately understood that the rockets weren't headed for an American college and that his old agent was up to some nefarious plot.

"You're engaged in charitable foundation work nowadays, are you?" Danny asked skeptically over lunch.

"Looks like it. That time of life. Brings me home a modest salary." It was a response Danny had expected.

"The deal is okay with me. Just promise me nothing gets lost in transit and ends up back here. I'll have the corporate signatures later this week. They trust me to keep them out of trouble. We don't want any public announcement. Those who we want to know about our good-heartedness will be contacted directly. All these conditions okay with you?"

Martin responded, "Of course, Danny. This is perfect. We will look after this in whatever way you want."

Martin had a sensitive question as they stood up after lunch. "On a completely different subject, do you remember Reggie Bain, that bright fellow from Newcastle who made our lives easier with his handling of unstable explosives? Is he still alive? Has he retired?"

"Odd question, coming from you. Looking for a mate to watch a cricket test match? Yes? In that case, I'll find a phone number."

At the front door of the restaurant, Martin confirmed one last detail. "Still keep the villa in the St. James parish in Barbados? The one on Hibiscus Lane by the grocery store? Let me know which weeks you're there. There's a chance we'll be down there ourselves. Love to take both of you out for an evening at Tides; it's still a great restaurant. If I don't see you, I'll leave you a note with a few English newspapers to keep you up to speed."

"That would be great," acknowledged Danny as he walked back by himself to the tube station. Martin would later let Juan know these details, and the appropriate packet would be sent to the Scotiabank branch in Holetown on Barbados' west coast.

MADRID, SPAIN

Winter 2009

Juan called his son about the wind turbines at his newly established Philadelphia office.

"Our engineers endorse the concept behind these wind turbines you found and would like to install them in a few of our trucks. It will take time to adjust them for Europe and the Middle East, but let's try them. We'll ship them here in a container early in the spring. It will also give us a chance to test our ability to move goods across the Atlantic. If we goof up on the logistics, we will be the only ones hurt. Our sales rep in London has come up with the name of an independent freight forwarder living in Buffalo who knows both North American and trans-Atlantic traffic. Don't you worry about these details. We'll pass on the information to your California manager when we're all set to go."

Even though Juan had made only a passing reference to this in his conversation with Angel, he was always mindful of unusual arrangements indicating that a new operative might be hiding something important. Apparently, Hugh had recommended that Martin support his hiring a longtime collaborator still living in Buffalo. He had explained his reason for choosing her with a high handed nonchalance that disturbed Juan. Martin recounted the conversation verbatim at Juan's insistence. "Never ceases to amaze me. The most reliable way to learn key business secrets is from an independent that's friendly with the local guys. She tells me everything she knows when I need info. She'll take care of us. I'll tell you how we'll build on this connection at a later point if we need to move goods across the border without a hassle. You're making a wise long term investment. It's best to let me handle it."

That's all he told Martin. Scratching his ear as if this conversation physically pained him, Juan put it aside for now so Angel, sitting patiently at the other end of the call, waiting for his dad to break out of his trance, wouldn't presume that there was an unspoken problem. Maybe Hugh's story was simply a cover for keeping a girlfriend on call. He returned absentmindedly to the conversation. "It's a little too loose for me. In any case, don't worry, Angel. Everything is going fine. We'll catch up next week. Whenever you get back here, be prepared for the onslaught of eligible girls looking for you. Your mom and her friends have been hard at it."

Angel ignored his dad's warning that his mom was out wife hunting for him, "A quick question for you, Dad: how many should we buy?" Angel had jumped in, knowing the call would end in Juan's normal, brusque style.

"Tell me how many will fill one forty-foot cargo container. Then we'll decide what to do. Look forward to seeing you again. Sounds like you're doing well."

"It will be good to be back." Angel heard the silence and knew his dad had hung up and was onto something else. He picked up his phone to call Heather and catch up on the gossip in his second city. They decided to leave work early and meet at Parc restaurant overlooking Rittenhouse Square.

At the other end, Juan turned to Amar, who was quietly taking all this in as part of learning the company's business; Juan chuckled as he threw his cell phone onto his desk.

"That call should put the listeners in a tizzy, as these shipments will be thought of as part of the everyday business of the trucking firm. They know that I don't usually use my cell phone. They will analyze this for several days before they get bored with me." He was underestimating the commitment of Todd to put him away.

Juan now spoke directly and intensely to Amar. "Here's the plan. We'll fill the containers mostly with the turbines in big boxes. Inspectors will think they are constructed out of metal instead of composites, which are a fraction of the weight. That leaves space for the rockets. The initial destination will be marked Madrid through the port of Barcelona. At the last possible moment, we will change this to another Mediterranean port to unload and take the rockets away by truck. I want you in on these decisions so that you can learn from the outset how to stay out of trouble. Do your research to find the best port for this shipment. Also, we'll need a small warehouse to reorganize the freight. Some of it, the wind turbines, will eventually end up here as planned. The rest will disappear. Our trucks will meet your team at the warehouse; the rest of the route is yours to be designated and protected. The Americans and Canadians are known to be pretty careless about what leaves their ports, and authorities at our destination can always be bought to guarantee our way into their country. At the same time the cargo leaves North America, I'm pulling my son back home until the job is finished, the money in, and everyone safe. He's not to know anything at this point."

VICTORVILLE, CALIFORNIA

Winter 2009

Caesar quickly learned how to deal with his youthful new boss. Angel anxiously demonstrated that he was there to learn about the transportation business by throwing out question after question about AT's operations. Early in the new year, Caesar decided he'd better fix his business accounts dating back several weeks and stay clean until Angel moved on to other interests. This would be good for both, he reflected. The business would look stronger with profits healthier and growth projections higher. All he had to do was deposit some of the cash he had been siphoning off for his own funds. Caesar noticed that Angel didn't object to illegal drivers or booze moving across borders, but he did rant about drugs, so Caesar warned his top drivers to be very prudent around Angel. As it was Caesar who provided the cash bonuses, they shrugged and went along with it. He also reminded them that, while it was a great pleasure to have an owner who spoke their language, it also meant he understood all their quiet side conversations—not at all like the last guys.

What Caesar didn't take into account was the watchful eye of the new analyst scrutinizing his books on behalf of the remaining minority owner, Aird. Marsha had assigned an ambitious, very young MBA graduate to take over Brent's job of protecting her, assigning Brent to find more money from his friends. His replacement, Jarred Slade, took the time to review each month's accounts and noted the sudden increase of cash into the business. Although it wasn't a lot of money, Jarred was committed to being extra diligent on his first assignment. He wanted to prove he was the smartest of newcomers who could see through every scam. It wasn't satisfactory to have unexplained money coming into the business, even though at first glance that might be good news. Finding the source of the money was the only way to avoid money laundering. Caesar had not antici-pated this.

Theodore had promised to keep an eye on this file on behalf of the inves-tors group, as they all wanted to go after Marsha. They were terribly dissatisfied and had concluded she was all show and no profit. They weren't sure what they were hoping for, success or failure, in this tiny trucking company. They did, however, want a better and clearer story to tell their bosses. They would use this tale to plainly express why they would never recommend investing again in Aird Investments.

As the economy was still on the skids and aerospace in particular was drift-ing in the doldrums, Jarred had time to take Brent for coffee to find out as much as he could about AT. "What do you make of this? Who is suddenly, in this rot-ten business environment shipping 10–15 percent more each month? And why does it not take any more resources?"

Brent was distracted and noncommittal but Jarred ploughed on: "The number of drivers, trucks, fuel—none of the inputs have changed. Suddenly, almost magically, AT is generating more money." Again Brent just shrugged and changed topics to other investment problems. This was unexpected and too uncomfortable for him, as it might lead Marsha back to his original study. She would be asking him to explain how he had missed what was happening in the trucking company.

Brent finally answered him defensively, as he wanted this problem to go away. He never took his eyes off the half empty cup of coffee. "I speak to Angel regularly. He's on top of his investment and speaks daily with Caesar. Why not give him a call?" He knew that the rookie would be too intimidated to phone Angel.

His hunch was correct but this new pest soldiered on; Jarred instead took a stab at finding answers on his own by making two quick calls that same afternoon to California.

The first was to Hutton. "No," replied the president, "our bills are about the same, and the service is as good as it was. We're okay with AT right now."

This implied that the biggest (and frequently the only) customer was not doing anything differently. The money had to come from another source.

The second call was to AT's chief accountant.

"Yes, I have noticed more business revenue. It appears to be from a com-pany operated by our general manager. He's never really given me the full story, but from what I can gather, he helps the families on both sides of the border move their packages back and forth. Say you shop more cheaply at Wal-Mart here than back home in Mexico. You buy for the bigger family, and Caesar gets it home. He has the driver collect, and the money goes into his account. He arranges that invoices for the use of the trucks be made out to his trust company, the CR Trust, after which he deposits money in our bank and reports it to me. Unusual, yes, but not out of the question. As long as he can show me paid invoices, I'm fine with it. You know, of course, that I don't work in the general office, so I don't pick up much gossip about his managerial style. I simply follow the paper trail to record this arrangement."

Jarred then asked him to explain where he worked, if not at the office. "Caesar hired me a few years ago and told me it was okay if I stayed in my hometown, Ensenada. It's about twenty minutes from the AT office. Makes it easier on me and my family. I visit maybe once a month. Really don't know those folks, only the books."

Jarred decided he would report this arrangement and the transactions; if it triggered the same response with Theodore as it did with him, he would take actions to clean up a potential embarrassment.

VANCOUVER, BRITISH COLUMBIA

Spring 2009

The Cascadia Pension Fund was particularly troubled by this turn of events when Theodore first heard Jarred's analysis. Several active ethical investment advocates followed Theodore's fund very closely, as its corporate headquarters were located in Vancouver, a city renowned for its social activists. They didn't want Cascadia to be anywhere near companies engaged in illegal activities. The advocates had made sure Cascadia had signed onto endless international agreements for the promotion of socially responsible investing. Fund managers had purposely avoided companies whose operations could have negative impacts on environment and labor standards. The list of what Cascadia should avoid was lengthy and widely circulated to NGOs, governments, and business analysts. If the lefties got wind of any shenanigans in the States, there would be trouble in the local media.

Jarred had surmised that AT was somehow money laundering, as cash doesn't usually suddenly appear, particularly in tough economic times. This might be okay for their Spanish partner, a tightly knit family firm operating away from public scrutiny, but this was definitely not the case for Aird Investments. Jarred pushed hard to call the culprits to task. His career as a champion of the little investor could be launched by his successfully attacking Caesar who did not stand a chance of defending himself in the investment world. Jarred knew this and proceeded hastily, this time by bringing in Aird's outside communications expert, a consultant troubleshooter on retainer to keep aggressive, bonus-driven investment teams such as theirs out of the news.

After mumbling self-deprecating excuses about his inexperience, Jarred explained the situation in the most circumspect fashion, waiting for the reaction from a professional. It was instantaneous.

"Show it to Marsha right away. Although it's a petty sum of money, the actual amount has nothing to do with it. You cannot let yourselves get tagged with any criminal activity, let alone money laundering. No one will read the small print. We should call Marsha for a meeting later today. As your chief legal counsel will tell us, I'd be surprised if we don't have to get in touch with the FBI sooner or later." He picked up his Blackberry, typed a message, and within a few moments, they had their response: lunches were to be cancelled, and a meeting with Marsha was scheduled for noon.

With Jarred's discovery of Caesar's business within AT, Marsha ordered him to build a case for their withdrawing from the business or maybe going so far as shutting it down if they could. Emboldened by her mandate, he immediately phoned Theodore. Jarred prepared his notes to ensure that he could answer all of the obvious questions and to defend his favored recommendation that they liquidate their position as soon as possible. He would eventually inform the FBI, but he wasn't convinced that he should make that call right away.

"Mr. Williams," he began, almost apologetically, "I've finished my analysis of AT, based on what I've seen over the past three months. We're making more money, but I think it's for the wrong reasons. We've got a real problem here."

Theodore listened and took notes as Jarred outlined the negative implications for everyone. He thanked Jarred for his analysis. "Well, to take a well-worn cliché in this industry, our interests are not aligned with AT, and possibly not even with Aird. Sorry to say that, but the consequences might be pretty dramatic. I have a reporting obligation here to brief our president, Paul Livingstone. I'll see him late this afternoon and get back to you. Given the three-hour time difference, you better wait around until eight o'clock or so. Make sure Marsha knows what you're recommending, and give her a realistic assessment of my initial reaction. Thanks for your work. Talk later."

Marsha did not take the news any better; nor did she appreciate that Williams had found out first. Jarred anticipated this and said, "I'm sorry; that's how I read the minutes of the investment advisory board meeting." She scowled and dismissed Jarred from the room with no further words. It was at that moment that Jarred realized that he, too, was vulnerable. Brent immediately came to mind as his scapegoat. Jarred would make sure Marsha knew that this had all started under Brent's watch.

WASHINGTON, DC

Late Spring 2009

Todd listened to Marsha's predicament. "You're in a jam, alright," he answered, "of your own doing. I hadn't factored in the way the deal was struck with Angel and how deeply involved you'd suddenly find yourself. Unfortunately, you have to stay put. If Juan hears about your withdrawal based on this story, he'll first ream out his son for such incredible stupidity, and then they'll make themselves disappear. One morning your legal team will open an envelope with a document inside announcing that Angel's holding company has folded and that the investment sold off to Caesar for next to nothing. Rodriguez is your worst nightmare: a new partner with no credentials and the track record of a minor hood. At that point, what do those high-status pension plans want to do? Only one answer: blame you."

Too many problems were quickly arising in Todd's bailiwick. It sounded as though Theodore and his boss in Vancouver, Paul Livingstone, already disappointed in Marsha, were looking for an excuse to get out of Aird. Since they were domiciled in Canada, he could only hope they'd respond helpfully. It appeared now, without a doubt, that he was already stretching his authority by not telling anyone in either Washington or Ottawa about what was happening in Winnipeg. Todd knew that his day as an independent, good old-fashioned American sheriff were about to end.

Todd decided to make one last move on his own. He called Marsha back and asked her permission to talk to Henry Bennett, her chief legal counsel. She balked but remembered she had few options left if she wanted to survive.

"Okay, I'll put him on the line, but I want to listen."

"Whatever," was all Todd muttered in his response.

Once Bennett was on the line, Todd told him he couldn't reveal what was happening in his security operation and that he anticipated his silence would continue for several more weeks. Aird could best help their government by sitting tight.

Bennett's response was cleverly constructed to protect Aird's interests. "You can talk to Theodore Williams. In his capacity as the lead on the investment advisory board, he is subject to all sorts of nondisclosure arrangements. You'd be taking your chances with his boss, whom I've never met. Remember, they're Canadians, not Americans. If you do this briefing session with a conference call, I don't think they have to do anything to please you. They have clear obligations to their own stakeholders and are subject to the laws of Canada. Out of goodwill you might get a few days' grace but not much more. They'll recognize the danger they are in, and their lawyers will urge them to run for cover."

"Thanks. Marsha, we'll talk later." With that, Todd shook off his feelings of impending doom and asked his staff to arrange a conference call with Livingstone and Williams as soon as they could.

He outlined to them late the next morning why he had contacted them.

"We're making this call so that our international undercover operation doesn't fall apart. We are in the midst of an important sting operation. The thinnest thread, your investment, is the lynchpin to our work. I'd like you to suck it up and sit tight."

After those abrupt and succinct words of introduction, Todd summed up in obtuse language delivered in skimpy sentences the international investigation centering on their investment. With that out of the way, he zeroed in on their vulnerability. "Your trucks are not only carrying all sorts of drugs as well as illegal immigrants into the States, but it looks like you're getting ready to carry rockets halfway around the world into northern Africa. Furthermore, your real partner is not Angel Moreno but his dad, Juan, whom we've been chasing since the Lebanese civil war of thirty years ago. We have him pinned down in Spain; he's paid off enough local policing agencies to find peace and quiet there. He uses his own people worldwide to carry messages, make all sorts of arrangements, and return to Madrid with the cash. He usually deploys his own fleet of trucks for delivering armaments, but not all the time. When we've managed to stop one of his trucks, it's clean. He knows all about me and taunts me whenever he can. It sounds like fun, similar to a good spy movie, until you attend three or four funerals of close colleagues. So, just sit tight, ask no questions, and everyone will be okay, except for Juan."

His message was greeted by total silence. He waited for questions but when none were forthcoming, he added to his remarks. "There is one more piece of the puzzle you maybe can help me understand. We think he's brought a large North African or Middle East sovereign investment firm into the trucking business and maybe into the armament game. What do you know about these funds in general? What are they looking for?"

Livingstone responded first, "I can't help you too much. We've visited all of them from time to time to see if we can come in as junior players on some deals. Lots of discussions. In the end, we think that they operate too differently to be a long-term partner. Most are well connected, though."

"In the arms business? What's your guess?"

This time Williams spoke. "Totally off the wall? I've read many regional histories during my long flights over there. In my opinion? They are brutal societies. The alliances are old and secured within themselves, but they readily go after their enemies, some of whom date back for centuries. If you look closely, you'll find their animosities have roots in Africa, and consequently, they watch the battles there pretty assiduously. Often it's simply Muslims helping Muslims. Would they use rockets to win a skirmish? Absolutely. Therefore, would they help finance and transport armaments to help their friends? Again, yes, without a doubt."

Todd appreciated the candor. "That's my conclusion, too. I think they're now testing a major new pipeline for procuring armaments on our soil. I've checked you out, and believe I can trust you to be quiet for the next few weeks. One of their first shipments could originate in western Canada before the end of the year. They will likely ship their treasure out of your country through the Port of Montreal, or perhaps Halifax, depending on the destination but, honestly, I'm simply guessing. If it happens this way, it's mostly out of our control as nothing passes through our country. It's all up to you folks. I'm informing security people in your capital later today. Our ambassador in Canada is coming here tomorrow to be brought up to speed. He'll call you in a few weeks to give you the latest on our plans. I welcome your help."

He was finished. "Thanks for taking this call. Remember, Mr. Williams, to tell the young analyst Slade that you thought his work was terrific and that he is sworn to secrecy. Just keep him dead silent without a hint of this conversation. These young guys all have girlfriends they like to impress. Very dangerous."

WINNIPEG, MANITOBA

Winter 2009

Professor Goldstein taught Arthur to think in broad strokes as one might expect from a brilliant social scientist reminding him to keep his focus on the big picture. Consequently, the details of everyday life often escaped his attention, a fault that Todd and Myron had to judge harshly in their world. His indifference to details proved costly when Arthur missed the significance of Hugh's role in the science exhibition. Despite his mandate to review proposals to make sure no one associated with the fund was embarrassed, when it came time for Arthur to draw up his recommendations for Jessica, he failed completely to recognize that the damaging aftermath of their contribution would far outweigh the immediate benefit of displaying local scientific inventions. For the longest time, he sat alone at Bar Italia in front of a small, cold vegetarian pizza, not ready to go home and even less prepared to write the memo Jessica was expecting before the end of the day. He was torn between Hugh's seductive personality, one that he was quite open to, and the suspicion he carried that Hugh was always up to no good. He chose to buy himself a few more minutes and reached for his cell.

His indecision bothered Annie to no end when he outlined the proposal over the phone. As a young researcher, she was perplexed that he was calling her for advice; after all, she had absolutely no experience in assessing funding applications. If he was indirectly looking for moral guidance, he should know better than to ask a neophyte about right from wrong. While he foresaw the possibility of Hugh's profiting by siphoning off funds and covering his tracks as he stole from the truckers, he explained, Arthur was about to recommend that Jessica designate the last week of April for the celebration of science; Hugh's idea was a good one that her fund should support.

Annie wondered if the professor noticed her shrug when he announced his decision at the end of the call. Probably not, since lately he was bumbling along where an older man should have been more surefooted.

Once he had received Jessica's blessings, Hugh had arranged through his Bison Board to stitch together several sites where researchers and manufacturers promoted their unique contribution to scientific innovation. The mayor's idea was to re-make Winnipeg's image, turning it into a progressive city where the community supported scientific creativity. The media loved it. Hugh also had arranged it so that schools had support from his travel subsidies to conduct afternoon site visits. There was such a charged atmosphere of enthusiastic support that no one actually noticed that Hugh had obtained permission from England to move several rockets out of storage.

The most popular stop turned out to be Cando Composites. Inside, Bertie and Bill had constructed a perfect display showing off a wind turbine on top of a local delivery van. Bertie was proud of Cando Composites' demonstration as the wind turbines with their bright colors were by this time being spotted on city streets.

But the real attraction was the rockets put on display outside. Local artists painted an elaborate backdrop, perhaps with far too many military overtones for Arthur's liking, yet the kids loved it. Bertie, who had started out with a contemptuous view of the whole idea, turned into a staunch supporter. He wrote an enthusiastic description of the rockets for his blog claiming that he had checked all the scientific data he could find and every assertion about their superior performance was supported by outside experts.

Arthur again stared blankly at the jigsaw puzzle on his desk. He had failed to uncover from the paper trail where Hugh was grabbing the cash from the science exhibition project although he remained convinced that it was the case. Jessica made light of his worries. While she was younger by close to two decades, she was already wiser about the ways of devious men. However, she thought best not to show Arthur how Hugh was operating less he sidelined her ambitions by unnecessarily attacking somebody who was a big help to her.

Jessica recognized that Hugh didn't always jump at the cash; he was far more subtle in his gamesmanship. This particular exercise was his opportunity to use her cash to build credibility for future considerations, whatever they might be. After staging a successful show, Hugh had paid for the allegiance of some key players such as the mayor who loved the positive spin in the national media and Bertie who put aside his jaundiced views long enough to cash one of Hugh's checks. A brazen Hugh had boasted to Arthur during a visit to their offices about Bertie's newfound, animated commitment. "Do you know he took the rockets apart to make sure that he could guarantee their safety? He even brought over his own equipment, making us stay away while he worked. Who knows what he was really doing, but he was having fun. Once, I watched him sharing his ideas with a bright immigrant kid who dropped by one day. This young Iranian was a student in electrical engineering at the college. Bertie was overjoyed at the chance to exchange ideas about the rocket's electrical systems and later disappointed that the student had to move away to Ontario with his uncle before he finished his diploma."

Arthur didn't twig to the significance of that story but others did. Bertie had mentioned the student only in passing during an interview but his comments immediately made the rounds among the listeners in Washington who were following every lead to determine whether they were unearthing new cells populated by recent émigrés from the Middle East. They shared the widely held view among American operatives that Canadians were far too tolerant of potential terrorists, frequently taking the initiative among their own agencies to track down potential threats. Eventually Myron conveyed this suspicion to Shelly, who was continuing her own shadow research on this file through her Canadian sources. She quickly confirmed for Myron their suspicions about the student, whom national security agents had finally traced to Ottawa, where his uncle directed a cell focused on damaging diplomatic residences. He was being recruited to drive a taxi to move fellow conspirators around the capital while attending Algonquin College. When Shelly passed her completed profile on to Myron, he sat still for a long time. In exasperation, he phoned her at the embassy. "Shelly, where do you Canadians stash all these terrorists? Does no one pay attention to our dire warnings?" She had no answer.

If he hadn't already suffered enough humiliation by being outfoxed, Arthur had to review Hugh's expenses as a final task before releasing the foundation's remaining tranche of funds. He didn't mind the $50,000 contribution, especially since Hugh gave freely of his own time and managed to pay for transportation costs, including meals on the buses for a number of schools. He heard from others that the local gadfly, Bertie, had dibs on a few thousand to help out at the facility. What caught his eye was the $20,000 spent on the shipping costs to get the rockets to the display area at Cando Composites. In fact, he phoned Hugh a few days before signing off on his report to Jessica, asking him directly about this invoice. Hugh had his answer all prepared, as he never liked to be caught unready.

"Yes, it looks like a lot, doesn't it? I started by getting Stomper, who knows about these things, to prepare a note reviewing all the transportation and environmental regulations for moving a rocket. Turns out, there are plenty of rules and regulations. Stomper drew up a plan, and I went out to make sure different authorities were okay with everything. Had to pay Stomper about $5,000 for his work; I did mine for nothing, as you know. The Cando Composites shop knew very little about how to do this, so they followed Stomper's instructions and built the special containers to move the rockets. We found out that the requirements are the same whether you're moving a rocket down the street or across an ocean. It costs the same, about $15,000. I would have been over budget if I'd paid a local transport company to deliver them and pick up afterward. Luckily, I found out that AT, an American trucking company, was going to be in town with a delivery and a pick-up at Bill's facility. Its new owner was happy to help out and volunteered to return the rockets to the storage facility at no cost. It will give the driver and the young Spanish owner something to do while here in the city. I'm spending time with them. They sound like good people."

When the science exhibition ended, Brown's staff efficiently packed the rockets carefully into their individual boxes before loading them into the same container being used for the boxes of wind turbines that were destined to be Angel's first shipment to Europe. As usual, the packing was arranged in the evening, without any casual spectators asking why the rockets went in first or why the boxes all looked the same shape and size. Bill had his employees carefully follow instructions from AT, as he personally had no experience in overseas shipping. Angel dropped by after his dinner with Hugh to watch the last of the loading. In the morning he would fly out to Montreal; there he would spend the weekend before completing his travel back to Madrid via Halifax. These arrangements were known only to Heather and him. Hugh, too, would leave the following day for Montreal. Neither had mentioned his travel plans over dinner; they talked only about the transportation business and general economic conditions in Canada. Angel hadn't noticed Martin walking into the restaurant to confirm with Hugh, out of sight at the back by the bar, their final arrangements for meeting in Montreal.

Hugh wasn't at all surprised when Angel didn't get back into the truck to head south. He knew the container was being delivered that evening to an intermodal transportation hub where it would be shipped by rail to Halifax. The truck itself was picking up a container at a nearby food processing plant and hauling it into the Chicago area.

AT's truck made its way across the dark city to its cargo's first destination on the long trip to North Africa. Caesar had instructed the driver to wait and confirm Angel's last-minute instructions about its routing. The container was to be taken off the truck and be put immediately on a train bound for Halifax via Montreal. When Angel was planning his own itinerary to return home, he had decided to cross the Atlantic as a passenger on the same cargo ship. Playing it coy with his family as well as Caesar, he did not tell them that he would be on the same ship as the container. Instead, he played it as if he were learning about shipping lanes and costs. This complicated the logistics of moving the container, as only one shipping line had room for Angel and his container, and its ship stopped in Halifax, not Montreal. Investigators afterward found that both Angel and the container were originally destined for the Port of Barcelona on the east coast of Spain. At the last possible moment, Martin passed on anonymous instructions from Madrid for a new destination for the cargo. A very few were kept current that the container's final stop was changed to Algeria. This is where Hugh's deviousness came in handy to Juan. Martin's message on his Blackberry was abrupt. Phone the agent in Buffalo and tell her the new plans. He could not blab much as that's all he was learning from Martin. Within a week of leaving Winnipeg, the two were at sea, leaving Canada from the Nova Scotia port. Angel was to disembark in Spain, while unbeknownst to him; his cargo was destined to travel onto two more ports, followed by a final truck trip. After the cargo arrived in the warehouse, Juan's Algerian partners were to divvy up the two sets of boxes for the very different clients. Caesar, who did not know the whole story, was told by a very scary Martin to pay the freight agent whatever she asked for in additional fees and to not trouble the holidaying Angel with these details. When he finally caught up with Martin in Montreal to confirm shipping arrangements, Caesar had no idea where Angel was during that weekend or that he planned to be on the same ship as the rockets.

WASHINGTON, DC

Spring 2009

Bertie's new blog posting brought an immediate call to Todd's home. It was his former boss at the DEA, anxious to pull Todd back into agency wars.

"Check your fax; it's only one page. Read it now and phone back. No more than fifteen minutes." Todd saw the problem and froze. It had been posted after midnight, not many hours ago. *The Mad Scientist* blog read:

I have lots of good news and maybe even some great news.

First, the good news. Our city held a very unique science innovation exhibition here. Everyone was encouraged to visit eight sites where a business or university, successfully using state-of-the-art technology, opened its doors so locals could come and look it over. Some great projects, good tours, and solid publicity for science. My dear friend Bill Brown of Cando Composites put together a display at his place, "Old and New," to remind us that scientific research has been critical to our growth since the Second World War. He brought the old rockets out of storage (some of you readers will recall my discussion of these in an earlier blog) and had them all cleaned up. Since I was there when they started production, I could help them out. They left me alone and gave me the run of the place to fix them up for the daily showings. I opened one up so the kids could see the inside of a rocket, including where the weapon went. The boys loved it.

Bill also put my new wind turbine on display along with the specially designed batteries we've ordered from Japan. Bill has now sold another twenty of them.

There's a new kid on the block who is buying these. You should bookmark his name: Angel Moreno. His family apparently owns a big trucking company over in Spain; does anybody know the name? Send me an e-mail, as I'd like to know more. Angel has established their first company in North America. He apparently runs it himself. He's a real go-getter who rode in one of his trucks up here to get to know his customer better.

The only problem is that this jerk, Hugh Parks—I told you about him previously—shows up as the host of the science exhibition. He claimed he found the money to do this project on his own. Doubt it. Word among the different companies who were asked to help out was that the mayor sent his niece, Jessica, to drum up support. I know she told Bill to expect a call from Hugh. Might be she threw in some money from a secret fund she supposedly manages. Beyond me. We'll find out the truth sooner or later.

The great news is that I've set a trap to put this idiot in his place. He's been showing far too much interest in these rockets. I had time when no one was looking last week to put a couple of devices on these rockets that will soon cause anyone thinking of using them in real life plenty of trouble. If the rockets had been returned properly to their original storage room, everything would have been fine. It's a long, complicated story, but I found a way to booby-trap the rockets. If they had been returned to the old warehouse as planned, I would have disabled them—not a big deal.

It will be no surprise for you to learn that the rockets were never delivered back to the warehouse. They're missing! What a shock! And guess who else is missing? Hugh. He flew out the next morning, now a week ago, and hasn't been seen since. Told Stomper he was off to Buffalo for a couple of sporting events and to work at a local university there. I think Stomper may actually believe this. They deserve each other.

Let's see what happens. We'll soon see how Hugh survives all of this. Check back in a few days.

Pinawa

Todd phoned back as requested with absolutely no enthusiasm for the conversation, only anxiety, curious to know whether Myron was in the loop. The director surprised Todd with his calm voice.

"Here's what we've found out in the last five hours since this was posted. The local police have confirmed that the Winnipeg warehouse is empty. There have been no sightings of the cargo at this point, although that doesn't mean much. We've just started tracking down possible shipping companies, but we'll have to wait until later this morning for responses. One of the sailing companies, Hapag-Lloyd out of Hamburg, has confirmed they accepted a container from AT last week, but again, the complete record won't be available until 9:00 or 10:00 a.m. this morning. Could have been shipped to either coast out of that rail yard.

"We now know that all the major suspects traveled to Montreal, including the European agent we still really don't know much about, Hugh Parks, who is in custody in a northern New York jail, and Angel Moreno who was, we think, staying at the Vogue Hotel in downtown Montreal before he left for Halifax. Apparently, his girlfriend came up from Philadelphia to spend the weekend with him. His credit card was used last week in Halifax after he arrived there on a VIA train. We'll get to the bottom of this in the next day or two, but I want your help right away. You'll have to open up and tell me what you and Myron Klass are up to with the politicians."

After that call, Todd waited until seven o'clock before calling Myron, giving a detailed summary of what had happened overnight, including the stressful calls a few hours ago. Abruptly, Myron's voice lost any pretext of remaining calm and together. "Can you help me, please? What exactly do I tell my political bosses? What is unfolding in real time in several countries?" Myron's voice was getting edgy. "Most importantly, where is the other shipment we've been watching? Let's hope that it hasn't also gone missing, although that's the word out of Kansas. You better be careful today. Your many enemies have a long reach."

The gray Washington sky didn't improve Todd's spirits. He hated crossing the Potomac, away from his comfortable suburban condo, into the danger zone of Foggy Bottom. Even the buses slowed down as they passed the lethargic headquarters of the state department. Taking a deep breath and hand combing his hair, he entered the tiny briefing room reserved on the second floor for failing officials such as him. Since this was only the first of five such briefings organized for him today, Todd was heading into a bruising day in the bureaucratic trenches.

The state department's lead on North American political affairs got right to the point.

"Do you have any magic number for the countries you thought you could piss off in one operation? At the moment, I would count Mexico, Canada, Spain, Algeria, Britain, and maybe Germany—but your listening post there was restricted to drug surveillance, not espionage. Thankfully, you were mimicking the Lone Ranger, so no other agency is implicated. Having said that, is there any chance you can recall what you've been doing? Say, for the last decade since you showed up at DEA? When did you first hear about Moreno?"

At least, Todd thought throughout the day, each questioner was posing the same questions so that by late afternoon, his answers actually had a coherent pattern and might possibly be a little believable. All he really thought about was spending the evening with Myron, someone he knew could bail him out of these troubles.

Off the Record was the basement bar of the Hay Adam Hotel. Its claim to fame was the view of the White House just across the street. Not from the bar, however, which was a dark, windowless room in the basement usually packed with the intensely chatty political crowd. This meeting had more urgency than their last one, as Todd was now completely at Myron's mercy for his own survival. After an hour of martinis and innocuous conversation, they moved onto Georgetown, where a less political audience at La Chaumiere would afford them the privacy they needed.

"This certainly is a difficult saga for a top-notch operative. What are the most recent headlines for me?"

"I've told several slightly different accounts today—about five times, in fact. Everyone from my own agency, to the military, CIA, the White House, and the Canadian Embassy want to know the story. It turns out that their ambassador is from the Winnipeg area. Did your contact tell you that tidbit? Had to be careful, as you never know who knows who in a small society."

Over dinner, Todd gave a very carefully laid-out narrative, and this time he didn't cut corners, as he knew Myron could read his face all too well.

"Let me take you back to my original interest in Moreno. I've been tracking him since the late eighties, a lot longer than most here think. When I came across him, he was the major supplier to the original Afghanistan fighters, but at the time, they were our friends. I saw his name again in a drug file from Europe. After the Taliban turned on us, he kept supplying them as though nothing had happened. I tried to line him up a few times, but he's incredibly smart and definitely keeps away when his cargo is being deployed. He's made millions, keeps it hidden, I think, in a family trust operating outside of Spain. I had no clue for years where that was. Now my guess is that his new business partner, NAF, has it stashed away, or maybe his Dubai bank is still involved; they continue to look after the family. All standard stuff in our difficult world, right?"

Myron nodded and gestured for him to continue.

"The plot recently changed dramatically and is far more dangerous. It's a mixture of amateurs looking for a quick buck and real pros whose operations have led to the murders of thousands of people. One more here of these," he waved to a passing waiter, pointing at his rum and diet coke. Myron quietly added another vodka to the order as Todd continued. "The amateurs think the murders in faraway places have nothing to do with them; they block what's really happening. Take Hugh Parks from Canada, for example; he's a con-artist who thinks he can ship out the rockets, make a lot of money, and then disappear off our radar. He keeps his thick-headed researcher, Stomper, in local business, so no one wants to get in their way. They operate a classic good guy/bad guy shop that we can blow up in a minute. Moreno's guy from London, on the other hand, is so smart that we know very little about him. Martin Belanger has worked with Juan for years and is fully capable of organizing a quick hit. He's very streetwise and knows how to get around without any watchers taking note.

"It turned out that Juan's guy stayed to supervise the packing of the container and left on a later flight the next day to meet Parks in Montreal. That's when the final payment was to be made, all in American cash. As far as we can tell, no one saw the young Angel Moreno leave Winnipeg, arrive in Montreal, leave that city for Halifax, or embark on the container ship as its only passenger. He was making his own way back to Spain with their first cargo from America. This boat has a few passenger cabins, so his traveling alone at that time of year would attract little attention. He was able to get on without any of us knowing—including, we think, his father. We now understand that it was only at the last moment that their Buffalo freight forwarding agent changed the container's destination from Spain to Algeria, with no explanation; the same ship stops in both countries. The agent has been interviewed, and she claims Caesar phoned from California and sent a confirmation e-mail. The money for the additional shipping charges arrived the same day. Who knows about her—I'm still digging. I suspect she's an old girlfriend of Parks. He probably saw her and not his daughter during his Buffalo business trips."

Todd broke off while the table was cleared for the next course and wine glasses refilled. Although he felt restless sitting in the same spot for so long, he continued his comprehensive summary, as it was essential that Myron be completely on his side. Fortunately, his dinner companion could sit still for hours listening to misadventures like this.

"We still don't know what happened next. The trip was expected to be twelve days. About eight days out of Halifax, there was a fire on the ship. Since AT's cargo was no longer being taken off at the first stop, we don't think it was high on the stacks of containers. The captain reported that an explosion came from the cargo area and blew a big hole in the side of his ship. He reported injuries, deaths, and missing persons. We're guessing the rockets were set to go off by the local scientist, Bertie Jackson, as foreshadowed in his blog, *The Mad Scientist*. He's being interviewed today by Canada's national police."

"Does this ever happen to ships in those waters? Do they explode and disappear like that?" asked a skeptical Myron.

"As a matter of fact, it does happen. Back in 1978, for example, Hapag-Lloyd reported that it received a distress call at three in the morning in stormy December weather off the coast of the Azores. It was a large, new ship, like the one Angel was on, and it simply disappeared, leaving no survivors and few traces of any wreckage. In the thick of the night, sailors often report erroneously about explosions onboard."

"Where's your guy Parks?" Myron interrupted Todd's musings about sinking ships.

"We have him in jail. We figured he'd go back to Buffalo after he received his final payment. He rented a car up in Montreal to be returned a few days later at the Toronto airport. We had his license plate number from Hertz, so it was easy to stop him when he crossed the border into northern New York State. He had the usual story about going to a sports event, but he had decided to take a chance on bringing along the money from Martin into the States without declaring it. He got caught, and it was enough to impound the car, from where we officially found out about his Buffalo residence from his extra driver's licenses. We will charge him, keep him in jail, and move to have him put away for a few years. Not much sympathy for a foreigner breaking our law. And no bail, of course. He's in Syracuse right now."

"You're not telling me that's the only guy you got, are you?"

"Afraid so. That's it."

"What about Belanger, Moreno's agent?"

"I'm not sure the Canadians could have charged Belanger with anything, since they had no inkling of what he was up to." In response to Myron's incredulous looks, Todd knew what he had just concluded. Shelly had not formally kept the Canadian police in the loop. This would lead to further trouble for the two of them.

"I had one of our young guys watching them in Montreal, mostly at the Marriott airport hotel. Hugh checked with his forwarding agent, who confirmed the container had left Montreal—that's where everything gets stolen in Canada—and was on its way to Halifax. He texted Rodriguez that all was clear; he was sure the container would be delivered to the ship. We couldn't figure out why it would leave from Halifax and not Montreal until we realized that Angel was on the boat. Apparently only one container company takes passengers from Canada to the Mediterranean, and they board the passengers in Halifax. After his girlfriend left him in Montreal, Angel took the VIA train to Halifax to see more of the Canadian countryside. He waited there for his departure.

"Meanwhile, back in Montreal, Parks returned to the Marriot and met Belanger. They sauntered back to the car in the hotel parking lot, looking deep in conversation, but suddenly they drove off. When our guy finally caught up, Parks was heading away from the arrivals level at the nearby Trudeau airport with no one else in the car. Panicking, he started to follow Parks, calling us on his cell. Our operations manager decided the one to follow was Moreno's agent, ordering the youngster back to the airport, as we are interested only in nailing Moreno. Of course, Belanger was impossible to find. Later we tracked him down through one of the airlines, learning belatedly that he had actually checked in earlier in the day while Hugh was downtown. Without any baggage except a small shoulder bag that we suspect earlier contained Hugh's money, he quickly boarded his plane after disappearing into the airline's private lounge until the last possible moment. Our poor agent was too inexperienced and didn't catch on soon enough as to what was happening.

"Since we weren't anticipating this, we took hours to track down Martin's route through Iceland. He's most likely somewhere in Europe, not to be seen for a long time. He hasn't checked in with Juan, at least on his cell, but we don't expect him to call for some time.

"What happened at sea was a complete surprise. As I told you, the ship capsized in heavy weather, probably without a trace. I'm guessing it was hit with an extremely high sea surge like the other disaster. I'm discounting the explosion theory, but it will dominate the headlines for several days. Salvage operations out there cost a fortune. Some containers might float for a while, but not the one we want. It's gone."

Myron was clearly uncomfortable with this update. "I'm afraid to ask, but here comes my dark question. I know you goofed up more than a little, and you and I suspect that this will cost you your career as a regular security type. But everyone is so crazed—what's the big deal?" Myron was still puzzled.

"Uh, I guess you're right about me." He stopped. Myron outwaited him.

"There's a second shipment."

"Where is it?"

"We don't know."

Myron now knew why everyone was after the DEA's neck. For once, he wasn't sure if he wanted Todd to continue.

"We knew the rockets were in two locations, one up in Canada, the other in rural Kansas. We actually found the Kansas site some time ago and had the local police looking into it. In return, we were going to help them break up a small-time local smuggling gang operating out of the Eagle Aerospace warehouse. It was a reasonable deal for all of us.

"Our communication intercepts left us a little up in the air about timing. When Angel decided to ride one of his own trucks north, to show his dad that he was learning the business from the bottom up, we were investigating how exactly he was tied into this operation. Was it a coincidence that he was headed for Canada? We didn't know. We were more worried about the cache in rural America, as damage that could be done by terrorists in our own backyard. We couldn't think of a scenario in which the two suspected operations could be unrelated. We made the decision to follow Angel's trail to find out exactly what was going to happen in Canada. We told only one Canadian, and she was sworn to secrecy until we knew more.

"AT's truck was stopped at the border in a random check by the Canadians. We held our breath. Much to everyone's surprise, it was totally clean of drugs, money, and anything else of relevance to our investigation. They were really only going to deliver the composite material as per the manifest prepared for Cando Composites, a local aerospace company in Winnipeg. What a concept. Then the border guards did one more thing that surprised us. When they saw Angel's Spanish passport, they became more curious. They took him into an interview room and found out, quite properly, about his owning the company. This passport check by the Canadians showed a clean record. He was wished a good visit and sent on his way."

"What happened next was totally unexpected. As you can imagine, the Moreno name is a trigger in many computers watching people move around the globe. The Spanish intelligence saw this flash on their screen as a message from Canada. The desk officer recognized the family name, and important government people quickly knew the story. Within a few hours, Juan's phone rang with the news. The official would always remember how surprised Juan was to learn of his son's border crossing at that peculiar time. Juan phoned someone in his network from a neighborhood pay phone at the Manuel Becerra, a Madrid Metro subway station, keeping the conversation very short. We assume it was to tell his agent, who by that time was in Winnipeg, that his son was there, somewhere in the same area of Canada, perhaps right in the same city where Belanger was in the middle of his heist.

"About the same time, we phoned the local police in Kansas for an update. It was reported that a patrol officer had driven by four days earlier, as we requested, and found no signs that anyone had been at the rocket storage site. Another officer had heard from an informer that an AT truck was coming in that night, meaning that all of the regulars who fenced goods coming out of Mexico were preparing to pick up their share of the haul over at the facility. There hadn't been a shipment of booze and drugs for a long time; everyone was anxious to see what would come in. The same informant thought it had been at least ten to twelve days since they last saw a shipment carried by AT. That one came without any special treats and left nearly empty. We think they were just testing us."

'If it happened tonight,' I asked the chief that day, 'do you have enough guys to make a raid?'

'Barely. I really don't think so.'

'In that case, I'd like you to watch and wait until next time.'

"Sure enough, the truck arrived; regular stock unloaded, and the contraband was distributed. A new shipment of airplane parts, manufactured right there in the Kansas plant, was loaded, destined to be installed on an older aircraft at the Victorville repair facility.

"Following a map given to him by Caesar, the truck driver and his sidekick made their way to the old road leading to the rocket storage site. He backed his truck down the road for a hundred yards or so, burned the map, and settled in for a few hours' sleep.

"He woke up surrounded by several policemen. His boss back in California had warned him something like this might happen. He had been trained to stay quiet, show all of the documents requested, and appear to be very cooperative. By this point in the game, we were in constant touch from here in Washington. One of the officers went down the narrow roadway to check on the rockets. A few minutes later, an urgent message came back. The rockets were missing.

"We immediately sprang into action. I called the chief directly. 'Please take the truck back to the plant. Management has agreed to help us take out the heavy stuff as soon as the early morning shift begins at six o'clock. They'll park it away from the building to be safe.' Unfortunately, that procedure put us out there front and center in front of the entire day shift."

"Of course, there were no rockets to be found."

Myron was completely engaged in the story, as he was seeing the implications for everyone in the American security world. He asked Todd, "No one knew what to do or what to say did they?"

For the first time, Todd laughed at the shambles he had presented to Myron.

"As you're speculating, no one asked that the truck be put aside for our detailed search. The driver waved good-bye and was permitted to pull away. At the first truck stop, one of the two drivers reported back to Rodriguez using a pay phone. As far as our investigation can ascertain, a message was relayed to Belanger, who likely talked again to Parks and finally to Moreno. They had the answer to what they were worried about: yes, someone was watching them. Belanger's earlier suggestion worked perfectly; his decision to create a sleeping cell of fully committed, patient killers was the right one especially here in America. We don't think like overseas terrorists. They sometimes wait for generations to get even with their enemies. By holding off for as long as they did, they had left us with the impression that we were on top of the situation, but they turned the table on us. The terrorists were really the watchers, not us. They set us up pretty good.

"It looks as though Rodriguez had sent in his most trusted truckers to case out the surrounding farm property since the last shipment and knew just about everything there was to know before they made their move; they came over one evening after dark from Kansas City with their own truck and a plain container. They were back in Kansas City before noon. Their transit paperwork was prepared expertly beforehand, leaving the container ready for rail and shipping routes. The agent was paid handsomely and has not been heard from again. The truck without any container headed back to California—more specifically, to the paint shop owned and operated by the aerospace company. Rodriguez had it changed by the weekend. We think another company will one day be called by a new customer to pick up a container headed for Spain via Mexico. The paperwork will be together, and payments made well in advance. They'll never know what they're shipping."

Myron pushed himself away from the table to be more comfortable. During the meal, they'd had to sit closely together to make sure that Todd's story wouldn't be overheard. With the restaurant now emptying, he could stretch out a little more. He asked Todd to pause so that he could absorb all of what he had just been told. After several minutes of quiet, he spoke to Todd about his problems.

"Let's recap based solely on what is happening here in the States. We'll leave for another day the problems overseas and in Canada, all of which appear to be severe. I always have to do it this way to get my mind around to the Senate committee. It's not easy for any of us to sort out what's a risk to national security, as there is so much noise in this policy field. Everyone has an opinion. In fact, since 9/11, it's been imperative for American politicians to express their concerns as aggressively as possible. Nobody can be soft on terrorism. I know Europeans and Canadians don't get this. It's too bad, but this situation will probably complicate your handling of this file.

"On a superficial level, the bungling of the surveillance job in Kansas is more than regrettable; it is beyond comprehension. We'll have to settle that problem another day.

"What do we want from the Senate committee?" Myron put the question out there not expecting an answer. Todd knew it was a rhetorical habit of his colleague to buy time while he thought through his answer.

"For starters, we're lucky that one of the committee members is a Kansas Democrat. She has ties to the aerospace industry there, so she won't want anyone she knows at Eagle to be embarrassed or implicated. Once we settle on a strategy for the committee chair, my guess is that she'll move whatever motion we'll need. Above all, the politicians will want to be seen as being totally informed and on top of a dangerous, open file. Our job is to make that possible.

"I want you to sit down tomorrow morning and put what you told me just now in writing, along with a few recommendations.

"Such as?" asked Todd. "What would you like to recommend?" His sharp question reminded Myron that his friend was a man much more comfortable sniffing about his world of intrigue than sitting still and writing memos.

"I want you to recommend that the committee chair speak immediately to the president about the danger this incident creates among several allies. I want you to emphasize the unknown, that we don't know where the rockets are, how they will be shipped, or their final destination. If you mention Juan Moreno, I'll suggest that the chair ask the president's national security advisor for an updated dossier on this foe.

"The president will grant this session, as the chair is one of the most important Democrats in the Midwest states. He'll want to take her advice as much as possible so that she considers herself a key participant in the inner circle on national security discussions. If she's happy, our work with the others will be much easier."

"I understand. I'll get back to you tomorrow." Todd hated sitting around once an assignment had been described to him; he wanted to get on with the task at hand.

"Not so fast. The president will ask what transpired to make this possible. Who's to blame? Democrats need enemies, such as oil companies or the Taliban, who are domiciled in faraway places. It suits the American psyche. Any suggestions?"

"Hmm. That's tough. I'll work on it. I would remind the president that our most elusive terrorist, Juan, is in his heart an anti-Israel combatant who will help all of Israel's enemies across the Middle East. And now, he's in our homeland."

"Should help with the pro-Israel lobby here in Washington. Anything else?"

"Yes, it's minor but important. Part of the funds supporting this terrorist plot came from a Canadian pension fund located in Vancouver. We've been fighting the flow of capital into America that ends up supporting criminal activity. The president can use this to scare the Canadian government into stiffening their backs in support of our efforts to fight international terror. So far, they haven't been there for us."

"Good, it'll give the Democrat senator and the president two enemies to serve as whipping boys for criticism. We'll let them decide where to start. Once I've read your note, I'll add my own, recommending that you become the senator's special advisory on armament traffic issues for the next year. Should protect you, right?"

"Yes, indeed. Let's go."

The next morning, Myron read a cursory report in the *Washington Post* about a ship sinking off Europe's coast. Soon, more news of the ill-fated container ship began filtering out across the Internet and into mainstream media. No one knew what had happened. Newspapers reported an explosion at night far off the coast of Spain or Portugal, the ship's instability in heavy seas, a loss of cargo, and missing passengers and crew. First reports could not confirm whether the ship would stay afloat, as the weather was too difficult for a major sea rescue effort to be launched. Industry experts assumed the ship would disappear about 300–500 miles off the European coast in waters too deep to recover anything.

Myron phoned Todd to tell him the story was now public, further complicating their plans to take charge of the file before they were both badly hurt by Washington and European rivals. "Look, you spend the morning writing the report as we outlined last night," Myron said. "But I'm not going to wait. I'm making a couple of calls as soon as I can. I'm going to send the FBI over to Buffalo to go through Hugh's apartment and talk to the university where he apparently made a deal. And then I'm calling our friend at the Canadian embassy so she can alert her colleagues about what's happening. I'm glad you're not objecting, as I'd just have to scream at you. We'll talk daily to make sure this all unfolds how we want it to."

The news spread that the son of an infamous Spanish armament dealer was lost at sea and presumed dead. Since no one knew of Angel's connections to America at the outset, the news was brutally curt, with no understanding of the devastation this brought to the lives of the survivors living on that side of the Atlantic.

Funeral arrangements were made in Spain and private to the family, so Heather and Brent were left to grieve on their own, which they did for weeks afterward. Angel's death left an incredible hole in their lives, as he was the first of their peers to die without cause. Such youthful promise brought to an unexpected end.

OTTAWA, ONTARIO

Spring 2009

It didn't take long for the Canadian government to swing into action in late May after the flurry of weekend calls and meetings. Security officials whom Shelly Spicer had been quietly informing for months were still surprised by the severity of the problems now leaking into public view. The crisis intensified early Monday morning when they were debriefed about a rare Sunday night meeting between the prime minister and his minister of finance.

Finance Minister John Fisher's regular flight brought him back to Ottawa by 9:30 p.m. most Sunday evenings. As usual, it was both dark and overly quiet with the sole local weather question for the residents of the nation's capital being would it be cold and damp or warm and damp? It may not be the worst weather among the tiny capitals of the world, but it made every diplomat's short list. He used the time on the plane to have a few drinks, read a small number of documents, and think about the problems that lay ahead. Were the headlines over the weekend correct? Was his country headed for more financial chaos? Was his finance department thinking about all of his options? It was too much some nights to sort it out. The biggest issue, he decided, was drawing up a script for caucus in a special meeting Tuesday night. The PM wanted him to go over the numbers with their parliamentary colleagues, who had grown uncomfortable with all the rumors that were swirling in harsh economic times. News from the States was so overwhelmingly negative that his officials were now constantly afraid the Canadian economy might go into a tailspin.

"That's not going to happen on my watch," he brooded as he left the plane, saying his usual thanks to the tired-out crew. He passed through the airport as quickly as possible, keeping his head down to avoid random, troublesome conversations, and then slid into the waiting limo so that his driver could quickly take him to his Rockcliffe apartment. No calls, he hoped, as late Sunday night was not the time to bring him arguments, diverting news, bad economic information—all these could be dealt with in the morning.

His team was good. It was always surprising how many smart people would come to places like Ottawa and Washington, spending a few years helping out and then settling in elsewhere with their own careers. In addition to his own inner circle of political aides, the finance department supported him with people and policies that could only be described as brilliant. Since finance officials everywhere loved to control governments, everyone worked their hardest to stay on top of every issue, making sure their minister had the strength to keep them on as top dogs.

Louis interrupted his thoughts. "The phone's for you. The prime minister needs to see you tonight." The two senior politicians had been close friends for decades, and both knew that there could be no space between them on any major issue. All differences were worked out privately before cabinet and caucus. No surprises. They had none of the troubles like the ones seen between Gordon Brown and Tony Blair. They worked hard at keeping the peace in the political family.

As there was no refusing Prime Minister Jimmy Caruthers, they drove to his residence quickly and were met by a somber leader. The fact that he didn't bother to offer a drink made it clear that he wanted Fisher's total attention and concentration.

"I had an unusual visitor yesterday. Paul Livingstone who, as you know, is the president of the Cascadia Pension Fund, called late Friday requesting a low profile but immediate meeting. I hardly know anything about him, but our cabinet minister from British Columbia also phoned, urging me to meet with him this weekend. You've met him a couple of times, right? But all the investment guys stay away from us here in Ottawa—they think we're crazy and irresponsible—look after their own shop, make pensioners good money. All that's wonderful. All tickety-boo."

"So what's so bad about that?"

"Exactly, I asked, what can be bad about this? The worse that can happen is that they make a bad investment decision and lose a few billion. Like the guys in Montreal with their pension plan. The story he brought me, however, has put us in the middle of an international crisis like Canada has rarely experienced, in North Africa, of all places. I'll bet nobody in caucus, including you, John, could name two capital cities from over there! In fact, I even had to have a brief conversation with the U.S. president today to let them know we're on top of this. His advisers all tell him that we're out to lunch on security matters."

They both were now ready for a scotch, needing some relief from the pressure. Along with the drinks, the finance minister's and the PM's chiefs of staff came in quietly to be briefed on the situation.

"Cascadia has about $60 billion in assets," the prime minister began. "A few years back, they decided to move some money offshore to gain some exposure to world markets. The Canadian investment communities in Vancouver, Calgary, Toronto, and Montreal were all over them with an endless number of bad schemes. They needed a bigger playground, so they set up contacts in London, Hong Kong, New York, and Brazil.

"At the same time, several countries were setting up sovereign wealth funds, often based on energy resource tax structures. Pull money from oil and gas revenues, put it to work elsewhere. These are big funds with secretive operations, set up to operate opposite from the way we do. There's no transparency, no reports to Parliament, none of the things we do.

"Most of our pension fund guys are small players. I hear the big sovereignty funds from places like Singapore are many times larger than the ones we have. But, of course, our guys want to make deals with them and get into markets we've missed because of our isolated history, culture, language, politics—I can think of many good reasons we could be left behind.

"Last week, the deputy director of the SEC arranged to meet the president of our own national pension fund by inviting him to Washington. He requested that the trip be camouflaged and that no information be shared with our ambassador. He used as an excuse that American regulators were apprehensive about a rogue trader in his organization.

"It was a very uncomfortable meeting. These guys were joined by the head of CIA operations in the Middle East, a crazed group at the best of times. They've been trying to track how so much cash was finding its way into several North African countries. The stories about Syria and Iran are well known to the American security forces, and we all expect trouble from them. What the Americans don't expect is trouble from us, their quiet neighbor to the north.

"So there's been a lot of research, a lot of informants giving the CIA bits and pieces. The Americans are frantic, because Cascadia appears to be working with a Spanish armament dealer to send rockets to Africa or the Middle East. The Yanks simply don't believe that these developments are not connected. We have to find out for our own interests what's happening—and soon.

"Once the Washington meeting was over, I got an urgent call. Apparently, all the guys in the pension investment field know each other. The Americans correctly anticipate that if they bring in our top guy, he'll immediately take it upon himself to contact Cascadia. Sure enough that happened immediately.

That's why this Livingstone character came here. Apparently, his fund is mixed up with this arms deal through an investment in a California aerospace company and now has a whole series of problems with the American government. There is a high alert on the terrorist watch. It's serious. And, believe it or not, there are guys in Winnipeg wanting to play in this game. They think they can sneak into a side deal, make a few bucks, and then disappear. They're in for a rude awakening. Your political chum, the mayor, is apparently up to his eyeballs in this. Winnipeggers should stick with hockey deals, not terrorists from unpleasant countries.

"Here's what I need you to do this week. Your department will have to research this investment business and tell you how it's run. You'll have to know everything by the time our caucus meets next week, as this might be public by the weekend in the States. I hope we can buy some time to stay out of trouble. The president is planning to talk to me by next Sunday, so move as quickly as you can. Thanks."

As Fisher sat back in his limo behind Luis, he rhetorically asked how events like this happen. Didn't anyone in the government know anything?

The finance minister called Yvonne Mebane, his chief of staff, into his office at the conclusion of two intense days of briefings. "Okay, I know what we have to do," he said. Yvonne cut in, "Nothing! Whatever the investors were up to in Vancouver has nothing to do with us. I'm telling you, this is their business, their mistake. They didn't ask you for advice; they don't report to you or anyone else in Ottawa. They made a big, stupid mistake. They should have checked their facts. Now they have the American government pounding them for financing and supporting an international armaments family—so what? It's terrible, but it's none of our business. We're not going to wear their problems. We're clean."

"Finished?" asked the annoyed minister.

"Probably not, given your desire to fix every problem in the world."

He chuckled, and both sat them quietly while he absorbed both the meeting and Yvonne's comments, which she had obviously used as a tactic to head off his instincts to always get more involved.

"Listen," he began, "I don't disagree with you. We weren't involved at all with this situation. But think about it. The next in line in the family armament business shows up in Winnipeg. We know nothing about this guy. Yet the Americans know everything. Why's that? Because the Americans actually care about who's bombing whom around the world."

After glancing at Yvonne's skeptical face, Fisher continued to present his case. "I know you lefties don't like real-world politics, nor do your fellow travelers, the anti-American nationalists who protest regularly from coast to coast." He knew she would take the bait.

"Get on with your absurd position," Yvonne answered, "and put aside your horrendous horseshit about your political opponents. I don't want the whole department to see me walking out of here slamming the door. They'll say it's cute while spreading rumors about your judgment. What's the deal here?"

The minister came to his point. "We have to be completely onside with the American president in his public fight against terrorism. That nation has now elected two presidents in a row, covering both parties, who demand cooperation of their allies in fighting their terrorist enemies. Since we have no choice, let's go forward with enthusiasm. We need to be clear on the one important message: we will join America and support its fight against terrorism at home and around the globe."

He sat back; proud that he had said something profound.

Yvonne could only fuss over the stacks of papers in her arms. "I've no clue what you're talking about. It's obvious you're dealing with information that I don't have. I'll have to assume the PM has given you clear instructions to do something. I know you'll do cartwheels to keep this job. So be it. What exactly do you have to do to please your boss?"

Fisher smiled slightly. "Finally, political realism survives another day." He instructed Yvonne. "Find the president of Cascadia and ask him to Ottawa. Tell him nothing. By the time he gets here, we'll have a plan that makes everyone happy; from you to the PM. Away you go."

Yvonne had known that this was to be the outcome of their meeting long before it started. Fisher was the quintessential leader whose moral ambivalence about worldly events had long ago become submerged and replaced by his pragmatic approach to solving whatever crisis popped up in his career. He was completely comfortable with his moral compass that had formed at Sunday church services. He believed his role as a politician was simply to accept events as they happened daily. Nothing untoward or overtly corrupt would happen on his watch, as he understood without any ambivalence the evil displayed in the lives of Juan Moreno and Hugh Parks. He was definitely not the political crusader that Arthur Crawford was aspiring to be.

PHILADELPHIA, PENNSYLVANIA

Spring 2009

The sinking ship and missing rockets immediately wreaked havoc among the many innocent bystanders. This was particular true for Angel's two friends in Philadelphia.

Brent had rarely heard from him in the months leading up to his death. He assumed that his friend wanted to prove to his dad that he could quickly learn a new business. While Angel was in Philadelphia, he was either out alone with Heather or the two of them were playing in a high society world that excluded Brent who they viewed as a likeable nerd without contacts in the city. Despite his tenacious commitment to arranging the original transaction, and his special interest in Angel's engagement on the ground in California, Brent did not discover until it was too late how his colleagues at Aird were having their own investment advisory committee, led by Theodore and Jarred, monitor monthly AT's statements searching for falsified records. Jarred had his supervisors perplexed enough to call in a major Los Angeles-based accounting firm to ferret out details in support of his suspicion about the company's finances. While Caesar and Angel had been looking for opportunities; Jarred was searching for fraud.

At the same time, Juan and Martin mostly tucked away in Europe were learning as much as they could about AT on their own. Could they use it when the time came to go ahead with their supplying armaments into North Africa? Juan talked daily to Angel under the guise of family business but he was busy pulling out valuable information that he passed onto Martin who in turn had found an innocuous way to strike a relationship with Caesar.

Obviously Caesar wasn't expecting any immediate review when Angel headed north as planned, especially since his new owner was quite happy. He casually explained away most questions from both Jarred and Angel so he wasn't worried. Aird's rep had sounded more exasperated by the shadowy deposits from CR. Trust, all in cash, that weren't supported by proper invoices particularly since no California agency or banks had any records of such a company. External auditors had walked several months ago during the ownership transfer because of this anomaly in order to protect their reputation. Besides, no staff wanted to spend extra days at an abandoned air force base on the edge of a desert searching out the truth. That left only the single-minded Jarred.

The day that Angel pulled himself up in the cab for his first long haul truck drive, Brent sat staring at the information Jarred had casually thrown his way as he passed by his desk. It was indeed bad news for Aird's investors, not so much on the scale of the thefts but on the likelihood something else was happening. Had Brent missed all of this in his own review?

When Brent chose to ignore Jarred's overtures to talk about his findings, in the hope he would go away, his colleague immediately phoned Theodore. His conclusions were too compelling to ignore. He barely could bring himself to consider where this now was headed. Jarred took a deep breath and continued against his better judgment that told him if this spiraled out of control, the police and financial regulators would be on their doorstep looking to blame someone. But, he thought, if he were going to make a career move over this file, now was the time. "I think Caesar has his own cargo on most trips and is getting paid pretty good money. He makes himself scarce whenever one of the accountants wants to clarify any transactions. We could pressure the drivers for more information, but I think they'll all claim they don't speak English. They will protect Caesar."

Theodore regretted the incriminating information he was hearing. He really liked Brent but now felt betrayed. He thought it through; AT management had a phantom business no one had noticed. Rodriguez used company trucks to make a lot of money. Marsha had been right: if they had sold the whole company, they would not currently be embroiled in a money-laundering scheme not of their own making. The last thing he wanted to do was to make Marsha look smarter than he was.

Theodore swiveled at his desk until he sat looking out over the Vancouver harbor. Cruise ships were disembarking passengers returning from Alaska catching a few days in Canada's most beautiful city. Better than the view out of Winnipeg's tallest skyscraper, he thought. He had one of the great perches in the pension business. He had income, status, reputation, and a spectacular view out his window. Again, he asked out loud to no one in particular: Was it worth protecting? Yes. He turned back to his desk and phoned Marsha. It was time to act.

When the FBI phoned during the same day to arrange a meeting, Brent knew this could only be trouble. He called Marsha, who blew a fuse.

"What do they want? What company? What file?"

"They didn't really say. They want to come by this afternoon to talk about some unspecified recent developments; claimed one of their sister agencies needed their help, whatever that means."

Marsha now understood what was happening. "The DEA has messed up somehow, and these agents want into the AT file. We're caught in an agency war that can only hurt us. Call our advisory board and see who's available by 2 p.m. to discuss this."

Brent protested. "This isn't my file any longer. Why doesn't Jarred arrange the meeting and talk to the FBI on his own? I'm busy with other stuff."

Marsha stopped dead in her tracks. "How dare you? You brought us this problem. You are sinking us. Get on it, and don't ever question my judgment again."

She wasn't the least bit surprised when Theodore interrupted her during the teleconference call. He asked to speak first. "We concluded something was wrong a couple of weeks ago after a senior security officer contacted us. We worked on a plan and received internal committee sign-offs to launch our own investigations. Cascadia's lawyer, Jonathon Appleby, is a graduate of the Yale Law School. He recommended that we contact the antiterrorist specialist in the Justice Department who, like Jonathon, was in the top ten of his class in the same year, though at Columbia. Jonathon then flew down to Washington last Sunday afternoon. We agreed to tell no one, including this group, what was happening. It's turning out to be even more complex. Both our government's foreign affairs department and your state department are now involved. Everyone is worried that we're accidentally caught in something big with consequences outside North America. Marsha, one of your assistants called this morning with very damaging information. My guess is that the FBI will want to talk with Aird right away."

There was nothing else to say. She had been turned in by one of her investors aided by a junior staffer. Why? Didn't they understand what this would do to her business? She was destroyed. Distressed, she heard them warn that any future meetings were subject to legal constraints. Going forward, they would require FBI approval to talk to anyone except each of their legal advisors. Meeting finished, Marsha lost it, walked into the hallway and stared at Brent who was sitting by himself, looking discombobulated waiting for the FBI interview. Mustering all her pent-up frustration, she screamed at him "Watch out or you're fired!" and slammed shut her office door.

Suddenly she reappeared. She wasn't finished with him. Marsha turned on Brent with a vengefulness that he could have never expected; her fierce mouth spewed out adjectives and expressions he had never heard before and never wanted to hear again in any situation. Years of arrogant control came into play as the helpless Brent looked aghast at his attacker.

"These are your last two hours on the job. You are to sit here by yourself until the FBI agent arrives. No phone calls, no walks around the office. I'm calling building security, which will send someone up to watch you. I will sit through the FBI session and explain to them that you've been a rogue employee arranging a favorable deal for your university chum, Angel. Your analysis should have showed you several months ago what was happening, but you chose to ignore it. Our Canadian investor found it first, and we've been humiliated. There's a good chance I'll be forced out of the investment business.

"You will answer all of the questions with answers from my script. For this interview, don't even pretend that you have your own thoughts or interpretations of events. If you follow my lead, I might think about giving you a few months more pay than the law requires. Don't ask us for a letter of recommendation unless you want me to pick up the phone and tell the prospective employer how poorly you performed. Here's the FBI coming in now."

Brent sat there not knowing what to say or where to turn. The agent listened quietly to Marsha's disavowing of her employee but was curiously unmoved. He thanked her, recognized her busy schedule, and asked her to leave. After she reluctantly departed, the agent began talking to Brent in his same calm voice.

"You can relax. Although she's probably threatening to destroy you, we have a different take. I simply need to go over the story to confirm details so that we've got the whole picture. Before I start, I want to tell you that we now know a very senior DEA officer came in to visit her a few months ago, told her what was going on, and literally forced her to sell the AT investment so that he could follow the trail of the new owner. Unfortunately, he forgot to tell the rest of the American security world what he was doing until this week. Let's go over the chronology and the facts as we know them."

This took about thirty minutes. Brent had to admit they had the story covered as well as one could expect from these plodding organizations. The agent wanted to confirm more precisely what Brent thought was going on.

Brent outlined his side of the story. "For weeks, I just smiled and thought how lucky Angel was to turn around a company by the end of the first quarter. It wasn't a lot of money, but as a percentage, the growth and profitability were impressive. It was later that we decided to take a closer look."

In response to questions about the Moreno family, Brent replied, "I think Angel and his dad had a solid relationship. Angel phoned his dad most days and returned to Spain when he could. He told me Juan was proud of his accomplishments and encouraged him to get out, meet more people, and demonstrate the family's skills. At the same time, his dad let him travel and play. He knew about Heather but said nothing, as Angel's mother disapproved of any North American girl.

"Heather? Was she involved in this business in addition to the affair?"

"I can't answer that fully. I know she pulled strings and introduced him to all the right players here in Philadelphia. I don't know if he told her much about the family business; each guy operates differently with his women. I know that they met in Montreal recently, if that's of any importance. She phoned me to say it was a great time."

"Did Angel ever talk about rockets or his family's friends in the Middle East or Africa?"

"Never. He was strictly a guy wanting to make big money in America. Nothing more. We never talked politics except that he said he liked Obama and loved to hear so much Spanish on the streets of our cities."

The agent gave him a business card and asked him to e-mail a forwarding address, obviously sensing the immediate and brutal end of Brent's investment career.

His office was already cleared, and Brent's final check was in a plain envelope with a note from the legal department indicating that cashing it meant he would keep all of the affairs of the company to himself.

Stunned by his own bad news, he phoned Heather, knowing she was having trouble accepting what had happened to Angel. They agreed to meet for martinis later that afternoon at Rouge, a bar and restaurant on Rittenhouse Square. He of course had to tell her about his being fired but he dismissed her efforts to find out all the details. Instead he learned of her meeting with the FBI, during which the investigator dwelt on the details of her time together with Angel by confirming that she arranged many meetings, dinners, and weekends in the country through her social connections. Heather and Angel were viewed as a new couple, fun to be with; people assumed he was rich enough to carry their life together. Heather was surprised that the FBI knew so much so fast. She told Brent that the agent wanted every detail about their time in Canada.

"He asked me: 'Did you know where Angel was going next after Montreal?'

"I replied carefully, as I didn't understand where the interview might be heading. 'At first, no, I didn't. I had to return here late Sunday afternoon for work on Monday. Before I left for the airport, he sat up in our hotel room and told me his secret. He was going to surprise his parents by showing up at a Spanish port as a passenger on a container ship carrying his firm's very first transatlantic cargo. He was so excited about his first overnight train trip in North America. Angel anticipated arriving in two weeks at Barcelona's port. He was so, so proud. He thought he would be back here sometime next month. We didn't talk long, as I had to shower, dress, and head off to the airport. I heard once from him since—he called from Halifax— I really wasn't expecting another call until he arrived back home.'"

Heather and Brent sadly finished their drinks. Neither said much more, as it was clear to both that their lives were about to change dramatically.

ST CATHARINES, ONTARIO

Spring 2009

Emma Parks had looked at her dad's keys for several weeks before she decided to Google the address attached on a card. She and a couple of her friends were increasingly bored after years in the same Brock University residences. They were always searching during the weekends for something different to do as St. Catharines was definitely a city more appealing to the elderly. The location seemed okay; one of her friends had a car, so they crossed the Niagara River and explored Buffalo. The three of them easily found the building; it turned out to be just the right place to laze about without spending too much money. She phoned her mom during her first visit to say that they were using dad's condo, remembering long afterward the quiet surprise with which this news was received.

All Joanne said was "A condo? I should have remembered that. Hugh never really mentioned it, and he's not there very much, is he?"

"Doesn't look like it. Not much here. TV works. We've made ourselves comfortable. Let me know if he's coming so we don't surprise him."

Emma finished her classes and was preparing final exams; after that came the harsh task of looking for work in Ontario's bad economy. Still not wanting to return home, she had even applied for graduate school in unpopular fields such as library science, in the hope of delaying any return to Winnipeg. From her perspective, it was better to keep going to school and to stay in the cocoon of education. She dreaded most of all that she might run out of options and be forced to return home to live with her gaud awful father. All too soon she would be facing a series of decisions with unknown consequences. Instead of enjoying her success as a graduate, she was suffering anxiety attacks about what came next in her life.

Although most of her friends were busy with exams, the one who owned the car, Bridgette, declared she could use an overnight break in Buffalo. Emma jumped at the chance to get away. They did their usual wandering around without spending a nickel, ending up back at the condo early. The neighbors, who had gotten to know her, were always curious about her dad, with whom they rarely spoke. Her presence reassured them that all was normal.

Suddenly, the next morning before 7:00 a.m., Emma's world turned chaotic. There wasn't even a knock at the door. A key slid into the lock, and two men, casually chatting with each other, entered. They startled poor Bridgette, sleeping on the couch, who yelled as though Emma could save her.

"What are you young ladies doing here?" asked the first officer. He and his partner flashed their FBI badges, identifying themselves as Tom Bates and Russell Smith.

Emma stepped into the living room, having quickly slipped on a light sweater and jeans. "This is my father's place."

"Really? Its owner is listed on the condominium document as a corporation, owned by other corporations. Who do you know at Fenwick Investments?" Smith's question totally caught her off guard.

"Nobody," was the one-worded sullen reply.

"Your dad's never mentioned Fenwick Investments, his employer?"

"No."

"Yet he tells you that it's okay to use this place, right?"

"Yes."

"How did you get in?"

"I have a key!"

"How did you find the building?"

"My dad gave me an address, and I found it on Google maps."

"That's how you found this place? No, I meant how did you find the key? Where did you come from? Your home? Are you living with your parents? Or just your dad?" Smith quickly questioned Emma while Bates watched Bridgette's reactions.

Emma was overwhelmed. "We came across the border from Canada. I go to university close by. Mom and dad live in the west. I moved out almost four years ago."

"Really? But you have a key to a condo in Buffalo owned by an American company, Fenwick Investments. How did that come to pass?" Same question, different angle.

Emma tried feebly to fight back. "I told you, my dad gave it to me." Instead of stopping, she volunteered more to these policemen.

"He visited me a few times after I came here to college. He liked to keep up appearances among his friends back in Winnipeg. He probably was appeasing my mom as they fought over me all the time. We'd go to the same place, the Keg, a Canadian steakhouse chain. He talked about his great life and left me a couple hundred bucks, usually American money for some stupid reason. Early last fall, he gave me this set of keys. He didn't think any of his business friends would be around a place he had in Buffalo." Emma paused unexpectedly. "Until now, I just remembered. He thought he might be back around the end of April, but I haven't seen him."

"Neither have we, but we know people who have—I'll come back to that in a minute. Who else did your dad give a key to?"

"I didn't think anyone, but I did notice a credit card receipt from one of my dad's business friends back home. I'd have to look around to find it. His nickname is Stomper," she shrugged as she finished, as if to say, 'he's no good, an idiot.'

"It's okay, we don't need the receipt," Smith responded. That was an easy answer, because they already had a copy of it.

"We never asked: what's your dad's full name?" Bates realized they had never asked the obvious, and the girls would later be second-guessing them, if they didn't do it sooner.

Totally out of character, Emma shot back: "You already know that I'm Emma, also Parks like my dad, and this is my school friend, Bridgette Garson. She's never met my dad."

Agent Smith had decided before this outburst to increase the pressure on the girls, as it might be his only chance; later there would be lawyers and more senior security types from different agencies engaged, poking holes in his work.

"We have reason to believe that you and your dad are illegally hiding guns and cash that you cannot account for. One of the owners from Fenwick Investments was here a few days ago. He described what he found and asked us to come over. Do you mind if we check around?"

Emma wasn't quick enough on her feet. The agents soon had the kitchen table covered with five guns, $5,000 cash, a key to a bank safety deposit box, and fake American identification for her father.

"Since you are sleeping here, we consider you to be in possession of these goods. You are now going to be taken to headquarters, where we will fingerprint you and charge you with weapon violations; we will consider how to deal with the money, to say nothing of the fake ID. Agent Smith is going to take down all the information he needs from Bridgette. You're a Canadian too? Well, he'll go down and check out your car. If it's clean, you can go; based on the signed statement saying you didn't know what Emma and her dad were up to. You'll need to tell the local police back home whenever you leave campus. Both governments will want to know where you are going to be until all of this is cleared up. We'll be on the phone with your university to set up this protocol by the time you get back."

Bridgette left dumbfounded. What had Emma been up to? Was her family into drugs? She made her way downstairs with Smith. Her car was, of course, clean. She was stunned and in more than a little trauma. At first she didn't know what she was going to say to friends. That hesitation passed. Bridgette crossed back to Canada and made her way to campus. By Tuesday, it seemed everyone knew her side of the story. The mystery increased daily with Emma's continuing absence.

Still in Buffalo, Emma was overwhelmed by the seriousness of her situation. She was living her life as a victim, not as a fighter. There was absolutely no evidence to support their allegations, but she had no energy to fight off their claims. The sheer aggressiveness of the law enforcement agencies broke her spirit. She shut down her limited communication skills and crawled into a shell of protracted silence. This reminded her too much of home, where the exaggerated self-importance of her dad overwhelmed Emma and her mother. Both she and Joanne had retreated away from Hugh in their own fashion, each employing different styles to cope with the constant intrusion of the abusive father and husband who minded his manners in front of others. The picture-perfect entrepreneur played the community leader role to the hilt but turned around to hurt them daily in their own home.

Emma's exodus from Winnipeg and the building of her own life had been nearly complete until that Sunday morning in Buffalo. She suspected the American police would get bored with her but that it might take a few horrendous weeks. In the meantime, no doubt, her school life would be destroyed by storytelling among classmates, as uninformed youth pass around misinformation in person and through the Internet with abandon. The FBI knew that, and agents were watching the various chat sites to get a better fix on this defeated young woman sitting in their cell.

Thankfully for Emma, it actually didn't take them long to decide that she was of little value. A life in jail would be too extreme of a court judgment against her. As the agents huddled after each series of interviews, they recognized the all-too-familiar family life that the real villain, Hugh, had created for this woman and probably her mother. The FBI also realized there were no small or intermediate steps within the American justice system. If they presented the circumstantial evidence in the forceful fashion required by their mandate, a judge would have no choice but to instruct the jury to secure the harsh sentence always meted out in national security cases. This, they decided as a team, shouldn't happen to Emma.

With the quiet help of Myron, Todd orchestrated a way out in which everyone could be seen as a winner. Emma's university had swung into action to protect one of its own by contacting the Buffalo-based Canadian consulate. Its top official, Brad Eliot, was smart enough to make his inquiries in a way that put everyone on notice about Canada's grave concerns without any unnecessary media attention. Eliot knew, as they did, that by Tuesday there had to be a clear path for her release before the weekend. Otherwise, the rush of lawyers, media, and state department types would overwhelm the regional FBI office. The word from Todd was that her father looked like a genuine terrorist supporter operating a sleeper cell in the States out of his Buffalo condo. Authorities would punish him. It was likely that Hugh would receive a series of sentences that would cost him his freedom, probably forever. There was, however, absolutely no reason to entangle Emma in this legal quagmire.

Lead agent FBI Smith brought Emma into a small room for a final interview.

"I don't think I have to tell you how close you've come to spending many, many years in a prison here, with little hope to transfer back to Canada where jail life is more pleasant. Your consul general is waiting to drive you back to campus. Although you are free to go, we still officially consider you a suspect in your father's American terrorist cell. Until we close that investigation, you cannot re-enter this country. In my experience, these investigations remain open for years. I don't anticipate seeing you for decades. We in this office sincerely wish you all the best with your life in Canada. And be more careful."

Emma was indeed back home in a few hours. A representative from Brock's student services met her, asked what she needed, and presented her with a revised exam schedule to accommodate her harrowing experience in Buffalo. "You can stay in residence, but the university arranged the option of you staying in seclusion with one of your professors." As of yet, she had no idea what was being said about her on campus; it took some gentle persuasion to put her at ease about the safer environment at a professor's home in nearby Niagara-on-the-Lake.

After an extensive interview with several administrators who were anxious to know how she was doing, Emma was eventually left sitting alone with Eliot and the dean, who was put in charge of her file.

"We've been in constant touch with your mom. She's beside herself. You can phone her from my office in a few minutes as she's expecting you to call right away."

"And my dad: what's happened to him?"

A long, dead silence followed. Finally, Eliot spoke.

"As far as we can tell, he's sitting in jail in upstate New York, probably in Syracuse. Criminal charges are pending, and they've allowed us one consular visit. He's not taking it well, as you can imagine. He's under the illusion that all of this is a mistake and that he'll be on his way any day now. The FBI came over to our embassy in Washington, along with the DEA. They spent over two hours reviewing the developments involving your dad that go back for several months.

"Along the way he's met a few characters that led to this mess."

WINNIPEG, MANITOBA

Early summer 2009

Joanne was not much help to Emma. The shock of her husband's escapade was greater than she anticipated. Even though she knew full well that she was living in a complex web of deceit that Hugh had created quite methodically, she couldn't bring herself to walk away. It was in her blood to stick it out and to show others how to make a life with her own grim determination, fighting back the odds that favored failure.

There wasn't much left in the family's bank account the day after Hugh was arrested; she was smart enough to move quickly and search through his hiding spots. Two briefcases produced more cash than she had imagined, more than enough for a couple of years, with her modest lifestyle. Within two hours, she was out of the house, driving around in circles, endeavoring to work out where to hide so much money. She settled on the soft-hearted professor; she phoned and then picked Arthur up for a coffee. She immediately drove toward the campus, leaving him no room to decline when she asked him to take the two briefcases to his office right then and there.

"Hugh's done something stupid. This stuff is mine, and I need it to survive. It's not his, and I must make sure his friends don't get it. I need to hide it right away, and no one will look for it in your office. Are you okay with this? You have to stay quiet no matter what the fuss might be. This is my life security right here in this car."

Arthur smiled as he accepted his new assignment. They parked at the nearly empty campus, and each carried a briefcase over to his office. Although the office was small, there was so much mess that no one, not even Annie, would notice two more briefcases.

Arthur looked around, satisfied with their decision. "This will be fine for now, as classes are finished except for a few grad student projects; there's not much happening around the department. There's not a soul here today, so we're safe. Let's talk for a few minutes and then be on our way."

They left fifteen minutes later, observed only by the security camera that recorded they no longer had their briefcases.

Joanne continued on to her sister's house for dinner, as she frequently did when Hugh was away. Her life further fell apart around 9:00 p.m., when she arrived home to find the local police with their search warrant in hand. They were backed up by a single RCMP detective, not in uniform, obviously ordered from Ottawa to be there. Arthur would watch the morning news, surprised by the raid, but not in a mood to second-guess his decision. It would not be the last time he had to help out Joanne.

It didn't take Stomper long to follow the visit from the police. He was at Joanne's door before noon the next day wearing the traditional grin of the stupid sidekick that he was.

"Hi Joanne. I just got a call from an American attorney who says he is representing Hugh. Can you believe this? The newspaper was crazy this morning about what happened. He's clean as a whistle. I'm calling a meeting of the Bison Board after work so that we can put together the $50,000 retainer the lawyer wants to get started on the case. We'll come back to you if we need money from the family."

Joanne, anxious to move the conversation away from this as quickly as she could, said, "I can't help you right now; he left the family bank accounts empty. I can cover expenses for two months, but that's about it. What's coming in from your business ventures? He was always so proud of the work you did together." Joanne was barely able to cover her sarcasm.

"Good question. We've certainly done well in the past, as Hugh was a genius. It was always a pleasure for me to do projects with him."

Noticing the past tense in Stomper's remarks, Joanne continued to ask questions that Stomper avoided answering. Finally, desperate to rid herself of this overbearing goon, Joanne asked, "Since you came by without calling, can I assume you are looking for something specific?"

"Well, yes," Stomper began rather uncomfortably. "Hugh and I were working together on a couple of files, including the very successful wind turbine project. He always insisted on taking the files home with him for safekeeping. That was fine with me, because, as you know, we often met here. Could I take a quick look for them?"

The memories of Hugh and Stomper together standing far back in the yard crossed through her imagination like a fast-moving prairie storm. Joanne shivered, remembering when she'd caught Emma staring out her bedroom window at the two crooks in the same fashion. Neither liked these meetings. Neither had ever spoken to the other about them.

After these thoughts had passed, she shrugged and stared into Stomper's aggressive eyes. She stopped to look more closely at his face. It was scratched, bruised, and covered awkwardly with makeup. One more sudden insight crossed her mind before she spoke: he'd be another great husband. "Did you fall? You're bruised, aren't you?"

Stomper was avoiding any discussion about his face no matter how long she stared. Finally he admitted what had happened. "Just when Hugh left town, some kids ambushed me downtown in a back lane. They were pretty rough until I pulled a gun. Sure surprised them." End of story. Martin would be disappointed to learn that his target had escaped.

She returned to the issue at hand. "I don't think you'll find anything. The police spent over two hours here and took away all the files they could find in his office and in the basement. They even went thought all the suitcases and containers to find if he was hiding things. I have no idea what they found there. They were super polite; some knew Hugh because he'd helped them get a community grant, but in the end they did what they had to do. I think there may have been an FBI agent standing beside the RCMP observer. Who knows? There were a lot of people at my humble house late into the night."

"I'll just be a minute." Stomper was nonchalant but determined to look around.

She hesitated. It dawned on her that she might learn something. "Come in. Is there anything particular that you're looking for? Maybe I can help."

"A couple of briefcases. Just like the ones from Office Depot that everyone uses to carry their papers to work. It's nothing special. Just our files in them." He was avoiding looking at her as he spoke.

Although Joanne was outraged by the obvious lie, she wanted to extract as much information as possible. She motioned him to come and look around wherever he wanted. She faked working in the kitchen while he searched. Sure enough, within a few minutes he was checking out the spot where she had found the briefcases. The sounds from the basement became a little more anxious after that; soon Stomper was back in the kitchen less confident and very much less friendly than he had been twenty minutes earlier.

He confirmed he found nothing. She made a suggestion.

"I have the contact info given to me last night by the lead police officer who directed the search of my home. Would you like it? I'm sure he'd love to hear from you. He told me he would return any file they didn't need as soon as possible. I'm sure that includes any file relevant to these wonderful wind turbines. Hugh talked about them all the time."

Stomper declined the offer, as she'd anticipated he would.

"No, that's fine. I won't bother the police. Why don't we leave it this way: you'll call me when they start returning files, okay?"

"Sure," Joanne answered as pleasantly as she could. She assumed the worst. The police would keep track of her until they were sure she wasn't an accessory to Hugh's crimes. She should, however, move these briefcases again soon. She didn't want to telephone the professor at work; perhaps she would camp out on the veranda to await his passing on his way home.

MADRID, SPAIN

Early summer 2009

Far away, Juan was recovering from the shock of losing his son at sea. The authorities had put together a story based on Angel's truck records, his weekend in Montreal with Heather, the arrangements with the container ship to be a passenger, and the loading of his first shipment destined for Spain.

Juan's wife sat through this discussion, totally stunned and overcome with grief by the sudden turn in their fortunes. Her husband knew full well that she could never be compensated for the loss of their firstborn; Maria would remain angry and heartbroken to her dying days. Other issues might fill his business day, but losing Angel would bring her unending sorrow. During the official briefings, there was no mention of any armaments of any sort. The sinking was attributed to a late spring storm that destabilized the overburdened container ship, one of the first out of the northern regions after a long winter. Nor did they mention that they found out during their investigation that the change in itinerary for the container was not matched by any modification in Angel's destination. What did Angel know about the contents of his first trans-Atlantic container? Did he not know about the rockets? Was the ship's insurance adjuster on the same path? What would Myron's reaction be as reports filtered back through the channels of international counterespionage agencies?

Myron, putting down the initial cryptic report from overseas, phoned Todd. "I see now that Angel was not likely part of his dad's gang. Can't imagine being Juan, sitting beside his wife, and explaining why his battles among the Muslims cost them their only well-educated and soon-to-be-wealthy Catholic boy in the family. Unbelievable what couples do to each other. In any case, we've heard back from the embassy that our views were presented forcefully. Juan was told in guarded tones, I imagine, that our government is not at all pleased with what we are hearing and that we will be formally asking for an opportunity to interview him. At some point, I'm sure, Spanish officials will visit Juan and offer their official findings on the shipping accident. I want you to call over and make sure they get the message to Juan that the White House is totally engaged in this story. Bluff, pull out all the stops. Juan has to know there will be consequences. Perhaps you should have someone bump into his wife while she's out shopping. Let's tell her the truth as to why she lost her son."

Todd responded briefly with the assurance that the Spaniards would know immediately what the Americans wanted to happen.

Despite Todd's intervention, the Spanish government arranged for a single senior officer to visit Juan a second time with its accident report. It was arranged that there were to be no witnesses to the conversation; Maria joined only for a cursory summary before the officer left.

"You should be fully apprised that there is no doubt," he whispered to Juan, "the Americans want to know what you were up to and where this shipment was heading. There will be no peace until they settle their score. They suspect there's another shipment out there somewhere. Better help if you can. Sorry about your loss. See you next week." The officer departed, knowing little more than when he had come. It was Juan who now knew what was happening in the intelligence circles.

Juan returned to his wife, dreading meeting her eyes. They had a comfortable relationship, a mixture of Madrid family and business tied together. Maria had been parading Angel for months, beating the bushes for the perfect bride to continue these relationships into the next generation. Angel's girl, Heather, had been a distant distraction; however, Maria knew that when it came time to set up a new powerful household back here, he would do the right thing for his mother. She now not only had the trauma of death but the disappearance of the opportunity to carry on her life through her only son.

She spoke first. "Let me be as direct as possible. I must assume Angel knew nothing of the family trust business, as I, too, know nothing, I assume it's profitable, dangerous, illegal, and not to be discussed. Fine, we live well with it. I also assume you bungled this operation. You always told me we would stay away from America, that it was too big and too complicated for us. I agreed then, and I still think that now. Why you allowed Angel to go to university there, to find a woman, and to set up his own business are discussions that today I am not capable of absorbing or understanding. Maybe in a few years, though I doubt it. You should be clear on one point. If I ever find out that Angel knew what was going on and was involved in your plan, I will leave immediately. Is that clear?"

Without looking at her, he nodded briefly.

Maria continued as she gathered her things to leave the room. "I wish you luck in dealing with the authorities, who are probably now considering these possibilities. I will be nothing but loyal to you, as you have provided me with a lifestyle beyond my greatest ambitions. However, if you fail in your defense, I expect all the wealth accumulated to be safely in my hands. You are, at heart, a criminal. We both understand that once they take you away, we will never be together again.

WINNIPEG, MANITOBA

Summer 2009

The Jacobs Foundation was curious about the lack of any substantive reports from Arthur's research project. The school year was completed, and the Foundation knew from experience that they had to rope in all their academic researchers by June before they disappeared to their cottages. "Could you bring us up to speed this week?" asked Clarke in his e-mail to Arthur. "Maybe I'll call you tomorrow," he added to bring urgency to his polite request. When there was no response, Clarke called early as promised.

"Are you making progress? Is your participation in the neighborhood committee helping you better understanding local politics in the so-called real world? It's a long way from your sociology department, thank God!" Clarke probed the worried and evasive academic.

Clarke had several solid academic questions, which Arthur both anticipated and had appreciated on the rare days when he thought like a researcher. Unfortunately, he wasn't fulfilling that role very often these days, making it all too difficult to explain what exactly he did with his time. Smiling cynically at the thought of another round of academic one-upmanship, Arthur launched into a rather convoluted explanation of his accomplishments and plans that he hoped would be credible enough to camouflage his general laziness.

He elaborated on his research activities, constructing a plausible narrative about his day-to-day routine. "On the positive side, there's no doubt I'm trusted. A new community fund has given me the authority to review all of the applications and to recommend whom it might support. By your standards, this is very small potatoes but here, this is one of the few sources of community money." He paused suddenly, berating himself for almost admitting he was being paid.

Clarke would undoubtedly be suspicious to hear of the honorarium, given that the Jacobs Foundation was also compensating him for research expenses. Arthur was happy that Annie wasn't around for this particular conversation.

Arthur laid out what he now saw as the in-and-outs of civic politics in response to Clarke's abnormally long list of questions.

"Corruption here is not acknowledged. Everyone is in denial. It's quite interesting. I found this out when Jessica Brown asked me to help out at her foundation. As background, you should know that our city already has one of the oldest and biggest foundations for any city its size in North America. Monies keep coming in via estates, their investment returns are reasonable, and the applicants know the boundaries. It is a traditional relationship that you would appreciate inasmuch as donors don't expect much influence over individual donations.

"But this is entirely different. In this fund, the money pooled under Brown's mandate is entirely from the trucking and construction industries. I've asked them why this fund? They say community projects should recognize the hardworking public service. If community leaders include in their application monies to pay advisers who work at city hall during their day jobs, that's cool. There is a catch-all category of 'experienced advisers' in the application that facilitates a positive response from the funder. Looking at this from a different perspective, it would be possible, say, for a senior policeman in the traffic division, to be called upon for advice on neighborhood developments. It all sounds very innocent. It would be easy for him to pick up $20,000–25,000 in fees, with no questions asked and little paperwork. But he would know where the money came from—understand? In other words, Brown's job is to run the monies through this organization to public servants advising community projects for which they get paid handsomely. They have the cover and legitimacy, because no one can officially link them to the payoffs. She, in turn, asks me if the projects sound okay from the perspective of an urban studies specialist."

"Wow, that's quite the story," Clarke responded enthusiastically. "You don't hear of corruption like that every day. And for you to be trusted so much to be this close to the action! It's amazing. Congratulations. Just be happy you're not on the take. Keep really good notes, as this is a great story. We'll keep funding you and your assistant and will include money for your trip to Europe—and for your assistant too, if she chooses to go along. If you hand in a brief report before you go and a second more substantial one when you return from Europe, there will be no problems. Next year, if this works out, as I think it will, you'll be a full member of our team. Talk soon." Clarke signed off abruptly, his task finished.

The knock on the door could only be Annie's. Good mornings were exchanged, and he smiled warmly as a sign of his appreciation of her being there every day since classes ended.

"Early start?" she inquired.

"Yes, indeed, I'm right into it this morning." His style was far too gregarious for the occasion. Feeling that Annie was pulling away from his unreasonable jauntiness, he explained the excitement of the Clarke conversation over the progress they were making. Since he had previously told her about the honorarium from Jessica, as it paid their way around town for lunches and café stops, she asked the obvious question hanging in the air. "Did you tell him about the money you were getting?"

"It didn't come up," he responded, narrowly defining the telephone exchange. "I can't imagine that it's an issue at this point."

"Better to tell, don't you think?" Annie cheerily challenged him.

He quietly responded, "Some things are meant to pass by without any words being spoken." This was the end of the discussion for Arthur so pointedly Annie moved on.

"Okay, what's next today?" was all she said.

Just then the phone rang. Hearing Joanne's voice, Arthur motioned for Annie to check the mail down the hall at the departmental office. This was Annie's routine whenever Arthur's wife called; this morning Annie knew because of the hour, however, that it likely wasn't Brenda. She was one curious research assistant as she headed toward the departmental office for the morning mail.

Joanne spoke urgently. "I'm calling after my yoga class, using their office phone so the police can't hear our conversation. Sounds a little crazy, but after I saw you, they went through my house very carefully, and yesterday Hugh's bozo sidekick showed up, no doubt looking for the money."

"You okay?"

"Fine, but I feel very, very tense. They even visited my sister for information. They didn't go through her house, so maybe it's safer than your office."

They spent the next ten minutes inconclusively discussing options. This was neither of their worlds. They had no way to tell where there was danger and where there was opportunity. Ironically, Hugh would have been a big help.

"I waited for you yesterday, but you didn't walk by."

Arthur paused, and then said, "I tell you what. Today's perfect. You'll see me after work."

Annie returned, caught Arthur's nervous sign-off, and was naturally inquisitive.

Quickly, to head off too many questions, Arthur volunteered, "Sorry about sending you off. I never know about her. It was Joanne, the wife of Hugh Parks, whom you've read about in the paper. Remember, I met her and your Auntie Susan at their house months ago. She wants to talk local politics, which is fine, so I told her I'd drop by after we finish up here. I walk pass her house most days, and she was looking for me yesterday."

As Arthur left the social science building on his walk home, he glanced up for security cameras; it never occurred to him that campus life had changed so much that all outside spaces were covered by 24/7 security cameras. Sure enough, he spotted the one covering his door. That suggested that their entrance into the building on Sunday was captured on tape. He now had unanswered questions about the campus security system. Were the tapes kept for long? If so, were they ever reviewed by outside authorities? What would trigger such a review? How was he to remove the money even if he were not observed coming in? All these questions caused him enormous anxiety, and he wanted nothing more than to walk quickly for his five o'clock cocktail at Joanne's.

He called Brenda as soon as he arrived at the Parks' home, mentioning that he ran into Joanne on his walk back from campus and that, given her stress level, he thought he'd stop for an hour or so. Did Brenda mind? Did she want to join them for a drink? She answered no on both counts.

Joanne was a mess, as he could have expected with all these events. They spent a lot longer than the scheduled hour together.

When he subsequently reflected about his day, Arthur had to acknowledge how difficult his life was becoming. Clarke's call had pushed Arthur back into his research project. His conundrum was not so much with general questions on his study as he was able to glide by critics with his pithy commentaries. He was smart enough to know that down the road he would be tripped up because his notes were so meager. How could he instruct Annie to draft reports when there were no notes? Every police constable knew that without notes, there were no convictions.

Annie now accepted that her professor was in over his head and naturally worried about the consequences for her. She observed somewhat ruefully that he sheltered Brenda from all the bad news as they still maintained a solid relationship that had brought both of them years of peacefulness in the midst of the usual turbulence around the university. Perhaps Arthur took to heart the homely advice proffered by Jack, his loquacious professor friend who told him "We academics are proud of expertly choosing partners who look comfortable in their library, in the kids' bedrooms, and occasionally in the kitchen. We usually specialize in these low-voltage arrangements or, if we're nuts, we end up in ones where all hell is breaking loose every day, usually at home and at the university at the same time. You can't survive that chaos without becoming a complete drunk, which most are. You're lucky: you have serenity." Annie knew Arthur was putting his comfortable life at risk with his unnecessary and risky involvement in shady politics.

Annie's knock the next morning reminded him that was time to re-engage in his work; after gossiping for a few minutes, Arthur turned to direct her to the day's work. Before he could outline his instructions, she broke in and asked:

"Do you want me to start planning our European research trip, as August is quickly approaching?" Arthur shrugged to avoid telling Annie exactly what he was planning for August. Instead, he explained, "I've already made my own travel arrangements. We just have to decide where to meet. If you use the university-approved travel agent, we can arrange everything so the Foundation is billed directly. You're all looked after."

Annie wasn't at all sure what this meant. Her quizzical look couldn't be ignored, so Arthur was forced to continue.

"Why don't you organize our research appointments in Europe? Start with the Jacobs Foundation project website. Find us six social scientists in different European cities, and then e-mail them about our specific focus in the Creating Vibrant Cities project. Arrange some interviews. When we go, I'll spend time with the professors; you can find their research associates and work in local libraries."

He continued, making it up as they talked. "Let's start in Brussels and then go to Paris. From there, we'll travel to Spain. Remember, it will be difficult to find people in these cities in August. It's their big holiday month."

"Why visit Spain?" she asked, not opposed, just inquiring.

"I'm interested in Madrid, as it's the capital city. The politics there are more vociferous than what you'd ever experience in Canada or even the States. They still hit the streets as though the civil war of the thirties continues. The political classes also have not finished settling scores dating back to the Fascists. I'm sure our contacts will have plenty to say about the political turmoil after the near collapse of the European economy. After that, we'll go to Barcelona.

"While you're checking out Madrid, I want you to research the death of that young fellow who was aboard a container ship. It didn't receive much play around here, but British papers have covered this as a possible armament story. Did you see anything in *The Guardian Weekly*? We heard all about Hugh Parks, of course, but the story goes deeper than a simple border problem. At least, I'm pretty sure it does. How else can one explain the FBI being in town? There are rumors that more than a few countries are upset and accusing each other of breaching security protocols. The overseas newspapers are filled with the usual code words that the rest of us don't understand."

Right away, Arthur knew he had made a major error. He had forgotten that all of his speculative conversations were with Joanne; Annie had no clue why he mentioned the FBI being in town. She was obviously lost by this story and how it related to this project. Arthur decided he'd better be smart and show his patience for this young star. "It's a long shot. Several weeks back, Hugh Parks, who was the organizer of the science exhibition, came by Jessica's office to review his budget. He was showing off in front of what I presumed to be a young Mexican—at least at first he stuck me as someone from a wealthy Mexican family, with an Ivy League degree. He had an easy manner with a sharp mind. I quite liked him. I remembered his first name, Angel, as an unusual one to come across in the Midwest. It turns out that he was a Spaniard; Hugh explained the young man's interest in green transportation and his purchase of the locally produced wind turbines for his long-distance trucks. At the time, it was nothing of great importance, just a chance meeting with a nice young businessman.

"However, there may be more to this encounter. The shipping company was slow to release passenger and crew lists. In May, *The Times* out of London reported that a suspected arms dealer in Madrid may have lost his son, named Angel, on that boat. Probably just a coincidence." He went on. "When you find our academic contact in Madrid, see if he speaks English—most do—and e-mail to set up an appointment. Ask him in the second or third e-mail if he's ever heard of this character. "

With Annie unhappily off doing research chores that she didn't understand, Arthur phoned Jessica to find out if she had any updates. In the pressing voice of a workplace superior, she suggested lunch sooner rather than later.

"Sure, tomorrow works. Right at 12."

"Let's try somewhere other than Sam and Benny's; it would make lunch more relaxing. There's so much gossip to discuss and dissect."

He agreed to Sorrento's, as it was conveniently close for both.

Arthur returned to the most urgent task at hand and called Joanne. She picked up her phone warily, as she assumed she was under surveillance. Arthur started the conversation using coded words, as agreed upon the day before. "Annie and I just reviewed those community papers you lent me. Thanks. They were useful for our local research project. I'm hoping to return a few of them on the way home today or tomorrow, just so they don't get lost in our piles here. University offices are too small, making us look like packrats."

"That would be fine with me," Joanne answered. "I'm usually around late in the afternoon. Check for me in the garden."

He was opening up one of the briefcases to stuff in some community brochures as cover when Annie breezed back in with a pile of notes from her time in the library. It was impossible for her to miss all of the $100 bills lying there in the open. Neither acknowledged this encounter, but Annie never forgot it.

"Let's go to lunch at Central Park. We can buy a sandwich there and talk about the upcoming trip." Arthur knew it was a little early to eat, but he had to get out of there right away.

As soon as they settled back in the office after the quick lunch, Annie kept on with her research tasks by chatting about the morning's finds.

"You may have come across something of interest. I checked out numerous media websites about this Angel Moreno. All of the coverage is tentative because of his father's reputation for settling scores. The braver columnists are speculating that this is the only son of a Juan Moreno, describing him as the scion of a Spain-based trucking empire. Some stories report Juan's international armaments reputation, although the references are quite obtuse. No one is writing why his son was on the container ship out of Halifax. I also found us a professor in Madrid who communicates easily in English. He e-mailed me back and said he can meet us in his mountain village retreat, where it's cooler, about two hours out of Madrid. Sounds like fun. And Barcelona is only three hours away by train. I can't wait."

"Great work. I think we should assume this is the same Angel. Maybe you'll find pictures in a European newspaper now that they've confirmed his death. Was there any news on why the boat sank?"

"Ah, I thought you'd never ask." Annie was totally engrossed. "It's a mystery. The captain hurriedly radioed that there had been an explosion, maybe a fire—probably in the cargo area—that ripped a hole in the side of the ship, which was quickly destabilized because of the weather. Further communications were only about abandoning ship in early morning darkness. It must have been so scary," she added. "The ship was gone by mid-morning, and it will probably never be recovered. Apparently, there were many containers floating for hours before they, too, went under. The shipping company has reported no survivors; not much other information is available about the accident. In *The Guardian Weekly*, there's lots of curiosity about the chatter and accusations flying among different national security forces. The tone of the articles is 'nothing definite, but stay tuned, because something's happening.'"

Looking at his watch and realizing he was running out of time, Arthur suggested they call it a day. "We got a lot done. You go ahead; let me make a couple of quick calls, and then I'll walk home. I'll see you in the morning." He shrugged and gave her an awkward wave.

As soon as the door closed, Arthur worked quickly to remove several thousand dollars from the briefcases. Annie would later spot that both were now stashed in a less visible place, although the office offered no hiding place; she would also notice that both briefcases were moved to yet another corner the following weekend, this time under a new stack of academic articles.

Arthur easily tucked a little money away in his shoulder bag and headed off to Joanne's. Seeing the parked police car not far from her house, he waited for her to call out from the garden, as they had arranged. Acting surprised, he crossed the street to greet her and to accept her invitation for a drink. He quickly moved the money to Hugh's desk drawer; later she would find a better hiding spot of her own. He looked around for a heavy novel and stuck it in his bag as a substitute weight in case one of the watchers was particularly observant.

Over drinks, they talked about nothing in particular, very conscious of the apparent surveillance and possible listening devices. He had to admit that he was finding himself being drawn into her predicament and into her emotional life, although both probably required a savior bigger than he was. Joanne looked a little more attractive than he had realized, despite the toll taken by the stress all around her.

She suggested that she walk him partway home. As soon as they felt comfortable, he explained where he had left the money. She acknowledged this with a brief nod of gratification.

"I should go visit Hugh—although I don't really know exactly where he is or what the charges against him are. There's no bail, but believe it or not, Stomper has raised some money for an American lawyer. I plan to leave Friday, be back on Monday or Tuesday.

Quietly he asked, "How do you want to move the money? We can't leave it in my office. It's too risky. We may have been caught on our security cameras going in, although I'm not sure. To be safe, you can't come back, and I can't use the same briefcases."

Joanne paused, thought about it, and finally laid out a solid plan. She was fast on her feet, providing him decisively with a strategy that would likely work better than anything he was considering. By Friday afternoon, before she left to visit Hugh in Syracuse, the money had been stashed with her sister, further divided, and hidden for as long as Joanne wanted. Annie was happy with the unanticipated, long weekend granted by Arthur, as she had some old high school chums from the country visiting for three nights. On Monday, she noticed the briefcases had been moved again for no apparent reason, but they still felt as heavy as before.

The police did come by his office on Wednesday morning while Annie was at the gym. He recognized that the officer, Bob Sampson, was recently one of his students. After exchanging pleasantries, the officer came to the point.

"We have been following up with the Hugh Parks story, as you probably guessed," Sampson began, obviously not sure where the questioning of his former professor might take him. "You know him?"

"Yes." Arthur let his thin response sit there for several seconds before elaborating about how they met, describing the role of the community foundation in financing the science exhibition originally proposed by Hugh.

The officer followed with many questions, starting with the rocket display.

"What did you pay him for his work on the exhibition?"

"I don't know. We may have paid him something, although he claimed all of it went to others. My guess would be $10,000 to $25,000, but that's just a guess."

"Did you notice his interest in the rocket display?"

"I heard about it from both Bertie Jackson and Bill Brown as I made my rounds to confirm displays and make notes for our fund."

"What is this fund? Is it the truckers' foundation?"

"You can ask Jessica Brown about that. I don't know the actual legal structure."

"How is money received and spent?"

"That's not my end of things."

"Do you get paid?"

"I receive an honorarium."

"How much?"

"That's private."

"How often do you get paid?"

"I'm not sure why you're here."

"Fair enough. There's a big-picture story here about the rockets, and we've been asked to find out where they went. We now believe the transport company, an American outfit largely owned by a Mr. Angel Moreno, who was also in town at the time, took them as part of a shipment of wind turbines sold by Cando Composites Aerospace. It looks as though Moreno lost his life at sea, although we're not privy to that investigation."

Sampson continued, "We do know that Parks was arrested in New York State with a load of cash on him. His daughter was also detained in the Buffalo area. We think there's more cash, or what we call proceeds from criminal activity, involving Hugh, here in our city."

Arthur sat silently, taking in the fact that the officer referred to the suspected criminal on a first-name basis. "We received a call from the university security manager, who showed us tapes of you and Mrs. Parks bringing in a couple of briefcases the other evening."

"Yes, indeed."

"What were they for?"

"She called and asked me to come over. She had been very involved with a local transportation community group, NAT, which Hugh has also supported, although I gather in a pretty minor way."

"How does this involve you, Professor?"

"Well, as you can imagine, Joanne was upset, and her coping mechanisms were shutting down. She remembered my academic interest in local politics. She asked me to take her papers from NAT, go through them, and keep whatever I needed for my research project. It is not uncommon that academics—especially historians, more so than a sociologist like me—are given what others think are valuable documents but turn out to be family junk."

"What did you find?"

"I don't know. I only had a peek at one case, as they're not a priority for me. I did tell her that I was finished with them and would return them. They're right here under some other papers. Do you want to see what's there?" He worried about whether he was keeping his story straight.

"Yes, if you don't mind."

Once the briefcases were opened, the officer quickly flipped through the flyers, invitations, copies of correspondence, membership lists, all the usual paper trail of an active community group.

"Want to take anything?"

"Nope," smiled the frustrated officer. "This is all crap, from our perspective. Do you know her well?"

"Not really." Arthur highlighted their casual encounters in her garden and at meetings. "Nice enough. Probably just needs someone to talk with these days. My wife and I will likely have her over for dinner in a few days. Is she under suspicion?"

"Can't say. Not likely. His bank account has next to nothing in it, so we're curious about her sources of cash these days. We went looking and found nothing. Word is that his business partner, Stomper, whom we know a little about, reported he couldn't find the stash of cash he went looking for at her house. When we got the call about you, they sent me over for this chat."

"Are you satisfied? Do you have any more questions?"

"No, not right now. I'll submit a clean report. If you're seen too often with Joanne, it will be noticed. So, be careful; keep your wife around."

After that, they relaxed and talked about his classes and about the community fund. The officer talked about his own application, along with that of a few other officers, to sponsor their youth softball team to play in tournaments around the Americas. "There is lots of travel for the team and all of the parents. It's expensive. Great for morale and gives everyone a good feeling about the fund. Hope we can get help from you and Ms. Brown."

They shook hands. Both had successfully completed their missions.

Arthur reviewed the situation with Joanne upon her return from visiting Hugh. As they walked over to his house for dinner with Brenda, he gave her details about his conversation with the police so she could have a better sense of her shaky situation. He didn't pursue any questions about the money, as her scheme had apparently successfully created multiple hiding places. Joanne would be okay for several months. She was quickly learning how to operate under the radar.

Although Arthur didn't ask Joanne directly, he had felt comfortable setting aside some of the money for himself. He didn't take that much, he thought, just enough to pay for an additional trip to Europe so that his wife could join him, and perhaps enough for a holiday together during next winter's study break. And he did want to save for a new car.

The following Monday morning, Annie found that the briefcases containing worthless documents were gone and that Joanne and Arthur were spending considerable time together after work. These "research" issues were becoming increasingly complicated.

TORONTO, ONTARIO

Summer 2009

Bertie Jackson's next blog was more measured than those he had written over the previous twelve months. He wrote once, in late May, about a month after events had taken a turn for the worse for both the Moreno and Parks families. Canadian police had interviewed him not many days after the ship's explosion to discuss his blog, where he had bragged about how he was going to hurt Parks through what he had secretly done with the rockets. Toning down his hyperbole, he told the investigators that he had set up a trigger that would most likely induce a puff of smoke, not blow up a large modern container ship. The authorities didn't leave him alone, despite his newfound modesty. Although they did let Jackson go home each evening, he was a critically important witness, as he alone knew both the major personalities under police scrutiny as well as the technologies underpinning the wind turbines and the rockets. His statements formed the heart of this international investigation, and the scientist grew to love every minute of it. Shelly Spicer pulled strings from afar so that an FBI agent was accommodated in the room to augment the work of local interviewers. They flew Bertie to Toronto in late June, ostensibly to accommodate more investigators but, more honestly, to keep him in a benign but isolated environment. Experts were linked in by teleconferencing to examine the scientist's expertise and his prowess as an inventor. When they focused on the wind turbines, they were quite impressed with the concept. They spent time between meetings contacting engineering experts who confirmed its possibilities, at least in theory, although no one knew of any testing in the States. That news made Myron even more curious: if that's the case, why did AT purchase several for delivery into the European market?

Otherwise, experts were less confident that Bertie knew what he was doing when he mucked with the rockets. He could have triggered a greater reaction than he anticipated, depending on the quality of the rockets after years in storage. The explosives specialists were not much help in evaluating the potential danger posed by the old rockets; in part, they were stymied by missing company records that apparently were scattered halfway around the world. Whoever had approached British Engines recently in London had carefully shielded their own identity and certainly had not left anything behind for investigators. In the past, the company admitted, many of their rockets were sold ready to launch so that potential buyers could see them during quick, unnoticed visits from faraway places, watch a demonstration, buy them for cash, and put them into action shortly thereafter. No authorities in Winnipeg were in the loop.

It was speculated among the NASA experts called in that it was possible that one or more of the rockets were battle ready unbeknown to Jackson. In that case, he may have ignited a chain reaction in the container that was more devastating than a doozy of a little joke he could later share with his readers.

Jackson was paying the price for stepping into a bigger, more menacing world than he had ever encountered. As he had only read about such perils through espionage novels and conspiracy-driven blogs, Jackson never dreamed this was an actual reality for thousands engaged in destructive actions and the counterespionage teams fighting to stop them.

To relieve the sheer weight of the nonstop interviews, Bertie retreated into his favorite space where his thoughts could turn to the antics of his cherished extraterrestrial forces. Only they could rid the world of such chaotic antics. He regularly waited until after midnight to blog, energized by his followers. Internet audiences loved his wild images and his breathless anticipation of his outer space allies, whose 2015 arrival was promised by their leaders, he believed. Experts worried that Bertie's real mission in life as a false prophet made him a tenuous witness.

His inquisitors weren't terribly interested in such antics. Every day, these interrogators pulled the scientist back from outer space into the immediate environment of their emergency. Before they tossed him aside to move onto more pressing targets, they had organized one last session where they could ask their questions about Parks. The answers were to be sent onto Todd so he could better gauge the nastiness of their prime suspect, who was now sitting in a New York State jail.

Bertie protested when he saw on the table the pages of questions compiled for their last day of interrogation. He regretted that he had innocently passed on requesting a lawyer to help him through this quagmire, as they had assured him that he was of interest only as a scientific witness. Bertie ventured that if he didn't take charge, they would batter him relentlessly for their own purposes; he wanted to be out of there in two or three hours.

He put his hand up in defiance, stopped the pre-interview chatter, and began:

"Listen: let's get to the point. This is about Hugh, correct? You want to know more about the man you're holding in custody: is he one of the most dangerous criminals in the terrorist world who has been in charge of a sleeping North American cell for the past decade? Or, is he a blithering idiot who has fallen into a world he never dreamed of, saw an opportunity in his own goofy way of making a few hundred thousand—not millions—by slipping a handful of rockets out of the country?"

He continued, uninterrupted. "I realize that most of you operate in smart worlds where, even if you don't like what you see, you at least appreciate the evil genius of those you're busting your butt to stop. You don't come across mindless stupidity very often. Just think of the best examples for a spectator like me: the suicide bombers—how mindless are that? But I've never met one. I don't know if they are bright or dumb. We guess when we view them from North America that they're not too bright. Occasionally, I watch an interview with a young person who at the last minute decided not to detonate the bomb attached to their body. That doesn't help me much to understand the thinking of a bomber, because the survivors we watch on the news have bolted from their handlers.

"With regard to Hugh, this is never going to be answered at one end or another of the polar extreme that I gave you. No, it's a continuum, as you already know. Where does Hugh fit on this measure of smartness? That might answer your questions: how involved was this suspect?" There were nods everywhere. They were back on his side.

Bertie continued holding court. "By now, you have all read my blogs and can guess how I feel about Hugh. I personally find him to be stupid and conniving. Gentlemen, my words cannot be harsh enough on moral and principled grounds. He works in tandem with another scoundrel, known locally only as Stomper, whom you should shake down as hard as you can." That produced murmurs of agreement.

Bertie pressed his point. "Sometimes we come across these guys who look so stupid that you ask yourself, 'how do they succeed?' That's been my question for months. Here's my answer.

"Hugh knows exactly what he's doing. He has the same approach as a banker with a subprime mortgage package or the infamous Canadian mining stock promoters who knew Bre-X had no gold. Hugh could sell you potash technology, diamonds, scientific breakthroughs, whatever you can think of, without missing a beat. That's the heart and mind of a swindler. We built the continent with their dreams. And we lost family savings when they came by as friends of the house, asking our parents to empty their tobacco cans for a new, sure-fire investment opportunity.

"Look, we have a pretty active scientific community in this region on both sides of the international border. Nobody from the big investment houses or pension plans comes looking here for opportunities. They think grain, oil, natural gas, and minerals when they think of the prairies or the Canadian Shield. That's the same for folks in the Dakotas, Montana and Wyoming. They don't think about finding innovations from scientific geniuses out here. They think, if you're so good, why aren't you at MIT or in one of IBM's labs in the East? Or at Lockheed Martin, making real rockets—right?"

Everyone was absorbed in Bertie's entertaining diatribe. He might be the Internet's feisty 'mad scientist,' but at this moment, he seemed a respectable intellectual giant driving home an important point to his receptive audience.

"Where there is an opportunity to make people feel better and to give them an opportunity to be recognized, that is where a figure like Hugh wins big, and in that respect, he is not stupid. He should be recognized for his smarts. I'll put aside my hysterical anger and paint you a more balanced picture.

"Imagine that you are an inventor, teaching, say, at a community college, a job that leaves you little free time to invent new contraptions. No one at work understands or, worse still, cares about what you're doing.

"Hugh is always cruising, not unlike the traveling housewares salesperson of a century ago. While he's selling his goods, he's always looking for an opportunity to steal away whatever you have. It could be that he's taking your cash for worthless stocks or maybe building your hopes that your property is the right place for an oil rig, or persuading you that your invention was perfect for his investment club. It doesn't matter what it is; that's not the point. He takes whatever he can. He'd ruin all his friends if they gave him a chance. What's his defense? Well, as I heard him say, 'They're all over 18.'

"As your notes will show, he has an investment group, the Bison Board. The greatest and most common attribute among them is forgetfulness. They are like a miniature NYSE." He stopped to enjoy the laughter.

"He orchestrates his scams perfectly. Hugh saw my invention as his way into a bigger deal. He took money from the investors and starting production right away. He dug up information about corrupt practices at city hall and where the truckers fitted into that scene. To his credit, he managed to string together a story line that seemingly makes everyone happy.

"The plot gets more complicated with the rockets. Here's where your knowledge counts more than mine. Somehow, he anticipated that this Moreno fellow would want the rockets. Nobody said boo to us at Bill's shop. I only heard the full story about the Spanish connection much later from your guys. I do know that Hugh went away on a couple of business trips but didn't bother to tell us where. I now assume that's how you picked up his trail in the States.

"His suggestion of a science innovation exhibition was over the top, but we all pitched in to make it happen. He let me know that he requested expenses only for himself while keeping Stomper and me, I must add, very busy. What it did accomplish was the release of the rockets from storage with all the proper documents from England, along with an agent of some sort who came over to supervise." You could hear the room stop.

"Excuse me," Bertie listened to the first interruption since he'd begun his monologue. "We haven't heard much about this shadowy character. What was his role?"

Jackson was running out of steam but still had some important points and wanted to avoid being sidetracked. "I promise I'll come back to him and give you all the details I can remember."

They let him continue, although all had made margin notes to return to this mysterious intruder. Only Todd, listening in from DEA headquarters, wasn't surprised.

"At this point, two critical decisions were made. I decided to place a bug on the rockets, as I feared they were somehow going to be misappropriated. At the same time, Hugh decided he was brighter than the rest of us and would be much better off playing with his new European partners. He presumed he could beat everyone at this game and make a fortune.

"What he apparently didn't understand was that Angel Moreno knew nothing, at least that's what I think. Angel was probably the only one who wasn't told what all was in the container; he just accepted that only his newly purchased wind turbines were going east through a port to be shipped to Europe. Hugh assumed that the clandestine agent and Angel were on the same team. Hugh left Stomper, who always did the dirty work, at home to continue spending time with Angel, not realizing that the lad was also leaving for Montreal. Stomper took him to Winnipeg's Richardson Airport the next afternoon, not really sure where Angel was off to, sneakily asking questions about where the container shipment and turbines were going and which port they would be unloaded at. When he was forthrightly told Spain and concluded that Angel had no apparent interest in rockets or terrorists, Stomper called Hugh in Montreal right after he dropped off Angel. Hugh was confused. I know all of this because Stomper was sent back to Bill's place to find out what we might know. It was obvious that Hugh was confused by the apparent duplicity of this Martin Belanger. No wonder he stayed clear of Angel; the boy wasn't on the team. Who was in charge if Juan's son was this far out of the picture? I'm speculating that Hugh was so nervous by the time he met with Belanger in Montreal—your agents have explained all of this to me—that he hurried to the border to hide his cash payout in Buffalo, if your part of the story is correct.

"Thus, he's cunning and manipulative, but he inadvertently entered a league in which his ambitions left him vulnerable. He was caught and should be punished as an active participant in an international ring of criminals." With that, Bertie hoped that he had sealed Hugh's fate and settled an important grievance on behalf of his blog followers.

Todd signed off from the conference call and phoned Myron for advice.

WINNIPEG, MANITOBA

Summer 2009

In late July, on one of her final days on the job before traveling, Annie passed her last research gem on to Arthur.

"I've made arrangements for our university and community visit to Madrid, as I mentioned last week. On a hunch, I sent another e-mail to the professor and innocently suggested we meet with Juan Moreno. I asked him if he personally knew the family."

Arthur was too nervous to turn around in his chair. "You took on a very interesting initiative. Thanks. What did he say? Does he know the family?"

"Not directly, as the family has sent their children outside Spain for their university education. Apparently the family is more than well-known; they're the heart of the Spanish elite. Juan's father built a major transportation company during the civil war. The company was paraded by the new democratic Spanish government as an example of how they could compete in the European Common Market. That helped them get into the EU in 1986. Juan himself has hosted parties with guests from London to Istanbul. It's quite the story, according to our new friend. But you should not plan on meeting anyone close to this family."

"Why not? Is there a problem?"

"Well, yes, if you ask the Americans. The English newspaper, *The Times*, has reported that his trucks are carrying more than fruits and vegetables for European markets. There are very substantial accusations that Juan is a supporter of international terrorism and on the wrong side of the States."

"What's the Spanish government doing about it?"

"They won't lift a finger to help the American security operatives, although there are hints in the European media that he's been told not to travel outside Spain for fear that another country might buckle under pressure from Washington and arrest him. Hard to say what's true from the little I've read. There are only a few English-language sources, and my Spanish is too limited. He doesn't travel very much and is thought to leave Spain very occasionally by private plane for unspecified Middle Eastern and African countries, always returning within a day or two. He literally returns before the Americans find out he's gone."

"Annie, you're being pretty obtuse; what's he supposedly up to?" asked the skittish professor.

"He deals in guns, rockets, and every sort of armament in demand by terrorists. That's why they were here in our city."

Annie knew full well at that moment how far Arthur had gone without telling her. His body tightened like that of an amateur thief on an old film noir who is caught playing with professional criminals. He had walked into the abyss and was now filled with anxiety.

She continued, pretending not to notice the change in his disposition. "You remember the science exhibition you funded?"

"Of course I do."

"Do you remember how you arranged for that creep, Hugh Parks, to get funded as its promoter?"

"Yes, again, I remember. He turned out to be a pretty good help to me at that time, although your aunt would disagree."

Annie ignored the taunt. "I saw the application on your desk months ago. Entries for the rocket show budget included monies to obtain permission from the owners to put them on display by moving them into the city. You set aside more money for Hugh's friend Bertie to fix them up for public viewing. Right? You approved those expenditures and the transportation costs. Right?"

"I sort of remember this. It wasn't a big deal at the time. What else?"

"You may recall you came back from a lunch with the same Mr. Parks and told me how community-minded he was. Your smug example was his personal contribution to the science exhibition as he volunteered to look after the VIP tours and all of the security arrangements. That was the deal, right, as you told me?"

"I suppose," he demurred, and then he fought back. "It was a good deal. He saved us money and promoted the city very positively for the many visitors from out of town."

"Such as?" Annie was angry.

"For starters, the British aerospace expert was most impressed with the show the city put on for everyone. He kept thanking us profusely for showing the world how to enjoy scientific breakthroughs."

"He was a bit over the top, don't you think?"

Arthur shrugged. "Who knows? Parks also gave that young Spaniard, who was on his first visit here, a wonderful tour on the last night. He was a great kid. I'm sorry if he turns out to be the one who lost his life at sea."

Annie could only stare at his back as Arthur refused to turn around. Instead, he focused hard on other matters.

Annie switched tactics. "I'm so glad we're going to work in Europe together. The itinerary is magnificent. I'll spend a few days on my own while you and your wife celebrate your anniversary in London. There's an interview or two for you there, if you have the time." She went on. "Afterward, we'll start in Brussels, where there are people at the EU interested in your research, and then we'll end up in Barcelona two weeks later. I'm so excited. I can't imagine how my first trip to Europe could be more interesting than the one that we've planned. Are you as hyped about this as I am?"

"Absolutely, I'm looking forward to every day." He still did not turn and face her. "This will be great; it will be fun to work together and we'll both learn a lot."

Annie started up, for the last time, on local politics. "Sounds good. Besides, it'll be good to get away from the mess here. I don't think we completely understand what we've been involved in."

That comment drew him out of his hostile aloofness as he turned in his chair to face her. He looked at her with uncertainty as to where she was going in this discussion. Annie didn't wait for encouragement. "Let me give you one wild example. Say Hugh did assist those who stole the rockets and the Americans are right to hold him in jail. They will come looking for money, as they probably think they didn't find all of it in his car. Suddenly, his wife is a suspect. How is she living day to day without her husband's income, with only a meager salary from her part-time work? She isn't just a suspect in helping a local, stupid businessman; she's tied into an international operation to supply the enemies of America with armaments. The Yanks are crazed by this. Anything can happen. Say my Aunt Susan innocently wants to help Joanne by stashing an envelope for a month or so containing, she guesses, a little money to help tide her over. Will she be publicly embarrassed, or worse, charged in the conspiracy? I can tell you, my aunt is scared stiff. And what happens if Hugh is let free because they only want the big fish? He coughs up some information they can use, and suddenly he's back in town. He doesn't really care about his family; he never has according to local gossip. No, he'll want his money right away. He'll kill for it, and Joanne probably knows this. She'll tell the whole story in two minutes, and he'll be on the prowl with that big oaf for every single nickel. Best wishes to all the good Samaritans who fell for Joanne's story. They'll be dead meat."

She finished her attack. "Sorry, I'm over the top. I'm spending too much time pretending I'm writing my first novel. I love conspiracies and coincidences. I'm not smart enough to tie together all of the bad stuff I hear, especially from Andrew, and now I just want to get out of here for a few weeks. Let's go to lunch right this minute and forget this whole thing."

"Yeah, that would be fantastic. I need a break. Let me go to the washroom first, and we'll be off right away." Arthur didn't return to his office for several minutes. He splashed his face with cold water in an effort to bring his anxiety attack under control. When he realized that the departmental secretary, a permanent fixture on the floor, was fixating on his pacing the hallway, his face still dripping wet, he disappeared back into his office to avoid further scrutiny by office spectators. Annie looked at him alarmingly but again did not think it her place as a rookie researcher to say anything. They soon departed under the watchful stares of curious colleagues for a favorite restaurant, a nondescript bistro on Corydon Avenue. Sitting across from him, Annie presented herself as the contented assistant of a brilliant scholar, leading the conversation off in different directions about each city in which they would be conducting interviews. She had found many good contacts and some excellent sites to visit. All of the interviews were organized. Arthur interrupted to confirm that the Foundation had accepted his detailed itinerary with both of their travel expenses largely paid through an advance. She acted as though she were happy with the arrangements.

Without any particular interest, almost absentmindedly, between spoonful's of his broccoli cheese soup, Arthur asked where she was going after Barcelona. "You know, you don't have to come back right away. Stay on for a week or two; that's fine with me. I'll give you a cash advance if you want. Anything else interest you?"

She winced at the suggestion of a cash advance directly from him, as she knew, without a doubt, where he had found the extra cash. She was nauseated but kept her best face on to answer his question.

"No, I'm fine with money. You've given me a good salary, and my parents have come up with a very nice graduation gift. I'm thinking about the south of France, because we'll be so close, and then off to Britain for a quick look at two or three campuses that interest me. I'm planning to be back in early September but haven't settled on an exact day. I didn't think you would mind, as that's such a busy time at the university. She looked at him. "What about you?"

He avoided her eyes. "I think I'll stay for two or three days in London. It's a great city, my favorite place to wander day after day. But I have to be back long before you."

"What about your wife; will she still be there? That would be a lot of fun to see her twice on this trip."

"No, she's back before then," he answered as if talking to a daughter.

He passed on the opportunity to talk about another woman on the trip. He had recently heard from Jessica who wanted to check out community foundations in London. She knew about his trip and had suggested dates and a hotel in London, all at the expense of the fund, where they could meet. He acquiesced without a murmur. She would be fun, he guessed, especially for a few days far away from home.

Arthur never had such good luck with money and women. This was much better than researching statistics alone in his office. With some finagling, he could put teaching aside next year, with the support of Jessica's fund and the Jacobs Foundation.

Annie disguised her disappointment from her preoccupied companion as they finished their last visit to the eatery where they had munched happily from the same menu dozens of times. Nothing Annie had speculated about that morning had surprised Arthur, but he was deliberately blocking all negativity. That's why he was looking forward to Europe: he would finally escape from it all.

What about her speculations about Hugh? Maybe he would duck his jail term. Arthur had never thought about that. Had Joanne?

His slow walk back to campus with his body slouched forward betrayed his emotional collapse; the sight of this humbled man beside her brought a chagrined smile to Annie's darkening face. Her speculation about the money was obviously bang-on; he was scared beyond belief. His including her aunt in the stupid plot by using her for safekeeping the stolen money broke every one of Annie's rules of decency. It was the final turning point that assured her she was right to get away from this corrupt research project and enjoy a year or two in Europe. All that was left to be done was a final lunch with her aunt. She flipped open her cell to start making arrangements; this meal would be more fun. "So, Annie, you want out of here, just like you had to leave your home in Russell. We will talk about it Sunday. Same time; same place."

They had much to catch up on but the time passed all too fast. Susan was as happily engaged in her immediate local life as Annie was with her imaginary future place. Susan had already heard from Annie's mom about her imminent departure and quickly picked up on her current discontent.

"It's not bad to want to leave, but it can be a struggle to find a new place to call home. While you are making plans to leave, I'm determined to improve life here. I'm doubling my efforts to save our older neighborhoods from all those noisy trucks and other unnecessary intrusions. It's actually turning out to be fun. And although I'm not going to fight you about you leaving, you're not altogether correct about Winnipeg. If you want to be a writer or an artist of some distinction, you can stay here and be quite successful. Lots have.

"You know, when everything is said and done, I don't think it really matters where we live. Some places are too cold; others are too hot. Some places have too much traffic; others don't even have bus service. You can dream of a better place, or you can build one. Right now, you're a dreamer and I'm a builder. But, before you go, I will add one note of certainty. More important than deciding where to live is settling who you are at your core. A solid moral compass, rooted in your self-awareness, including your weaknesses as well as your strengths—that's what makes a good life, one worth living for your own self. Develop that integrity, and don't let go."

As brunch drew to a close, Susan remarked just how much she had enjoyed their times together. When Annie looked back flustered by this compliment, her aunt elaborated. "It rejuvenates my spirits to listen to your ruminations on various topics. You are exceptionally skilled in expressing your ideals. I don't hear many undergraduates talking as you do; you shouldn't take it lightly as you have the potential to accomplish much more than most of your peers." While that comment was sinking in, Susan asked, "One last question: Why do you think so many young people leave Winnipeg? What's your opinion? A group of us forty something moms want to keep our babies here. We are asking for fresh answers. What's the rush to leave?"

Annie hadn't expected this. She didn't want to insult her aunt unnecessarily as she was indisputably her dearest relative but she was again driven by her youthful honesty and directness.

"I've thought about my ambivalence every day since I arrived in Winnipeg that first September—warning you now, this won't be a short answer." Susan encouraged her to take her time.

"Last year, I saw Guy Madden's movie *My Winnipeg* and I think he got it right. He has a great feel for so many of the paradoxical and contradictory situations we face here. I'll only pick one—winter's darkness—to make my point. We enter the winter season like zombies who have all forgotten about the last November or the November before that. Then it hits everyone: it's winter again, a dark and cold climate only rivaled by Russia's. The energy drawdown depresses each generation of those determined—for whatever reason—to continue living here.

I really felt it this year. Madden's image of train passengers passing out from too much booze, totally inert as the dim lights of the city go by, is brilliant. No one over thirty has a second wind after dinner. On a bad winter's day, you can't see anyone moving after 4:30 in the afternoon. Winnipeg is not the only dark northern winter city, but it may be the only big city that is *so* dark and cold. It's brutal.

"I watch couples cocoon for months at a time. Even students search for reasons not to go out at night. Winnipeggers are like Muscovites except those folks make no pretense that they suffer through the drabness totally drunk on Vodka.

"So what does my generation think? I don't know about the others, but I have to get out of here, at least for a few years.

"Listen, Auntie, I'm probably exaggerating to make my point.

"But then—how is one supposed to pass the teenage years? Where do you go? To whose basement should you go is the only text message being flipped from one lonely soul to another. Few kids have the money for bars, restaurants, taxis, movies, which are all basic essentials of a more public social life. Perhaps the cafés can be fun, but Starbucks has changed just stopping by into an unending series of $5.00 transactions. Basements and smoking too much dope are the only focus; that has the liveliness to put verve into this culture? Not the parents, clinging to their own survival on dark nights. Stop and think about what it takes to go out and bring home the kids after midnight. Everyone begs off. I've watched this. It's an awful life for kids to be stuck here, knowing that the winter sucks the energy out of their parents. What, they wonder, will they be like?

"I can't imagine being even younger than I am and sorting through this. Do you have to send them away to save them? Yes, in all likelihood—at least that's my conclusion about my own life.

"Some of what I see and think about has always been here, but nowadays, too many kids manage to finance themselves with drugs and thieving at a level that adults either ignore or cannot fathom. It may not be new, but it certainly is of a scale and intensity that freaks out more moderate youth peering into the mess. Is it the same everywhere in North America? It wouldn't surprise me if I come across this phenomenon elsewhere. I really don't know, but the question remains. Who will save the good ones? How?

"How did the city end up this way? I wish I knew; my professor spends a lot of time thinking about these problems. I listen to him all the time but have my own take. Corruption is embedded in the nonchalant ways our leaders approach young people's problems. They lack the urgency to make the world work positively for us. By ignoring us, they pass their corrupt practices to the next generation. Abandonment brings despair and legitimizes corruption; is that how we're supposed to get by?

"Here's where I think I am at right now. My wrestling with the great questions of my time at university is actually giving me the courage to confront the limits of my own lifestyle. Each day I should be making a determined effort to engage in what works for me alone. Hopefully I'll soon find a small conclave of like minds. This, I certainly believe, is the absolute key to my own peace. My next big question: is it sufficient only to think about it, or must I motivate others to change? I will personally have to find my own ways to tell my story. I think this is what I'm wrestling with—at least right now. Who knows if it will be the same the next time we brunch together!"

"I can't wait to hear about the next episode in your life," was the genuine and generous response of her aunt. "Don't forget us!"

Surprisingly, given his reluctance to open himself up to confrontation, Arthur was asking Joanne pointed questions on her veranda a few hours later. "Are you going to stay here?"

"Good question." Joanne paused and smiled at Arthur in a warm but not intimate way. "You've been such a big help to me and to so many others over the past few months. Good question." She repeated herself.

"Apparently, and I think I mentioned this to you previously, Stomper was able to pull together a $100,000 defense fund, mostly from the Bison Board, or whatever Hugh's group of investors call themselves. He told them this might be their best investment ever, as it was Hugh who brought them so many opportunities in the past. Don't you love it? It's so, so nuts. In any case, they bought in. Rumor has it that your fund also made a contribution."

Arthur passed on any comment. His mind was reviewing past conversations with renewed suspicion. Jessica had definitely given him some hints of that.

Joanne offered a second drink, which Arthur readily accepted. "Your fund has several connections with the police department, which followed up suggestions to phone the FBI to explain Hugh's longstanding support of local police charities. I have no idea what that's about, do you?"

He ducked the question with a shrug, and she continued. "The Americans agreed that he was a small-time player, but they still want to make an example of him. Our poor Emma has already been harmed beyond imagination with all of this. If Hugh, the little fish, turns out to be more valuable as an informer, then a deal will be made. Otherwise, I have no idea of what's going to happen. My great fear is that one day there will be a knock on the door, just like an old Hitchcock movie, and Hugh will be standing on the porch, all smiles and expecting to regain his spot as master of the house. I have no idea what I want—to see him in jail or back in the living room."

Joanne tossed her hair back and used her left hand to nervously give it some shape. She looked intently for a long time at Arthur while she gathered her thoughts.

"I know, Arthur, that I owe you an explanation. We came close to getting totally involved during the past few months. In retrospect, that would have been disastrous, but you should know I've been quite smitten with you." Arthur, who wasn't surprised to hear this but had thought he would be more pleased to hear it spoken aloud, barely smiled.

"You're probably asking yourself what my deal is with Hugh. Why am I still here? You know, it wasn't always this way, and our lives didn't have to turn into shambles the way they have. Hugh has a great heart and can be a caring fellow. He didn't start out by lying about everything, nor does he have to continue on as he does. When I first met him, I was working downtown in a branch of a major Canadian bank. I ran into Hugh regularly at a coffee shop in the basement of one of the big office towers and I would see Hugh in the branch doing an American dollar transaction. Never thought much of it at the time. Soon after that, we started to date, married the same year, and had Emma the next. She turned out to be our only one; he was always disappointed in her but I never knew why. You probably have some idea of how badly he's treated my Emma. She'll never come back."

"Yes," Arthur acknowledged, "I've heard that. But you're still attracted to him. I don't get it."

"My life is quiet except when Hugh is in the room. He brings an excitement to conversations and to meetings. He's able to convince others that his way will be successful. If they invest with him, he'll make them rich. Believe it or not, sometimes he does it right and they make a lot of money. That brings them back to his circus, and they bring along their friends. It's hilarious; he jumps around the house all happy at the deal, and, honestly, it makes me smile.

"He genuinely believes his scheme will work, every time. He has no doubt about it. My guess is that he's surprised when it fails. I think he's fortunate that he can block all the bad things he's done. He forgets the promises solemnly made, the monies borrowed and lost, the disappointed faces of those he has lied to, including me."

"But you stay." This time Arthur's voice had more than a hint of accusation in it.

"Yes, I stay," she said; she shrugged and grimaced weakly. "Maybe it's better to go to a bad party than to no party at all. That's no defense, I suppose, but I'm not going anywhere.

"Even though I really like you, Arthur," she added, "I'm glad now that we didn't get more involved. Can you imagine what it would be like if he sent Stomper after you? It's going to be bad enough with the money. If he comes back, he'll want to know where every penny is and how I spent it. I'm keeping a detailed list. I hope nobody took some for their own spending. Only Hugh seems to know the real amount that should be accounted for. He'll do damage through Stomper to get it all back."

Arthur sat there, stunned. Danger had finally come to his own doorstep. Joanne waited a minute, endured the silence, and finally encouraged him to go home. As they stepped onto the porch, she broached another subject.

"I hear the three of you are going to Europe." She laughed at the thought. "What a sight for our little city. You and your wife will have a great visit to Britain, and I hear through Susan that your assistant has put together a fabulous study trip for you two.

"Luckily for you, Professor," she gently mocked, "all of the women watching you trust you with such a pretty young thing. You'll have fun. Do drop in as soon as you come home." She gave him a hug and sent him on his way.

By now, Arthur couldn't wait to get to Europe. Being away from local intrigue would afford him the chance to sort out his various problems. The first week in early August was pleasant enough with his wife. He had prepaid Brenda's airfare and their hotel room with the stolen money and had plenty left over for her visits outside of London. After Arthur had left for the continent, she stayed with old friends who had found themselves teaching and researching positions in England. Nothing that Arthur and Brenda did back home was particularly extravagant, but her holiday lifestyle was definitely a cut above academic life. She returned to Winnipeg full of grand stories and heard frequently from Arthur, who was busy with his interview schedule.

EUROPE

Summer 2009

Annie had befriended the university's travel agent to get some terrific deals and to make a number of changes without too much fuss.

"I love your boss!" the agent gushed. "He made the arrangements for his wife without bothering you, saying, 'no reason that a research assistant should have to look after my wife. It's simply not fair to a young professional.' He pulled out an envelope of cash to pay for her trip and to treat her to really nice hotels. It was so cute. He told me how he put away $50 each week for months without her knowing. The professor was so proud of himself."

Annie held back her desire to scream. She wanted to be done with the whole lot of them. Instead she calmly put down on the counter a revised itinerary for herself. "I've decided to visit an old boyfriend in Frankfurt who left here a year ago. This would be a great chance to see him again." She smiled at the agent with a look that would leave her with the memory of a young woman pining for an old love from college. The change was easy to make, and she didn't have to reveal her own arrangements for taking a train directly from the airport to Berlin.

After this was settled, Annie returned home to finish packing. The student taking over her lease had kindly agreed to help her store a few boxes and to one day take the family car back to Russell; soon she was ready for her trip, leaving Winnipeg on her own for her first overseas trip. She did not bother to text Arthur about any of the changes in her plans.

When she disembarked from the train in Berlin, Annie was naturally disoriented after the long trip, finding it slightly overwhelming to cope in Europe for the first time and on her own. Nevertheless, she took a deep breath and headed off to the nearby inexpensive Meininger Hotel, close to the neighbor-hoods that she was keen to explore.

She was ready the next day to look around and find out what the artists were doing to make Berlin the new center of the creative Bohemian life she craved so dearly. She wandered freely for hours, settled into a local café for an early din-ner, fell asleep for a few hours, and headed out for a night life—one completely different from anything she had ever experienced on the Canadian prairies.

Annie found a suitable apartment on the border of Mitte and Prenzlauer Berg. Natural light flooded her tiny living room, so she would enjoy whatever time she spent there on her own. The apartment was near the busy Volkspark Friedrichain with its beer gardens, film showings, lakes, and family picnics. It was also in the middle of Berlin's super-trendy district, which was a favorite with the young crowds and artsy types she was planning to join. The neighborhood would afford her opportunities and allow her to attend as many of the terrace cafés, kitsch boutiques, and alternative-style bars around Kollwitzplatz as she wished. Ready access to public transit made her feel complete in living out her first fantasies of a creative metropolitan life.

She traveled on to Brussels as scheduled and immersed herself back into Arthur's research. It would be the last few weeks they worked together, making her quite determined to not give in to the temptation to have a fight or otherwise confront him. She doggedly kept him at ease as they moved from one city to the next. Although she was no more or less experienced than he was as a traveler in strange places, because of her youthfulness, Annie was capable of moving about with greater confidence. Each day was filled with interviews or work-related site visits. They were often free for dinners but again she took advantage of oppor-tunities to stay busy and not spend too much time alone. She had organized her checklist to keep moving while working with Arthur so that he wouldn't notice her increased aloofness in their work relationship.

At the end of the trip, she fretted about secretly returning to Berlin and about saying a final good-bye to her professor. Despite his failures, she knew she would miss him; she would grieve for him as for an older brother, for the role model he could have been. Her train left for Berlin at noon, and she wanted to go out later that evening on her own in her new city. She packed her bag, checked out, and arranged for a taxi.

Deliberate and methodical, Annie went back to the elevator, took it to Arthur's floor, and slowly walked down the hall. She knock on his door in the same fashion as she had for months at his university office, and he opened it with the same enthusiasm in seeing her for the first time that day. She smiled, stood aside, and waited as he threw everything into his two oversized suitcases.

She waited until he went into the bathroom to say her last words to him. Then she called through the door, "I'm going down to the lobby. I'll check my departure time. If I'm cutting it too close, I'll have to leave. Don't worry, we'll catch up soon."

He yelled back from the bathroom. "Wait just a second so we can have a farewell hug." The door closed silently, and she was gone.

WASHINGTON DC

Summer 2009

It was Todd's turn to host the interagency meeting in Arlington in the stifling August heat. Myron had put out the word that Todd was to be respected and protected. The Americans were joined this time by security force representatives from the key embassies. Todd began his presentation expectantly. "Let's first hear what's happened since we last met in June before the holidays started."

He started methodically going through the facts. "Some of you are new, so first I'll recap what we know for sure. After that I'll give you a couple of scenarios we have to think about.

"We now know that we came across a plot to export rockets from North America overseas to an unknown location. We know that Juan Moreno, a citizen of Spain and an armament supplier to terrorists mostly in the North African and Middle East regions, was involved.

"This story is complicated by the fact that we had at least two and maybe three games happening simultaneously. This is not entirely a surprise, as we all know that criminals like to hide themselves among unsuspecting citizens. We likely have two types of criminals engaged here: the first is petty thieves thriving in the usual drug, illegal immigrant, and investments world, and the second is hardcore, sophisticated, international terrorist operators. The former, being opportunity driven, landed in the middle of the rocket heist, while the latter were working from master plans organized to cover months of smart, detailed work. They're just like us in that important respect.

"Somehow, several months ago, these worlds collided. Small thieves came across the bigger game. Although we think they had no idea of what was happening, they thought that by nibbling at the edges, they could pick up the crumbs and make solid money, probably the most they had ever seen.

"Luck played a big part in our surveillance. The petty thieves appear to be Hugh Parks, a Canadian businessman, assisted by his colleague, known as Stomper, and Caesar Rodriguez, the general manager of a California truck company. Rodriguez doesn't really know the others. These circumstances, where the parties are literally colluding without knowing each other can often make it next to impossible to anticipate their next moves.

"However, we picked up Parks ingratiating himself to Moreno as his new best friend several months ago, based on an intercept." Catching everyone's impatience, he moved right to the point.

"Since then, Moreno has shown his excellent skill by leaving us wondering what will happen next. As far as we can tell from the events that happened last spring, there is a second shipment of rockets that disappeared at the same time the ship blew up, somewhere between Kansas and its destination."

"A little vague, don't you think?" asked the Spaniard diplomat.

Quick to push back, Todd asked in return, "Perhaps you and your colleague in from Mexico can lunch together at *Bodega*, across in Georgetown after our meeting. You can't find Moreno, and he doesn't know where Rodriguez is; you have something in common. Perhaps over tapas, you can see if your memories don't improve in Spanish. Your government studiously ignores one mastermind, while the other government has lost the transportation manager, who may have controlled both deliveries far across North America. Maybe after a glass of their excellent Spanish wine, your analysis will improve."

There. The room felt the crush of American anger over the inefficacy of the Spanish and Mexican governments. The diplomat flushed. Someone had to move the meeting along, or it would all fall apart.

"Is there a specific game plan you have in mind that we can all help with?" asked the Interpol rep, trying to rebuild goodwill around the table.

Todd nodded his appreciation. "We've concluded that we're watching over a sleeper cell about which we know very little. If Juan's the guy running it, and I know the official position of the Spanish government is that he's not involved—but just suppose that someone like Moreno is the one pulling the strings to make sure the job gets done. What will he do, and when? Any thoughts?"

Participants offered their opinions, gradually adding bits and pieces of information, supposedly to help measure the risk of possible scenarios, but also to show others that they knew what was happening in their own backyard.

After they ran out of steam, they returned to Todd for suggestions as to where all of this might be heading. He looked at his notes for a moment, as this part of the meeting had been well-rehearsed by the bickering American agencies. Despite their feuds, they knew they had to pull this one off.

"Our conclusion is that the rockets are still here somewhere on American soil. That makes it our problem and one we'd like to solve right away. We think they will only be found by accident or when Juan decides to move them to his target. We think there's both a patient seller and a patient buyer in play here. Both know the risks if they move too quickly. While they wait, they have the network to advertise their armaments, sell them, and move them to the target country. This could take a couple of years to play out. It will be like most of the cases we all work on: slow, tedious, mistaken leads—and then bang-o, we'll have it in our hands. The only question is not who is arrested but who gets hurt."

This time the British rep from MI6 spoke in his usual measured tone. "You're probably right. The case, however, has shifted in one significant way. There are now at least six or seven agencies whose operational knowledge is indispensable, as well as the concurrence of their governments, and most are still angered by recent events as they hold you responsible for not warning those organizations six months ago. And, before you express your frustration, I know how you've been ignored on this file. Furthermore, when this payload moves, we'll have to anticipate their target and let our friends at the other end know to help them defend their own country. That assumes we end up watching where one of us actually has a friend. The list is getting smaller, isn't it?" She concluded by staring at the CIA station-chief assigned to the Middle East. "So who's in charge, hopefully with some pretense of a communications agenda?"

"Thank you," Myron responded, speaking for the first time and barely able to hide his disdain for the British intelligence services. Their haughty attitude pushed away the likes of Todd and undermined the stoic commitment among operatives living by their wits under dangerous circumstances. "Our congressional committee met privately yesterday and listened to various players, including myself, talk about this operation, which will henceforth be known as Operation Angel." He stopped mid-sentence. Using his most innocent voice, he had introduced the code name Angel in its English pronunciation. It took a few seconds for everyone to realize that it was named after one of the innocents killed in the game. He also assumed this codename would be passed on to the Spanish government, meaning a very aggravated Juan would eventually hear about it. "The mission was approved under the committee's secret mandate and will be properly funded. The committee told us that Todd is to remain in charge." He shrugged. "He's not the first among you who has succeeded after being given a second chance. He'll be back to you as he finalizes his plans. I think he wants to leave you to think about one immediate problem we are facing."

Todd ignored the parting shot and the grins around the table. They all remembered their own errors, yet here they were, still in the game.

"One of the petty thieves, Parks, is facing significant charges and is still being held without bail in one of our jails in upstate New York. We are confident the minor charges will hold, but not the major ones. His cronies back home have put together funds for a solid defense lawyer who's jabbering at us every week in the media. We certainly don't want a cause célèbre case on the terrorist front, as it might be one of the first trials under our new tough legislation. We don't want it lost due to flimsy evidence. That would hurt. Our Canadian colleague here today can tell you that there are problems for their investors and politicians in this story. Don't ask; it would take too long to explain. Her government would also like this problem to disappear tomorrow.

"The point is that Parks claims he learned a lot about the rockets through his conversations with a British contact. We sort of know who this Martin is, but not enough to tail him or to peg how he works with Moreno." He nodded at the Spaniard. "Sorry, I meant to say, whoever might be the armament supplier to the terrorists we've been chasing."

"We're thinking of letting Parks go after a total debriefing with his lawyer to make sure we actually find out something. We'll send him over the border to Canada and tell him he can never come back."

Looks of surprise appeared on several faces around the room, as the Americans weren't known for their generosity and deal making with the supporters of terrorists, especially in their own country.

Todd put his hand up to stop the murmuring. "I know, I know, it doesn't sound like us, and we haven't come to a final decision, but do you have any questions?"

"Is he important to us?"

"No, he's a petty thief and a con-artist who wormed his way into this."

"Do the Canadians want him back?"

Spicer answered this time. "We don't care. Our government just wants peace and quiet on this file."

"Will we be compromised by charges from the local police who are left dealing with this character?"

"Don't worry," she piped up for the second and last time. "He's bought everyone off for the past couple of years. Even the mayor likes him. He's arranged for the police to have their favorite charities—run by their brothers and sisters, of course—sponsored. He's all over paying people off. There's no chance of any further charges that would hurt this operation."

"Good, he sounds like one of us," someone from the back called out. The participants laughed darkly as the meeting came to a close.

Todd left the room with his mandate to get Parks out of the States.

SYRACUSE, NEW YORK

Late Summer 2009

Todd looked at Parks and then at his lawyer; he shook his head, thinking about how people get into so much trouble when they understand nothing. When Todd came across a character like Moreno, he bore down with all the energy and skill he could muster to bring the mastermind to justice. Parks wasn't innocent by any means, but he was more of a nuisance than someone worth the time and energy of a major federal agency. Todd just wanted him out of the way as soon as he could make a deal.

They were all there in the little police interview room to talk price. Everyone except the unskilled and inexperienced Hugh recognized that when the international security community focuses on a big picture sting, they badly want everyone else out of the way. Marsha now knew that. They didn't want newspaper stories, specialty television profiles, messy courtroom appearances, and diplomatic flare-ups because of simple stupidity. The price was the measure required to show the law-and-order types that justice was being served when Hugh was returned to the Canadian border.

Todd was humorless and abrupt in his approach. There was no warm-up commentary, and no niceties were exchanged.

"We have most of your story and have had time to check out the facts. You had a major role and are at the point where you have to decide what you want: an American prison life or Canadian suburbia. What is your preference?"

Silence. Everybody knew who was in charge and what could happen if it turned out that Hugh had bluffed in previous interviews.

Todd started up again by addressing the one outstanding issue in the case. "As you and your lawyer have probably speculated, we don't have a good fix on the guy you chauffeured around back home. We figure that's where your money came from. By the way, thanks for that cash in your suitcase. We'll let the local guys take it to help pay the bills for all the work they've done to keep you in good spirits as a visiting Canadian. You've had a good time here in Syracuse? The food's been good; the cell, clean? They deserve a reward for their efforts. You don't mind, do you?"

At first, Hugh didn't know what to do. He had thought he could keep the money as part of his deal. He glanced at his lawyer, whose look immediately disabused him of that notion. He nodded. "I'd love to help out the local guys. They've been good to me."

Todd wanted the nicety of a gift to the local police. The paperwork would flow more quickly. "Great, we'll sign some documents shortly.

"The major contribution you can make is to tell us more about this character, Martin. We have the notes from your earlier interviews. I can tell you now, for the first time, that the agent beside me was tailing you in Montreal. Some of your story doesn't make sense, from what he reported. We'll come back to that. You think he's from Europe. All we know is that some fellow you met with went into the Trudeau airport and hasn't been seen since. The name you gave us has led nowhere. Before you start giving answers, let's make sure we understand each other. First, I think you are an incorrigible, lying con-artist. You'll say what you have to, to get what you want. Second, you've never dealt with guys like us who thrive on putting much bigger players in jail or killing them if need be. We find them sending their underlings across borders with hundreds of thousands in cash. Do you know how much money the kingpins have in order to shrug at that loss? More than you've ever dreamed of. They came to you, and you agreed to help smuggle rockets out of your country. What for? It's petty change, maybe two fun weeks in Monaco for these guys and their women.

"Our first conclusion is that you don't have a clue about Moreno. If he'd ever thought you would be so stupid as to take this money across the border in a rented car, someone would have shot you dead in that Marriott. They would have left the money in your room, because the hotel staff would have hidden your death as long as possible while they divvied up the cash. Are you beginning to understand what is going on?"

Hugh didn't know what to say, and for the first time, neither did his lawyer.

"The second point is this: you have had the charges described to you and to your lawyer. You have probably been advised that these will not all stick. I won't threaten or belittle you; that advice is not altogether wrong. However, if you don't give me enough information, I will pull the trigger and start court proceedings in the morning while I'm still in town. I'm sure your counsel has told you we're all scheduled to be in court by 10 a.m. We may fail on several charges, but this is trial by jury. Your question to your lawyer is rather straightforward: Is a jury likely to let an alien arrested with more money than they have ever seen go home without being found guilty on at least one of the charges? Tell me the side bet you want, and I'll place my money right here and now. So, bad luck gives you thirty, good luck, five years. We'll recommend a Texas jail with Mexican drug dealers and no air conditioning. Now, let's listen to your story."

Todd never took his eyes off Hugh. He had guessed right, however. Their guy was scared stiff, as his lawyer had painted the same bleak picture.

At that moment, it occurred to Hugh that he found it nearly impossible to be honest. He had spent so much time cutting corners with even his closest friends that telling the truth was almost beyond his capability and certainly outside the range of his experience. What did he really know about Aykroyd? Which tale could he start with that would leave him without the looming prison term?

No one spoke for several minutes. Hugh asked for pen and paper but was denied. Todd had previously seen liars take notes so that they could recreate the same stories. The truth was easy to repeat time and time again. He refused Hugh another consultation with his lawyer; they had had time together earlier in the day.

Hugh was hanging on to the belief that he was still a valuable asset to Moreno. If he managed to escape this crisis by protecting that gang, he convinced himself he would be okay. They wanted to have someone like him in North America.

Todd's conclusion, one that he didn't share with anyone else, was that Hugh was of no further value to any of them, whether they were thieves, terrorists, or investigators.

To Todd's surprise, Hugh spoke out with a strong voice. He had obviously come to the same conclusion as Todd during the half hour of silence, or so the investigator believed. Hugh had hurt many over the years; he had worked painstakingly to take down those who opposed or undermined him.

"I can't say definitively that my story will hold up, but I'm willing to wait here while you search out my lead. Is that a deal?"

"What, we tell the judge we're waiting? He'll tell the jury you should wait in Texas. Go on, tell me what you have. There is absolutely no choice."

"I take it you know the Internet 'mad scientist' and his blog?"

"We don't follow him closely but our experts came across him some months ago. We've read his blogs ever since. Where are you heading?"

"I think there's a connection between Bertie and Martin that might be helpful to your investigation. When we held the science exhibition, the two sort of met."

"Sort of?" Todd was impatient.

"Give me a chance to set this up for you. I get a call from Juan's man in Europe. When we discussed how to get the rockets out of storage, make no doubt about it, he knew everything about them. I was the amateur, as it took me almost two months to dream up the science exhibition idea and convince some locals to support it."

Todd leaned forward and was immediately more attentive when Hugh introduced these two characters into his story. They were known to Todd through the notes taken by investigators but he had dismissed them as being among the immoral petty thieves on the edge of this major operation. He sat there quietly rethinking his position. Both of them were bright people who could do a lot of damage if they put their minds to it. Todd moved his head back and forth as if considering the next move in a chess game; however, in the end he let Hugh continue on with his story.

"You also know that Martin came to our city to see the science exhibition and to use this as a pretense to visit the rocket display. He stayed at a middle-of-the-road business hotel and kept a low profile. He rarely called anyone in my presence, stepping away to make sure I didn't hear."

"Can you give us times, dates, and exactly where you were when you saw him make the calls?"

"Sure can for at least three or four days; always before noon or after dinner. You should know he had several SIM cards with him at all times in his sports jacket pocket. Never made consecutive calls on the same card. I know that for a fact as I saw him fussing with his phone all the time. "

Todd made a note to instruct the computer team to work through the records of the local cell tower. They would use Juan's office phone for the morning calls and a California exchange for the evening. They might get lucky.

"Okay, that's a good start," Todd responded. He was in no mood to deny what was a good lead in favor of bullying for more information. He now knew the information would come. "Please continue."

"His interactions with these people were interesting. First, he stayed away from Angel, whose visit overlapped by a few days. When I casually suggested a dinner together, I was ripped apart for not understanding the dangers of such an encounter. He told me they had to have complete deniability in this operation. I left it alone. Angel certainly never gave me or Stomper any sense that he was expecting someone. Martin always kept an eye open for Angel. When he saw him once across the hotel breakfast room, he went outside right away ostensibly to place a call. He never came back. My impression was that although he wasn't expecting Angel to be around here when we planned this operation, he wasn't at all surprised to see him. Someone had told him about the likelihood of spotting him."

Yes, thought Todd, the link would be from the border-crossing message into Spain and on to Moreno, who would have called Martin.

"The second guy he never spoke with directly was the AT driver. I thought these two guys, working on the same deal, would at least acknowledge each other. It was just the opposite. He watched and listened, obviously understanding Spanish. He asked questions on the phone but not to the driver directly. Remember, this all took place over a period of thirty-six hours. Martin left no trail. Once the AT truck turned out of sight, I was out of the loop until I arrived in Montreal."

Todd looked on in casual disbelief as Hugh drove home a point no one else had thought of: the local climate. "Remember that we were working in Winnipeg in early spring. Weather hasn't warmed up back home. It's still more dark than light. After dinner, not many folks are out driving around. Few would notice a truck headed for the rail yard."

Todd shook his head about the climate. Since he had spent years watching Ukraine and Russia, he gave Hugh the benefit of the doubt.

"Okay, who is the third link?"

"He and Bertie only met once when Bertie was visiting Bill's shop to talk to visitors about the rockets. I had other things to do to finalize the shipment of the wind turbines, so Martin decided to linger near Bertie. At one point, I looked across the shop and caught the expression on Martin's face as he listened to Bertie. It wasn't a smile, exactly, but their gestures and mannerisms had a familiar quality to them, as though they had dealt with each other before."

Todd was waiting for some more concrete details. He urged Hugh to continue his thoughts about the relationship between Bertie and Martin.

"The only thing Martin said in passing as we left was, 'Nice to meet a writer.' I asked myself, 'how did he know that?' Only one way: he must have read his blog. I have never paid it any attention but I hear others do. The next question was, had he contacted him? Suddenly, I had the answer: they had e-mailed or twittered each other, or had participated in an online discussion of some sort. Bertie wouldn't think twice about engaging with someone he didn't know; he would assume goodwill among like-minded scientists. I suspect they entered into a dialogue about the rockets."

Hugh waited for a response; none came. He waited as long as he could before starting up again.

"Someone who knows about these communication systems could likely find out if they were correspondents. It apparently does not take much, if the computer sleuth knows his business. You might be able to find out more than you imagine by following this trail. It's worth a try."

Todd never failed to be impressed with how small-town criminals knew every angle of breaking the law and getting away with it, at least initially.

After he offered a short break so Hugh could eat some lunch, Todd phoned in to his office to recap what he had heard so far.

"We can check out the Internet pretty quickly, within a few days, for sure. We'll know who's staying in touch and where they might be living. It's worth a try at this stage." The analyst was standoffish in his commitment, forcing a direct order from Todd to begin immediately.

"Okay, okay. I'll be back to you tomorrow. It's more complicated than your informer thinks."

After lunch, Todd offered Hugh a short-term deal.

"We don't know what to make of this right now. It's very vague, and internet traffic is not easy to trace. None-the-less, it could be a break in the case." He turned his attention to Hugh's lawyer. "I'll ask the judge to meet us in private and ask to delay jury selection for a month."

"It will take us," he continued, "about three weeks to find out if we're onto something. We'll communicate positive news to the Canadian consulate in Buffalo. You can have a very limited number of visitors, including your friend waiting outside. Do we have a deal?"

"Sounds fair," the lawyer piped up, without asking his client.

Subdued, Hugh slumped in his chair. After everyone else had left, a guard ushered Stomper in. He waited for Hugh to smile, and then he relaxed. "Okay, I think my helping them solve the international terrorist plot will put us in good standing. Check with my lawyer for more details. Right now, I'd love some gossip from home." Both knew the camera would still be rolling in this interview room.

Later, outside the room, Stomper quietly explained to Todd that Bertie told him that Martin had been in touch with Bertie at least three times to clarify information about the rockets. It was obvious to Bertie from the questions being asked that he knew what the right answers were; Martin was only confirming what someone else had told him.

Stomper didn't have to be instructed during his brief meeting with Todd what had to happen. His task was to set up a credible scenario in which Martin, who had vanished, was staying in touch with Bertie. This was the trail Stomper would provide to Todd over the next month. After that, Hugh would be out of jail and on his way home. Stomper and Hugh's lawyer went over the strategy until Stomper could remember what to do without carrying reams of notes. Hugh's lawyer paid for Stomper's research trip to Europe as the Bison Board had instructed, all in cash up front.

WINNIPEG, MANITOBA

Fall 2009

September was a busy month. University had started again with another influx of anxious undergraduates looking for professional guidance. They were the ones to renew enthusiasm within the institution, pulling faculty out of their summer doldrums and forcing them to put on their happy, thoughtful faces.

This fall, Arthur was more emotionally at odds with himself than had been the case for many years, perhaps ever. His time in Europe had been so sweet; he never could have imagined spending such interesting times with three completely different individuals in various cities, each wanting to spend endless time with him, although each in very different ways.

When he returned, he immediately found out that Annie had left. At first, he worried about her safety. Talking to her Aunt Susan was a delicate conversation, as he worried she might be aware of some of his less-than-honest involvement with the Parks.

"I think her mom said she had decided to stay behind in Europe. Did she not send you a letter of resignation?"

"Not really necessary, as her job was ending at the end of August and she was thinking about where to spend a year before starting graduate studies. That's the trend nowadays, to take a year off."

"So you haven't heard? What an abrupt departure, considering you appeared to be good friends as well as professional associates."

"Ah, young people, sometimes they don't appreciate how much we care and fret about them. She'll call or send me a postcard at some point. Thanks, and see you soon at one of your community meetings."

Susan relayed the news about the call to her sister. Although they didn't know what had happened, they understood that their role was to protect Annie. The professor wouldn't extract any information from them; it was up to Annie to decide whether to contact him.

Luckily, Professor Clarke put life back into his project when he responded enthusiastically to Arthur's initial report on the European consultations.

"It sounds as if you'll fit right in. I had very positive feedback. Welcome aboard. Is your research assistant going to stay on? I've heard she's a real find."

Hesitantly, he told him no. "She's been great, but she's currently spending a year outside the university world before grad school. Next year, I suspect she'll be back on campus. Everyone needs a break."

"That's too bad. It's hard to find someone good at that age. We'd like to know as soon as possible what you are going to do." His voice had an edge to it, almost a warning.

"I think I already have a replacement. She's much different. She's already been in the urban field as a policymaker for the last few years. We've collaborated informally on assessing local activities. She'd love to have a reason to help on this project, as it would pull her away from other, less satisfying duties. She's not as sharp as Annie but makes up for it in street smarts."

"I'm leery of your taking on someone different like this. Why don't you outline your program for this year, including her resume and a budget? I'll review it with my colleagues. Hopefully it will be okay."

It was Hugh who phoned to arrange a meeting. He kept the chatter light, saying he had wanted to meet with both Jessica and Arthur about a brand new project.

"First, before that meeting, could I drop by your office, say at 3:00 p.m., to show you a draft of the proposal? It would take only fifteen to twenty minutes."

"Sure, why not? That will speed up the process. Nice to hear your voice and to have you back in the city."

"Thanks. It's great to be with Joanne again, as this has been a miserable time in our lives. Joanne told me that you were a great help and were more than honorable in your dealings with her. I appreciate that very much. See you at three."

Joanne had told him about Hugh's return, and until today, Arthur hadn't thought much about that conversation—that is, until he heard what Hugh had mentioned on the phone. What exactly did Joanne mention about his being so helpful? Given her fear of her husband, the professor had to assume that she'd told him everything, including his keeping the money for a few days.

Promptly at three that afternoon, there was a heavy-handed knock at the door. Following the academic tradition of never getting up to receive a visitor, Arthur called out for his visitor to enter on his own. The footsteps striding across the doorway didn't belong to Hugh—but to Stomper, who shut the door softly behind him.

"I certainly wasn't expecting you," Arthur said roughly. "What happened to Hugh?"

Stomper shrugged. His bulk overflowed the chair, and his menace filled the tiny office. His aggressive face set the tone for the next several minutes.

"Hugh had another meeting suddenly pop up in his agenda. He asked me to come over and see you. Besides, it's usually my job to help him and the Bison Board out in these situations. It's the way we work best together."

Arthur wasn't catching on fast enough. "What job? I'm not sure I'm following you." He now wished the office door were open.

"Well, I'm sure you agree that it's great to have Hugh back in the city."

"Of course. Jessica and I valued his judgment on community projects. I told him that this morning."

"Right; the feeling is mutual, from what I understand. Joanne told the two of us last night that you were also a big help to her. She's very grateful."

"Thanks." Arthur was asking no questions yet.

"Did you know that Hugh is a terrific investment leader? We have a small group of knowledgeable local people; we named the group the Bison Board, which he calls to order frequently. We talk about opportunities to invest locally. We don't waste their money. He keeps track of every penny. My role is research and report writing to make sure the opportunity is legitimate."

He paused and looked around the office.

Arthur broke the long silence. "Sounds like a good deal for the investors."

"Really, the key is, can Hugh show them exactly where all the money is, all the time? There can be no complaints about sloppy bookkeeping or unprofessional use of the funds."

"Sounds fair."

"Take the decision last year to invest in wind turbines. It really caught on locally, and sales are picking up internationally. That's why Hugh went east; he was so excited about the first shipment."

"That's what Joanne told me."

"A lot of the investors are older and grew up believing in cash. Often Hugh has to deal in cash, which makes his accounting so important. Everyone is careful with cash so that nobody gets hurt. Nobody trusts the banks, as they are always running to the government about large cash deposits, so we often keep the money at Hugh's house, sometimes at mine. No big deal."

Arthur had still to vocalize a single substantive comment. He was not inclined to encourage Stomper although he was quite curious how long Hugh had spent prepping him for this performance. This was beyond the reach of Stomper.

"We often laugh at our informality and pretend we're mobsters from the '30s in Chicago. Nowadays, you have to be careful lest others think you're drug dealers. Just before Hugh's trip, we received a dividend from one of our investments and were paid in cash. We had all the proper expense receipts; the whole arrangement was in perfect order. We were getting ready to meet our Bison Board for a much-anticipated distribution. Everyone was happy. The money was in two briefcases—matter of fact, they look just like two that you have there on the floor. Remarkable coincidence. Then again, it's a common brand found in all of the stores. We got ours at Office Depot. Where did you find these two? On sale, I hope. Profs' salaries don't go far." Stomper laughed.

Arthur didn't. He finally began to understand what was being played out in front of him. "Don't remember. I get lots of gifts from the parents of graduating students who have told them about their favorite professor. That's probably where they came from."

"Great; you must be a wonderful teacher. Just think, two sets of parents buying the same briefcase from the same chain for the same professor, maybe even in the same year. Surely even an absentminded professor would remember that."

"Probably not Jerry Lewis."

Stomper grinned. "No, that nutty professor didn't notice anything."

Dead silence coated the room, but Arthur stuck to his silent role.

Stomper picked up where he'd left off.

"When Hugh left for Montreal, he called me and reminded me about the distribution that was due ten days later. We talked about our own briefcases that were stored at his place. You never know what can happen with accidents, bad weather, and travel, so we figured it was safe to leave them there. Joanne never knew what exactly was being stored."

Stomper tossed him another question. "Were you surprised by his arrest?"

Arthur thought for only a second. There could only be one answer. "Yes, of course. I never saw him do anything untoward."

"When Joanne called me, I knew what he would want me to do. He'd want the Bison Board to receive their money on schedule. They didn't know it was coming, as Hugh loved to surprise them, but we always kept to our deadlines and to our commitments.

"I didn't do anything at first, because the seriousness of the situation escaped me. I couldn't comprehend what was happening. I waited a couple of days, called Joanne, and went looking for the dividend money. I didn't find anything. She said the police had already been there with a search warrant and had taken away some documents. I was nervous, to tell you the truth.

"Later that week, I met with the investors who, instead of receiving a surprise distribution, got a cash call from me to help get Hugh back as soon as we could. At that meeting, I raised a lot of money for him. We found a fantastic but expensive lawyer. That took up most of my time over the summer. After that, I went to Europe on business and just got back this week. I hear you've been there recently too, right?"

Arthur nodded. "On a research project."

"Me, too. Boy, it was sure expensive."

"I had a foundation support most of my travel, thankfully."

"When Hugh came back, he asked Joanne if she'd moved anything around. She immediately explained that she'd taken the money from the house before the police came knocking. She was one smart cookie. Hugh asked her to go around and collect it, as everything was fine with the authorities. She did that quickly. Hugh is dying to know who these friends were. Joanne has told him it's none of his business. I would have loved to have heard that conversation."

"So you must have your money back, then," Arthur said, after another long pause.

"Well, yes and no. Hugh explained to her that since this money belonged to the Bison Board as their dividend payment, he had to account for all of it. He made it clear that they would understand her stress and why she took out living expenses for the last several weeks. She gave him a good breakdown of how much she spent, although privately, Hugh is angry over their daughter getting some of it. We can't easily sell the Board on that."

He paused and looked straight at Arthur. He was quite menacing.

"We counted, and we counted again, but each time we came up short. Easy to do with $100 bills. Probably two bills from each pile; suddenly a guy has $40,000. If he took only four thin bills from each stack, why, he'd soon have $80,000. And so on. A lot of money for, say, someone teaching at a university. I got to thinking about the cost of Europe when I was over there. Now, I only spent a modest amount, but I was thinking that if I were there with two or three women for a month, yeah, I would go through twenty to thirty grand so fast that I would come back without a trace in my pocket.

"You know, we live in a small city. When I went to buy my airline ticket, I ended up at the same travel agency as you. I paid her in cash, and she began telling me about this wonderful professor who paid in cash for his wife's tickets and even her hotel in London. The Brown Hotel, I think she said. Apparently this wonderful professor had been saving twenty or fifty dollars at a time for a couple of years to give her this anniversary gift, although he paid with hundred-dollar bills. Just think: saved with twenties and paid with hundreds. I agreed with the agent: he would be a pretty special guy."

Stomper didn't take his eyes off Arthur, who by now was sitting chained to his chair in terror. He couldn't have moved even if he had wanted to.

Stomper threw up his hands as though he couldn't unscramble all the new information. "On top of all this, one of Hugh's new friends in the police department, Bob Sampson, the one who was recently in your class, told him he was forced to go interview you, I guess in this very office. He was chatty; you and Hugh had helped him out with a large community project run by his family. He cleared the air immediately about the two briefcases you carried past the security cameras that weekend. Apparently, you pointed to them, opened them, and showed Bob the community documents you had picked up from Joanne. Small world."

He stood up. "I don't like universities at all. Too snobby and too chummy for my liking. Hope I don't have to come up here again to see you. Maybe you can phone Hugh, as he thought he'd be free by the time we finished. It'd be best for the two of you to sort this out." He moved his hand a few inches in a half-hearted wave. "Take care."

Now what? Arthur did not want to place the call, although he clearly knew the grave consequences if he didn't. They had figured out how much he had stolen. It had never occurred to him that he would be found out by these crazies, as he took it for granted that the Americans would never let Hugh go. He had been wrong.

His phone sounded, interrupting his panic attack. Hugh wasn't waiting for him to make up his mind about calling.

"Hi, Arthur, how's it going? Sorry I couldn't make it. I hear you had a fruitful chat with my good friend Stomper. Good guy. Smart. Thoughtful. Why don't you think about your options? The Bison Board meets next week. As long as everything is in order by then, we should be okay." His voice trailed off; he said "Cheers" and hung up. Arthur hadn't said a word.

Arthur realized that he wasn't built for a fight like this. He was best in other struggles, like writing a book or teaching hours and hours of class each semester or maybe even telling someone in administration to get lost. He had never considered taking on bullies who spent their life stealing from the likes of him.

It was now five o'clock. He didn't dare walk by Joanne and Hugh's house lest one of them see him. What then? Stop for a drink or ignore them? Pretend that nothing had happened or admit he was a thief?

It was hard to claim he had taken the moral high road, which it was okay to steal from Hugh because Hugh had stolen from other people. To steal is to steal, he reminded himself. He sat frozen at his desk, pondering the enormity of his mistake. It wasn't just a mistake; he deliberately stole thousands and thought he could get away with it. He didn't.

He obviously needed to find the cash quickly. He had very little money sitting in any saving account, and a loan against the house would require his wife's signature. He was too embarrassed to phone any of his friends, as he would likely need some explanation as to why he was suddenly under such duress. The story in itself was so unbelievable. No one would understand why he helped Joanne in the first place—or why he afterward thought it was okay to steal from the briefcases.

He had made so many wrong moves during the past two years that even he was stunned by his bad judgment. He thought back over his dealings with Annie, his colleagues, his students, his wife, and the Jacobs Foundation. He had moved his life from that of a highly respected professor to one of a common thief. The transformation was so utterly complete that he couldn't fathom how to rescue himself.

He was scared right to his soul. The youthful, energetic student he had been, capable of explaining complicated theories of social change to the uninitiated, had ended up as an ordinary thief with no explanation for his base behavior. The kindly, supportive professor had taken advantage of every relationship to fulfill his own desires while thoroughly destroying trust and friendship. Colleagues who appreciated his sharp observations about corruption would be shocked to learn that he himself had fallen from grace for a few—okay, many—hundred-dollar bills.

It wasn't necessarily the amount of money. Long after the fact, professional friends would whisper that they could have easily helped. That wasn't the point. Two emotions were tearing at him and causing his collapse. One was the humiliation of trying to explain actions that could not be justified. The trail leading up to the theft constituted a series of immoral decisions. This wasn't how he had planned to live out his life. He was fiercely attached to his own self-image of a man always trying to do the right thing. He had anticipated mistakes, but ones for which he would be forgiven. In his final judgment of himself, however, the last two years were unforgivable.

His other emotional drain was fear. He had managed to conceal his private fears through all sorts of defenses to which no one else was privy. He remembered ducking away from family and neighborhood violence as a child; he'd continued this avoidance throughout his adult years. He ran from any confrontation. He hated bullies and walked away from any interaction where aggressive hostility could have led to physical fighting. He was incapable of drawing a line where he would fight back. Bullies beat up Arthur the moment they started after him. He had no stomach for the big fights that could have defined him as a strong leader. Fear made him into a lesser man.

He told himself he had no other choice. He picked up a pen and wrote his wife a final note.

OTTAWA, ONTARIO

Fall 2009

Shelly passed the message to Ottawa that the second effort in one year to sell AT was not going well. Todd half-heartedly fought to keep it going in case it might attract some unsuspecting criminal, leading them back into Juan's stealthy networks. Angel hadn't had a chance to put in place a succession agreement with management before he had his fatal accident, and he was far too young to have a will back in Spain. Juan's lawyer had triggered a clause in the shareholders' agreement that forced the immediate sale of the assets or a significant payout by the partners. Marsha was making every effort to ditch the company; the low quotes being garnered were a blotch on her record and a visible barrier preventing her from raising new capital. That scenario, she worried, would likely put her out of business within a year. Various law enforcement agencies, including several in Canada, wanted detailed financial, personnel, and transactional records some of which were destroyed about the time Brent was fired. Rodriguez remained in California until friends snuck him off to Mexico. His English language skills had disappeared along with the trucks and their drivers. It was a nightmare for Marsha.

Cascadia may have been dissatisfied with Marsha, but the suspicion remained that Theodore woke up only once he saw that his fund was left holding the bag. The fund's interest in Aird Investments was on the cusp of becoming a Canadian political problem. Ottawa's finance department had phoned him far too many times, obviously on behalf of national politicians, to ask for updates. It was beginning to look like a case of money-laundering, which could be prosecuted on both sides of the border. Politically embarrassing questions would be raised about who knew what and whether Ottawa had failed to pay enough attention. Topping it off, both Theodore and Livingstone were aggravated by having to spend several days in Ottawa getting beat up by politicos who knew nothing about the pension business.

The minister of finance found out that he had the same problems as Cascadia's management after his most recent briefing. In a convoluted and unfair turn of events, he was now to be held responsible for events far from his office. The prime minister, too, would be held accountable for Moreno's entry into Canada, as Angel was a member of a family internationally rumored to be active in providing arms in the Middle East. Thus, the prime minister's party was at risk of losing the Jewish-dominated constituencies. As security issues were always reported up to his office, parliamentarians would be asking why he didn't read the report on the missing rockets, or on Moreno's departure, or on the rockets being shipped to the Mediterranean.

A more subtle but equally precarious complication was unfolding in Winnipeg, which, like Vancouver, was important in the government's political calculations. The more detailed briefings suggested that Aird's investment in AT could be tied into events unfolding in Winnipeg about the stolen rockets. Although Mayor Patterson was not directly implicated, the briefing note referred to his promotion of Parks as an outstanding innovator in the Manitoba economy. It was unlikely this would cause the demise of the mayor in his next local election; however, it definitely took him off the list of star candidates for the upcoming federal election. There would be no further evenings spent entertaining the mayor in Ottawa.

When Cascadia's CEO was asked to join the prime minister and his finance minister for a final chat before his return to Vancouver to determine what exactly his fund was doing with the savings from their pensioners, Livingstone couldn't explain his own chain of command governing investments in America.

He tried lamely, "We govern ourselves within the context of obtaining benefits for our pensioners in all situations. There are moral risks in the safest of investments, as governments are as guilty as a private company. We were offered bonds in Africa, as many Canadian mining companies think it's now clean. We declined that investment. We also thought that an honorable and historic democracy like Greece would be responsible and never walk on debt held by foreign pensioners. In the end, they screwed everyone. The investment world is not usually one of transformation; it's a place where you can protect yourself as much as you can and take your gains in a quick, civilized fashion."

The prime minister, who had been listening to the comments, took the opportunity to outline briefly how interstate relations had changed in the wake of 9/11.

"The Americans have fundamentally changed how they deal with even the most established of allies, including us. And we haven't had a border incident in two hundred years!" Everyone laughed at his reference to the time the Americans had tried to take over parts of Canada in the War of 1812, episodes that rarely made it into American history books.

"Americans have put new borders around their country. Daily they watch every single person and dollar that crosses into their territory. Most people don't realize that the Department of Homeland Security has about the same number of employees as our whole national government.

"You know full well that our own national pension plan investment fund is subject to the same rules as the sovereign funds out of Asia and the Middle East. It's all quite insulting, but that's life in the new America.

"Now, to get to our problem with you," the prime minister said to Livingstone. "Your investment in Aird Investments is interpreted by Washington as supporting terrorism by financing an American-based transportation company that intended to move rockets from North America to the battle fronts. The country is in the middle of its global war on terror, which doesn't seem to be going well. Because terrorism is played by their media as a universal problem, their politicians and advisors link stories in big cities, mountains, poppy fields, and oil deltas, as if they are one and the same, as if they are fighting a single enemy.

"They have told us in very frank conversations at the highest levels that they don't want any hint of terrorism on this continent. Domestic police forces are already overwhelmed by the drug cartels. They don't want to see that money being deployed to buy rockets for the Middle East and moved through a sophisticated trucking firm partly owned by you and partly by international terrorists."

Paul was terrified. What should he do now? The investment was so small that it hadn't even been reported up to his board of directors, let alone noted in the annual report.

The minister was ready for this. "I know you're already winding down your current position with Aird, and I'm sure you'll be out of there as soon as possible. We've heard that the head of this investment firm is looking for your participation in a second fund. I would prefer if you didn't go ahead with it, but that's your decision, not mine, and that's the last we'll ever speak about it.

"You may also want to develop a new speech for the annual meeting season in which you trump good governance as a core value in your organization. Show people how you avoid mistakes in this era of instability in promising investment fields. That speech will resonate well with those I'm making."

WASHINGTON, DC

Early 2010

Myron was worried about whether the Canadian government could outlast this latest money-laundering scandal. He knew all too well that even the most stable governments can unravel during unanticipated events. He called Shelly after dinner for her opinion on the durability of Canada's government. She told him not to worry.

"Canadian prime ministers and their finance ministers are usually the most seasoned and embattled politicians, so most episodes that destabilize others have little impact on them. Mind you, minor characters like Mayor Patterson immediately disappear from their agenda books, and few in the national media take any interest in their sudden departure. The investment entanglement is more complicated; all that means initially is that the prime minister turns the file over to the finance minister and wishes him well." They both laughed at the reality of politics.

Shelly curled up on her couch and spoke in a relaxed frame of mind as she described as best she could what had been happening in Ottawa since they last had dinner together.

"Canadians, as is their habit, took exception to what happened. We hold ourselves in high esteem, and, broadly speaking, we adhere to our international commitment to socially responsible investments—although we, like our northern cousins, the Scandinavians, are reticent to spell this out in much detail. Having said that, everyone was surprised to discover that an investment in the United States landed them into so much trouble."

It seemed like an eternity had passed since Marsha had mopped up the messy scenes at Aird Investment when the misfortunes of AT egregiously weakened her fortunes. She had driven hard, pushing everyone away from the file so she could evaluate what had gone wrong. Marsha thrived on punishing her enemies. She desperately wanted to fire Caesar, but he had surreptitiously disappeared into Mexico, protected by extended family and business allies. She moved on not wasting a precious minute chasing someone beneath her despite her anger. Brent was gone, as at least one head had rolled in her shop. After Angel had disappeared at sea, his local lawyer had written that the estate was exercising its right to sell its interest in AT back to her investment house. This was a problem. She didn't know what to tell the financial community. Everyone was quietly asking: Was she dumping a worthless asset into a weak market because it was owned by a reputed armament dealer? Did they all believe the European newspapers with their whispering campaign against Juan Moreno? Maybe she should find a way to keep the family involved with Aird. This she would work on as a priority despite Todd's admonition that her investment career couldn't possibly survive if she were viewed as Juan's agent. When she pushed back and tried to bully Todd out of the way, he quickly responded with his deadly message that he was prepared to deliver personally to the Wall Street pros she needed onside for her survival: "I will tell them this. If you invest with Marsha at Aird, you'll be watched as a possible conspirator for laundering overseas terrorist money. The president of the United States will not forgive you for working against your country and his campaign to free us of terrorism." She knew she had to find a way to squash any missive like that.

Her self-imposed deadline for raising funds for her second fund came and went without a single dollar flowing into the firm. Cascadia digested the news, and its private investment team decided to divest itself of Aird. They had all had enough and were pleased to be away from Marsha. Her meanness was an affront to Theodore's personal style, and he let this be known; he resented the caustic, unrelenting tactics hammering home her uncompromising efforts to win each and every struggle, hiding as it did her prevaricating personality.

When Cascadia told Marsha they were winding down their current position with her and would exit as soon as they could, she flew into a rage, calling other investment houses to complain about their audacity in abandoning Aird. When she settled down a few days later, she recognized the damage she was doing to herself. Fed up with being hounded, she phoned Todd. "I need help. I'll come to Washington. Meet me at Acadiana, the restaurant near the corner of New York Avenue and K Street. It's a little out of the way for the usual suspects who like to spot political deals in progress. I want to make an arrangement with you."

Todd could only chuckle when the call was over. She was such a control freak she even chose the restaurant in his home town. It always had to be on her terms and on her turf. To make matters worse, he had to put on a suit, as Myron was always after him to dress the role while working in Washington's political crowd. He hated to feel so cramped in his clothing as the current style certainly was not designed for middle-aged, big men like him long removed from active combat duty. The outdoor casual look suited him best but Todd knew that Marsha would arrive perfectly tailored in a black outfit. She did not disappoint him.

She had reserved a table along the window, closer to the kitchen than the front entrance, to afford them more privacy. They both dispensed without a fuss the ordering of their meals as neither was very adventuresome at lunch time.

Over her seafood chopped salad, Marsha outlined her survival plan.

"I've been watching you over the past year," she started. "You've managed to recover from some errors and have quite obviously reestablished yourself as a respectable spook. I say, well done. In business, we do this all the time. It's getting harder right now, given the attacks on the industry.

"I bet your next big question, now that you've put a kybosh to Juan's direct involvement in our transportation investments, is to monitor what his gang will do next. You're smart enough, Todd, to know that laundered money will continue to gravitate to this country. The great dealmakers from the Middle East and China will organize their minions who are spread across the States, put on the right garb for meetings in restaurants like this, and offer money that's cleaned up and ready for investment. The problem you face is that no one is telling you what's happening in real time. You're always finding out too late, by which time the hot money has disappeared. Money moves too fast for government bureaucracies, even if your mandate is to stop the flow. All you're doing is chasing case studies."

"I appreciate your analysis, especially since you're paying for lunch," Todd responded, uncomfortable with Marsha's aggravating tone. "Where does it take us?"

"I've concluded that right now we are compelled to cooperate with each other. I suffer for cash badly; my business is about to collapse. This, of course, is of little concern to you. From your perspective, what are you getting in the meantime by way of really solid information? I'm willing to wager big poker chips that it's next to nothing. Certainly you're not any closer to the very thieves you've been chasing for years. It's not great for you. A plague on all financial houses that play in this arena. That's the nub of your anger. Correct?"

Since this was exactly what he had been thinking as he sat on the Metro making his way over to the restaurant, he nodded and indicated she should continue.

"If we were sitting on Wall Street, we wouldn't be having this conversation. The banks have proven over the last few years that most are too big to fail while they continue to promote and reward their senior ranks who propose and execute plans that are so immoral that the rest of the world is left gaping. It's beyond comprehension."

Marsha was nearing her point. "Nobody outside the States wants to partner with people like that. Remember that in the middle of the Great Recession, Washington convinced a sovereign fund to buy a big chunk of bank debt for which it is unlikely to see any return for months and months. Our government and our banks are contaminated with assets that no legitimate dealer will touch. Check it out. Have you seen any offshore buyers of our financial institutions? No!" She answered her own question less Todd wasn't paying attention.

Todd gestured his agreement; he was observing how she negotiated. He was intrigued by the complexity of her strategy.

"Last month, when Aird was about to accept that we were failing to attract new capital and that our firm was about to close, I had a visitor from a major Spanish law firm based in Madrid. They're significant and influential professionals who advertise their advantageous connections in the Middle East. Ostensibly, the lawyer was in Philadelphia working with a local law firm to close down the transportation company since we had no intension of carrying on without their financial backing, as we've discussed previously. He really wasn't compelled to see me on that issue, yet he was quite insistent on a private meeting."

Now Todd was totally interested in the conversation. Marsha sat quietly as their plates were taken away and replaced with coffee cups. Since he did not want to be seen as having absolutely no knowledge of Spain, he broke into her monologue. "We know about this character. He acts as the major figure for Juan's company whenever they decide to move into new markets or if they're having any problems with transport regulators. At least that's the official line. We think he's a major link to both North Africa and the Middle East, where Juan has several terrorist organizations as clients."

She shrugged, knowing that her information about this Spanish visitor had shifted the power to her in the course of this lunch. "The very fact that you didn't know he was in the country supports my position that you are obligated to be more engaged with a financial institution such as mine. You must find a way to be kept better informed. When you're asked by Congress what's going on in Europe and the Middle East, you want to be in a position to tell them exactly what is happening the very day they pose the question. You don't want to give the predictable bullshit answer that there's a well-coordinated international conspiracy of Al-Qaeda organizations threatening American interests all around the world. You don't want your voice to echo that mindless analysis of global terror."

"And why not?"

Marsha waited several seconds. Was he pretending to be dumb, or had she miscalculated his shrewdness? She concluded that it didn't matter, as she had to plow on with her pitch.

"The bright analysts know there are a myriad of interests working to destroy America. Some are big institutions supported brazenly by hostile foreign governments; others are so tiny that even the most dedicated analyst can't remember their names. But even the smaller ones can recruit some poor young fellow to load his body up with explosives and walk by one of our embassies. As most of this is planned and carried out in Arabic, we never catch on until we hear the boom. Arabic dominates communications in big chunks of the world, and we don't have a clue, not a clue, what they're advocating against us. We're so out of it that we don't want their television network on our cable system. What, we're so scared we don't want to hear their voices? It's preposterous."

Marsha finally took a washroom break as Todd ordered more coffee. She returned with the same hardened look that Todd found very disconcerting. After stirring in a bit of cream, she continued. "In the drug trade, where you've officially spent most of your career, it's pretty black and white. Criminals make money through drugs; then they store their outrageous piles of small bills, all American currency, spend some on wives and girlfriends, and look at ways to make it all legitimate. Hard work for you to pursue these characters, but let's face it: it's a straightforward business model that works. You agree?"

He nodded and added his thoughts about the Juans of the world. "The terrorism world is no different. As a starting point, not all terrorists are bad, and some are bad only for a while. When they win their struggle, they often are treated as our equal and celebrated as legitimate powers in their countries. Some battles, like in Ireland of all places, keep on going for generations; other insurgents are wiped out in three good raids. To be involved in this world and live to talk about it, you have to be really smart and lucky."

"It all requires money," she replied. "Not all of it comes from the drug world, but some certainly does, and that's where I imagine you got your start following these modern-day gangsters." She looked across the table but didn't wait for an answer. "In my business the money can come from religious organizations, multigenerational and successful family businesses, oil, and even competing states. Makes it complicated to follow the money trail and to be outrageously opinionated about what's right and wrong.

"So, back to my new friend from Spain. He came with an overture. I immediately concluded that Juan has a new financial partner. My guess is that it's a small off shore sovereign fund or they wouldn't want me—an American woman. Making it perfectly clear that he was representing another interest, he tells me that his client liked our prospectus for the new fund. Of course, it's widely known that no American investor fancies Aird running their money these days. So why this foreign fund? Only a couple of possible explanations. One is that they want to control a fund to find out how to operate in the States as a venture capitalist. That gives them their much-needed cover-story for whatever else that they might be up to with their nascent terrorist cells. Second, they're the only ones who have done their due diligence without asking a hundred questions about the AT story. It probably means they know all about what happened, confirming how closely they're tied up with the Moreno family."

That in itself was enough of a story for Todd. She was correct. A low-profile sovereign fund not asking Marsha questions about the AT scandal could only mean that it was one of Juan's invisible financial partners. This was big news, because it could provide new leads.

"How can I help you?" Todd asked.

"The lawyer suggested that I restructure this second fund around one investor only. This unidentified group will provide the original $1 billion I've been looking for and want an option in five years for a second tranche of the same size. It will keep me in business, although I will effectively become their agent, as they'll be the ones making all of the key decisions.

"Do you want a window into this world? If so, you have to go to your bosses in the intelligence community to clear the way. I'll later give you a list of all the approvals Aird will require to operate with such a dominate foreign investor. The paperwork will be sufficiently sophisticated that all your friends in high places can turn a blind eye to what I'm doing. I'm assuming that my new partner will camouflage some activities, but you'll have plenty of fresh, current information to pass around. I'm meeting their representatives for a late dinner tonight in Philadelphia, where we intend to map out a deal. What do you say?"

"I'm in," he replied without hesitation. The deal wouldn't produce leads anytime soon, but Myron would appreciate the unparalleled access to people associated with the Moreno family. It would take weeks of hard lobbying to get approvals, but Todd knew Myron was up to the task.

Marsha gave him one last morsel at the door after she paid the bill. "I think Juan desperately wants to retain and build the transport company. That was the message delivered during that meeting. A few months ago, they pushed me hard to close it down but now it's a different story. AT's a mess, but it's his money.

Apparently, he wants to convince his wife that Angel's life was not in vain. I doubt she'll agree, but men will try anything."

With one lunch, Marsha had saved her company and would go on to make millions in this new partnership. She fed bits and pieces into the American intelligence agencies while managing to keep her new partner up-to-date on these communications. She thrived as a double agent, one tolerated in bemusement by both sides. They were smart investors and took out significant dividends over the years. At the same time, with new cash and a new Mexican-American president, AT grew into a large conglomerate beyond trucking. Juan often talked about it at home as a tribute to his much-missed son.

Marsha never once mentioned Brent or asked her colleagues what happened to him. As for the Canadians, she quit badmouthing them, although she managed to provoke several congressional hearings regarding foreign ownership of big infrastructure investments, ones that her client wanted stopped.

WASHINGTON, DC

Fall 2010

Todd's hooking Marsha into their web of espionage surveillance was about as good of a coup as could be expected within a failed mission. She now could be counted on as part of the team. Myron had conferred with Todd and organized their approach heading into 2011. Although Myron was convinced that Juan was a fading threat given the demoralized state of his family after losing Angel quite accidentally, Todd was doggedly determined to bring him down. Myron relented. Todd was assigned surreptitiously to yet another congressional committee whose mandate included tracking radicals in faraway places. He took to travelling more than he had in the past, and the two of them saw each other less frequently.

Myron, however, wasn't satisfied with leaving so many loose ends, simply because the file lay dormant in his office safe. After much thought, he invited Shelly who had told him that she'd be back in town for a few weeks of quiet research to lunch nearby at SushiAOI, an innovative and modern-looking Japanese restaurant where the traditional noon-hour sushi crowd would not be comfortable. It was a good place to talk, as few would suspect finding old-fashioned Myron in such a trendy eatery. When Shelly accepted his invitation, he caught her a little off guard by asking her to prepare a few notes about the Canadians who had been caught up in the fracas when the rockets went missing. There were a few matters he wanted to discuss over lunch. "Anyone or anything in particular?" asked the skeptical Canadian not familiar with a friendly face in Washington's power circles.

"Yes, as a matter of fact. I want to talk about people. Is there anyone still at risk after our adventure with the Canadian rockets? Let's limit our research to the young. Can you find out about Emma Parks...and also, there was an ambitious young woman we heard about who hung around the professor who disappeared on us—Annie I believe is her first name. I'll do my share of the work by tracking down Brent and Heather from Philadelphia. I don't think there were any other innocent bystanders. See you next Tuesday."

They talked initially less spontaneously than was usually the case. Instead of openly debating the merits of various offerings on the lunch menu, they hurriedly deferred to the waiter giving him instructions to bring whatever he fancied to their table. Shelly recognized how differently they were reacting to the fallout from what had been a most difficult file perhaps because she was from her own experience stubbornly locked into her world view for dealing with tragedy. A miserable divorce, dating back for more than fifteen years, spawned her tenacious refusal to look back. Shelly was adamant and remained true to her character in every difficult personal problem she subsequently dealt with while Myron's commitment to bachelorhood since his university days made him the opposite: a very compassionate and caring individual. That was typically a surprise to newcomers who assumed he would be as jaded as the next among the national security cliques. He was largely unscarred by personal failure so had an endearing capacity for generosity. Responding to her unasked question, Myron volunteered that he liked to keep track of individuals overrun by circumstances beyond their control. "There's more collateral damage than you might want to acknowledge in our line of work," he elaborated, "especially when there are young people involved. They're too innocent and trusting to see the train wreck ahead, and more than a few are too headstrong to ignore warnings from more experienced players. I like to know where they end up in case we can help in some subtle way."

The restaurant was indeed a superb change from the stuffiness of the Cosmos Club. They at last relaxed and bantered around for quite a while, obviously enjoying each other's company more than Shelly initially had anticipated given Myron's odd proposal. She begrudged him that Myron had a solid knack for finding reliable and worthy friends in his very dark and sinister world. And it caught others off guard to watch him track down those who had unnecessarily Become victims when more powerful interests were seeking their own rewards.

"Let's turn to the business of the day," he suggested as he put his napkin aside and reached inside his suit jacket for his notes. "Shelly, you go first. Whatever happened to Annie?"

"You've chosen the most interesting one to start with," she responded with energy, as she had enjoyed the chance to review the state of these young people.

"She stopped working with the professor from Winnipeg over sixteen months ago to take up a new life in Berlin, of all places."

"Cheers for her," he interrupted good-naturedly.

Unfazed, Shelly continued her story. "Berlin has turned into the great launch she was hoping for. She wasn't lonely for those back home, including her professor, as she found new friends with different expectations. Crawford was already inconsequential before she left, as his reckless swimming into life's gray areas left him without the tools to avoid the black zone, where his lack of morality became unforgivable.

"The city symbolized faraway freedom; she probably could have moved anywhere. She didn't want any more anonymity; indeed she wanted to be in front of a parade where she could show her spirit, originality, and determination to rise above mediocrity. Annie had to prove she was truly as strong as she had told herself she was. Although her exit from North America was sudden and dramatic, it was the direction her spirit needed next. It would work for her, as her previous decisions had brought additional strength to her character.

"It took only a few days to find a job. An American artist had been commissioned to create dramatic art for new buildings back in North America. Her works were incredibly large, so she employed several young people to mix paints, draw lines, grab coffee, and otherwise be on hand at all times while being quiet and invisible. Annie knew she fit the bill and argued her way into the coffee job. Soon she was the chief organizer, taking charge of the morning's work before the artist arrived. For months the job expanded, until the artist chose her as the one to go with her to America and help mount the art. Annie lost her anonymity when the *Wall Street Journal*'s Friday art section last spring ran a photo announcing their arrival in downtown Chicago. Winnipeggers found out about this, but before they could track her down, she was off to the next big project, having fun, achieving success, and finding, most importantly, creative peace. She may go back to school, but not in Canada—at least that's my best guess.

"Okay, Myron, it's your turn. Start with Heather. She was such a curiosity to me."

"No doubt you recognized a kindred spirit," he teased before launching into the sad story of Heather.

"Heather has not fared well in the aftermath of Angel's death. Disheartened at the loss of her very dear friend and lover and thinking that others would be sympathetic to her plight, Heather had completely misjudged what was going to happen to her. As the full story unfolded, implicating Angel in the family's unseemly dirty armaments business, her predicament as a young woman fending for herself was untenable. Heather was now viewed as dangerous, particularly among her women friends. She was the one who had introduced their boyfriends, fiancés, and husbands to a menacing character who could have ruined their lives. At the same time, she was strangely more attractive to these same men as a femme fatal, someone who didn't live a protected life. They thought of her as being enticingly sexy because of her involvement in such intrigue. Their side glances were caught by their own girlfriends, who immediately dismissed her from their lives.

"Her busy professional life stopped abruptly. With apologies from everyone, Heather was on her own four months later with little support. She returned home to Huntingdon in western rural Pennsylvania where she was still seen as everyone's local cutie pie, albeit one with a well-known reputation for her crazy liaison with the heir to some mysterious Spanish murderous cartel. Her mom and dad forgave her, loved her and brought her back into their church. She is living a quiet life looking after them although lately a local man, also wanted to be cared for in the same fashion as her parents, intends to marry her. She's never heard from college friends again.

"Back to you for the update on Emma. How is she doing? Where is she living?"

"Emma moved after graduation to Toronto, where she hoped the hustle and bustle of a metropolitan life would give her the opportunity to create a new life. In a very determined fashion, she is working her way into the city's well-paying financial service businesses by taking advantage of progressively more important assignments. Lacking a mentor and missing a single big score she could boast about, Emma is still finding ways to succeed and support herself. She came across her niche almost by accident. Since she spent her formative years watching distastefully the likes of her father and Stomper, she has an insightful jugular skill for spotting fraudulent players. The superstar dealmakers who are her bosses appreciate how Emma keeps them out of trouble. Sitting quietly during their negotiating sessions and looking every much like the librarian she had planned on becoming, Emma follows-up meetings with potential clients like the toughest of private investigators in a detective novel, coming back with information that protects her colleagues. They owe her big and are making sure she survives well in the difficult world of finance. Living on her own in Toronto's west end among various new European immigrant groups seems to be a life that is making her happy."

When she finished, Shelly looked over to Myron to tell him about the last of the four youthful bystanders. "At first, it was a sad, sad story but Brent is currently showing a determination to live his life on his own accord in a new city: it takes guts to do it, but he is succeeding. A few months ago, I asked the FBI to find out what happened to Brent, a kid who I concluded was caught in a game far too big for anyone as inexperienced as he was. Exactly as I had anticipated, Brent was reasonably quick to realize that, in the middle of a recession brought on by reckless financial institutions, he was more than just damaged goods. He was finished. All his training, the family's several hundred thousands of dollars in education support and the many friends across the Northeast were worthless assets in a world moving into new and untried circumstances. The FBI reported back that he had hung around his shared rented house as long as he could but his roommates soon needed his share of the rent. Each day he journeyed further out of Philadelphia looking for work, initially scared of taking anything that looked like failure. He was numb from rejection, failure and now poverty. Public transit replaced the car he sold and soon walking replaced city buses. After four months of this, he settled into Baltimore a couple of hours on the freeway and a lifetime away from Philadelphia, selling hotdogs, chips and sandwiches to sporting crowds and downtown office workers. Many evenings he parks his cart outside the open air Pier Six concert stage, giving himself a chance to listen to some great touring jazz musicians while selling ice cream to the tourists.

"He's ended up living alone, proud that he is still alive because of his own determination, making friends among new immigrants from Somalia and Nigeria, competing for the same vendor space on the street and yelling for the attention of the same customers. Unlike many others whose lives fall apart, he's stayed away from drugs and his favorite but expensive martinis are long gone from his daily routine. His family is apparently embarrassed beyond their imagination, treating him gingerly as the mentally-ill misfit who wasted their money.

"But he's never given up. A few months ago Brent created interesting seasonal work in Baltimore at Otakon, the quirky festival featuring Japanese cartoon characters. He loves the kids and young adults who come downtown in late July dressed as their favorite character. He made a presentation event showing how to make the most of the surrounding streets and expand their program. He is gradually incorporated into their team, taking home a modest stipend for his efforts. It is not the life he planned but he was no match for the older and more destructive Marsha, who had cleanly laid to waste whatever dreams he had."

By the time lunch was over, they were both struck by the resilience of these four inexperienced victims who had shook off potential defeat to find blossoming lifestyles, maybe not of their original dreams but certainly of their own making. They escaped; Angel didn't.

WASHINGTON, DC

Late 2011

After the death of Angel, Todd spent two years leading his team in an increasingly frustrating effort to trap Juan. As far as Todd's agents could tell, Juan had withdrawn from any new ventures into America but might be setting back into the business of moving armaments from Eastern Europe and Russia into his favorite Middle East and African spots. On Myron's advice, he did not share any information about Aird's mysterious new partner. It was reported from a listening post in the Persian Gulf that Juan's elusive Algerian banking partners were bringing African customers to the transportation company; Todd took for granted that Juan's so-called family trust was once more growing in wealth but it was well shrouded from the DEA's watchful spies in Europe, the Middle East and America.

Todd was reflecting on his frustrations, holding his hands perfectly still on his lap less his fidgeting would betray his frustration. After hitting rock bottom among counter espionage agencies, he struggled hard to regain control of the file. His first break was when he and his colleagues quickly unscrambled Hugh's messaging with Stomper to avoid American jail. Todd had learned a long time ago that petty thieves were just that: crooks who stole a little bit from everyone who crossed their paths. Hugh and Stomper had chosen to play brinkmanship not only by stealing time and resources from Todd's professional life but also by tampering with his reputation. Neither thought about what was at stake: if he failed again, he would be more than embarrassed. His career among the elite antiterrorist units in the Western alliance would be finished. He loved his work and couldn't allow it to be threatened in any way. Todd was grimly determined to push aside these Canadian lightweights so he could return to more serious work.

His computer team had followed Hugh's suggestion that there might be a trail between Bertie and the mysterious Martin. His lead was not insubstantial or inconsequential, as they uncovered e-mails linking the two. This led them to a Gmail address that they put under watch. They quickly realized how professional their opponent was; Martin, if that was indeed the correct suspect, never used the e-mail address again. Wherever their quarry had learned his craft, he had learned well. After several false starts chasing down too many leads, Todd relented, retreated from the trail and put his efforts elsewhere. Occasionally a staffer sent a note observing that Hugh was checking out Bertie's blog, asking the odd question about rockets and wind turbines, almost, she opined, to let the scientist know that he was being watched regularly. It was all interesting but not germane to the American security forces preoccupied with uncovering what was happening in Moreno's big-picture world. They kept waiting for Martin Belanger to misplay his hand, but Juan's operative stayed ahead of them all the time. There was not a single visual sighting of the two visiting each other; consequently, Todd's team tentatively concluded that he may no longer be on the scene. That was off the mark, another example of how American intelligence was inexperienced in monitoring sleeping cells of international terrorists burrowing into its society. Juan's partners had agreed to fund fully Martin's mission once he acknowledged that it would best if he disappeared for several years. The two combatants who were so comfortable and trusting of each other, were naturally despondent about their separation but agreed to stay apart while Martin built the infrastructure for a powerful terrorist cell in America. Todd had to admit that he was confused by Martin's disappearance but didn't have enough evidence to raise his concerns with Myron.

When Hugh returned to a rather normal life in Winnipeg, Todd pondered how to bury him without leaving many tracks. Stomper was an easier read because of his heavy-handedness as he continued to play the role of the menacing fool. Todd kept asking staff the same question at their monthly meetings: does he not know we're always keeping an eye on him? Can he not camouflage himself better than this? In exasperation, Todd called together a low-level interagency meeting to explain his game plan to separate Stomper from his patron.

"We'll continue to follow leads, but as for Stomper's trips, find out his destination but let him go. Their so-called investors on the Bison Board are wasting funds on these guys. I hope it's costing them a small fortune. I'll keep pressure on the two of them through a friendly bureaucrat who is back in Ottawa after a stint in Washington. She'll contrive a quiet but thorough investigation that will put both Hugh and Stomper through the hoops with a coordinated effort among different agencies. It may not lead anywhere from our perspective but it sure won't be pretty from theirs. Hugh will end up spending the rest of the investors' money on their local lawyers. On one of his alleged business development trips, we'll help the Canadians apprehend Stomper on his return at the border. We'll set a drug trap, scare the shit out of him, and tell him never to leave Canada for either the States or Europe. He won't know what to do. I wouldn't be surprised if Moreno doesn't take him out with his people."

"Is that also the end of Hugh Parks?"

"Guys like him never disappear. You always need to have a hammer over their head, or they start up again. They're like dumb dogs. The only memory they have is of the last stick that hit them."

Everyone chuckled at the prospect of sting operations against both these characters. "Knowing you, you must have some plan for putting him away? What are you thinking for Parks?" an agent asked.

"We made arrangements several months ago when we let him off the hook to pay him in advance-remember we first took all his money in Syracuse and, we thought, his wife a good chunk back in Winnipeg- and in cash to watch over the scientist. We anticipated that, being who he is, Hugh would never declare this cash as income. We're right and I'll guarantee you, it's the tip of the iceberg. We've already talked to Canada's tax department through our embassy. It was not a surprise to find out that they already want him, but he's so slippery that they've had no solid evidence. Well, we've filmed the transaction, put it into the back of a file drawer, and are waiting for the right moment. We'll hand the evidence over to the Canadians, who'll run the prosecution for us. They'll do what has to be done to a tax evader."

MADRID, SPAIN

Winter 2012

Time passed, and the media moved on to more pressing events. First there was yet another political crisis in Pakistan with it being destabilized by an embold-ened Islamic anti-American bombing campaign. Then a wet summer in Europe upset the normal life of millions living close to river beds; this naturally caught the attention of television reporters loving the dramatic visuals of people living on the edge of disaster. The Moreno family had disappeared from public scru-tiny as if nothing had happened.

Juan's wife, despite her grief, had stayed with him. The transportation empire was running smoothly under the leadership of the new Algerian inves-tors. They were intelligent and determined to build a dominant firm in Euro-pean markets. It would eventually extend financial clout, respect, and mobility for their many family members and friends back in Algiers. Juan plunged back into business with renewed vigor as soon as he thought it decent to do so.

It was time he personally welcomed Amar back to Madrid. On this trip the Algerian brought with him his most senior investors, Rashid Medelci and Said Ghoul, along with their political strategist, Mahmoud Khadri, who had been at the first meeting. "As you've suggested, perhaps it's time to talk in more detail about my dreams." Juan said vaguely as he never let down his guard while on the phone. "Let's deal with as much as we can during your visit here."

They resumed where they had left off in their previous discussions. "I understand the battles and the compromises in dealing with colonial pow-ers," Juan began. "I understand Algeria and France. My family lived in Spain hundreds of years ago, only to be forced out because they refused to accept the

Catholics as their new masters. After centuries of our family eking out a miserable living, my grandfather gave up his Spartan life in Morocco and moved the family back to Spain. I know firsthand the complexity and moral ambivalence of straddling European and Muslim lifestyles. We never formally switched our religion. We have stayed on the sidelines, although my marriage to a Catholic woman was certainly viewed as turning our back on Islam. I remain agnostic and stay away from all religious trappings except marriages and funerals.

"My political strategy in Spain is to abstain from all fights involving the government. If you've done your research thoroughly, you know that I've refused to help the Basques. I personally don't understand what they want; they have all the money in the world for arms and munitions. In the same light, I talked to the highest security people in Madrid after the 2004 bombings. They believed I was the perpetrator, but I was able to calm them and point to the productive leads that found the actual culprits.

"Where does that leave me? What I won't do is supply any campaign operating in Europe. This is where my family makes its money, and I'm not about to destroy that. I have no forgiveness for the Americans, who campaign around the world to demolish any opposition that they arbitrarily consider a threat to their national interest. I like to render them useless whenever I can. I favor faraway battles so that I'm personally safe. Maybe in your country, it's harder to know whom to support and how to do it effectively."

Mahmoud led off the response from their team. "Our positions are quite similar so you can understand our position. If we stick it to the Islamic moderates at home, only the Europeans and Americans will stand up and cheer. The rest of the region will be outraged. What should we do? We're positioning ourselves as the guardians of Islamic enclaves living in poverty, ignored by their current government, and up against international forces led by the Americans. Our government cannot commit itself to these fights on its own, as there will be terrible repercussions from other nations. The government will enter the armament business through the back door with us but without any public discussion. When it's time, we will let the Algerian Islamic leadership know enough to allow them to claim a new political clientele." He stopped in mid-sentence searching for the right words to express his frustration with the opposition in his own country. No one helped him through his long silence. Finally, he waved for someone else to take over the conversation.

Said filled the room with his heavy heart. "I hope that you're wrong. The world around Algeria is marked by dangerous and inexperience insurgents. They cannot be trusted to fulfill the dreams and ambitions of their people no matter how much we want them to succeed. With their monumental mistakes, they could easily take down others. It's best to help as a friend but not own their cause."

"Your national leaders have good reason to be afraid," offered Juan in an unusually blunt tone. "They're known throughout the region for their corrupt lifestyles. They live well by making others live poorly. I have no patience for your government, but I don't want to be drawn into any cabal in your nation. Still, I'm willing to be your business partner. Today I'll simply re-iterate my earlier commitment to join forces between my family and NAF. The battles are important, and we with the resources to change the circumstances of the downtrodden have a historical mission to rebuild our strength to the days before the Crusades and to create a new empire. It sounds grandiose but I'll do my bit to support this campaign."

The conversation continued about what pitfalls they could avoid while signaling support for legitimate Islamic fighters taking on tyrannical regimes.

It was Amar's turn to speak. "Your comment about staying out of Europe, Juan, is perfectly reasonable, but it's easier said than done. All of Algeria's leading families are approached incessantly by religious leaders who demand that they show their commitment by financing European terrorist cells. You can probably imagine the temptation to get even with France after the way their citizens treated earlier generations of Algerians. With so many Muslims living in Paris suburbs, we would have no trouble finding volunteers to be jihads. Some cells have been sitting silent for over a decade. Young people are open to the appeals of leaders from North Africa, particularly the Al-Qaeda in the Islamic Maghreb."

"Okay. There will be complexities no matter what, but I stand by my original position: no activity of any kind in Europe. I know all about the AQIM. They're aggressively pursuing me for help, but the answer is no."

"Where do you think we should go to show our support?"

"Right now, the world is slowly waking up to the situation in Yemen. The Americans are planning to battle from a distance using drones. It won't work. We have to teach them that they can't run this region from Stuttgart up in Germany. It will take a few months, but if you and your investors want to support the battle against the States in that country, I'll find someone for you. That's all I can say right now."

Rashid spoke earnestly about their complex relationship with the existing regime. "The government has signaled its support for our building wealth outside the Middle East and North Africa. When we do work closer to home, such as financing the local construction companies for the North Africa super highway, we're fed up with the corruption. We hear that the Japanese and Chinese offered hundreds of millions to secure the big contracts—this is money lost to Algerian citizens as their leaders fill their pockets. Our strategy is to borrow the tax profits from our national oil company, Sonatrach, and from other private operators like France's Total, and engage our wealthy families who understand what can be done with this exceptional pool of money but who stay away from politics. We call them advisers, although in reality they run the fund and frequently put in their own capital. We now have close to $70 billion to invest. We also want to show people at home how we're helping them. The only thing we won't do is invest in French companies, for obvious reasons.

"Now let me finish this talk with a closing comment about our political agenda. Our nation has struggled. Life has had its ups and downs for too many generations and we Algerians would all appreciate greater stability going forward. The Islamic political movement is strong here, despite our official announcements to the contrary. Too many bombs are going off; we cannot pretend to be a peaceful place. We want to help others because their situations are so disastrous but we can't destroy our own society at the same time. We are under a great deal of pressure from other Islamic partisans to be more involved in their fights. Given the many battlefields, we must choose carefully."

Juan nodded his assent and left them with one last story on their way out. "A final word of caution. The Americans won't stop until they find who's behind me. Also, did you hear what happened in February? The Italians arrested seven people for selling arms to Iran. Can you imagine the humiliation if we were the ones arrested? These thieves were moving small items such as rifle scopes, bullet-proof vests, scuba vests, and parachutes. So far, who cares? Then they decide to think big and deliver a helicopter! What's their preferred route? They go through Romania and stay in contact by constantly using their cell phones. That way, they brilliantly plotted, they could better coordinate their delivery times. They're lucky to be in Italy where even dumb crooks go free. Let's never be that dumb, please."

Everyone laughed heartily. They knew that Juan was back in the game.

The next day he ordered shipments from Slovenia and Romania into Afghanistan, taking advantage of the expertise found in central European countries after many decades of producing armaments and shipping material for export. New alliances were struck, and more cash was kept on hand to smooth their dealings with officials. They saw his predicament and gladly accepted his generosity. Juan was climbing out of danger by using every means at his disposal. The summer months afforded him a reason to be away from Madrid. He moved casually around different resort towns, sometimes with Maria, more often than not on his own, as had been his habit for close to twenty years. His watchers failed to catch every meeting. Timing and location were remembered year after year without fail by his associates. No communications were necessary for arrangements to spend three or four hours together exchanging plans and cash and to cement relationships in the face of immense pressure from the Americans. The Americans wanted him badly but weren't able to trap him.

With Angel gone, the NAF was encouraged to advance their management track more quickly. A team of three took up temporary residence in Madrid to begin learning about European transportation systems. Younger siblings in the family were given the opportunity to begin more formal education in these fields, creating a magnificent pool of future managers. It would take a decade, maybe fifteen years; given the incentives, no one doubted that the mission would be a success. Everyone was committed to making this work properly.

A few months later, his prized rockets from North America had finally arrived in Algeria. They had been brought into the Algiers port that was now being run by his old banking friends from Dubai who had taken over the management of DP Ports. It was a roundabout route, more expensive than usual— yet, as they were originally stolen in Kansas, Juan could afford to be generous to those helping him transport them in so many different ways. The wooden boxes were pulled out of hiding a long twelve months after being stashed in Mississippi, taken to the Mexican port Lazaro Cardenas for another long stretch in storage, shipped to Amsterdam, transferred to his trucking company, and stamped for Israel...but lost in Algeria.

The Islamist Movement of Society for Peace paid Juan handsomely and immediately into the family trust's new account under NAF's management. They quickly moved their newly acquired armaments out to their target country. This was to be Juan's last deal. He didn't covet the money or bask in the thrill of besting everyone on his trail. His mission to support almost every cause whose purpose was to beat back European imperialism was now drawing to a close. He checked his watch, picked up a new cell delivered by one of his drivers, and waited patiently.

The pre-arranged call came at a busy time of day in faraway Yemen. He answered promptly. There was no one there, only screams, pleas, and the sounds of explosions that Juan was expecting to hear. There was no message, nor did he expect one; it would only make the call easier to trace. He didn't end the call; instead he went over to a second cell and calmly entered a number in Virginia. When Todd, a little drunk at a private cocktail party, picked up his cell and said hello, all he heard was a man with a vaguely European accent whispering "boom" and the sounds from a distant chaotic street scene. The line went dead. Todd knew the rumbles were bringing terror to a distant part of the world. He also knew, as did Juan, that at some unknown security listening post, an alert desk officer would excitedly report the commotion, and a new round of bureaucratic horror would begin in the morning. He punched in a familiar number to find Myron.

THE END